Maisey Yates is a *New York Times* bestselling author of over one hundred romance novels. Whether she's writing strong, hardworking cowboys, dissolute princes or multigenerational family stories, she loves getting lost in fictional worlds. An avid knitter with a dangerous yarn addiction and an aversion to housework, Maisey lives with her husband and three kids in rural Oregon. Check out her website, maiseyyates.com, or find her on Facebook.

Nicole Helm writes down-to-earth contemporary romance and fast-paced romantic suspense. She lives with her husband and two sons in Missouri. Visit her website: www.nicolehelm.com.

Jackie Ashenden writes dark, emotional stories with alpha heroes who've just got the world to their liking only to have it blown wide apart by their kick-ass heroines. She lives in Auckland, New Zealand, with her husband and two kids. When she's not torturing alpha males and their gutsy heroines, she can be found drinking chocolate martinis, reading anything she can lay her hands on, wasting time on social media or being forced to go mountain biking with her husband.

USA TODAY bestselling, RITA® Award–nominated and critically acclaimed author **Caitlin Crews** has written more than one hundred books and counting. She has a master's degree and PhD in English literature, thinks everyone should read more category romance, and is always available to discuss her beloved alpha heroes. Just ask. She lives in the Pacific Northwest with her comic book artist husband, is always planning her next trip and will never, ever, read all the books in her to-be-read pile. Thank goodness.

Also by Maisey Yates

Confessions from the Quilting Circle
The Heartbreaker of Echo Pass
Rodeo Christmas at Evergreen Ranch
The True Cowboy of Sunset Ridge

Also by Nicole Helm

Shot Through the Heart
Mountainside Murder
Cowboy in the Crosshairs

Also by Jackie Ashenden

The Wedding Night They Never Had
Pregnant by the Wrong Prince
The Innocent's One-Night Proposal

Also by Caitlin Crews

The Sicilian's Forgotten Wife
The Bride He Stole for Christmas
The Scandal That Made Her His Queen

Sweet HOME COWBOY

MAISEY YATES

NICOLE HELM · JACKIE ASHENDEN
CAITLIN CREWS

HQN

ISBN-13: 978-1-335-63996-7

Recycling programs for this product may not exist in your area.

Sweet Home Cowboy

Copyright © 2022 by Harlequin Enterprises ULC

Teddy
Copyright © 2022 by Nicole Helm

Joey
Copyright © 2022 by Maisey Yates

Georgie
Copyright © 2022 by Jackie Ashenden

Elliot
Copyright © 2022 by Caitlin Crews

Copyright © 2022 by Jeff Johnson, interior illustrations

HQN
22 Adelaide St. West, 41st Floor
Toronto, Ontario M5H 4E3, Canada
www.Harlequin.com

Printed in Lithuania

MIX
Paper from responsible sources
FSC® C021394

Contents

TEDDY   7
Nicole Helm

JOEY   127
Maisey Yates

GEORGIE   231
Jackie Ashenden

ELLIOT   345
Caitlin Crews

TEDDY

Nicole Helm

For Peggy

PROLOGUE

IT WAS NEVER comfortable for people when four sets of violet eyes zeroed in on them with the level of intensity the Hathaway sisters could manage.

A fact the half sisters had learned when they'd first met at summer camp, thanks to their families, who'd been careful to give the girls the opportunity to meet each other, without the pressure of having to become friends or even real sisters.

But sisters they had become that first day at the age of thirteen. In each other, they'd found kindred spirits. Not just in the unusual color of their eyes, but in the depths of their passions, and in their driving need to forge family out of the fragments their father had left behind when he'd impregnated all their mothers at different points in the same year.

So that, as adults, though they lived in different parts of the country, they were the best of friends. Sisters, through and through, and when Georgie had informed them of Grandpa Jack's heart attack in Jasper Creek, the rest had rushed to the small Oregon town to see what they could do.

Grandpa Jack looked at each of them with his usual squinty-eyed suspicion. Though their father had never made any effort to be a part of his daughters' lives, Grandpa Jack had always made it clear he'd be there if needed.

But not to expect him to be cheerful about it.

"Didn't all have to come," he grumbled, shifting in his hospital bed.

"Well, of course we did. And we'll stay until you're on the mend," Teddy said, patting his hand. The squinty-eyed suspicion became a full-fledged scowl as he pulled his hand away.

While Teddy was all about gestures of affection, Grandpa Jack was decidedly not.

Which made the fact Georgie was the only local grand-daughter a blessing as she shared the discomfort with such goings-on. He turned his glare to her. "Didn't have to call them."

Georgie shrugged.

"She was right to," Joey said firmly, meeting Grandpa Jack's scowl with her own. "We won't hear another com-plaint about it. A waste of time. You know how stubborn we are."

Grandpa Jack grunted.

Elliot smirked. "Wonder where we got it."

A nurse knocked on the door, then poked her head in. "Sorry, girls, it's time to head home. Visiting hours are over."

"Girls," Elliot muttered under her breath with a consid-erable amount of disdain for the word.

But Teddy pressed a kiss to Grandpa Jack's wrinkled forehead, Elliot touched his shoulder, and Georgie and Joey hovered at the door until they all left the room, chorusing goodbyes.

"I hate leaving him all alone," Teddy said as Elliot linked arms with her. Teddy reached out and took Joey's arm.

"He'll be home soon enough," Joey reassured her. She gave Georgie an apologetic shrug, then linked arms with her too, so they were a unit as they walked out of the hospital into the cool spring evening.

"He's not going to let you fuss over him, Teddy. It isn't his way," Georgie said pragmatically as they walked to her truck.

Teddy frowned. "I think you misjudge my tenacity."

Elliot's eyebrows winged up. "Do we?"

Teddy wrinkled her nose, but didn't argue with Elliot.

"I found an Airbnb closer to the hospital," Georgie said, sounding tired as she climbed into the driver's seat. "I knew this wouldn't be a quick visit and we'd need more room than Felix and I have." Georgie had grown up with her half brother right here in Jasper Creek.

The four sisters climbed into Georgie's truck. Whatever belongings they'd packed were strapped into the bed of the truck from when Georgie had picked Joey and Teddy up at the airport this afternoon, after Elliot had driven down from Portland.

Georgie drove onto the highway, and it was only about fifteen minutes later she parked in front of a pretty little farmhouse just outside of Jasper Creek.

"This place is amazing," Teddy said.

"Much better taken care of than the main house at Grandpa Jack's property," Georgie returned.

The women got out, grabbed what they'd need for the night, then headed inside.

"I'll make us some dinner," Teddy said, already moving for the kitchen.

"The host said she left some things for us to eat when we arrived," Georgie replied, dropping her stuff in the front room.

They all descended on the kitchen, which was quaint

and old-fashioned—something that suited all four women to the bone. On the table were a variety of baked goods.

"I found a teapot and some tea," Teddy said.

"Scones and sweet rolls for dinner sounds good to me," Joey said, already unwrapping the plate of baked goods and digging in.

Elliot found plates and set the table, shoving one at Joey as she'd already plowed through three-fourths of a scone.

"Do you think Grandpa Jack is stressed about the ranch? And that's what caused this?" Teddy asked, fiddling with the stove.

"I think he's an old man who eats poorly and smokes cigars regularly. But…" Georgie sighed. "He's been talking about selling off the last piece of land to Colt West next door. He'd keep the cabin and about an acre around it, but the rest would go to Colt."

"Even the main house?" Joey asked, as she licked crumbs from her fingers.

"You could hardly call it that these days. It's falling apart at the seams."

Teddy frowned. "That's just not right."

Georgie shrugged. "He hasn't lived in that house in decades. He's a single, old, grumpy man. He's finally accepting he can't really take care of the ranch. Why not sell?"

"It's our legacy," Joey said. Then she looked around the table. "Isn't it?"

"It's our absent father's legacy," Elliot returned. "Assuming he's still alive."

All eyes turned to Georgie, who was the only one who'd ever had any contact with Mickey Hathaway. She lifted her shoulders. "Far as I know."

Silence filled the room until Teddy's teakettle began to whistle. She poured tea for everyone, then took a seat at the kitchen table. As far as she was concerned, this was all fate. The timing, the chance of all four of them coming here at a point in their lives where they got to decide what came next.

"We've always talked about how much we wanted to live there, so why don't we?"

"Why don't we what?" Joey replied, mouth full with her last bite of scone.

"Live there. Do what we all love to do. Put together some kind of…business. Honey, eggs," Teddy said, pointing to herself. "Produce," she said, pointing to Joey. "Ceramics." Elliot's specialty. "Our sweet Georgie's baked goods," she said, grinning at Georgie's negative reaction to being called sweet. "Most of us are already selling our wares anyway. Why don't we do it here? The four of us."

It would be more than the year her mother wanted, more than just learning some independence. It would be actually, hopefully permanently, forging that independence. Well, with her sisters. Which suited Teddy better. She didn't want to be alone. She wanted to be a part of a family. Her family.

"You'd move here all the way from Maine?" Joey asked dubiously. "Leave your mother?"

Teddy sniffed. "I can leave my mother." Then she wrinkled her nose. Subterfuge wasn't her strong suit. "She wants me to move out anyway."

"Why?" her sisters demanded, offended on her behalf.

"She thinks I need a year of independence. To *find my own way*. Apparently twenty-five is too old to have always lived with your mother, according to her."

When none of her sisters argued, she glared at them. "You *agree* with her?"

Elliot shrugged. "I don't *dis*agree with her."

"Well, anyway, this would solve that, wouldn't it? We

can fix up the house. I'm sure some people need bee removal around here, so I'll start a new hive. Buy new chickens. Elliot can drive her ceramics van down here. Joey, you could start the farm of your dreams with local produce and flowers—a brand-new challenge, all yours. Georgie, you can design the baking kitchen you've been planning since childhood. And we'll be close enough to Grandpa to help him—and far enough away he won't beat us away with sticks."

They looked at Teddy, varying looks of consideration and concern on their faces. But as the idea took shape in Teddy's mind, she knew it was exactly right. This wasn't some new dream out of left field; it was an old dream.

And if she had to be independent, why not make that old dream a reality?

"We always wanted to live in one place. Like a real family," Teddy said. She would have reached out and grabbed all their hands if she had three herself. As it was, she only looked at them imploringly. "Sisters. Live together. Work together. It's the dream. Maybe something good can come out of Grandpa's health scare. If Grandpa lets us live in the house, and we pool whatever our savings are together, it's not a financial stretch. Elliot and I can keep our independent businesses running while we get our joint business set up. Then we split the farm profit four ways."

"Profit. That is optimistic at best," Georgie said.

"You know I am *all* about optimism," Teddy returned.

A wind chime tinkled from the front room, which was odd considering there shouldn't be enough wind to make it move here inside.

"Did someone leave the door open?" Joey asked, pushing back from the table. The girls got up and walked toward the door, which was indeed open.

"Look at that," Elliot said.

They stepped out onto the porch together. Beyond the dogwood in the front just beginning to bloom, the sun was setting in a riot of colors—bright magentas, deep oranges, fading into lavenders and lighter pinks.

"It's the most beautiful sunset I've ever seen."

"That's a tad dramatic, Teddy," Georgie said gently, though her voice held all the awe of someone who agreed, but would never admit it.

"We have to do it," Teddy said, her voice almost a whisper. "This is a sign. Don't you believe in fate?"

Elliot nodded. "Yeah. I'm mobile. I go where I please. Why not right here?"

Georgie shrugged. "Don't know about fate, but it wouldn't change much for me, except you guys would be close. I'd like that. Felix is talking about leaving Jasper Creek."

Teddy reached out, but Georgie stopped her with a quelling look. "It's fine." She offered a smile, or Georgie's version of a smile anyway. "Especially if you guys are here."

All eyes turned to Joey.

"I have to talk timing over with my mom. I don't want to leave her short-staffed," Joey said, her eyes still on the sunset. Then she pushed out a breath and looked at her sisters and grinned. "But why the hell not?"

Teddy smiled at the sunset, feeling a bit teary over the whole thing. But it was meant to be, she was sure of it. "Four Sisters Farm." She looked at each of her sisters. "That's what we can call it. Because it'll be ours. Always."

Everyone nodded. Because this was exactly where they were meant to be. Four sisters. Living and working together.

Finally.

CHAPTER ONE

"I THINK IT looks great." Teddy Hathaway always preferred optimism—even when there was very little to be had. Like now.

"It's a shithole," Joey said.

"It has potential," Teddy replied, with a smile. Because she saw it as it could be, not how it was. "I've done a lot of work on the basics to clean it up and make it livable. Georgie said her brother and his friend can give us a hand with the more complicated repairs. We can get a professional for the rest as finances allow."

She'd never gone back home to Maine after hopping on a plane to see Grandpa Jack in the hospital. Mom had supported the decision and packed up all her things and shipped them to Oregon. Teddy had been a little afraid if she'd gone back, she would have chickened out. By just staying it felt more like a trip with her sisters, than permanence.

It was better that way. Easier. And she'd kept herself busy. She and Georgie had gotten Grandpa settled back in his cabin, and fussed over him until he had in fact threatened to beat them with sticks.

He'd never do it, Teddy knew, but he'd looked healthy enough to try, and so she'd started backing off some.

He'd agreed to let them live in the main house on his ranch property, claiming he didn't care one way or another how the land was used long as he didn't have to concern himself with it—or them.

Teddy fretted a bit that they were cheating him out of the money he'd get from selling it to Colt West, but that only made her more determined to make Four Sisters Farm a raving success. Grandpa Jack could haunt his small cabin tucked into the north side of the property, and here on the southern half, she and her sisters would make everything *flourish*.

Teddy loved a flourish.

"You did all that on your own?" Joey returned. She'd just arrived from Texas to settle in, and Elliot was driving down from Portland today.

"Georgie helped when she could. The first step was just getting it cleaned out and patched up in a few places," Teddy said with a wide smile. "We didn't even touch the barn. There are a bunch of tractors and things cluttering it up. Grandpa Jack said we can use whatever we want, but he isn't helping anyone fix them."

Joey winced. "That bad, huh?"

"But they're free," Teddy said brightly, being careful to sidestep the hole in the porch. "I had an inspector go through and he assured me the foundation is in good shape."

"How much are you sinking into this place, Teddy?"

Teddy kept her wide smile in place as she opened the door and led Joey inside. She didn't answer Joey's question because *Everything* made her heart pound a little too hard.

But she was twenty-five. This was the time to sink in everything.

She didn't want her sisters to know she had put a lot in already. She just wanted to…do it. Everyone would put what they could, and once they were settled as a joint venture, the financials would be more even.

But for right now, she felt better…doing what she could. How she could. Without letting anyone know how *much* that was.

Luckily, Joey didn't push for an answer because she stepped over the threshold and laughed. "Oh my God, Teddy, you never fail."

The insides definitely didn't match the outsides. Aside from the necessary fixes to make it livable, Teddy had spent her weeks cleaning like the devil, sewing and hanging curtains. She'd bought Joey some houseplants—though she knew Joey would also bring a truckload of her own, on top of the ones for the farm. Teddy had also arranged all the ceramics she'd bought or received as gifts from Elliot over the years, and though she knew Georgie wanted to build a full-on baker's kitchen in the barn, had made this kitchen as baker-friendly as possible for the interim.

Teddy had laid rugs, put as many knickknacks as Mom had sent her on every available surface—glass chickens, stained glass bees hanging in the windows. She'd put dried flowers in vases and she'd even decorated every bedroom upstairs to her sisters' tastes.

Everyone would add their own additional touches, but she'd laid the groundwork for *home*. For family.

She watched Joey's amazed face, pleased down to her toes. Then she checked her watch. "I want to run into town before Elliot gets here. Do you want to come?"

"No, I want to get started on that atrocity of a yard."

"Okay, there's a feed store I think I might be able to order some chickens from. And I need a few more things for the hives." Teddy slid her bag on her shoulder. "I can get anything you might need. I think they sell gardening supplies too. No cell service out here, but you can call me with the landline if you want me to pick up anything."

"Teddy?"

Teddy stopped in the door and looked back to see Joey staring at one of the glass chickens on the freshly polished hearth around the fireplace. Joey turned to look sternly at her.

"No house chickens," Joey warned. "I mean it, Teddy. Not one chicken in the house."

Teddy only smiled.

What was a house without a house chicken, after all?

BEAU RILEY WALKED INTO Riley Feed & Garden Supply on a pretty afternoon. Though his morning plans had been derailed by a swarm of bees, he had a smile in place as he walked up to his sister standing behind the counter.

"I'm needing something that'll kill bees."

"Morning to you too," Pru said, scowling at him. But she studied her store. "Not sure I've got any of that. Wasp spray might work for the time being." Pru pointed him in the direction of a shelf of insect repellent cans.

Beau didn't relish the idea of spraying the little pests. Surely there was a more humane way to get rid of them, but they'd been harassing his dog, him, and he hadn't even been able to get the pallets Mom wanted out of the shed.

"Sure, I'll take it."

As if that can conjured a fairy, a small woman appeared at his elbow from seemingly out of nowhere.

"I'm so sorry, but I just can't let you buy that." She put her hand on his arm.

Beau looked at the frothy little picture in front of him. She was tiny, but a riot of color and…something. She reminded him of the cover of a book his little sister would have read in middle school. An old-fashioned-dressed young woman, windswept and earnest.

He looked from those blue eyes so vivid they might as well be purple, down to the hand on his arm. She looked awfully serious for flirtation, but surely the hand touch and interruption was a *little* bit of a flirtation. *Wasp* spray wasn't exactly life or death.

Except for the bees, he supposed.

"You can't, huh?" He grinned at her, tapping the top of her hand on his arm with his blunt, calloused finger. "Why not?"

"Bees are an incredibly important part of our ecosystem. They're the world's largest pollinators—which we need for plant and crop life. But insecticides and harmful chemicals have been murdering bees at a disastrous rate. I just can't let you contribute to that."

Beau blinked. Not flirting. Environmentalism. He wasn't against it. Truth be told, restorative agriculture and sustainable ranching were two of his interests. Contrary to what city folks tended to believe, being a rancher wasn't raising and killing cows for fun.

He didn't *want* to kill the bees. He just wanted to clear out the shed and get his mother off his back.

"That is a shame, but they're in my way. And stinging my dog while they're in my way."

"Oh, poor baby," she offered with some concern. Then she dug in her oversize bag. She handed him a card and flashed a megawatt smile.

He reluctantly took the offered card, expecting some sort of hippie commune with some become-one-with-the-bees bullshit. The card had her name, Teddy Hathaway, a drawing of a hive with a little bee flying out of it, and the words *ethical bee removal*.

"You remove bees," he said. Which was a step up from

what he'd been picturing, as he did need them *gone*, not to learn to live with them.

"Ethically," she added. Then she amped up that smile, and Beau figured most guys would allow her to ethically remove just about anything, long as they could watch. "Then rehome them where they can be useful and out of danger. Win for you. Win for the bees."

"I imagine you cost more than that bottle of bug spray," he returned, because while Riley Ranch was doing well enough, he *was* his father's son. A penny saved was a penny earned.

"In the short run," she agreed. "But do you want to only have a short run?"

He gave her a once-over. It sounded like innuendo, but those earnest eyes made him wonder if it was by accident.

Remove the bees. Re*home* them. It sounded a bit much, but he figured his mother would like the sound of that. Wasn't she the one always planting things that attracted bees and butterflies and too many godforsaken birds to count?

"So, how does it work?" he asked.

"We'll set up a time to take a look at the bees and their hive and then I'll give you an estimate. Once the price is agreed on, we sign a contract, I remove the bees, and voilà. You have helped save the world."

It was a bit over the top, but he appreciated her enthusiasm if nothing else. "I need the bees out now."

She looked at her watch, then pulled a little notebook out of her bag and flipped through. "I can do three o'clock for the initial meeting. Depending on the size, and your agreement, I could maybe have them out of your hair by Monday. Midweek at the latest."

It took Beau a minute to get past the fact that she wore a

watch and had some paper calendar decked out in flowers and…chickens in her hands. And no sign of a cell phone. "Uh, sure. Okay. Three."

"Address?"

He rattled off the address for the ranch.

"And your name?" She looked up at him and smiled that bright smile.

So, he returned it. Maybe she was very invested in bees, but that didn't mean she couldn't enjoy a little flirtation too. "Beau Riley."

"Riley? You must be related to the store owner."

He jutted his chin toward Pru, who was watching with rare *silent* interest. "She's my sister."

Teddy jotted down both their names, and Beau read her upside-down notes from where he stood.

Pru Riley. Riley Feed & Garden Supply—followed by a list of things Pru carried. Then *Beau Riley. Bees.* And his address. *Brother and sister.*

Then she slapped the notebook shut and looked up at him again. "Perfect. I'll see you then." She turned the smile on his sister. "Thank you."

Pru nodded. "I'll call you when the chickens are in."

"Awesome." The woman—Teddy Hathaway—waved and then was off, frilly skirts flirting with her knees. She wore tights the color of his mother's bluebells and boots that laced up past the ankle.

"Looking forward to it," Beau called after her, tipping his hat and flashing his most charming grin.

"You're an imbecile," Pru said from behind him once Teddy had disappeared.

He turned to his sister, keeping the charming grin in place. "You're a shrew. What's that got to do with any-thing?"

Pru rolled her eyes. "Hathaway? I'm guessing any daughter of Mickey Hathaway isn't falling for your over-zealous cowboy charm. Rightfully so."

"Ah, but you're admitting I've got charm." He winked at his sister. "Say, where's my best friend you stole away from me?"

"As I don't recall you planning to marry Grant, there was hardly any stealing. But he's helping our landlord deal with a busted pipe at our place."

Beau shoved his hands in his pockets. As happy as he was for his sister, and even more for his best friend who'd gone from stressed and dour to...well, still a little dour but definitely not so dark-hearted about it, all their domestic bliss made him bone-deep uncomfortable. "So, you're, ah, planning on getting married?"

Pru's expression changed; she got all smiley and soft, which was strange coming from his smart-mouthed, decid-edly unsoft sister. "Yeah, he asked me last night. Don't tell Mom. We're telling her tonight at dinner. She can finally stop praying over us living in sin." Pru waggled her fin-gers at him. "And since it's not catching, you don't have to act so squirrelly about it."

He opened his mouth to say he wasn't acting squirrelly, but if he did that, he'd spend the next hour arguing with Pru rather than heading back to the ranch and getting some chores done before the bee lady showed up.

So, he looked down at the card in his hand and thought about more pleasant things.

Like charming the strange little bee lady this afternoon.

CHAPTER TWO

TEDDY DROVE TO the Riley Ranch with a smile on her face. She usually only visited Oregon once a year around Christmas or New Year's—her and her sisters descending on Grandpa Jack for some forced holiday cheer. So she wasn't used to all Jasper Creek had to offer in spring as the world began to rebirth itself—all freshly turned soil and tentative buds in the shadows of mountains that were beginning to hint toward green.

She loved the idea of rebirth, of seeding an idea and growing it to completion. For twenty-five years her orbit had been mostly Mom, and now it could be Grandpa Jack and her sisters.

Still an orbit, she supposed. Maybe not quite the independence Mom had in mind, but Teddy wasn't looking for independence. She was looking for family. *Home.*

She turned into the Riley Ranch drive, and the curving gravel road took her through pretty pastures full of uninterested cattle. There was a white ranch house that looked in such ruthless good shape, it did indeed make the house back on the Hathaway property seem like Joey had so crudely put it.

A shithole.

But that hardly mattered. Teddy wasn't interested in perfection. She was interested in…home. A home that melded her and her sisters' interests and gave them all room to be fiercely themselves.

That was what her mother had always given her, and she had always been determined to give it to other people—particularly the other people she loved.

She didn't stop at the house. Though it looked inviting, it didn't look like anyone was about. So, she kept following the gravel until a barn came into view. She saw a truck, a horse tied to a post, and Beau Riley walking out of the barn.

He was wiping his hands on a dirty towel, a smudge of dirt was on his cheek, and he was scowling. There was a fat brown-and-white border collie following him into the sunlight.

Teddy didn't particularly care for scowling, but something about how classically beautiful Beau's face was made the scowling seem suitably romantic brooding.

She nearly laughed at herself as she got out of the car. Surely cowboys didn't brood romantically. Her grandfather was the only cowboy she knew, and he was nothing but grit and vinegar. It might hide a squishier heart underneath, but that was only because no matter what he said or did, he had a soft spot for the girls his son had abandoned.

"Afternoon," Teddy greeted, walking over to Beau.

"Sorry I'm running a bit late. Fighting with some stubborn machinery or I would have met you at the gate."

The dog greeted her with enthusiastic barks, but had clearly been well trained not to jump, so she knelt to scratch his ears. "Aren't you sweet. What's his name?"

"Benji." Beau pointed beyond the barn. "The bees are back a bit farther. Do you want to follow me in your car?" He studied the compact car with some suspicion. "Not sure it'll make it."

Teddy could see a little cabin down the way he pointed,

and pretty wildflowers dotting the landscape from here to there. "Well, we can walk, can't we?"

He flashed a grin. She couldn't help but like his smile. It crinkled his eyes and had a pleasant little flutter expanding in her chest. "Billing me by the hour?" he asked good-naturedly.

"Consultations are free. I want to check out your wildflower situation."

"Do I have a wildflower situation?" he asked, sounding concerned as she began to walk down the road.

"You've got lupine just about to bloom, and it'll be just gorgeous when it does. And those patches of green there that are a little darker than the grass, I think that's phlox. You might have some Shooting Stars over there, some Paintbrush for sure. Oh, Mule Flower!"

"Mule Flower," Beau echoed as if she was speaking a foreign language. "Well, you sure do know your flowers."

"The bees and I have that in common. I imagine that's what attracted them to this spot." She lifted her face to the sun. It was a chilly day when the breeze drifted over her face, but when it was just her and the sun it was almost warm enough to consider taking off the cardigan Mom had knitted for her.

When she glanced at Beau, he was watching her even as they walked. There was something considering in his expression, but she really didn't know him well enough to know what he was considering.

"Here," she said, rummaging around in her bag as they continued their walk. She pulled out a slim folder, decorated with bees, naturally, and slid out a piece of paper. "You can go over the rates while we walk. It's broken down between supplies, labor, transportation and so on. It'll depend on how big the hive is and how many hours, but you can get the idea." She handed him a sheet of paper. Though the column of numbers was neat and practical, she'd designed the flyer with drawings of bees and hives and flowers.

Just because something was practical didn't mean it had to be ugly or dull.

"Definitely more than a can of wasp spray," he muttered.

"Yes, but also solving the actual problem. Not only will the bees move, but once you clean up the shed, they shouldn't return. Of course, if they do, I'll only move the next colony. Presuming you're willing to pay the price."

He huffed out a breath. It didn't insult her any. She'd been doing this for years now, and she knew farmers, or in this case ranchers, tended to be frugal. But they were also stewards of the land, given to understanding that every action had a reaction or consequence.

Teddy eyed the cabin as they passed. It was clearly being used. Curtains hung in the windows, which were open to the cool breeze. Behind a screen door, the main door was open. There was a rocking chair on the short porch and a welcome mat liberally covered in dried mud. The dog waddled up the stairs and flopped into a spot in the dappled sunlight.

"That's a cozy little place."

He smiled over at her. "Glad you think so. It's mine. This is my part of the property here, going on up back there." He pointed beyond the cabin to a picturesque pasture where cows grazed. "And here's the shed," he said, frowning at the old, ramshackle building that didn't look like it fit in with main house, barn or cabin. "I don't think anyone's used it since my parents got married, but suddenly my mother wants things she put there before I was born."

"Where's the hive?"

"No idea. I just know there's bees everywhere."

She nodded as he opened the creaking, crooked door to the shed. Sunlight streamed in from the open door and from windows that had been without glass for some time. Teddy stepped inside to the familiar sounds of buzzing.

"Be careful," he said, following her inside though he had to duck to make it through the frame.

Teddy studied the inside of the shack. The bees swarmed toward one corner, and she could tell from the sound and the bees she could see, that this would definitely be a bigger job. "Do you mind if I pull this plank back?" She pulled a crowbar from her bag.

He stepped forward, though his step hitched a little when he saw the crowbar. "Uh, okay. Here, let me do it for you."

She waved him away, placed the flat head of the crowbar in a gap in the wood and carefully pulled back. The plank splintered a little. "Here, hold this," she said, not wanting to break the walls of his shed even if they were old and crumbling.

He moved forward and took the handle from her, keeping the plank right where she'd pulled it. "Aren't we supposed to be wearing those big suit things with the mesh helmets?" he asked.

"You can tell when a colony is angry, and when they're happy. These are happy. You won't get stung if you exude calm."

"Exude calm in the middle of a horror film," he muttered. But he held the crowbar right where it was and while he didn't look *comfortable* exactly, eyeing the bees with blatant distrust, he didn't look terrified.

Teddy fished a flashlight out of her bag and shined the beam into the small crack she'd made. "My, that *is* a sizable colony."

Beau cleared his throat, almost as if covering up a laugh, though she couldn't imagine why.

"It's a big project," she continued. "I can't predict the exact amount of hours or cost, but if we go outside I might be able to give you a range."

He took the crowbar out of the hole, studied it, then handed it to her. He led her back outside around to the back of the shack. She studied the wall. She could see the crack the bees were entering and exiting from. She had a feeling the colony might inhabit most of the wall.

"It's going to be at least four hours. Possibly longer if it takes too long to find the queen. Material costs are fixed, though, and while I'll be careful not to damage the structure too much, any damage isn't my responsibility." She pointed to the sheet of paper in his pocket and he pulled it out and unfolded it.

She stepped next to him. "The final cost would likely end up somewhere between this and this," she said, pointing to the prices on the paper.

He knocked his cowboy hat back on his head as he studied the figures. She looked up at him, trying to decide what the best tack to take to convince him to sign the contract would be.

Beau's expression was inscrutable as he studied the prices. He made quite the picture though. His brown hair was burnished with gold streaks, presumably from the sun. It was thick, a little wavy where it poked out from the hat. His eyes were a cool blue, flecked with gray that glinted silver in the pretty sunlight. Though she'd always sworn off cowboys—it had seemed best not to tempt fate the way her mother had—the way Beau wore the hat, and the T-shirt that was *just* tight enough over his biceps to give the impression of impressive strength, and the jeans that seemed to accentuate that particularly narrow hip thing men had going on was something to look twice at.

Besides, looking was free. And Teddy didn't hate men like her mother did. Though she understood. If she'd been treated like her mother had by the man who'd impregnated her, she'd probably hate men too.

Men were fine enough. She wasn't sure she *trusted* them, but then again, none had ever gotten through her list of questions. A woman had to be careful, hatred of men or not. Women always had more to lose. *That* was the lesson she'd taken away from her mother. The lesson she agreed with. Not that all men were *evil*, but that a woman needed to be *careful*.

So, it seemed a moot point to sit here and dream about this man.

"If you want more time to consider, you have my contact information. My schedule is fairly open at the moment, so I could jump in and do it pretty quickly."

He lowered the paper, flicked those cool blue eyes down at her. It felt a bit like he was returning the perusal she'd just given him, which made heat begin to creep up her neck.

Which made her uncharacteristically uneasy. "I've got to get to my next appointment. Just promise me you won't use wasp spray."

His mouth quirked upward on one side and her heart did that fluttery thing again. Oh dear.

"I suppose I'll promise you that," he offered.

"Good." When she was tempted to smile at him for far too long, she turned. "I'll see you around, Beau." And she began to walk resolutely back to her car.

BEAU WATCHED HER walk away. Her strides were much more urgent than they'd been on the walk over. She didn't spend much time looking at the wildflowers. Her arms swung, her skirts flapped between her legs and that ridiculously oversize sweater flew behind her in the wind.

She looked like she was trying to escape.

He grinned. She'd been checking him out when he'd been a little knocked back by bee removal prices, that much he knew. When he'd returned the favor he'd *sworn* the faintest blush crept into her cheeks.

So, it wasn't an *un*interested escape. Perhaps, if anything, it was an *interested* escape.

She was pretty and interesting what with her complete lack of fear over what seemed like millions of bees buzzing about, so he figured he might as well give it a shot.

He followed her and quickly fell into step beside her. "You doing anything tonight?"

She blinked, nearly tripped over her own feet before she caught herself. She looked up at him, those unique violet eyes wide. "I'm sorry. What?"

"You could go out with me," he said, flashing a charming grin. "Dinner? Drinks? I can show you around Jasper Creek."

"You're asking me on a date," she said slowly, as if she didn't understand why.

"Yes."

"Oh." She chewed on her bottom lip and studied him. "Well, there are a few things I have to ask you first."

"Shoot."

"How many women have you slept with in the last six weeks?"

His jaw literally dropped. Quizzing him on his sex life was not the *common* response to him asking a woman out. Particularly one who looked like a transplant from the 1800s.

"It's a judgment-free zone, of course," she continued with a fluttery wave of a hand. "I just need to know in order to inform my answer to your invitation."

Inform my answer to your invitation. Beau adjusted his hat. "Er, do you interrogate every man who asks you out about their...past six weeks?"

She shrugged. "More or less."

"When is it less?"

She smiled, any sign of the blush from before long gone. "When I'm not interested, so there's no need to ask any questions."

Well, that was something, he supposed. "Do I get to ask you the same questions?"

"That's only fair."

He studied her. Pretty. Odd. He'd always liked odd. He'd found women who were odd usually meant they had interests, a sturdy sense of self. He'd always appreciated that.

"One. One woman in the last six weeks." Was he really answering this question? Out loud. He wasn't *desperate.*

But he was interested.

"And was it a relationship type thing or...booty call, one-night stand, et cetera?"

He opened his mouth, but found he was speechless. *Booty call.* He was nearly thirty-eight years old, and this woman had just asked if he'd engaged in a *booty call.* "Either you want to go out with me or you don't, Teddy."

She looked so solemn at his answer, he didn't know what to make of it. "Life is far more complicated than that."

"Only if you make it so." He tipped his cap. "You go on and think about it. Let me know when you've changed your mind."

"I do not date men who don't answer my questions," she said firmly.

"And I don't date women who require a final exam before the first date."

She crossed her arms over her chest and gave him an imperious glare despite her much smaller stature. "I guess it's settled then."

He shrugged. He'd been rejected before. Not *often*, but it happened. There were plenty of women who'd go out with him without concerning themselves about his *booty calls*. "I guess it is."

"Well, let me know about the bees, Beau." She climbed into her tiny little car, out of place in a ranching landscape like this.

He grimaced. The damn bees. "You got time tomorrow?"

"Sundays are Sister Sundays. How about Monday morning. Say, eight?"

"Yeah, sure. Eight." *Sister Sundays.* "What's a Sister Sunday?"

She smiled back at him. "Hard to explain. See you Monday at eight."

Then she was gone, and Beau was…left very confused.

And still far too interested.

CHAPTER THREE

"WELCOME TO THE inaugural Sister Sunday," Teddy announced.

They'd decided Sundays would be dedicated to togetherness. Everyone would take a turn hosting each Sunday, pick a theme, and then everyone would bring their own contributions. But most of all, it was about being together in a way they hadn't been able to be growing up.

Teddy had chosen the ranch itself as the theme for their kickoff. She'd decorated the table with a tablecloth she'd sewed from some of the fabrics she'd found in the old house. Old curtains, dresses, blankets. It was a colorful display despite the faded pieces. It looked homey with Elliot's gorgeous dinnerware and piles of Georgie's baked goods. Joey didn't have any yield of her own yet, so she'd gone to the farmers market and picked out the ingredients for brunch.

"I need to find some chickens for sale," Teddy said, frowning at the egg casserole she'd made. "It'll take forever for the chicks I ordered to mature."

"The eggs at the market seemed pretty decent," Joey replied, pouring fresh-squeezed orange juice into little pink juice glasses they'd bought at a flea market. The tin pitcher had been found in the kitchen and cleaned to a shine. "It'll hold us over."

"I'm going to have my own chickens. Enjoy this chickenless time. For there *will* be chickens."

"The title of the horror movie I'm making," Georgie said dryly, sliding onto the long bench they'd dragged out of the barn. She and Joey began to fill their plates with pastries while Elliot pulled a cart over to the table.

"A cat is following me," she announced, pointing to the little gray striped fluff ball.

Teddy went over to the cat and bent down to inspect. "Well, who do we have here?"

"It's just a stray barn cat," Joey said. "I saw her or him slinking around when I was checking out the tractors."

"She's been following me around for the past hour. Not getting too close, but not letting herself be too far. I think we've got ourselves our first pet."

"We should give her to Grandpa Jack," Teddy said reluctantly. "He could use some company."

"Or, we could name her and keep her for ourselves," Georgie said. "Since Grandpa Jack is likely to chuck her out the window."

"He wouldn't," Teddy said, though she wasn't convinced he would let the cat in the house.

"She's a barn cat," Joey insisted.

"What should we name her?" Teddy asked, ignoring Joey's skepticism. "Remember those books we used to read? Junie B. Jones. She looks like a Junie."

Georgie shook her head. "She should have a boy name like us. Jasper?"

"Jasper Junie Hathaway." Teddy scratched the cat's head, then sighed as she stood back up. "We should put posters up, just in case she's somebody's."

"She is a stray barn cat," Joey insisted, again. "But I suppose Jasper Junie is as good a name as any," she added with a smile when the cat wound itself around her legs.

They took seats around the table and Jasper Junie attempted to jump up onto the seat next to Teddy, but she was a tiny thing. Teddy lifted her and placed her on her lap and set about pouring a little cream into a saucer.

"How'd the bee meeting go?" Elliot asked as they settled in to eat their brunch.

"Good. It's a *sizable* colony."

Elliot snickered and Teddy frowned. "I don't understand why that's funny."

"Something about the word *sizable* is *very* funny."

"Anyway," Teddy said. "He was skeptical of the price, but I'm going back tomorrow to begin the removal process. Should be a decent chunk to help keep us going until we can open Four Sisters Farm to the public. I do think we should try to at least have a street stand up in May to start selling things. I know Grandpa Jack said we could have this free and clear if we didn't ask him for anything, but I was thinking we should pay him some rent. Surely he could have gotten a lot more out of it if he'd sold the land to Colt West."

"You don't speak Grandpa Jack," Georgie replied. "He gave it to us because he wants us around, even if he pretends he doesn't."

"Do you really think so?" Joey asked skeptically.

"I know so. Miserable old coot will *never* say it, but if he really didn't want us around, and if he really needed the money, he'd sell."

Teddy thought that over. She knew deep down Grandpa Jack *needed* them, but she hadn't been so sure about the wanting part. But what Georgie said made sense. She pulled out her planner and made a note to take any leftovers to Grandpa Jack before she went over to the Rileys' tomorrow.

Looking at the entry for going to the Rileys', she was reminded of what had happened yesterday that she hadn't mentioned to her sisters. She didn't have to, of course, but when they'd finally met at thirteen, finally found other people who understood, Teddy had made a promise to herself to always appreciate what she had. To create the kind of relationship she wanted by always reaching out, always being there for her sisters. By being an open book, she created a sense of trust so that if her sisters needed her, they didn't feel afraid to reach out. At least not because of *her*.

"He asked me out," she announced, spreading some locally churned butter onto a thick piece of bread Georgie had made this morning.

"Who asked you out?" Georgie demanded.

"Beau Riley. The one with the bees."

"He asked you out on a date, sans bees?" Joey asked through a mouthful of muffin.

"I believe his exact words were, 'dinner, drinks, I can show you around Jasper Creek.' As if I don't know my way around Jasper Creek." She realized it came out sounding petulant, and she knew she was being petulant because he'd so rudely brushed off her questions.

"Maybe he wanted to show you around *his* Jasper Creek." Elliot waggled her eyebrows.

Teddy allowed herself a moment to consider *that*, then shook her head. No. "He wouldn't answer my questions, so it's a no go." Well, he'd answered one, but that was neither here nor there. Some guys had even gotten to question number ten. None had ever gotten through all thirty before giving up, but one was a terrible showing.

A shame, really. He was awfully handsome, and really did have a killer smile. But her rules were her rules. She had been determined not to be her mother and paint all men with one brush, but she had also been determined to protect herself. She considered her questions the best step in protection. She would make sure she knew the exact measure of a man before she even dipped a toe in the water. So she wasn't completely denying the possibility of a relationship at some point, but she wouldn't disappoint her mother either by getting hurt.

Teddy considered it a great compromise, and fancied herself above the declarations her mother had always made about men.

"No guy ever answers your questions," Georgie pointed out. "Maybe there's a problem with your questions."

"Maybe there's a problem with most men. The right guy will answer my questions." Teddy was sure of it.

"And if no guy ever answers them?" Joey asked, curious.

"I have my sisters," Teddy replied firmly, because of course she'd asked herself the same thing before. And always come to the conclusion it was better to be safe than sorry. "I have Mom. My chickens, and my bees, and my sewing machine. And Grandpa Jack. And now Jasper Junie. What more does a girl need?"

"I'm glad we rate above the chickens and bees," Elliot said, bumping her with her hip.

They spent the rest of the day eating good food and enjoying each other's company while Jasper Junie curled up in Teddy's lap and fell asleep.

Because her sisters were her fate. Not Beau Riley and his bees.

BEAU PROBABLY COULD have found a date Saturday night. Instead he'd sat through the family dinner where his mother got teary-eyed over Grant and Pru's engagement announcement. He'd uncomfortably sneaked out the back with JT, Dad not far behind, and they'd had a beer and let Grant deal with all *that*.

Then Beau had worked all Sunday. He found himself

thinking about Teddy more than was strictly comfortable. Because he didn't know her. She was just a pretty woman who wanted to remove his bees.

Not a euphemism.

So why should she be on his mind and why should he look forward to paying far too much money to have a woman remove bees from an old, unused shed on the property?

He didn't have an answer for that.

At breakfast at his mother's on Monday morning—a routine she'd requested ever since he'd insisted on his own space on the Riley Ranch—Beau found himself *anticipating* the arrival of the bee lady.

"You're unusually quiet," Mom commented, pouring him more coffee. Dad and JT had already finished their breakfast and gone out to the barn, but Beau found himself lingering. Watching out the big picture window toward the front gate.

"Am I?"

"Perhaps your much younger sister's engagement is making the two of you realize you're not getting any younger," Mom said, her tone so sweet he almost didn't pay enough attention to realize she was needling him.

Mary Riley would never be called *subtle*, though. Beau tended to appreciate that about her—more when she was needling JT over him, but nevertheless. "She's marrying a guy *my* age, so I wouldn't put the emphasis on *much* younger, Mom."

"Grant is younger than you too," Mom replied loftily.

Beau didn't bother to point out that he was only two months younger. It wasn't what his mother wanted to hear, so she simply wouldn't.

Beau finished off his coffee, ignoring his mother's careful perusal. "I've got an appointment," he said, pushing the chair back and getting to his feet.

"An appointment?"

"You wanted those old pallets, but I can't get to them because the whole shed is infested with bees. Got someone coming to take care of them."

"Beau James Riley, you cannot exterminate bees. Did you know—"

"They're being murdered at disastrous rates?" he returned sweetly, using Teddy's words from the other day. "Why, yes, I did, which is why I hired someone to remove them. Not exterminate them." He smiled at his mother, enjoying the rare moment when he got to make her speechless. He dropped a kiss on the top of her graying head. "See you around, Ma."

He supposed he didn't need to meet Teddy at the front gate now that she knew where the bees were. Still, he found himself dawdling. He decided to walk all the way back to his cabin. Benji would be out with Dad, so it would just be a quiet, solitary walk.

Almost back, he heard the rumble of the engine, the pop of gravel as a car got closer. He didn't look behind him. Kept his leisurely pace toward his cabin until the car got close enough he couldn't ignore it any longer.

He looked over his shoulder and winced at the way her low-slung car rattled along the gravel. She gave a little wave as she drove past, parking in front of his cabin just as he approached.

He hadn't expected her to arrive wearing a similar outfit to the other day. He'd expected one of those bee suits, or jeans at the very least. But she was wearing a purple dress with blue flowers on it. Thick blue tights on her legs, another pair of boots that went over the ankle. Her curly hair was pulled back into a braid, and she wore a scarf that matched the flowers on her dress. She was wearing the same chunky blue cardigan.

There was something...well, he didn't care for the word *breathtaking*, but it was the only word that seemed to explain the effect she had on him.

She opened the back car door and pulled out a bag. It was different than the one she'd had the other day—that she apparently carried a crowbar around in. He had no doubt this one was similarly full of bizarre tools. But it looked a bit more professional. Canvas and sturdy, instead of some patchwork thing.

Still, there was colorful embroidery on this bag. Bees and flowers, and...possibly a few chickens.

"Morning," she offered cheerfully.

"Morning," he returned.

"You're welcome to watch me work, but you're also welcome to leave me to it," she said. "Whatever works for you."

"I guess I'll watch for a bit."

"Can you grab the box in the trunk?" she asked, pushing a button in the car so the trunk popped open.

"Sure." Beau went around to the trunk. He grabbed the box—bees painted all over the glossy white. The rest of the trunk was filled with the oddest collection of floral fabrics, a collection of straw hats, rain boots, tools and...

A pitiful meow sounded from somewhere deeper in the dark trunk. Frowning, Beau reached forward and moved a quilt out of the way. Curled up behind it was a little gray cat.

"I don't think you're supposed to be in here," he said to the cat, who only blinked at him.

Since he'd known a few vicious cats in his time, he tentatively reached out. Luckily, the cat let him grab her and pick her up.

In one arm he carried the box, in the other he cradled the stowaway.

He met up with Teddy at the back of the shed. She'd already pulled some things out of her bag and pulled a few of the boards off the shed, exposing a jaw-dropping amount of buzzing, crawling bees.

"You've got a stowaway, I believe."

Teddy looked from the hive to the cat, then started forward. "Oh no! She must have crawled in. That's Jasper Junie."

"A two-named cat."

She petted the cat in his arms, standing close enough to him to pick up on the fact she smelled like flowers.

"Well, she had to have a boy name like us, but she also felt like a Junie. Do you mind holding on to her while I work? I wouldn't want her running off."

"Sure, long as she doesn't decide to scratch my eyes out." Beau set the box down next to Teddy's other stuff, unable to take his eyes off the horror in front of him even as he still cradled the cat. "That's a hell of a lot of bees."

"Oh, I bet that's only about an eighth of them," she replied casually. She stepped forward toward the swarm of bees. She reached her ungloved hand right toward the swarm of bees.

"Whoa, whoa, whoa. What are you doing?" he asked, grabbing her wrist with his free hand and stopping her from putting her hand in the middle of *swarming* bees.

She looked at his hand on her wrist for a beat too long, a beat long enough for him to think about how warm and soft her skin felt under his hand. A beat long enough to wonder what other parts of her might feel like.

She looked up at him, those violet eyes a punch. After a moment that seemed to echo through him like thunder, she smiled politely. "I know it's a little alarming for some people, but I know what I'm doing."

Slowly, Beau released her. Because it took a beat too long to realize she meant the *alarming* part was her touching bees, not that…thunder thing.

"Right."

"If they begin to get aggressive, I have a suit in the car. For now, I'll move some comb into the box—their new hive, then move as many as I can manually."

She got to work, removing a shockingly large chunk of comb from inside the wall. She secured it into the box. Sometimes she hummed to herself, sometimes she talked to the bees like they were a preschool class she was teaching, all the while she transferred comb.

"Now I'll just scoop them like this—" She demonstrated, literally *scooping* her hand through the buzzing maze of bees.

Beau had to fight back a full body shudder.

She studied her *hand full of bees* and then plopped the bees into the box. "What I'm doing is looking for the queen," she explained. "The entire colony will follow the queen." Over and over again, she scooped her hand into the swarm and studied what she pulled out. "Once I find her, get her to the new hive, they'll do all the work."

"They will, huh?"

She grinned up at him. She had a little dimple on the right corner of her mouth. "I guarantee it."

He'd promised himself he wouldn't subject himself to her ridiculous questions, but his next words came out before he'd fully realized that's what he'd planned to say. "All right. Hit me with the next question."

"Question?" she echoed, still scooping.

"From Saturday. Your questions."

She studied him before a small, satisfied smile crept over her lips. "You never answered my last question."

He tried not to grimace, though he doubted he managed. "The term *booty call* is offensive."

"But that's what it was? This one woman you've slept with in the last six weeks."

"It was two consenting adults enjoying each other for one night—a predetermined agreement."

"Hmm."

"Next question?"

"How's your relationship with your mother?"

It was a jarring change of subject from sex to his *mother*. He shook his head. Why was he doing this?

But something about the way she looked at him, like she didn't expect him to answer all her questions—let alone to her satisfaction—aroused his competitive spirit. "Just fine."

"Are you close?" *Scoop, inspect, plop.*

He pushed the hat back on his head. As a man who'd occasionally been accused of being a *mama's boy*, he was about as comfortable with this line of questioning as he was with the booty call one. "Suppose."

"Would you do anything for her?"

"I don't know about anything, but she'd probably find a way to make me."

Teddy nodded, and the moment of silence reminded him that she'd said he could ask her the same questions right back.

"What about you?"

"I *love* my mother," she said fiercely.

"Where is she?"

"Maine."

"So far away?"

"She moved about as far away from Oregon as she could

CHAPTER FOUR

"WHERE DO YOU see yourself in ten years?" Teddy asked, more than a little surprised that though she'd been scooping bees for two hours, he hadn't left. The cat dozed lazily in his arms after one brief break to figure-eight around his legs.

The large, handsome cowboy cradling a tiny cat was really splitting her focus. Both from finding the queen and remembering all her questions. Very, very important questions. Because surely he'd answer one poorly, or refuse to answer one like the other day. Proving that he wasn't a safe bet and she was better off letting sleeping dogs—or cowboys—lie.

"Ten years? Doing what I've always done. Ranching. Here. Helping the folks out."

She supposed at the end of the day, she liked his answers to most questions, because even if she didn't agree, what she saw in his answers was a man who loved and respected his family—deeply. And what could be more important than that?

"Did you ever want to do anything else besides ranch here?"

"Nope. The Riley Ranch has stood for generations, and I always knew I'd take my place in that legacy. Always felt right, being a steward of this land, right here."

Teddy liked the idea of roots and generations. Mom had grown up here, but she'd cut all ties with the place when

when she found out she was pregnant with me and… Well, anyway." She waved that away. "I've lived with her ever since, but she thought I needed to try my hand at independence, and then Grandpa Jack had his heart attack and my sisters agreed to start our dream business, so here we are."

"Removing bees."

"Oh, that's only a tiny bit of it." *Scoop, inspect, plop.*

The bees swarmed around her, but she looked perfectly at ease, crawling with *bees*. It was mesmerizing—though he wasn't sure if it was interesting mesmerizing or train-wreck mesmerizing, he just knew he couldn't take his eyes off of her easy, gentle movements as a small cat purred in the crook of his arm.

Maybe this was a dream. Nightmare? He wasn't sure.

"You didn't ask me about *my* six weeks," she said casually after a while.

"I figure your last six weeks—and however many years before, come to that—are your own." He smiled at her, maybe pointedly.

When she frowned, he knew he'd scored a point. At least in his book.

"So, going to go out with me yet?"

"You've got about twenty-five more questions to answer."

"Twenty-five?"

"Maybe it isn't worth it to you," she said, peering at the bees in her hand.

He wasn't sure it was, but he sure as hell wasn't giving up just yet. "Fine. Next question."

she'd gotten pregnant. Maine was home to Teddy, but Oregon was her family's roots.

Beau used the word *legacy*. Joey had used it too. Teddy had always been fascinated by it. Every generation before her had been born and bred in Oregon going back a century. What would it be like to step into that line of succession?

To be a part—an actual step—in the generational legacy of both Hathaways and her mother's Taylor family.

Because ever since she'd first visited, she'd felt a connection to this place. One she could never describe—certainly not to her mother, but even to her sisters. She'd had to chalk it up to some blood or ancestral soul connection to that *legacy*.

"Do you really ask every guy who asks you out these questions?"

Teddy returned her thoughts to the bees. And Beau. "Well, some of the tangential questions come up because of answers to the main ones."

"Uh-huh. So, what's with the bees?"

"Mom put a hive in at our farm when I was eight. I was fascinated by how the bees worked, and when I started to read about them, and realized how important they were, but how people felt about them, I knew I wanted to protect them."

"Ah."

"Ah, what?"

"You're a protector type. Creatures great and small and all that." He made a move with the cat on his arm as if she was an example. "Plus your grandfather."

"He wouldn't call it protecting."

Beau laughed. "Not to your face anyway."

"You know my grandfather?"

"The way I know any of the ranchers around Jasper

Creek and Gold Valley. My dad probably knows him a little better."

Teddy nodded, her heart beating too loudly in her ears as she thought about who else Beau might know. What he might be able to tell her. "Do you..." Did she want to know? She blew out a breath, frowned down at the bees in her hand.

She'd honestly grown out of any curiosity about her father. Mom had painted an ugly picture, and Mom had... Well, Teddy wouldn't have wanted to have grown up differently. She *loved* the childhood Mom had given her, loved being this close to her mother—even if Mom was insisting upon independence now.

Sometimes Teddy had wished for a father, or a father figure, but she'd never wished Mickey Hathaway was it after what he'd done.

"Teddy?"

She looked up from the bees. Beau was looking at her with a kind of sympathy she figured meant he knew about her father. She couldn't tell what Beau thought of Mickey, but that wasn't the point of this. The point of this was him and her.

"Who's your favorite poet?" she asked, though it came out a bit more like a demand.

"Do I look like the kind of guy who reads poetry?" he replied.

She glanced over her shoulder at him after making sure she hadn't found the queen yet. "Yes. Every night by the fire." It wasn't true, but she kind of wanted it to be.

"You are very wrong."

"Are you telling me you don't have *one* book of poetry in that cabin of yours? Not even to impress women?"

"I..." He pulled a face without finishing the denial.

"So you do!"

He hunched his shoulders. "My grandmother gave it to me before she died. Doesn't mean it's a favorite, and I have never once used it to impress a woman."

"Do you read it?"

"Rarely."

"And when you do, why do you?"

He shrugged. "Missing her, I guess."

Well, wasn't that the sweetest thing? "So, who's the poet?"

"They're all anonymous dirty Irish limericks."

She laughed in spite of herself. He was full of it. "Liar," she accused with a grin.

"Fine, it's Emily Dickinson. But don't get any ideas. I don't understand a lick of it."

Emily Dickinson. Her heart did another little flutter. She tried to keep it at a manageable level. There were still questions. Steps.

She found herself wanting him to pass the questions, make the steps, in a way she'd never really allowed herself to hope before. Because this wasn't about hope or futures, it was about protecting herself. About making sure she didn't disappoint her mother by getting heartbroken.

She took another scoop of bees. "Ah, there she is!" She grabbed the clip from her bag, carefully secured the queen inside. She moved the clip to the new hive and stood.

"So, now the entire colony will follow her and move in to their new home. It's a siz—" Teddy remembered what Elliot said about the word *sizable.* "It's massive."

Beau snorted, much like he and Elliot had over *sizable.*

Teddy frowned, but continued. "I imagine it'll take quite a few hours for the bees to all move. Best bet is for me to come back tomorrow morning and make sure all the bees are moved. Finish up then."

"So, that's it?"

"For today."

He stepped forward, nearly toe-to-toe so she had to tilt her head back to meet his gaze. He handed the cat off to her, but remained just that close.

"I pass your test yet?" he asked with that wide grin that made her knees feel a little weak.

"There's one more question," she admitted. One she'd purposefully saved for last, and one she really, truly hadn't expected to get to.

"All right. Shoot." He didn't take a step back. She could smell some kind of woodsy, piney scent coming from him, and the brim of his hat shadowed her face so it felt like they were cocooned in this little world.

It made her breathless, just as it should. Though nerves battered around inside of her, she really hoped he answered the next question well. If he did... Well, this could be the beginning of something special.

The severity of the nerves fluttering around inside her made her wonder if she really *wanted* something special. But she was this far in. No place to go but forward. "Why do you want to take me on a date?"

He pushed back his hat, opening that cocoon up to the sun. She noticed he did that when he didn't know how to answer a question right away.

"Well, you're pretty."

Not that she minded the compliment, but she frowned. "Do you ask every pretty woman out?"

He shrugged. "Mostly. Unless she's taken, or I know her too well. Or she's, God forbid, friends with my sister."

Teddy wanted to pout.

"But I'll tell you what, Teddy, I sure as hell wouldn't answer a hundred questions in order to ask every pretty girl out. Why, I wouldn't have time to eat."

She still wasn't sure she liked that answer, but he was smiling so cheerfully it was hard to resist a smile back. "So, why did you answer all my questions then?"

"Well..." He looked beyond her shoulder, to the hives with bees moving in. His blue gaze returned to her. "You're different."

"Not like other girls is such a cliché—an outmoded way of trying to make one woman seem superior to another," Teddy said, not realizing how much she sounded like Elliot until the words were out of her mouth. But she liked the idea her sisters were rubbing off on her.

"That's all fine and dandy, but I don't know any other women who scoop up bees with their bare hands. I've never had to survive an interrogation to go out on a date. Maybe those women exist out there, but I haven't met them." He reached out and gave her nose a little tap. "Like it or not, sweetheart, you are not like other women *I* know. Dinner. Tonight?"

She hesitated. She did want to go out with him, but she was under no illusions he took dating seriously. There was no way he would take this date as seriously as she did.

Then there was the fact Mom would not approve of him. Well, if Teddy really liked him, Mom would *try* to approve. But she'd be suspicious. Always. Because Mom felt men were evil. Particularly the cowboy kind.

Teddy hadn't been able to take that on board, or so she'd told herself. But she hadn't exactly ever been on a real date before, had she? Because no one had answered all her questions.

Until Beau. She couldn't picture the man before her

being *evil*. Maybe careless, but not mean. If nothing else, she truly believed Beau was kind, even if he wasn't serious.

She wanted to make her mother proud, and going on a date or two with a handsome cowboy—even if he *had* answered her questions—would not make Mom happy. Teddy should say no.

But Mom had insisted she take a year to be independent. To do things outside of her shadow. And Beau had answered every question, many of them while holding her cat. He owned a book of Emily Dickinson poetry and loved his family.

Besides, he was the most handsome man she'd ever seen in real life. What would one date hurt? Not her heart. She wouldn't let it. She'd take a page out of Elliot's book and enjoy a man without expectation.

She smiled up at him, ignoring all her nerves and back-and-forth thoughts and doubts. "All right."

TEDDY DIDN'T KNOW how to feel as she finished her errands for the day, and so nerves took over, making her feel nothing at all.

She had a date. He was going to pick her up at six, and take her to Gold Valley for dinner and maybe some dancing at some country-western bar.

Teddy didn't have the slightest clue how to dance, particularly country-western dancing. But she didn't know how to have *dinner* with a *man* either.

She'd get through it the way she always did. Chin high. Because a date, a man, a choice didn't define her. Only *she* defined her.

Teddy stopped by Riley Feed & Garden to check on the status of her chicks and inquire about finding some laying chickens. By the time she got home, she'd purchased three adult chickens, had to pull over and referee a fight between said chickens and Jasper Junie, and only had about thirty minutes to get ready for her date.

She had a date. She had chickens.

It was a good day. She was determined it would be *good*.

She parked her car in front of the house. She grabbed Jasper Junie in her arms, then opened the back door of the car and shooed the chickens out. "Welcome to your new home," she offered. "I've got a place all set up for you out back, but first Jasper Junie needs to eat."

She was gratified when all three chickens followed her up to the house. Teddy opened the door and the chickens squawked and flapped and fought their way in ahead of her and Jasper Junie.

"Get them out of here," Joey ordered from where she stood setting the kitchen table.

"I will. I promise. I'm just running late." Teddy put Jasper Junie on the floor and then filled the cat's food and water dishes.

"Running late for what?" Georgie said from her spot at the stove. "Dinner's in a few."

"I'll have to skip dinner. I have a date, and I've only got thirty minutes to get ready." She started to head up the stairs, but her sisters followed.

"He answered *all* your questions?" Georgie demanded.

"Every last one. Plus some tangential ones."

"We need Elliot," Joey determined.

"You need me for what?" Elliot called from downstairs. "I am *starving*."

"Teddy's guy answered all her questions," Georgie yelled. "He's taking her to dinner."

Elliot appeared on the stairs, a chicken trailing behind

her trying to peck at the strap of her overalls that was hanging down. She was scowling. "Really, Teddy?"

"Her name is Cluck Norris, if it helps."

"It does not."

Teddy stepped into her room and flung open her closet. Her sisters crowded in and with all four of them in the small space, there wasn't much room to move.

"What should I wear?"

"What's wrong with what you're wearing?" Joey asked, taking a seat cross-legged on Teddy's bed.

"He already saw me in this today."

"He asked you out in it, so he must like it."

Teddy looked down at her clothes. "I'm covered in pollen, cat fur and chicken feathers."

"Aren't you always?"

"From an artistic standpoint, go for something…red or pink, since you never wear those colors. And no tights," Elliot instructed.

"No tights is from an artistic standpoint?" Teddy returned, going through her dresses. She found a springy pink one with little red roses all over it. She'd bought it because it was beautiful, but almost never wore it because bees couldn't see red or pink.

"Okay, it's from a personal standpoint of I don't know how you stand them. Besides, bare legs is sexier than knit tights. Let yourself be a little sexy."

Sexier. Teddy wasn't sure she could pull off *sexy* of any kind. Cute. Pretty. Sure. Maybe even beautiful if she put an effort into her hair. But sexy?

Sex.

That was all getting far too ahead of herself.

Teddy quickly switched out her dresses, and then figured she might as well take Elliot's advice and lose the tights. She looked at herself in the old full-length mirror she'd found in the attic. It was a little warped, but it gave her some idea.

Without her usual layers she looked... She blinked.

"I think that's perfect," Elliot said. "Less pioneer girl, more sophisticated woman."

Teddy tried not to grimace. Pioneer girl was her favorite aesthetic. But it was one night. One date.

"You sure about this?" Georgie asked, concern deepening her frown. "I don't know Beau Riley personally, but he does have a reputation as a bit of a...flirt. Not like a womanizer or anything, but he's hardly boyfriend material."

"I don't mind a flirt. It's just a date." An experience. *Independence.*

"Just a date with the first guy in your entire life to answer all your questions to your satisfaction."

Teddy's stomach swooped uncomfortably, but she waved it away and gave her sisters a determined smile. "Twenty-five is about time to go on a first date. I don't expect him to be Prince Charming. Just a nice...start." And if he *did* turn out to be Prince Charming...

Well, there wasn't anything so wrong with that, was there? Fate had brought her here; bees had brought her to Beau. She wasn't *expecting* happily-ever-afters. She was just entertaining the possibility.

CHAPTER FIVE

BEAU WHISTLED AS he drove toward the Hathaway Ranch. He always looked forward to dates. He liked getting to know people. He liked the dance of flirtation with a woman.

Which was usually an easier dance, for sure. He'd never worked so hard to get someone to go out with him in his life. Not just because he didn't often have to, but also because he knew how to take no for an answer. Plenty of fish in the sea and all that.

But Teddy hadn't been uninterested. Just... Teddy. She really was different, and he couldn't get over the fact she just scooped up bees with her bare hands like it was nothing. There was a straightforwardness about her, even with all those frothy layers.

And her eyes. It wasn't just the unusual color, it was the way she wielded that purple gaze. All straight on and guileless. It left an odd, unfamiliar feeling dead center in his chest.

He rubbed at it. Hunger probably, as he hadn't been nervous over a date since something like middle school and didn't plan on returning to that feeling these twenty-some years later.

He pulled off the highway to the dirt path that would lead to the house on the Hathaway property. Word on the Jasper Creek grapevine was that the sisters had moved into the house Jack Hathaway had vacated after his wife had died some forty years ago. Jack lived in a bachelor cabin way off the beaten path on the Hathaway property, and the girls were fixing up the formerly mostly abandoned ranch house.

Beau pulled to a stop in front of it. The house didn't look abandoned per se, but it didn't look good. Did they really live here with the sagging roof and peeling paint?

But there were signs of colorful, cheerful life everywhere. Flowers in pots on the porch—sagging as badly as the roof. Ribbons and wind chimes hanging from tree branches and porch posts. There was a big picnic setup toward the back of the house, and he could see fairy lights hanging from branches back there.

It somehow suited Teddy down to the bone.

He took the porch stairs, worried they might give under his weight. But everything held firm and he pulled the screen door back. It screeched loudly. He knocked on the door.

Teddy answered, looking her earnest windswept self from the neck up. But from the neck down she looked different. No tights. No cardigan, so he could see the pretty peaches and cream complexion extended beyond her face. Her hair was completely down rather than falling out of some band, and though the dress was the same floral kind he always saw her wearing, it seemed to fit a little better, offer more of a glimpse of the curvy body underneath.

"Wow," he said, without meaning to.

She grinned at him, violet eyes sparkling. "I like wow."

There was a shout from inside. Then the booming yell of another woman. "Teddy, I swear to God…"

Teddy winced. "I'm sorry. I have to take care of a chicken problem real quick and grab my bag. Come on in for a second."

He stepped inside into a small, dilapidated and outdated

kitchen that somehow looked cozy because of all the little touches. Lace curtains. Set table with colorful pottery. The smell of bread baking.

He wasn't sure what to make of the three chickens currently trying to terrorize Jasper Junie. He reached down and picked up the cat to save her from the chickens.

Teddy managed to get one chicken out the door with simple shooing motions, then in an impressive feat, grabbed the other two under either arm.

"You're an expert animal wrangler," he offered, opening the screen door for her.

"Something like that," she said, a little breathlessly. "Stand tight. I'll be right back."

"Sure."

She disappeared outside and when he looked back at the kitchen, three women stood at the base of the stairs studying him with varying expressions, but the same violet eyes as Teddy.

Her sisters. He offered his most charming smile. "Hi, all. I'm Beau."

"Like *B-O*?" the one in a ratty T-shirt that had a longhorn cow on it asked.

"Uh, no. *B-e-a-u*."

"Is it short for Beauregard?" the one in overalls asked him, with a bit of a smirk.

His smile didn't falter. "No, it isn't."

"What time are you going to have her home, Beau?" the third asked, hands crossed over her chest. He knew this one. Or had seen her now and again, though he didn't remember her name.

"Well, you Hathaway women sure like your questions."

The overalled woman's eyes widened. "Women," she whispered to the sister next to her. "He said *women*."

"Did you prefer…another term?"

Teddy reappeared before they could answer. "Sorry about that." She was all smiles. "Have a good dinner," she said to her sisters. "I'll be back later."

"Your sisters didn't introduce themselves," Beau pointed out.

"Oh." Teddy turned back to the trio, a smile on her face that meant he'd earned some points for showing interest. "That's Joey," she said of the cow T-shirt. "Elliot." Overalls. "Georgie." The one from around here.

He gave them all a charming smile. "Nice to meet you."

They murmured varying responses, but the one thing that united them all was suspicion. As he had a little sister, he understood that. Respected it even. But he was certain he could win them all over.

He placed Jasper Junie back on the floor. Then followed Teddy out into the pretty spring evening. She had her bag on her shoulder and one of her chunky cardigans slung over her arm. But her legs were bare.

Maybe the questions were worth it after all. He beat her to the passenger side door and opened it for her so she could climb up into his truck.

She beamed at him as he offered his arm to help her leverage into the seat. "Thanks."

He found himself struck…dumb for a moment. Something about the smile, the way the sun hit those violet eyes at a new angle, gave him the strangest sensation he was making some drastic change in his life, just by setting this date in motion.

Beau didn't do change. He didn't upset the easy rhythm of his life. Ever.

But how would this sweet, cheerful woman who scooped

bees change anything? They'd have a fun time for a bit, and then they'd both move on.

What other options were there?

DINNER WAS DELICIOUS, and Beau had put her instantly at ease. A childhood on a farm in Maine wasn't all that different than one on a ranch in Oregon, so they'd had a lot in common. He told stories about terrorizing his siblings that made her laugh, and stories about his interfering mother that had her telling stories of her own.

She could forget she was on her first date *ever* for long stretches of time. Of course, then he'd do something like touch her hand, or brush elbows, or help her into his truck and the nerves came back tenfold.

Now, they were in some poorly lit bar and he wanted her to dance.

"I don't know how," she insisted, while he grinned at her.

He took her hand, gave her a little tug at her laughing denials. "Come on now. You can't *not* dance to this song."

She didn't recognize it, but his grin lured her to her feet. He gave her a little twirl, and she was half-afraid she'd trip and fall, but he had a good grip on her and no loss of balance sent her sprawling.

She didn't know anyone as…fun as he was. Lighthearted. Oh, she loved her sisters and their passions, their craft days and meals. But they tended to be…serious. Deep. Intense. Just like Mom had always been.

Teddy wasn't sure Beau was intense about anything. It was new and exciting.

The music changed, slowed, and Beau brought her close. He slid one arm around her waist, held one of her hands against his chest, and then they just swayed. It was a strange sensation, all these people around, and yet she felt like it was just the two of them. His large form enveloping her much smaller one. Until she was resting her head against his shoulder. Her eyes even drifted closed as the soft twang of the song settled over them.

She tried to stifle a yawn, but getting up before five to deal with a whining kitten was catching up with her.

"You're beat," he said, giving her a little squeeze before he released her. "I'll take you home."

He grabbed her bag and her sweater for her, then kept his hand on the small of her back as they weaved their way out the door. He helped her into the truck and then he held her hand while he drove.

Teddy had always considered herself a *touchy* person. She hugged, she held hands. She gave exuberant back pats when the person on the receiving end wasn't a big hugger. She was used to *touch*.

But it amazed her how much different it was when the touch was initiated by someone else. When the touch was from a man who looked like Beau. *A man at all.*

His thumb brushed over the inside of her wrist, making her shiver.

"I have to ask about the tattoo, because you don't seem the tattoo type."

Teddy looked at the delicate violet bloom on the inside of her wrist. "Well, the year we all turned eighteen my sisters and I got to take our first solo trip together. I believe Elliot was the instigator. I'll admit, I wasn't very into the idea, but it was about…connection. We didn't live in the same place, never had. It was supposed to be about…marking our connection. But keeping our individuality. So, we got it on the same place, but we chose different flowers."

"Why the flowers?"

"It was something pretty, something we all liked that

could be individualized. I like violets. They're one of the first wildflowers that bloom in the spring, and they pop up just about anywhere. Small, but sturdy. And purple. Bees love blue and purple."

"I can't imagine getting matching tattoos with my siblings," he said with a chuckle.

"That's because you grew up with them. You can't imagine life without them. It means more when you have to… make the relationship yourself."

He shifted, a strange, serious expression flitting across his face so quickly she was sure it must have been a trick of the moonlight. "Yeah. Of course," he said, then grinned at her in a way she didn't quite believe.

She wanted to press on that, that odd hitch in everything he'd been all night, but it was just a first date, and he pulled to a stop in front of Hathaway House, as she'd begun to call it.

It looked different in the moonlight. A little eerie, but eerie was just magic with a dark filter on it.

"I had a good time," she said, turning to look at him, but he was getting out of the truck.

"My mother taught me manners, Teddy," he said, somewhat scoldingly. "I'll walk you to your door."

Before she could think what to do he was opening the passenger side and offering a hand to help her down. She took his hand and stepped out into the cold spring night. He didn't let go, instead laced his fingers with hers.

The air was cold, the moon bright. And a handsome cowboy was holding her hand, walking her up to the door on a house her ancestors had built.

"Is Teddy short for anything?" he asked.

Teddy wrinkled her nose. "Yes."

"What, like, Theodora?"

She shook her head. "I prefer Teddy."

"Oh, come on. You have to tell me now." He took both her hands and gave them a little jiggle, making her laugh.

"It's nothing that interesting. No feminine *a* at the end. Just Theodore."

They weren't walking toward the door anymore. They were standing at the base of the stairs, both of her hands captured in his much bigger ones.

"Theodore. I'm going to have to meet your mom someday, Teddy. She sounds like a character."

Teddy's heart did an uncomfortable dance in her chest. He was mentioning meeting her *mother*. She couldn't imagine Mom approving of Beau, but she would try if Teddy asked her to.

Another possibility, and Teddy felt lit from within by all of them. "I had a really good time, Beau."

"Me too. And don't ever say you can't dance again. You can. With a little help."

She laughed. She would have let his hands go, but he pulled her to him, gently. She looked up at him as her chest bumped gently into his.

There was all that intensity she could have sworn he didn't have, deepening the blue in his eyes. Making her heart beat so hard against her chest she didn't recognize it as her own.

She had thought she didn't want that, but her body was telling her other things when his finger traced the line of her jaw.

He looked down at her, studying her in some way she didn't understand. When he tilted his head down to hers, her heart gave an uncomfortable jerk and part of her wanted to bolt.

But then his mouth touched hers, and her heart settled

and her feet were firmly planted to the ground, not want-ing to go *anywhere*. She didn't know quite what to do with herself, but Beau knew enough for the both of them. His mouth cruised over hers as he held her gently in place.

"You can touch me, you know," he said against her mouth.

It was only then she realized her hands were hanging limply at her sides. She laughed; at least she hoped that ex-hale sounded like a laugh. A sound more worldly than she felt as he ran his hands down her arms, then lifted them to rest on his shoulders.

Then he touched his mouth to hers again. A soft, lull-ing magic.

Was a simple kiss supposed to feel like she was *melt-ing*? Like her bones no longer functioned and her heart was beating at such a rapid rate she might actually burst. Was she supposed to want to *cry* and want to dance about in the moonlight all at the same time?

He eased back and stared at her for the longest time. As she had no words, she could only stare back. But eventu-ally, slowly, he began to release her. Step back, the cool air rushing in between them making her shiver.

"Good night, Teddy," he said softly.

"Good night," she returned, watching him walk back into the night and to his truck. She didn't bother to go in-side until she no longer heard the steady rumble of his truck.

She knew she couldn't tell a single soul what she was feeling, because it was ridiculous. Everyone would tell her it was too soon, and she didn't know any better, but what else could this sparkling giddy thing be?

Jasper Creek was fate, wasn't it? Maybe the bees were. Maybe Beau was.

And she went to bed dreaming of maybes.

CHAPTER SIX

BEAU WOKE UP the next morning unsettled. Not a normal feeling for him, not one he dealt with particularly well.

There was a simple enough solution. He wasn't going to ask Teddy out again. Sure, she was fun and they got along and that kiss was... Well, any guy would want more.

But it was dangerous ground, and Beau didn't take chances with that kind of thing. He'd learned his lesson a long time ago on that score. Teddy asked too many questions. She made him feel like...someone else. Someone who cared too deeply about things, and he simply refused.

He'd keep his distance. No matter how many times her violet eyes seemed to pop into his head over the course of doing his early morning chores. Teddy Hathaway was boggy ground, and he'd always stayed far, far away from boggy ground.

At breakfast his mother asked him to do some errands for her, so he found himself at Pru's store at opening. Pru and Grant were bickering while Pru got the seedlings together Mom wanted. Beau waited, an uncomfortable and uncharacteristic restless feeling making him irritable.

"What's up with you?" Pru demanded.

"Nothing's up with me."

"You're grumpy." She flicked a glance at Grant for confirmation. "Doesn't he seem grumpy?"

Grant eyed Pru, then Beau, as if deciding whose side to take. "You do seem a little off," he said at length.

"Traitor," Beau muttered. He wasn't about to tell them their wedding talk really brought home that things *had* changed. Vows and forevers, and it would no doubt end in *children*. It opened things up to all sorts of bad possibilities. Pru didn't even have a clue. "Look, I've got to get back to the ranch. Can we hurry this along?"

Pru pushed the seedlings toward him. "Grumpy," she reiterated.

"Obnoxious," he returned, taking the tray of seedlings and heading outside without even a goodbye. He drove back to the Riley Ranch with more speed than was expressly necessary.

He didn't like this jangling feeling inside of him. Hated even more that people could *see* it. He had to get a handle on himself. He'd solved the problem. He wasn't going to see Teddy again, so why did he still feel so unsettled?

But of course, when he drove toward his cabin, he realized not seeing Teddy again was going to be a little more difficult than he'd considered. Her car was parked back by the shed.

Beau had the cowardly thought he should just turn right the hell around. But he wasn't a coward. If he made a bed, he was going to lie in it.

When he saw her though, he realized the bed metaphor was a bad one because what he'd really like to do was talk her into one. Her dress was a dark green today, which seemed to tease out the red in her hair or maybe that was the sunlight. She had on one of her cardigans—a bright blue that practically matched the sky.

And as he approached, she was talking. To Benji. About bees as she worked.

When she finally heard him, she looked over and offered a bright smile. "Oh, hi. I wasn't sure I'd run into you. Looks like all the bees made the move."

Right. The bees. She'd said she'd come back today.

"I've just got to load up the hive and take them home." She frowned at her car. "I tried to borrow Grandpa Jack's truck, but he was being a mean old thing this morning and said he didn't let women with more chickens than sense drive his vehicles." She blew out a breath, fluttering the strands of hair that framed her face. "I don't suppose I could borrow your truck to haul these back to my place?"

More chickens than sense. Maybe, but clearly Jack Hathaway didn't appreciate that what his granddaughter had more than anything was...

Ah, hell. He didn't know, he only knew he wanted to taste her again.

Surely last night had been a one-off. They could have fun. So, maybe the intensity in this one took a little longer to fizzle out. That just meant there'd be more to enjoy.

Without saying a word, he bent down and captured her mouth with his. She reached out and grabbed on to his arms, for balance or because she wanted to. She melted against him like wax, sighed a little dreamily into the kiss.

When they both came up for air some time later, she was still clutching his arms as she blinked at him.

"You got plans tonight?" he asked. Because why not have fun together? Why *not*? Determining he was going to stay away hadn't lifted his mood any. The prospect of another night with Teddy did.

"I should say I'm very busy," she said, just enough *dazzled* in her eyes to have him grinning. Yeah, this could definitely just be fun for a while.

"Why *should* you say that?"

"Because I have more of a life than going out with you at the drop of a hat."

"Except tonight," he supplied.

She laughed. "Except tonight." She released his arms, took a bit of a step back. "What did you have in mind?"

"Go on, take my truck. I can't do dinner, but if you come back around seven or so with the truck, we'll go for a horse-back ride. You know how to ride?"

"Yes."

"Then that's what we'll do."

What harm could come from a horseback ride anyway? He had spent his entire adult life keeping things light.

So, light it would stay.

"You're going out with him again tonight?" Joey asked with a frown.

"Yes. We had fun last night." She wasn't sure *fun* was the right word for the way he'd kissed her last night *or* this morning, but she didn't *have* a word in her vocabulary for that. "Besides, it's just a horseback ride."

"Do we need to have 'the talk' with you, Teddy?"

"Don't be silly," Teddy said, waving Elliot away. The temperatures were supposed to dip tonight, so she picked a sweater dress and fleece-lined leggings since they'd be riding. "My mother has been having 'the talk' with me since I could walk. I've been on the pill since I was in high school. If there's a mother who prepared her daughter for all the consequences of sex, it's mine."

"Maybe that's why you haven't *had* sex," Elliot said dryly.

"Well, maybe," Teddy agreed. She'd never really thought about that correlation. That all the dire warnings her mother had given her about sex and how easy it was to get pregnant might have made the whole possibility...less than appealing. "But I'm not planning on having any tonight." She thought of the way Beau had looked at her last night after that kiss. The way he hadn't said a thing at first this morning, just walked up and kissed her like he couldn't help himself.

For the first time, the idea of sex was *very* appealing. Teddy didn't know quite what to do with that, but it *was* independence. So there was that.

"Moving a bit fast," Georgie said from where she stood by the door. It wasn't judgment in her tone, but concern.

"It doesn't feel that way," Teddy assured her.

"Maybe he should come to something on Sister Sunday," Joey said, looking at Georgie and then Elliot. "So we can give him the once-over."

"You gave him the once-over last night when he picked me up. You said he passed the test."

"Sure, the date test. Not the is-he-good-enough-to-have-sex-with-you test," Elliot replied.

"That is not a real test," Teddy replied, giving Elliot a stern look. "Certainly not one you'd ever subject anyone who you wanted to have sex with to."

"You have no idea what I'd do," Elliot replied loftily. "I am unknowable."

"I know you can't stop drooling over Colt West," Joey said under her breath.

"Drooling and sex are two very different things," Elliot returned. "Besides, his physical form is infinitely drool-worthy. From an artistic standpoint."

Georgie scoffed, but Joey was suspiciously quiet as if deep in thought.

Elliot grinned at her. "Perhaps you've noticed Hollis's *physical form*."

Joey frowned, but said nothing. Teddy tried to take the lull in conversation as a moment to escape, but Elliot stopped her and took her by the shoulders before Teddy could scoot out the door.

"Your body is your own," Elliot said, violet eyes direct and serious. "And he should see to your pleasure first. If he doesn't, he isn't worth a thing."

Something about the word *pleasure* had heat creeping into Teddy's face. "Well, of course," she agreed. Technically, she *knew* what Elliot meant, but she was having a hard time imagining what that meant when there was an actual person to picture. When there was *Beau* to slot into the partner place.

He was so…large.

"What are you blushing about, Teddy?" Joey demanded.

"I'm guessing it has to do with something *sizable* or *massive*," Elliot said with a grin.

"I'm not thinking about bee colonies."

"I wasn't suggesting you were."

"How *can* you tell if a guy is massive?" Joey asked thoughtfully. "I'd hate to get his pants off and then be like… accosted by a tree trunk."

Teddy made a choking noise, while Elliot howled with laughter and Georgie fell into a coughing fit.

Joey threw her hands up in the air. "It's a fair question."

"Trust me, far worse to get his pants off and find a toothpick instead."

"I have to go," Teddy said, wriggling out of Elliot's grasp. The last thing she needed was to be imagining the different *sizes* a man could be in Beau's company.

"Make sure to call us if you won't be home," Elliot called after her.

"I'm the only one who ever answers the landline," Teddy pointed out, already halfway down the stairs.

"Call anyway," Georgie insisted.

Teddy waved, then escaped outside. The cool air helped with the heat in her cheeks. She hoped. She tried not to be missish about things. She'd grown up on a farm. Her mother had always been frank with her about sex and sexuality.

She chewed on her lip. Frank to the point of making it sound…distasteful. Elliot on the other hand, had always made it sound…well, Teddy didn't have the vocabulary for Elliot's free-thinking views on sex, but it didn't seem *bad*.

Still, to Teddy, sex seemed so *private*—good or bad. Shouldn't a person keep it to themselves?

She got into Beau's truck. She couldn't quite believe he'd lent it to her, few questions asked, considering her own *grandfather* hadn't. Now she had the bees in place, and she'd begun to hang flyers about her bee removal business, and there'd be honey to start selling next week once they got the roadside stand up and going. Four Sisters Farm wasn't solvent yet, but it was on its way.

And she had a horseback riding date with a handsome man who made her laugh and took her breath away when he kissed her.

The choice to move to Jasper Creek had *everything* coming together. Maybe her mother did always know best what with her insistence on independence and trying new things.

Of course, that would mean Beau was a bad idea. Mom was quite convinced all men would disappoint you eventually. But when she arrived at the Riley Ranch, Beau stood outside the barn with two pretty horses, throwing a rope bone to Benji. He heaved the bone, then lifted a hand to wave to her as she pulled the truck to a stop.

No, Mom wasn't right about *all* men. And, technically, Beau was a very new thing.

She got out of his truck and walked over to him.

"Meet Apple and Carrot," he greeted, pointing to each horse.

"Beau, that cannot be their names."

"Why not?"

"It's a fruit and vegetable."

"It's their favorite snack. We've also got Sugar, Hay, Banana," he said, gesturing back toward the barn.

"You're killing me. Those are the worst horse names in the world."

"Surely not the *world*."

"I think the world. Actually, I think the entire universe."

"Well, next time we get a horse, I'll be sure to consult you on names."

"But you have a theme. A terrible theme, but a theme. You can't just ruin a theme."

"*You* can't, maybe. I can ruin a theme just fine. My mother always tries to put some theme on Christmas presents, and I never follow it."

"You're a terrible son," she said solemnly.

"Truly, but she's crazy about me anyway." He grinned.

"I'd like to meet her sometime."

"Oh. Sure. Yeah. Anyway, let's get you on up." He patted the saddle and helped her with balance as she got her foot into the stirrup. She swung herself over and settled herself into the saddle.

Then she watched him do the same. Such an easy, practiced movement. All muscled and male. She sighed a little dreamily, and realized he caught it when he looked back at her and winked.

"Carrot will follow easily enough. I've got a spot I want to show you that I think you'll like."

"Okay." She settled into a rhythm with Carrot. Poor horse. What a name. Still, she couldn't dwell on his or his family's poor name choices when they climbed a rocky trail. Everything was pretty. That vivid green of spring, the sky slowly starting to take on color.

After a while, Beau stopped his horse and swung off, tying the reins to a little tree. He helped her down and did the same with Carrot's reins.

"Just a bit of a hike up this way," he said, gesturing to a pile of rocks. He held her hand, helping her over the jagged boulders they needed to climb. She didn't really need the help, and she suspected he knew that, but she liked her hand in his all the same.

He helped her up over the last rock. Below, a valley stretched out, wildflowers carpeting almost the entire view. The sunlight was fading, and the colors danced vibrantly in the golden hour light.

"See any Mule Wart?" he asked, and she knew he was teasing her, but she couldn't quite catch her breath to tease back.

"Mule Flower," she corrected. "Beau, this is gorgeous."

"Bee paradise, huh?" He slung his arm around her shoulders.

"It looks like *anyone's* paradise," she said, too awed to do anything but stand there and try to drink it all in.

When she thought she'd memorized it all—the colors, the textures, the sheer, giant awe of it all, she looked up at him. "This is perfect."

He smiled down at her. "Knew you'd like it."

Their gazes held for a moment, and when he lowered his mouth to hers, she figured she knew what to expect now.

The ease into it, gentle and sweet, until it turned a little darker, more insistent like this morning. And she liked all those different flavors, the journey Beau could make a kiss take.

But this one didn't stop. It became its own entity. Not just mouths and arms, but their bodies pressed together. Their hearts beating against each other. His hand slid down her back, over her butt, pulling her closer.

Her heart jerked an odd beat once, a little trickle of nerves, but it was drowned away by the way he kissed her. And when his hand stroked up her leg, under her skirt, she didn't mind. She wanted to know where it would go.

"Teddy."

For a moment, she thought it could be that easy. This was beautiful and he was nice. And she loved that buzzy feeling inside of her as his hand moved up her leg. The way he said her name a little ragged. She wanted more of it.

But when his hand traveled up far enough under her dress to hit bare skin, about a dozen of her mother's warnings came crashing down on her, and they were outside, and it was a bit hard to not *panic*. She thought of Georgie warning her it was going too fast.

She pulled her mouth from his. She didn't push his hand away, but she touched his arm—keeping him from any forward movement. "I'm sorry. I just…"

He studied her for a moment. "You want to wait?" he asked, carefully.

She was so embarrassed she wanted to look away, but that would have been cowardly. "Just a little while longer yet," she managed to say, even as she was sure her face was as red as a tomato. "It's not that I don't want to. I just…" She didn't have words for what she *just*. Something like *my mom brainwashed me and my sisters warned me*.

Brainwashed wasn't the right word, but she didn't know what was. She felt…conflicted and confused. But he didn't press or demand explanations. He nodded. Once. He didn't frown or argue with her. Just nodded. "All right."

That was not…what she'd expected. "You aren't mad?"

"I'm not an asshole, Teddy." He tucked a piece of hair behind her ear. "I can take no for an answer without getting bent out of shape about it. I figure not being ready has more to do with you than me."

She nodded. "I've never…" She swallowed. "It's just I've never…" She really couldn't bring herself to say it and wished the world would swallow her whole.

"No worries," he said, and he didn't seem the least bit uncomfortable. "You just let me know if and when."

If and when. She looked up at him but his gaze was on the sunset. Like it wasn't a big deal at all. He hadn't even taken his arm from around her, or said something snide. He just accepted it and…seemed fine.

The antithesis of every dire warning she'd ever gotten. She didn't know what to do with that. That a man like Beau could exist. Could answer her questions. Not pressure her for more. That all those things she'd built to keep herself from danger…could be breached.

It was scary, but scariest of all was the fact that she didn't want to run away. She wanted to settle in. To be here. With him.

So, she leaned in and enjoyed the setting sun. And Beau.

CHAPTER SEVEN

IT TURNED OUT, dating Teddy was easy as could be. They liked to do the same things and talk about the same things. She never pushed for more, and Beau never pushed for less. They enjoyed each other's company.

He hadn't been bothered by her virginity admission. In fact, it suited him just fine. He figured few women settled down with their first or wanted to. And if they never got there, things would just fizzle out naturally.

As the weeks passed, he stopped worrying that he was getting a little too used to Teddy in his life. Didn't get grumpy over the way kissing her turned him inside out, made the earth below feel a little off-kilter.

It didn't matter. Because there was some kind of expiration date, as there needed to be. Which meant he could do what he did best. Enjoy.

Particularly when she came over and cooked for him, which generally led to making out on the rocking chair on his porch. Right now she was just sitting in his lap as they rocked, watching the stars.

"Tell me about your best day ever," she said. She often asked out-of-the-blue questions, like she was still quizzing him. He'd asked her if she had a list of them somewhere, but she'd only laughed. And decidedly not answered his question.

But he didn't mind answering them. He didn't mind talking to her about things. She was a great listener, and whenever she answered her own questions, she usually surprised him with something. Teddy wasn't easy to pin down, and there was something enjoyable about finding all those different facets of who she was.

"I'm guessing you don't want to hear about the first time I touched a girl's breast," he said after pretending to mull it over.

She swatted his arm. "I'm serious."

"All right. Best day ever. Hmm. Well." He thought it over, and she absently stroked her fingers through his hair, and it lulled him. That was the only explanation for the story that came out.

"Pru was about three. She'd finally convinced Dad to let her ride a horse." He could see it so clearly in his head. "Mom was telling him no, but Dad put his foot down— might be the only time I've seen my dad put his foot down to anything when it came to my mom. But he's carrying Pru out to the barn, Mom's yelling at him, and JT and I are following along because we don't know what's going to happen, and it seemed...important somehow." After the years of quiet, and grief, it had seemed like something was about to explode.

"Dad puts Pru on Sally—do you have anything to say about a horse named Sally?"

"Better than Hay."

He chuckled. "So, Dad plops Pru on Sally—this old, bored mare that wouldn't hurt a fly. And Pru's in heaven. She's giggling like a maniac. Dad holds her the whole time, walking in the slowest circle *ever*. At some point we realize Mom stopped yelling, and she's laughing maniacally right along with Pru. That's when I knew the dark days were finally really over."

Teddy shifted in his lap, looking up at him with concern. "Dark days?"

He stiffened. "I didn't mean..." He cleared his throat. "That sounds really dire." He tried to laugh it out. Why had he said that last bit?

But Teddy's violet eyes were fixed on him. All sweet and sympathetic. "Why were they dark?"

If he didn't tell her, it made it into more than it was. Waving it away would only make her wonder. He just had to explain it as quickly and concisely as he could and then move them along.

Because those dark days didn't matter. They were a blip, and they'd ended and everything had gone back to normal. Everything had settled into the way he liked things. The way he kept things.

"Just... I had another sister. Before Pru. She was born really early and she didn't make it, and... Mom almost didn't, and my grandma had a stroke about the same time. So, it was a bad year. Buried the baby, Grandma died. Thankfully Mom got better. But everything was kind of muted for a few years after. Even when Pru was born healthy and loud, it took a while, I think, for everyone to believe things could be okay again."

He didn't know what anyone else had felt that day, but he had felt relief. So big and life-changing he'd cried himself to sleep that night. Embarrassing for a ten-year-old boy, but the weight of the years was gone. And he'd determined they always would be. No more *years* of grief. Not for him.

"I'm not sure Pru even knows about her," he heard himself say, as though he were someone else not in control of his mouth. "Mom and Dad never spoke of it. There's a marker in the family plot, but she's never asked. She wouldn't."

"Why not?"

"We don't talk about things like that." And it was time to *stop* talking about things like this. "What was your best day?"

She studied him for a long time. Deciding, he supposed, if she'd let him move on or if she wanted to push the issue. She settled back into him, resting her head on his shoulder, her legs dangling over the side of his lap and the chair.

"It's hard to choose just one," she said at length. "One that stands out is the day I met my sisters."

"Met them?"

"Our mothers sort of bonded over what our dad did to them. It's a small town, and it didn't take long for anyone to connect the dots. For the whispers to make it clear to all of them that they'd all been impregnated by the same guy."

"Rough."

"It was. They all handled it differently. My mom moved to Maine. Joey's to Texas. Elliot's up to Portland. Georgie's mom…she was still a bit hung up on Mickey, I think. And in the end, didn't stick around for Georgie like she should have, but they all kept in touch. Knew what was going on with each other. I'm not sure whose idea it initially was, but when we were thirteen, our moms decided to send us to the same summer camp—and convinced Georgie's half brother to send her too. I know my mother wanted me to have some friends my own age and I wasn't making any at the farm. None of us were very good at…blending in with other teenage girls. Too intense, I guess. So, my mom at least figured if we became friends that would be great, but if we were at camp and we didn't really like each other, we wouldn't have to."

"But you did."

"Immediately. Suddenly there were three other girls with

the same eyes as me. We were all different, but we…fit.
Like pieces of a puzzle. It was like we complemented each
other, were *made* to be sisters. We were a unit that summer."

"And ever since."

She smiled up at him. "And ever since." Her expression
went thoughtful again, but before she could say whatever
she was going to say—something likely far too *thoughtful*
for his tastes—he kissed her.

She melted into it, as she always did. He knew not to
expect too much. She'd cut things off when she got uncomfortable, and maybe it made for a restless night for him, but
there was something fun about the anticipation.

And some relief in knowing if it never happened, they'd
part ways having had a nice few months together. There'd
be no grief. No complications. No *loss*. And that was the
important thing. Always.

"Oh," Teddy said, sliding off his lap. "I brought some
cookies Georgie made for dessert."

"Can't complain about the perks of dating a woman
whose sister is a baker," he said, following her inside.

She was already in the kitchen area, digging into the
bags she'd brought. "Do you have milk?"

"Sure."

He moved for the refrigerator and then she started poking around in his cabinets. She knew where the glasses
were, but she liked to poke around for something "prettier" than his spartan dishware, as she called it. He never
stopped her, knowing she'd never find anything that suited
her tastes.

Tonight though, she reached for the top cabinet that no
one ever reached for. He nearly leapt across the room to
try and stop her, but she managed to fling it open before
he could get there.

"What…is this?" she asked.

The top cabinet he would have said was too tall for her to reach was full of wooden ducks. Ones he had to keep in close reach in case his mother ever visited. "Well… They're wooden ducks."

"I can see that," Teddy said, turning to face him very carefully. He couldn't read her expression.

"My mom thought the cabin needed some decorative touches when I moved in and she gave me all those," he explained, watching her violet eyes, but they revealed nothing.

"Why are they in a cabinet?" she asked, as devoid of any inflection as he'd ever heard her.

"I can't stand to be stared at by wooden ducks all damn day. But I could hardly tell *her* that. We made a deal when I moved into the cabin that since I was staying on the property, but decidedly moving out of her house, she had to call before she popped in. So, when she does, I put them out."

Teddy blinked. "You…put them out when she comes over so she doesn't know that you hate the wooden ducks she gave you."

"Yes."

She nodded. Studied the ducks for a few more seconds. Then she carefully closed the cabinet and turned to face him, her expression very, *very* serious. "Remember when you said to let you know if and when?"

It took him a minute, but then he got it. "Oh."

She smiled at him, and for the weirdest moment of his life *he* felt like the nervous virgin.

But only for a moment.

HE WAS ACROSS THE ROOM before Teddy fully realized what she'd said. He lifted her off the floor, crushed his mouth

to hers, and all she could do was hold on and laugh breathlessly against his mouth.

"I take it you're interested," she managed, wrapping her
arms around his neck for balance.

He carried her all the way into his messy bedroom.
"Very astute. I'd have shown you the wooden ducks weeks
ago if I'd known that would do the trick."

She laughed and he tumbled her onto the unmade bed.
She didn't even feel nerves. It was just…joy. Laughter and
smiles and *fun*.

She trusted Beau. He wasn't going to hurt her. Mom was
wrong, and that was okay. Teddy was choosing to be right.

He pulled his shirt off in record time, kneeling there on
the end of the bed, her sprawled out where he *slept*. This
was where she was going to let him…

Well.

She wished she had any of the vocabulary Elliot had
about these things. She wished she could feel like her body
was her *own*. But she couldn't help it. Part of her personality was a prude and no attempts to change it had stuck.

Beau's…enthusiasm, after spending weeks letting her
stop things whenever she started to feel panicky without
a complaint or hint of disappointment, was something of
a relief. He *did* want to sleep with her. The same way she
wanted to sleep with him.

This time she wasn't going to let her fear of the unknown hold her back. He'd told her a heartbreaking story
from his childhood, and while she knew it had made him
uncomfortable, it had allowed her to understand him on a
deeper level. He kept things light to mask the loss, the hurt.
Those *dark days* as he'd called it, and the happiest day of
his life had been when his family had felt healed. When
they'd stepped into the light again.

She wanted to be part of that light.

But it was really the ducks that had done it. He kept them, put them out whenever his mother came, because he cared about his mother's feelings.

Who wouldn't fall for that?

The flutters inside of her were a mix of anticipation and nerves, but the nerves were for the unknown, not him. He made her feel like she belonged right here. Like they'd both been waiting for just this. Always. *Fate.*

"You just tell me to stop if you don't like anything," he said, taking the time to unbutton each of the buttons of her dress—from collar to hem. Then he grinned at her. "But I'm going to work very hard to make sure you like it all."

Whatever tiny piece of her heart she'd been trying to hold back, to wait on him, fell. Hard. So hard, she didn't think twice about him parting the fabric of her dress, gazing down at her in her underwear.

She was too busy dealing with that word. *Love.* Love. She was in *love* with him. Here. Now. Probably irrevocably. He was everything her mother warned her didn't exist. Kind and funny and thoughtful. Mom wouldn't believe it, but for the first time in her life Teddy found she really, truly didn't care.

Mom had been hurt, and lived in that hurt ever since. Believed in that hurt ever since. But it wasn't Teddy's hurt. She didn't have to live in it too. This wasn't about her mother. It was about Teddy herself.

She wanted this man, wherever this led.

Ranch work seemed to have chiseled him into marble. Smooth skin over hard muscle. Coarse hair over a chest like a brick wall. She didn't know *why* that was appealing, only that all that hardness, and the size of him, made her feel like the perfect complement—soft and small.

He kissed her, slow, leisurely. His clever hands molded over her curves until it didn't seem strange at all she was naked underneath him. It felt elemental and right. Maybe she jolted a little when his hand slid up her inner thigh, but he didn't stop. He only changed the angle of the kiss.

He kissed her deep, then trailed those kisses down her neck. Even as his fingers touched *her*. Her brain couldn't even latch on to this very new situation, because his mouth seemed to be everywhere—new sensation after new sensation—until she was just made of feeling. Sparkling, building *energy*.

Until it all spilled over. It was like…an explosion. Like metaphorical fireworks. All bright and booming, echoing through her in absolute pleasure. She was panting for air when he lifted his head. He grinned down at her and her heart swooped. He was everything she wanted.

Everything.

He made quick work of protecting himself, and then he was over her again. So perfect. She didn't feel those nerves anymore, as he cupped her face, kissed her with a gentleness that simply undid her.

Then he was entering her, and it wasn't nerves now. It was something like panic. It was too much. He was. Surely. Something was wrong and this did not work. But he said her name on a whisper, nuzzled his mouth against her neck as he stroked a hand down to her hip.

Like she was magic for him. Like she was *his* everything, all reverence and amazement.

Some of her panic unwound, warmed, relaxed into acceptance. Into him. It didn't feel so impossible when he kissed her like they had all the time in the world, like they were the only two people *in* the world.

He moved, until she moved with him. That same need building within her all over again. She kissed him, sliding her hands down the strong, muscular breadth of his back then back up to those impossibly wide shoulders.

They were one. They were *right*. She held on to him, moved with him, gave herself over to every sensation that poured through her, unraveling once again. Her name on his lips, as he followed into that release, collapsing on top of her.

She let her fingers drift through his thick hair, enjoying the heavy weight of him. The ragged rise and fall of their breathing that seemed to match along with the pounding hearts that slowly eased into something...lazy, and sweet.

He groaned a little and then rolled off of her. "Right back," he murmured, pressing a kiss to her mouth before leaving the room.

She pulled the blanket up to her neck, snuggling into his bed. His *bed*. Her body felt warm and sated and *perfect*.

Exactly as it should be. He returned, lifted the blanket and scooted into bed next to her.

Naked.

She wanted to giggle, but she supposed she should be more mature than that. She was hardly a teenager, even if she was new to this whole being naked with a man thing.

He slid his arm around her, pulling her into his chest. "Good?" he asked.

"Are you asking if *I'm* good or *it* was good?"

He laughed. "You. I know *it* was good."

She grinned and snuggled deeper into the heat of his body. "I'm great."

They lay there for a while. Not talking. Not doing much of anything, and yet it was perfectly comfortable.

"What are you thinking about?" she asked, drawing little patterns on his chest while his fingers combed through her wild, tangled curls.

"That those wooden ducks got me laid."

She barked out a surprised laugh. Not the romantic nothings she might have hoped for, but somehow better. Because it was so perfectly him. So perfect for her.

She sighed heavily. It was getting late and surely they couldn't just...sleep here in his bed. Naked.

Could they?

No, probably not. "I guess I should go."

"Why would you do that?" He looked down at her, genuinely puzzled.

"I...don't know."

He tugged the sheet away from her, then rolled her under him and grinned down at her. He kissed her, until she forgot what she'd even said. "Stay," he murmured against her mouth.

Stay. Yes, she thought she'd do exactly that.

CHAPTER EIGHT

BEAU HAD NEVER spent enough time dating any one woman that she practically became a fixture in his home. He'd never planned to, but somehow most days saw Teddy in his cabin, most nights in his bed, and he didn't mind at all.

Any time the worry that things were getting a little too domestic cropped up, she'd do something to make him forget. He was an enjoy-the-moment, go-with-the-flow kind of guy after all. He'd molded himself into that—purposefully—and he had no plans to ever, *ever* deviate from it.

His life had been marked by loss once, and he wasn't about to entertain dark years again.

This particular morning was a Saturday, which meant he wouldn't see Teddy until Monday, and there was that uncomfortable tightness in his chest. But why should he be bummed that he wouldn't see her for a day? It was always good to have a little breathing room.

Great, actually. In fact, he should suggest they take a little break. Just a little one. Give both of them that breathing room that would keep things on even ground.

But she was somehow braiding a colorful scarf into her hair, chattering on pleasantly about some bee removal she had later that day. She was fully dressed, ready to go. He was still in bed. Naked.

He loved watching her flit about in the morning. He'd always considered himself an early bird, but she was routinely up and moving, ready to see to her day before he even got dressed.

"Oh, I almost forgot," she said, digging in that giant bag of hers. He never knew what she'd pull out. From that crowbar the day she'd inspected the bees, to baked goods, to a bandana she'd embroidered for Benji, or some candle that made his cabin smell like Christmas morning.

Today, it was a pink envelope. His name was printed on the outside. She walked it over to where he still sat in bed and handed it to him.

He took the envelope a little warily. It was just so... glittery.

"Open it," she instructed.

So he did, half expecting confetti to explode out of it. He pulled out the piece of paper inside. In pretty script he had no doubt Teddy had written herself, it said:

You are cordially invited to attend the brunch portion of
Hathaway Sister Sunday
Theme: Flowers!
May 1st
11am
Hathaway House

He found his mouth curving in spite of himself. "*I'm* invited to Sister Sunday tomorrow?"

"Just the brunch portion," she said, pointing to those words on the invitation. "Certain aspects of Sister Sunday are wholly sacred and sisters only, but brunch can be attended by anyone, so long as they're formally invited."

He chuckled. "Do I have to RSVP?"

She pointed to the envelope and he looked inside again. There was another piece of paper. Smaller. An RSVP card.

"I see. Well…" He reached over to the nightstand and opened the drawer, pawing around inside of it until he found a pen. He pretended to consider, then used the pen to check the *attending* box.

He handed the card to Teddy. She glanced at his answer and grinned. "Bring your appetite."

"I always do. What does one wear to a Sister Sunday brunch? Do I have to wear flowers?"

"Do you *have* anything floral to wear?" she asked speculatively.

"Probably not."

She shook her head, waved it away. "What you usually wear is fine enough. You can interpret the theme however you like. You have to be prompt though. Brunch starts right at eleven. But don't be too early, because we'll be preparing."

"Yes, ma'am."

She leaned down, gave him a quick kiss. "I'll see you tomorrow then."

He grabbed her by the waist and pulled her back onto the bed before she could turn and leave, settling her in for a much longer, more involved kiss.

"You don't have to go," he murmured against her mouth.

But that seemed to remind her that she did indeed need to go because she pushed against his chest and wriggled out of the bed.

"I *do* have to go. As I have work and you have chores and breakfast with your mother." She stopped for a moment as she smoothed out her skirt. "Oh, do you think your mother would want to come?"

He blinked, something clenching tight and uncomfortable in his chest. "To Sister Sunday?" he managed to say without sounding as strangled as he felt.

"Of course. And your sister."

"Uh, probably too little notice this time around." He was fine with getting a little too wrapped up in Teddy, but letting her anywhere near his mother and sister was…dangerous. Begging for complications and grief.

She nodded thoughtfully. "Okay, next time I'll get invitations much further in advance," she determined, and he didn't know how to argue with that. So, he kept his mouth shut. There just wouldn't be a next time. It just…couldn't happen.

She said goodbye again, this time darting out of reach before he could grab her, though he was still a little…tense over the idea of involving his mother and sister in this and his grab for her was only half-hearted at best.

Hadn't he been thinking about breathing room? Now he'd agreed to see her the *one* day they didn't see each other as a rule. The *one* day he could remind himself this was just…fun. And eventually it would fizzle out and she'd find someone else more suited for all her plans.

Better suited. Much, much better suited.

The kind of better suited Beau wouldn't be able to *stand*.

He got out of bed and got dressed. Sister Sunday would be fine. They'd be with her sisters. He'd go, and then maybe make an excuse for Monday. Go out with JT and Grant instead.

So convinced he was that his plan was good, he found himself looking forward to brunch. He went through Saturday in a cheerful mood, and was ready to go Sunday morning long before he needed to be.

He played fetch with Benji for a bit, then figured he could be a *little* early, and he'd offer to help "prepare"— whatever that entailed.

He drove off the ranch, and decided to take the short-cut onto Hathaway land through a road that bisected the Hathaway-West border.

This direction led him past Jack Hathaway's cabin. Maybe Beau would stop in and say hi. He'd always enjoyed Jack Hathaway. The man was grumpy as a devil, but he was downright funny with it. When Beau saw him sitting on his cabin's porch, looking off in the direction of the main Hathaway house which was out of sight thanks to distance, trees and rolling hills, Beau figured he'd stop.

He knew Teddy was worried about Jack's isolated nature. He knew she'd appreciate Beau stopping in and making some conversation.

He frowned at himself. He was not supposed to be earning more of Teddy's appreciation. He was supposed to be working toward *breathing room*.

But Jack was there, and he could find breathing room *and* talk to her lonely grandpa. He stopped his truck outside Jack's cabin, got out and offered a wave. "Howdy, Mr. Hathaway."

"Howdy yourself," he said with his telltale gravelly drawl. "Which Riley boy are you?"

Beau's eyes were drawn to the shotgun leaning against the wall, right next to Jack's chair. Jack's hand was on it.

Beau cleared his throat, uncomfortable with the old man's grip on the shotgun. "Beau, sir."

Jack made a scoffing noise. "And why the hell are you here?"

"Well, I've got an invitation to go to Sister Sunday brunch." He tried a charming smile, but Jack was squinting off into the distance. Toward Hathaway House, as Teddy's invitation had called it.

"That why there's some pink doodad on your hat there?" he asked, pointing to Beau's cowboy hat. Where he had indeed fastened a broach in the shape of a rose he'd "bor-rowed" from his mother. Not that she knew he'd borrowed it.

"You got it in one," he said with a pleasant smile.

"Goddamn brunches," he muttered.

Beau shrugged. "I don't mind being fed. Georgie's a great baker."

Jack's sharp gaze turned to him. "So, you're defiling my Georgie."

Beau nearly choked on his own spit. *Defiling.* "No, I'm with Teddy, not Georgie. But not defiling her. Or anyone." Had the old man really said *defiling*? "Just… She…"

"You hurt any of them and they won't find the body, son." The gun came to rest across his lap.

And much like the defiling comment, he said it so casu-ally Beau just nodded along. Though he backed away from the end of the shotgun not so subtly pointed in his direction.

Surely it wasn't loaded.

Surely.

"Well, I better be going. Teddy told me not to be late." He backed away to his truck, but the barrel of Jack's shot-gun followed Beau. Not just into the truck, but all the way down the path as Beau drove away.

Beau figured the gun was still pointed at him, even as he descended the roll of land that hid Jack from view. He parked his truck in front of the house. He knew there'd been work done on it, Teddy had mentioned Con Stone had been doing some repairs, and they'd hired someone to patch the roof. The porch still sagged, but it didn't look dilapidated really. It looked well lived in and well loved.

Then there was the backyard. There were flowers every-where. The picnic tables were covered with colorful table-cloths, more flowers, candles. Ribbons and wind chimes and beaded doodads hung from tree branches—with more flowers threaded through.

Georgie and Elliot were bringing big plates of food out of the house while Joey and Teddy were adding more flowers to the vases on the table. All the women were dressed in bright colors, and florals, though they were different styles. Teddy with her usual fare of dress, leggings and big cardigan. Joey wore a bright blue T-shirt and jeans, with a Rosie-the-riveter type scarf in her hair that had bright blue flowers on it. Georgie's choices of flower were darker—black backgrounds and dark red flowers, while Elliot seemed to be dressed from head to toe in yellow, with a puffy thing in her hair that made her look like a walking flower.

A bouquet, in and of themselves.

Teddy turned, her whole face brightening when she saw him. Nothing ever quite got to him the way she brightened.

He rubbed at his chest. *Breathing room, remember?*

Teddy crossed over to him. "Hi, you're early." She sidled up next to him, though she didn't offer him a kiss. He thought it was cute how uncomfortable she was with any kind of public displays of affection.

He dropped a kiss on the top of her head anyway and slid his arm over her shoulders.

"You found a flower," she said, pointing to the pin on his hat.

"Raided Mom's jewelry drawer. I guess I should have found more to really fit in."

"You're perfect," she said, then lifted to her toes and kissed him. He would have let it linger, but there were a few too many pairs of violet eyes on him. And her cheeks were turning bright red.

"I had an interesting drive over," he said, keeping his

arm around her as they moved to the table. "Took the short-cut and thought I'd stop by and talk to Jack."

"Oh." Teddy stopped walking, looked up at him with a slightly troubled gaze. "Did he talk to you?"

"Not really. Mostly just threatened me with a shotgun."

Her expression immediately went to concern. "Why on earth would he do that?"

"I assume it's his version of protecting you." Beau winked at her, but she seemed wholly baffled and a little horrified.

He squeezed her shoulders. "It means he cares. Trust me. I don't think it was loaded." Probably.

Teddy nodded thoughtfully. "Well, I guess that's nice then and not horrible?"

He grinned down at her. "Promise."

Teddy led him to a seat where there was a place card—in the shape of a violet—with his name on it, and an incredible spread of food. Beau couldn't deny he enjoyed the whole experience. Oh, it was all a bit girly, but he'd grown up with a little sister who'd had a bunch of female best friends. There'd been slumber parties at the Riley Ranch and Disney princess movies and boy bands being blared and sung over by out-of-tune teenage girls.

As he enjoyed brunch, he was reminded of what Teddy had said about her sisters complementing each other. They did, and they were…a family. One they'd cobbled together themselves, though they did share some DNA. Georgie was grumpy and standoffish, and as Beau had JT, he knew that every sibling group needed one of those. Joey reminded him of Pru, the straightforward tomboy type. Elliot the worldly artist with a sneaky humor that always made Teddy laugh.

He loved that laugh, so easy and natural like nothing could really bother her. He loved the way she flitted around, like her bees she loved so much, always making sure things were in order, people were happy. He loved the way she held hands with him under the table, and blushed and smiled if he did anything that might even remotely be considered PDA.

But didn't pull away.

He loved…

Her.

Shit.

Well, this had to end.

And quick.

"Isn't he great?" Teddy could admit she was a little buzzed on the wine Elliot had insisted they share under the stars, all perfect and beautiful. The night was warm, like summer could arrive at any moment.

And she was most definitely in love with a sweet, handsome cowboy. Who'd stop in and talk to her grandpa and raid his mother's jewelry drawer to fit the theme.

"Kinda ran out of here fast, don't you think?" Georgie offered.

"I told him he couldn't stay," Teddy replied, though he had seemed a bit…odd there at the end. But she assumed it was just all the girly, sister stuff he didn't understand. He might have a sister, but only one and she was so much younger. He was used to traditionally male pursuits and likely had chores to do.

"I'm going to tell him I'm in love with him," she announced, to no one in particular. She'd been keeping it to herself so long, but today had done it. She wanted to shout it from the rooftops. She wasn't even scared to tell her mother.

Beau was not like all the men her mother had warned her about, and after today, Teddy was certain that with time and charm, Beau would win over even her mother.

And if he didn't? She sighed. It would hurt, she couldn't deny that, but she also was moving into a place where… She just didn't agree with her mother. With that one awful—and understandably so—experience guiding her through an entire life.

Some men were like Mickey. Some men hurt and broke.

But some men were like Beau. They were good. They healed and fixed and…loved.

Maybe Mom couldn't understand that. Teddy hoped she would at some point. Really hoped.

"He hasn't told *you* yet?" Joey asked.

"No." She'd been waiting for him to, she could admit that to herself now. But he'd shown up today with his mother's sparkly broach pinned to his cowboy hat. With Beau, it was about the actions. "He's not so good with words. He's more an action guy, and all of his actions say he's in love with me."

"Are you certain?" Elliot asked gently.

Teddy thought it over, really thought about it. She knew she could be a little overly romantic, but she'd never transferred that love of romance in books and movies and other people's lives onto her own. She'd had too much of her mother's voice in her head.

"I am." She knew he loved her, and if she had to be the one who said it first, that was okay. Better even. It would be on her terms.

"Well, then. Good for you." Her sisters echoed varying sentiments, but there was a mutedness to it all. Teddy understood that though. Men and love were thorny topics, and everyone had their own little hang-ups, their own cowboys they were currently trying to work out.

But Teddy had worked out hers, and she knew that with time they'd all work out theirs. They'd be happy.

They closed out Sister Sunday with the ridiculous dance under the moon Elliot always insisted on. Every week Teddy felt a little less self-conscious about the whole thing.

She crawled into bed, didn't even bother to change her clothes. Just curled up and dreamed of cowboys and bees and fate.

SHE WOKE UP GROGGY, a slight headache dull at her temples. But it didn't stop her from getting up and getting ready before anyone in the house stirred. Monday mornings she always did the same thing—took leftovers to Grandpa Jack, refilled his weekly medicine organizer, tried to make conversation with him and convince him to come out to the big house for dinner.

She packed up the leftovers and got in the doohickey—the doorless, windowless flatbed truck that they'd decorated with ribbons and brightly colored seat covers. She drove down to Grandpa Jack's cabin. She'd have to carefully warn him off threatening Beau with bodily harm.

A shotgun, for heaven's sake.

She hummed to herself as she drove over the swells and rises of the Hathaway Ranch. It was a beautiful place. Peaceful. It was like home, but different. She loved the farm in Maine, but Mom had built something of a...commune. There were always people about. There wasn't a lot of quiet. Teddy had enjoyed that growing up.

Now, she enjoyed the quiet. She enjoyed her sisters. And she enjoyed that...she was a *Hathaway* here. Even if her father was a bit of a blight on that name, people thought more about Grandpa Jack, and the Hathaways who'd come before. The ones who'd settled here and built this ranch.

They weren't all like her father. She'd determined he was an aberration. And *she* and her sisters were a part of a long line of Hathaways who were part of the land, part of the community.

Her headache was nearly gone when she parked in front of Grandpa Jack's cabin. She went up to the porch, knocked, then let herself in. He never said come in. Never answered the door to her.

He also never complained when she let herself in.

He was in his little kitchenette, sitting at the table, sipping coffee. He didn't even look up when she breezed in.

Because this was their routine, and though he never thanked her or acted like he appreciated it, she got the sneaking suspicion he did.

"Morning, Grandpa," she greeted, unpacking the leftovers. She found a plate, arranged some of the things she knew he liked best on it and set it in front of him.

He grunted. Sipped his coffee.

She had to hide a smile when he dug into the food.

She checked his weekly medicine organizer, pleased to find it all empty, then set out to fill it for the week ahead. "Did you talk to Beau yesterday?" she asked casually.

Grandpa only grunted.

"With a gun?"

"Not *with* a gun. Just had one nearby. You know, to scare off the possums."

She stopped what she was doing to stare at him. "In the middle of the day?"

"Daytime possums are the kinds you got to watch out for."

Teddy didn't think there were really daytime possums, but if there were… "You shouldn't be shooting at anything." She finished putting all his pills in their slots, then went ahead and poured herself a mug of coffee.

He'd clearly made enough for her.

She took the seat across from him. "Beau said it was your way of protecting me. I don't know if he's right, but I can take care of myself."

He gave her a sharp look. "Everyone thinks they can take care of themselves. But you get hearts mixed up in things and that's never the case."

Teddy blinked, something…foreboding shivered through her, but she pushed it away. "I suppose you're right. And I appreciate you care."

He scowled.

"You know we'd love to have you down for dinner." She gestured at the breakfast he'd already scarfed down. A few times he'd wandered down while they were eating outside, but never had he come inside for a meal. He'd never once gone anywhere near the house.

He looked straight at her, something he rarely did. His eyes were a dark brown, so she'd always assumed Mickey had gotten from his mother the violet eyes he'd passed down to all his daughters.

Her grandmother. Teddy didn't know a thing about her, but the few times she'd asked, she'd been shut down. Hard. So she'd stopped asking.

But she would never stop trying to get Grandpa Jack to be more involved with all of them.

"I'll never step foot in that house, no matter what you girls do to it," he said. Firm, but not with his usual vinegar. It was a different answer than he usually gave. Not just a brush-off, but something sincere.

"Why?" Teddy asked, figuring he'd never answer.

He looked down at his coffee. "I left that house in an ambulance with my wife. She never went back, so I never did either."

Teddy had to sift through it all, combined with what she

knew. He'd never set foot in the house after his wife had died. "So, you loved your wife, and in your grief... You couldn't step foot in the house you lived together in again?"

He didn't confirm or deny. Just sat there looking hard and mean. She had never really been dealt that kind of blow. Never lost so deeply.

Beau had. The way he'd talked about the baby sister who hadn't lived, his grandmother who'd passed away. He'd told her his story and then wanted to change the topic, so she understood Grandpa wouldn't want her pushing into his feelings. She was beginning to understand that sometimes love was space and time. When the space and time came, and Grandpa Jack was ready, he'd let her in further.

Just like Beau.

When she offered a goodbye, he spoke. Looking her right in the eye.

"I'm warning you, girl. You've got hearts in your eyes over that man. Hearts aren't worth having. Yours is far too soft for your own good. Only going to end in heartache."

It was the longest sentence he'd ever said to her at once, and it made her sad. But also...hopeful. Because he was opening up, wasn't he? Giving her advice and telling her things he hadn't before.

So, on her way out she did something she'd never done before, because she knew it wouldn't be well received. She wrapped her arms around him and squeezed. Maybe like so many things it was something he didn't want—but needed.

He didn't hug her back. She hadn't expected him to. But he didn't push her away. He even kind of patted her shoulder a bit.

Because what Grandpa Jack might not understand, but what was clearly true in a way she'd never fully understood until now, was that love was always the answer. Love allowed you to be yourself, fully and wholly.

Her mother had always loved her enough to give her that. And then her sisters. And now she was learning that she could give that to her grandfather, to Beau, and it wasn't a danger simply because they were men.

Love was the answer. Always. And she was ready to give it, without fear of hurt.

CHAPTER NINE

BEAU SPENT MOST OF Sunday night tossing and turning and talking himself in and out of too many things to count. But in the end, there was only way to handle this.

Be a man. Rip off the Band-Aid. Let Teddy go.

It was the right thing to do. It had been wrong of him to let it go this far. His fault, and he owed her an apology. Face-to-face. He wasn't going to lie, and he wasn't going to take the coward's way out.

She deserved more than that.

When she showed up, her usual whirlwind of colors and smiles, he had the strangest sensation.

He didn't want to do this.

Would it really be so wrong to enjoy each other for a while longer? She put her bag down, was already chattering a mile a minute and came over and gave him a casual *hello* kiss.

He wanted to reach out. Hold on to her. Possibly forever. But he wasn't about to commit himself to forever. He couldn't bear it.

He knew what it was like when the forever went away. When excitement and hope turned to grief. When love and comfort just suddenly wasn't there anymore. Darkness and quiet and questions to God no one could answer. He knew the interminable *years* it took to find a way back to normal, to calm. To that place where everything didn't feel like a constant, depressing end.

He wouldn't do that to himself.

"Have a seat, Teddy."

Her smile sobered at his serious tone, but she took a seat on his couch. He sat next to her, but kept a careful distance between them.

She smiled at him as if waiting for him to deliver great news. He felt like *slime*. But he was doing the right thing. He knew he was.

He cleared his throat. "Look." He couldn't remember ever feeling this...awful about telling someone something. *Emotional*. But it was the right thing, no matter how much he preferred to avoid emotion. What was right trumped his idiot feelings. "We've had a lot of fun, and you're a sweet girl—"

"*Girl*?" she interrupted, that tentative smile melting off her face. "Don't be patronizing, Beau. That isn't like you."

He hadn't meant to be. Truth be told, he'd never had to break up with someone, so this was new territory.

He hated it.

He cleared his throat. Again. "I'm just trying to say we should...take a step back. Not see as much of each other."

She blinked. Once. Then sat totally motionless. "I'm sorry. What?"

He looked down at his hands. What other words were there? "I like you a lot, but... It can't go anywhere. So we should probably stop pretending."

"Pretending," she echoed.

"I know you don't want an emotional scene any more than I do." Okay, he didn't know that. He just desperately wanted it to be true. Because her eyes were starting to get shiny like she was about to cry, and he didn't think he was strong enough to withstand that.

Any of this.

Why was he doing this? *You decided a long time ago you weren't doing the wife and kids things and that's all she'll ever want.*

It wouldn't be fair to her to pretend like he had any inkling of being willing to give that to her.

But if you were going to give it to anyone...

He stood abruptly. He'd made the choice. He'd stuck with it. He was nearly forty years old. He'd damn well stuck with it this long. He wasn't going back now. There would be no grief for him. No more than he'd already had to endure.

"I had a lot of fun, and I really like you."

"Yes, so you keep saying," she said. Her voice was quiet, and she still didn't move. "But you're breaking up with me."

"It's just…" He blew out a breath. "It's not you. It's me. You'll find someone else…" He meant to say *better suited.* But he couldn't get the words out, because the thought of her with anyone else made him downright violent.

"Of course." She was nodding now, and she stiffly got to her feet. She retraced her steps to her bag. She didn't say anything else, but she didn't cry and that was a relief.

This wasn't so bad. He could survive this. They would both be better off. He'd done the right thing.

It felt like utter shit, but sometimes the right thing did.

He stayed where he was, standing in his living room, as she opened the front door. It took everything in him not to race forward, slam the door, and kiss her with a million apologies and promises.

But he had done the right thing, damn it. He was a strong enough man to watch her go knowing he'd made the right choice for her. He wouldn't give her what she wanted. So, he was being *noble*.

She didn't step forward into the pretty evening though. She stood there, looking out the open door, her hand gripping the knob tightly. Her breathing began to get more shallow, and he was deathly afraid she was crying. He even took a step forward with the idea he'd have to comfort her.

A strange sensation as he usually ran in the opposite direction of tears, but with Teddy he wanted to be the one to comfort her. To…

Damn it, no. No, he wasn't doing this.

And then, like she'd read his mind, she said her own *no* out loud.

"No." She dropped her bag and spun around, slamming the door in the process. Her eyes were pure fury, her fists clenched like she meant to punch him as she stalked toward him. "No *fucking* way."

TEDDY NEVER SAID the f-word, but if it wasn't appropriate now, when would it be? "This doesn't make sense." She stopped in front of him, having to tilt her head back to look up at him.

She'd never wanted to cause someone physical harm in her life. Never felt the violence curling her fingers into fists. Oh, she knew she wouldn't do any damage if she punched him, but she was sorely tempted to do it anyway.

But he was standing there looking so… Hurt. When *he* was the one trying to break up with her. When she'd come over here planning to tell him she loved him. *Loved* him.

"What brought this on?" she demanded, narrowly resisting poking him in the chest.

"Nothing *brought* this on. I've been thinking about it for a while."

"A *while*?" Maybe she should be embarrassed by the screech in her tone, but she couldn't find embarrassment or decorum when she was so desperately furious. Emotion swirled inside of her and she had no control over it. Didn't *want* to control it.

She wanted to drop f-bombs and kick him in the shins.

Because he'd made her believe that she could trust him. *Made* her believe he wouldn't hurt her and… She'd thought she understood the world better than her mother because she wasn't defined by one hurt but…

Well, this felt like it would be pretty *damn* defining.

"Teddy, I like spending time with you."

"And that made you think, 'Gee, I should *stop*'?"

A strange expression crossed his face, and it reminded her of that night he'd told her about his family's dark days. There was something akin to grief in his eyes. And that awkwardness with having expressed it.

"I'm sorry. Really."

She supposed she should leave it at that. A *sorry* was more than her mother had gotten, and Beau wasn't leaving her pregnant and alone. He was just ending things. He was being very mature about it, really.

She didn't want to be mature. Or fair. She didn't want her pride.

She wanted to *wreck* him.

"Well, bad news for you, Beau." And then she really did poke him in the chest. Hard. "I *love* you."

He staggered back like she'd *shot* him, not poked him. "No."

"No? You don't get to say *no* to my own feelings."

He looked so comically shocked she might have laughed if she didn't want to cry.

He cleared his throat for what felt like the hundredth time. "Teddy."

"Can you really stand there, look me in the eye and tell me you don't love me back?"

He stood there, looking frozen. Horrified. And when he opened his mouth, she was terrified that's exactly what he'd say. *I don't love you, Teddy. You are quite unlovable, actually. Passed down in the blood from mother to daughter.*

Not all that far from something her mother had said on occasion. When she was trying to explain it was *okay* to be unlovable. To never have a partner in life. Mom meant well, but Teddy... She'd held out hope for that partner, even when she'd been scared of actually doing the looking for one.

"Listen to me," he said, his voice very low. But not mean. Not scathing. He did not say the words she was afraid to hear. "You will want to get married. And have kids. I decided a long time ago I don't want those things."

For a brief moment, she thought about lying. Telling him she didn't want those things either. It would solve the problem, wouldn't it?

But he knew her better than that, and why should she lie just to keep this idiot man in her life? No matter how much she loved him. "Why?" she asked instead. She didn't understand why a man who was so close with his family, so good with people and *her*, wouldn't want those things.

"I can't. I'm sorry. I do care about you, Teddy, but that future is not one I want. Not with anyone."

Which wasn't an answer. None of this was an *answer*. "Why won't you tell me the truth?"

"I *am* telling you the truth."

"I can't decide if you're lying to me or yourself."

He crossed his arms over his chest. "You should go," he said, looking a little angry for the first time tonight.

Which sparked her own. Because he had no right to be angry. When he was just…ending things. He wouldn't say he didn't love her. He wouldn't say why he didn't want to get married and have kids.

Just. *It's over. Be gone.*

Oh, she'd go. She would go and she would… She stopped in the kitchen, fury bubbling up all over again. She'd finally gotten over her own hang-ups about love and sex because of those damn wooden ducks.

He did not get to keep them. She grabbed a chair from the table and dragged it over. Stood on it and opened the cabinet, then scooped *all* the ducks into her arms.

"What are you doing?"

"I'm taking these ducks," she said, climbing down off the chair and looked right at him. "I'm going to name them and sew clothes for them and display them *proudly* in *my* house. Because I am not a coward. And you are."

She whirled away from the kitchen, and this time when she got to the door, she went right out. She dumped the ducks in her car and drove away.

She didn't cry on the way home. She was propelled by a violent anger that would have scared her if she'd been able to step back and really think it through. She parked the car, gathered her ducks, then strode into the house.

She walked into the living room where her sisters were sitting in various states. They all looked up at her, waiting for her to explain. Her violet-eyed sisters, who'd always be there for her. Who'd never need space, or abandon her, or scoff at her hugs or brunches. They loved her.

And the worst of it was, she knew Beau loved her too. He just didn't *want* to. There was no way to fight that. No way to fix that for him. She just had to accept it.

She plopped onto the ground and began to cry, holding

on to the wooden ducks like they were babies. Because she'd gone and done the one thing she was so sure she'd avoid. With questions and waiting to be intimate and a million other things.

She'd gotten hurt. Her heart broken. Utterly and completely. And it *sucked*.

Her sisters were immediately around her, murmuring soothing words and rubbing her back.

"What did the asshole do?"

"He broke up with me."

"I'll break his face," Joey said loyally.

Teddy shook her head. "It's not even face breakable. It was all about how I'd want marriage and kids and he didn't."

"I'm not sure that explains the ducks," Elliot said with some concern.

"He didn't deserve them," Teddy said, and since she was with her sisters, since she was safe and loved here, she let it all out. Because he didn't deserve the ducks, or her for that matter.

But she really wished he did.

CHAPTER TEN

BEAU HADN'T GONE OUT with JT and Grant that night, but he sure as hell had finished off a bottle of whiskey in the comfort of his own home.

He was paying the price this morning. He forced himself out of bed, way later than he usually got up. He checked his phone.

Nothing.

Not that she should call him. It was over. That was right.

He ran through the shower, figuring the pounding head-ache was his due. Penance. He should have stopped this after that first kiss.

He'd learned a lesson.

A lesson he'd put to use *never* since the idea of touching anyone who wasn't Teddy made him sick to his stomach.

Just the alcohol. Just the... He'd get over it. All this.

He wrenched the shower off, ran the towel over his hair, and then he heard... He pulled on his pants and rushed for the living room. He had no idea what he'd do if it was Teddy. All his shouldn'ts were falling apart. He just wanted her to...

But it was his sister standing there.

"What the hell are you doing here?" he demanded.

Pru frowned at the scathing note in his tone. "Warning you that Mom's on her way. You should thank me." She made a face. "You look like hell. What's your deal? And for the love of God put on a shirt."

Beau grumbled a non-response and went and hunted up a shirt. When he returned, Pru was still there.

She was studying him with a narrowed-eyed clarity Beau didn't care for. "Bee girl break up with you?"

He stiffened. He knew he should blow it off, but his words were stilted. At best. "Bee girl and I came to the mutual decision not to see each other anymore."

"Oh, you broke up with *her*."

"Fuck off, Pru."

"You're really messed up about it too. Why'd you break up with her then?"

"Did you not hear the 'off' in fuck off?"

"Wow. She did a number on you." She looked at him speculatively. "Unless you did a number on yourself."

He decided to say nothing. He stalked over to the kitchen and began to make coffee. God, he needed coffee. And to have his sister anywhere but near him.

"Maybe I'm off base since you've been hiding her away, but I almost made some mistakes by pushing Grant away. If you want to talk about it—"

"I don't."

Pru hesitated, then barreled on because of course she did. "It's just you seemed really happy. I mean, you always seem cheerful, but this was different. Happy cheerful. But now… This is about as awful as I've ever seen you. And I know how it feels… So, maybe—"

"Maybe nothing. She wanted more than I was interested in giving. The end."

Pru frowned. "Are you *that* afraid of change?"

"I'm not afraid of change," he muttered, shoving the

coffee carafe into the machine. Change was life. Life was change.

It was the *loss* of it all he couldn't stand.

"Oh, please. Your entire life is dedicated to keeping everything the same. Hell, the only reason you even live here is because Mom and Dad wanted to raze the place, but no, Beau Riley couldn't stand the thought of something being *changed*."

"You don't know a damn thing," Beau said darkly, staring at the coffee dripping.

He heard the front door open, knew it was his mother without turning around.

"He broke up with the bee girl because she wanted *more*," Pru said to Mom. "Just like JT and Marianne all over again."

"JT didn't love Marianne," Beau muttered, then realized that made it sound like he…did love Teddy. Which he did, but his mother and sister certainly wouldn't understand why that was bad.

"Look, I'm fine. Just need my coffee. Sorry I missed breakfast, Mom. But I'm not in the mood."

"Because you're an idiot," Pru said scathingly. Getting his back up. "Go apologize to the girl. You want more. *Clearly*."

"The hell I do."

Mom still hadn't said anything, and Beau was afraid to turn around and see the look on her face. So, he watched the coffee.

"You know, it's not so bad," Pru said, changing her tone to something he was deathly afraid was sympathy. "Scary at first, sure, all those dumb words you gotta say. But once you say them, it gets easier and—"

"I am not doing this. Not with her, and I'm not having this conversation with you."

"I cannot for the life of me understand why you and JT are so afraid of marriage. All we have in the Riley family are good marriages and long, happy lives. Knock on wood. Get over yourself and make a commitment."

He whirled on her, everything splintering inside of him. Long happy lives? "You don't understand *anything*. And you're going to get married and have kids and it's going to hit you over the head."

She didn't even look offended. Just mad. "What is?"

"Prudence. Go on up to the house," Mom said, in an odd voice Beau didn't recognize.

"He isn't making any sense."

"Prudence."

"Fine," Pru muttered. "I sure hope you can get through to him." Then she stalked out of his cabin, leaving him alone with his mother.

And he thought last night was bad.

"What was that about?" Mom asked, *very* carefully, and Beau didn't think Mary Riley had asked anyone anything *carefully* in her entire life. She was a bulldozer.

"Nothing."

"What do you think is going to hit your sister over her head?"

He didn't look at her. He looked around his kitchen. And there was the cabinet door hanging open. Nothing inside. No ducks. Just an empty cabinet. Just emptiness.

He reached up and carefully closed the door on the cabinet. "Can you just…not?"

"Very tempting, but I'm afraid to get rid of me you're going to have to tell me what you meant. What is going to hit your sister over her head?"

"I know you and Dad love each other. I'm sure marriage is great. Pru and Grant will be happy." Until they weren't. Because loss was *inevitable* when you opened yourself up to all that possibility.

"Beau."

It was the odd brokenness in his mother's voice that had him closing his eyes, resting his forehead against the cabinet in front of him. "Doesn't she know it's just more people to lose?" He shook his head. "Why would I want to put myself through that?"

It made him angry. That Pru didn't know better. That Mom was making him explain it. Furious, really. "I know that someday I'm going to have to lose you and Dad. I know that I will lose people I love, but that's why I plan on sticking to the ones I've got. I'm not adding any more to it. Those few years were bad enough. I won't put myself through it. I refuse." He hit his fist against the cabinet as a punctuation mark on the whole thing.

End of sentence. End of conversation.

When he finally turned, he didn't know how to react to his mother standing there...crying silently.

It just about ended him. "Mom, don't."

"We've never talked about it."

"We don't talk about those things."

"No, but maybe we should." She took a seat at his kitchen table, gestured for him to take a chair.

He shook his head. "It's old news. It happened. I learned a lesson. Love is grief. So, no thanks."

Mom pointed to the seat again, and this time he knew he had no choice but to sit. Listen. He'd weathered last night. He'd weather this. Because nothing could change his mind.

"You are right. Love and grief go hand in hand." She reached across the table and took his hand in hers. Smaller now, when in all of his memories of holding his mother's hand *his* were the smaller ones.

See? Didn't that just prove his damn point?

"You can't have one and not experience the other. Beau, I wouldn't have chosen to lose my mother and daughter in the same year, while I was struggling to survive myself, but I wouldn't change the fact that I loved them. I got a lot of years with my mother, and too precious few moments with my daughter, but I'd hardly erase them."

"I'm not erasing anyone. I'm choosing not to step into all that."

"But, baby, you're miserable. Because you already love that girl you've been hiding from me." She used her free hand to wipe away the tears on her face. "It's a loss all the same, and loneliness is no replacement for love."

"I'm not lonely. I have you all."

"All right. Let's pretend for a moment that I agree with you. Love is too hard. Loss is too heavy a weight to carry— despite the fact I'm still married to your father, had a child after we lost Elizabeth, could not be more thrilled for Pru and Grant and the little family they'll hopefully give me no matter what struggles we might all face—let's say you're right and avoiding it all is best. You'll be happy because you have this ranch and you have us." She leaned forward until they were practically nose to nose, her grip on his hand tighter than she had a right to be able to hold on to him when her hand was so much smaller than his. "I want you to picture your life, ten years down the line, without that woman in it, and *really* ask yourself when you're nearing fifty and alone if you'll be glad *you* chose to lose her now. Because you couldn't bear the *chance* a little tragedy might touch your life."

He frowned. "You make me sound like a coward."

She released his hand, got to her feet. She brushed imaginary lint from her shirt. "If the shoe fits," she said with a shrug.

And left him with that.

He wasn't a coward. He'd done the right thing. No one could convince him otherwise. Love was loss.

Ten years down the line? He'd still be who he was now, in this cabin.

Mom and Dad would be older but here, same with JT. Maybe Grant and Pru would have kids. He'd be an uncle. More chances to love and lose. Because there wasn't a choice there, of course. If he had a niece or nephew, he'd love them. He'd always liked kids, and they'd be related by blood, by family. There wasn't a choice there. He'd deal.

But there was a choice with Teddy. She would...find someone else. Maybe he hated the thought in the moment, but he could picture his life without her, and it would be *fine*.

Except no matter how he imagined those fictional ten years down the line, he *couldn't*. All her colorful dresses and happy smiles were right there in the middle of it. All his. He couldn't picture her anywhere but at his side. He couldn't erase her from it.

Damn it.

WHEN TEDDY WOKE UP the next morning—abnormally late—she had another headache. Though she hadn't had any wine, it felt like a terrible hangover all the same. She'd cried it out, cursed Beau to hell and back, all with her sisters around her.

She wanted to feel better this morning. She'd gotten all those firsts out of the way, love, sex, breaking up. It was like a rite of passage.

It was a stupid rite of passage and she hated it.

In fact, she was going to lean into that. In a way she

never had before. She was going to be grumpy today. Stay in her nightgown and her robe and stomp around the house *growling* at people. She'd been watching Georgie do it for weeks now; she could do it too.

"It'll be cathartic," she told Jasper Junie, who looked at her skeptically out of one eye from the end of the bed.

Cat skeptics aside, Teddy was certain she would feel better. She had to. And maybe if she leaned into it now, she wouldn't…let it mark her forever. Because she didn't think Beau had hurt her simply because he was a man. He was hurting her because he was *hurt*. Because he didn't know how to get over it.

Didn't make her hurt less, but she felt for him. She still loved him—couldn't turn that switch into anger and blame.

No matter how hard she tried.

She pulled on her fluffy robe and found some fuzzy socks and went downstairs in search of coffee.

She found Georgie standing next to the coffeemaker, brewing coffee with her patented scowl. "I've been thinking about it," she said by way of greeting. She poured Teddy a mug and set it on the table as Teddy sat down. "He's a no-good rat bastard, and rats deserve poison."

"Oh, are we talking about the no-good rat bastard?" Elliot asked, entering the kitchen, already covered in clay— or more likely she'd never gone to sleep last night and was still in yesterday's clay. "I like poison. But only if it's really painful. Like a liquefying his organs so he pukes them out type situation."

"It should be bloodier," Joey said. She was carrying Henrietta down the stairs without complaint. She even gently placed her on the ground. And while Georgie eyed her water pistol, she didn't use it on the chicken.

Joey plopped herself down at the table. "Maybe I can

run him over with the mower attachment to the tractor. Mulch him up."

It was all rather horrible, and Teddy knew none of them actually meant it. Which she supposed was why it was so comforting.

"I love you guys," she managed, feeling weepy all over again.

"I know it's not Sister Sunday, but why don't we go into town? Hit the thrift stores, get a picnic lunch. Just...be with each other," Elliot said, eyeing Teddy carefully.

Teddy had planned on moping, but maybe this would be better. *Healthy.* Stop crying and thinking about the no-good rat bastard she loved, and enjoy what she'd come here for: family.

She didn't have to wallow. She didn't have to be changed. She could be sad, and then she could move on. And she didn't have to choose the same path Beau and her mother had chosen: letting loss and grief shut her off from everything.

No, she was going to live. *That* was independence. This, right here. Making the choice that was right for her. Oregon. Her sisters. Chickens and bees and the belief that if Beau wasn't her fate...

She couldn't finish that sentence. Not yet. She'd get there though. "All right," she said, letting out a cleansing breath. "I'll be right back."

She went upstairs, Emily Peckinson following her, to get ready, and tried to find a dress that wasn't tied to a memory with Beau.

Which was impossible. Luckily that didn't make her weepy. It made her mad. She considered her options, then stalked down the hall. She wouldn't wear a dress. She'd wear *pants*. She decided her best bet was a pair of Elliot's linen, spacious overalls.

So, she found herself a pair, went ahead and borrowed one of Joey's more colorful T-shirts and headed back downstairs. She picked up Cluck Norris on the stairs.

When she returned to the kitchen, no one was at the table. Everyone was crowded in the hall between the front entry and the kitchen.

"What's going on?" she asked as Cluck Norris chirped in her arms.

There was a slow, parting of the sea of bodies.

And Beau was standing there.

He looked terrible. Bloodshot eyes, his hair at crazy angles. She'd never seen him look so tortured. For a moment, her heart soared.

Until she quashed it. The man who had broken her heart last night was not already at her doorstep to beg forgiveness.

Please be here to beg my forgiveness.

She held on to the chicken for dear life. "What do you want?"

"To talk to you. You're...wearing pants."

She lifted her chin, trying to do her best Georgie impression while wearing Elliot's clothes. Withering disapproval and worldly disinterest. "Why?"

His gaze moved from the pants to her face. "I... We need to talk about last night."

"Do you want us to go, Teddy?" Elliot asked quietly, coming to stand behind her, her hand on Teddy's shoulder. "Or kill him?"

"You can certainly kill me after, but what I've got to say I'll say it in front of everyone." Beau kept his gaze straight on her. "I know you'll never forgive me if they all hate me."

"Forgive you for what?" Teddy managed to say, sounding quite unaffected if she did say so herself.

"I messed it all up last night."

"Yes," she agreed. She reached back with her free hand

and found Elliot's. Elliot squeezed. It gave her the strength to stand here and not throw herself at him. She wouldn't.

She needed a lot more than *I messed up*.

"It's just…" He stepped forward, but one sharp look from Georgie had him stopping. It was a strange tableau. He stood in a hallway with Joey behind him as if she was contemplating ways to stab him in the back. Georgie stood slightly in front, between him and Teddy, as if she was protecting Teddy from him, and Elliot stood behind her.

Varying kinds of support, and Beau didn't wither surrounded by all these women shooting violet daggers at him. He just looked at her with heartbreak in his eyes.

And that soft heart Grandpa Jack accused her of having *throbbed*. She didn't want him to be heartbroken. She just wanted…him.

"I let an old decision I made a long time ago in a place of grief cloud my judgment. Maybe if I'd met you a long time ago, I would have seen that a little clearer. But I've gotten kind of…set in my ways, I suppose. Because no one I ever met made me question what I thought I didn't want."

"Did you ever question being a no-good rat bastard?" Georgie asked casually.

He didn't even look at her. His blue gaze stayed on Teddy. "But nothing has been the same since I met you, Teddy. I told myself the first time I kissed you I should end it, because I knew… I knew it'd be more. It *was* more. Every time I told myself to back away, there you were and I… I didn't want to push you away. I wanted you right there."

"Funny way of showing it," Joey said from behind him.

Beau took another step toward Teddy, but Georgie's body blocked him from getting any closer.

It didn't stop him. He just kept on talking. So serious. So unlike him.

"I've never told anyone about my late sister, my grand-mother and my mom and all that. Never. And I don't even know why I told you. It's not like I wanted to share that. I *hate* that time and remembering it. But with you, it came out. At least part of it, because I didn't tell you the rest. I decided after all that loss in such a short time, I wouldn't put myself through it again. I had to love my family, and I'd suffer those losses if it came to that, but I wasn't going to add to that potential. It was my family. That was it."

She wasn't going to get all softhearted over this. Grandpa Jack had warned her. That's how you got hurt. She was going to remain strong. Let him get this out, but she wasn't about to give in.

"I made that decision when I was young and…confused. I never talked about it with anyone. Never had to. No one ever once made me question those decisions I'd made as a kid, until you."

Okay, maybe she wasn't going to remain strong.

"I was damn sure I was doing the *right* thing last night, because I had made a decision to never get married or have kids or hurt myself that way. I knew you wanted those things, and should have them. You should have everything."

"I just wanted you." It wasn't a fully true statement, be-cause she'd put the *want* in past tense when even now, mad and hurt, what she really wanted was him.

He nodded, never taking his gaze from her. He didn't even look down at Cluck Norris when she began to squawk.

"Maybe I messed that up too badly. I hope I didn't."

"You just woke up and had a change of heart?"

He shook his head. "No. I woke up, and you hadn't called or texted, and I'd wanted you to. I was getting out of the shower and heard someone in my cabin and I wanted it to be you. But it was my sister, and my mother, and they both started laying into me."

"I think I like your mother and sister," Elliot interrupted.

Beau didn't even send her a sharp look. He just kept explaining.

"After talking a little bit about…everything, my mother asked me to picture my life in ten years without you in it. So I kept trying to picture myself alone because I thought I had to be, but no matter how hard I tried you were always there. I *wanted* you there."

No one had anything scathing to say about that. Georgie even looked back at Teddy, as if asking her if she really wanted the barrier anymore. Teddy swallowed. It was reassuring having them here, but this was… Her deal. She had to deal with Beau, and what she wanted, on her own two feet.

That independence Mom had impressed upon her she needed to find. Because Mom's experiences didn't get to determine her life here—and maybe that was what Mom had really wanted for her. To develop her own. To make her own choices.

Regardless, Teddy wanted it. Wanted to choose her own life.

"You guys can give us some space," she said, giving Elliot's hand one last squeeze.

There were murmurs. Everyone touched her as they passed. Hand or shoulder squeezes. And then it was just her.

On her own two feet.

"This is all very…" She struggled to find a word. "I appreciate this. I understand your decision better now."

He frowned, stepping all the way forward. He took the hand Elliot had let go. "But that's what I'm saying. It's not my decision anymore."

She didn't pull her hand away, but she didn't hold his back. She did understand him. It connected to what Grandpa Jack had said about never coming back to this house. His grief had kept him solitary. Alone. Like Mom—one bad experience had kept her from even wanting to attempt to find a partner. Like both of them, Beau had kept himself separate. He loved his family, she knew, but he hadn't cried in front of them. He hadn't told them what he was afraid of. She remember what he'd said about those "dark days." *We don't talk about things like that.*

He'd made a decision. Hidden it.

Until she'd come along.

She should be flattered, but she just felt like…something was still missing.

He wanted her in his life, but he hadn't said the three words she wanted to hear. "So, what is your decision?"

"I don't want to break up."

"And that's it?" she asked, carefully, doing everything she could to hold herself together.

"Is that not…it?" he asked, eyebrows drawn together. Confused.

She sighed and blinked back the tears. Maybe he wasn't a no-good rat bastard, but if he didn't love her, there wasn't much point to all this. "I'm sorry, Beau. I don't think this is going to work."

BEAU DIDN'T UNDERSTAND what was happening. She was turning away from him, in overalls that clearly weren't hers. The only part of this scene that made any sense was the chicken in her arms.

He'd run out of words. He'd told her everything, been as honest as he'd ever been, and she was still walking away. Toward the stairs.

Why the hell was she walking away after he'd just spilled his guts? Prudence had said that's all it took. Dumb words.

Scary at first, sure, all those dumb words you gotta say. But once you say them, it gets easier and—

"Wait." It dawned on him then, the words he *wasn't* saying. Words she'd said, heartbroken and teary.

Didn't she know he felt the same?

She stopped her forward progress, stiffened her spine then turned to face him. "Beau, really—"

"You don't get it, and that's my fault. I'm not all that great with words."

"You explained yourself very well. I just—"

"Teddy, damn it." He was distracted by the incessant meowing happening at his feet, and Jasper Junie's little claws digging into his pant leg. He picked up the cat so it would be quiet and allow him to say what he needed to say.

He stepped to her, standing on that top stair, looking at the cat with tears in her eyes.

"Teddy, I love you," he said. Her gaze flicked to his, so much surprise flashing over her features, he just…said everything. "Maybe from the first time I kissed you, definitely after that Sister Sunday and you were just so beautiful and happy. I didn't want to be anywhere else, even though it was the most ridiculous thing I'd ever been a part of. I love that you're fearless, and so uniquely you in the midst of doing whatever you can to make everyone else around you happy. I love that you're shy about kissing in front of people and the way you look when you're dead asleep in my bed. I love everything about you and you in my life."

He waited, but she only looked at him wide-eyed, clutching the chicken.

"Are those enough damn words now?" he demanded,

feeling wrung out and uncomfortable, because if he had to come up with more...

And then she began to cry. Big fat tears, and little sobs. His typical response to tears was a quick retreat, but when it came to Teddy... He didn't want to run away. He pulled her to him, cat and chicken between them.

"Come on, Teddy. It can't be all that bad, can it?"

She sniffled into his shoulder. "It's not bad at all. That was beautiful."

"Good, I guess?"

She looked up at him, touched his cheek. "Oh, Beau. I love you too. And I do want all those future things, but not if they'll make you unhap—"

"*You* make me happy. It was never that I didn't want them. I was...scared. I'm still scared. But I figure you can hold my hand through it." He wiped some tears from her cheeks. "Can we put the animals down now?"

She laughed and bent over to put the chicken on the floor, and he managed to get the cat off his shoulder and put her on a chair so she could hiss at the chicken below.

Then he picked Teddy up off the stairs and held her to him. Really held her. "I love you beyond reason, Teddy. I don't want you to ever doubt it. I don't want to make you cry again."

She wrapped her arms around his neck. "I love you too," she said. "And you can make me cry—for good reasons and bad—as long as we both say that at the end of the day."

"I promise."

And he sealed that promise with a very long kiss.

* * * * *

JOEY

Maisey Yates

For my mom. Who loved these Jasper Creek books
a whole lot, and even more, loved my friendship
with Megan (Caitlin), Jackie and Nicole,
and was always excited to hear about how my books
were doing and how theirs were doing too.

And for Jackie, Megan and Nicole,
for being there profoundly while I was losing her,
and when I lost her. She knew you would
take care of me, and you have.

It's all love and bluebonnets.

CHAPTER ONE

JOEY HATHAWAY HAD never met a problem that couldn't be solved with a cheerful, determined attitude, a can of WD-40 and a roll of duct tape. Unfortunately, none of her past experience was proving to be applicable with her grandpa Jack's old farm equipment. She didn't have the money for all new things, and anyway, she liked the antique stuff. But none of her mechanical know-how was getting her anywhere with the rusted out machinery, and she was at her wits' end.

Going off of a suggestion from Pru Riley down at the feed store, she had gotten the contact information for Hollis Logan, who supposedly specialized in restoring old equipment. They had a meeting in about a half hour, and she was looking forward to meeting the man. She loved old men. They were filled with curmudgeonly wisdom and great war stories. She had always liked talking to the hands at her mom's farm in Texas. She was sure this would be no different.

Right. Because you have had such an easy time connecting with Grandpa Jack?

Well, she hadn't gotten a chance to spray Grandpa Jack with WD-40, had she?

Maybe that would work. Get some of the creak out of his soul.

Joey had just put her boots on and stood from the

crooked little bench by the stairs, and looked at Teddy, who had just come in from tending her bees.

"I'm going out to—"

Her words were abruptly cut off when Georgie came into the living room, presumably from her kitchen, and deposited a chicken into Joey's arms.

She looked down at the small, black-and-white hen, but before she could do anything with her, Teddy appeared and gingerly lifted her from Joey's arms, opening the back door and setting her outside.

"Cluck Norris," she said in a scolding tone. "You know you aren't allowed in the house." She closed the door behind herself, her floral dress swirling with the motion. "What were you saying, Joey?"

"I was saying that I was going—"

That was right when Elliot came down the stairs, her fingertips brushing Joey's climbing ivy plant that was just beginning to wind around the banister, cradling a chicken in her other arm, which she also deposited in Joey's arms.

Teddy turned to Joey, and carefully lifted the little red hen from her arms. "You can't be in here either, Henrietta. I don't make the rules."

"Where is Emily Peckinson?" Georgie asked, looking suspicious.

"I'm sure I don't know," said Teddy, her expression a portrait of near comedic innocence.

"You are limited to *one* house chicken," Georgie said. "It feels more than fair."

Teddy nodded solemnly. "It is."

Somehow, Joey had the feeling that Teddy did not think it was fair. Not at all. But, her sister wouldn't make an issue out of it. She also had a feeling that Teddy did, in fact, know the current location of Emily Peckinson.

While Teddy had an affinity for most creatures—in particular bees and chickens—she did understand that her affection for them was much greater than what most people felt for them. And for all that she was wholly fantastical, she was also reasonable when it came to such matters.

"Where are you headed, Joey?" Elliot asked. Her sister was already covered in a healthy layer of clay, and Joey had the feeling she was headed out to her spot to throw more. Or whatever the terminology was. Joey tried to take it on board, because she did find it interesting, but she had tried sitting at her sister's pottery wheel once.

She had not enjoyed it at all.

Joey wasn't opposed to struggle. In fact, she liked a challenge. What she didn't understand was engaging in something that was supposed to be fun when it was actually just a lot of work. If she wanted to work, she would work. And if she wanted to do something leisurely, well, she would lie in a hammock for four hours.

"I'm headed out to meet with a man called Hollis Logan? Pru Riley recommended him…"

Teddy's face took on a delicate flush at the mention of Pru, who was sister to the man Teddy was dating.

Dating.

Teddy, who had never dated before ever. And was now very much involved.

It made Joey feel…

Well, she'd come here to feel closer to her sisters. And that made her feel perilously close to being an odd duck. Or chicken, as the case may be.

"Who is Hollis Logan?" Georgie asked, crossing her arms. Georgie was the closest thing to a local, and as such, often expected to know exactly who someone they mentioned offhandedly might be.

"He owns a ranch somewhere around here. But his specialty is fixing antique farm equipment. Pre-1975. Which is exactly what we need."

Joey was spearheading the renovation aspect of Four Sisters Farm. It was a natural extension of what she'd done on her own family spread back in Texas. She'd seen to minor repairs of equipment—she'd learned to fix most things as the need arose, to save on both money and time. She'd been involved in planting and harvesting, and while that was her true passion, she'd fixed more engines, roofs, fences and plumbing problems than she could shake a house chicken at.

She could not, however, fix tractors this old.

"Oh yes," Georgie said, brightening. "I wonder if he's any good with replacing parts on other things. There's an old washer that I'd love to get going. It would be really fun to do the aprons by rolling them through the crank."

Elliot wrinkled her nose. "You have to be careful with those. I had a great-grandmother whose finger was never the same after she accidentally got hung up on one of those as a child."

"On second thought, maybe I will stick to the newfangled washer."

"That sounds like a plan," Joey called, heading out the front door. She could still hear her sisters continuing to chat. She was just so…happy. She had expected to miss Texas a lot more than she did. She looked down at the simple bluebonnet tattoo on the inside of her wrist, a tattoo that she'd gotten at eighteen, along with her sisters.

It was a reminder of home while she was here. But when she had been in Texas, it was a reminder of the bond she shared with her sisters. Well, it was still a reminder of that. A reminder of why this place felt like home, even though she hadn't grown up here.

Her mom had been okay with the move, mostly because Janine Brown was a woman who believed a woman had to make her own way in the world.

It was a value that she had instilled in Joey from the time she was a little kid. She knew that some people had thought her mother was hard on her, but as often as she'd made Joey grit her teeth and get through something difficult—she could remember struggling with a can opener for a half hour one time while her mother stood there and watched—Joey had always appreciated it. Because she had learned a keen sense of problem-solving, determination and grit.

All things that had come in handy since they had taken over the farm.

She got into the doohickey—the doorless, windowless, DIY flatbed truck—and batted some of the ribbons away.

They had maybe gone a little bit overboard with decorating the ugly old vehicle that they used to putter around the farm and carry supplies. It was more garland than anything else at this point.

But it was utterly and perfectly *Hathaway*.

She had always wondered why her mother had given her her birth father's name. She hadn't liked it when she was a child. Not having the same name as her mother. But she understood it now. Her mom was giving her ties to her sisters. And she appreciated it very much.

The little truck bumped cheerfully along on the pothole-filled road. The mid-April weather was bright and cheery, if not still a bit chilly, in spite of the sun doing its best to warm the air. When she worked the roadside stand, selling little bouquets and her fruits and veggies—which at the moment was primarily rhubarb, so business was...niche—she still needed a light jacket to combat the afternoon breeze.

She rolled up to the barn that housed all the old farming

implements. Joey was fascinated by them. By all of them. She just couldn't fix them.

But, that was where Hollis came in.

She could see a big, black truck, all state-of-the-art and fancy parked outside of the red barn. The barn was a bit weatherworn, but she counted it as charming. The epitome of what a barn should look like. Though, they were going to need to give it a fresh coat of paint eventually. Brightening up the red, crisping up the white. That sort of thing. Joey didn't consider herself an expert on aesthetics generally speaking. But when it came to barn aesthetics, she felt like she knew what she was doing.

She knew a barn.

Apparently, she was going to have to adjust her idea of Hollis, though, because she had been certain that an antique tractor mechanic would show up in an antique truck.

But no.

She put the doohickey into Park, curling her fingers around the knob, which was a giant crystal fixed to the end of the gearshift, with a pink ribbon wrapped around it, and turned the engine off. She left the keys in the ignition, because why not.

She got out, and looked around, but didn't see him. He had clearly already gone into the barn.

She made her way in, and she stopped. The man was facing away from her, much taller than she had imagined him being, a black cowboy hat on top of his head. Both hands were shoved into his pockets, and his posture was straight, rigid. His shoulders broad.

"Hollis Logan?"

He turned around, and frowned. "Can I help you?"

And she was near knocked flat on her behind by the force of his…everything.

His face was sculpted, dark stubble covering a square jaw, his nose straight, his lips of interest—and Joey could not ever recall a man's lips being *of interest* before. His eyes were the kind of blue she'd only ever seen in the sky before, a shock on a man with such dark hair.

She was nearly speechless, and she could say for certain, she had never been rendered speechless by a man. Interesting mouth or no.

"I'm Joey Hathaway," she said, looking at a man who was probably barely over thirty, and not at all what she was expecting. "We had a meeting today."

"I'm aware we had a meeting, or I wouldn't be here."

"Right," she said, taken slightly aback by his general... gruffness.

Among other things.

"*You're* Joey Hathaway," he said.

"Yes," she said.

"You're not what I expected," he said.

"Why not?" She frowned. "Did you think I would be taller?"

"In a manner of speaking. I assumed that you were a man."

Joey had spent a lot of her life feeling like she didn't fit in well with other girls. Until she'd met her sisters, that was. At thirteen they'd met and spent the summer at camp together and she'd felt...like she fit. They showed her there were different ways to be a girl. Elliot, so confident, artistic and certain of her convictions. Georgie, assertive and opinionated and not afraid to ruffle a feather. Teddy, soft and fluffy and a friend to all. It made Joey's plainspoken nature feel...not so odd. But as much as she'd moved past feelings of inadequacy where all this was concerned, his words stung a bit. "Well, I'm not."

"That is clear."

His response was deadpan, his face... Lord, his face. He was the most handsome man Joey had ever laid eyes on. And... That knocked her back. Because she was not used to being bowled over by men's looks.

It wasn't that she didn't like men, she did, more or less. Especially when they were useful. It was just that she didn't really have much use for them as decorative objects.

Sure, in theory, she liked the look of a handsome man, but her mother had taught her to be self-sufficient, and she had never felt that there was a deficit in her life that needed to be filled by a member of the male species.

Looking at this man made her feel all kinds of deficits. In places she would rather not feel them.

"Well, you're a bit different than I thought too," she said, feeling the need to score a point of her own.

"How so?"

"I thought you would be old."

"Why?"

"You're an *antique* tractor mechanic," she said.

"The tractors are antique," he said, his voice flat. "Not me."

Was he joking? Because if so, it was pretty funny. But, she honestly couldn't tell. He didn't crack a smile.

"Well. Unexpected all around." She tried to imagine what Elliot might say in this situation. "And we won't discuss the inherent sexism in your assumption that a farmer is going to be a man."

"Is it sexist to assume that someone named *Joey* is a man?"

"Probably," Joey said. "Yeah. Probably. If we asked my sister Elliot, she would say definitely."

"Great. Elliot? Sister?"

"Yes," she said, trying to keep her tone patient. "There are four of us. Georgie, Teddy, Elliot and myself."

"Your mom had a theme going?"

She laughed. "We don't have the same mothers. We all have different mothers. Same father."

"Makes my family look downright boring," he said.

"They can't be too boring, you grew up to be a tractor mechanic."

They stopped talking for a moment, and his eyes lingered on hers, and she wondered if he was flirting. Was it flirting? She had never flirted before. So she honestly didn't know.

"Well, my father was a tractor mechanic."

"Was?"

"Yes," he said.

"I'm sorry," Joey said. "Of course my father might as well be dead for all I see him."

She had always been just a little too free with the things she said, and she regretted that tendency toward frankness now that she'd just blurted out her familial issues to a stranger.

It stung a little, to think of it, and she thought that was odd because she'd never done much dwelling on her dad.

Her mom hadn't been wounded by Mickey Hathaway. Sleeping with him hadn't changed her, and men always thought their dicks were instruments of transformation.

Per her mother.

But they were wrong. They didn't have that kind of power.

It was Joey who had changed Janine. At least, that was how she told it. She'd been happy Mickey hadn't wanted any part of the raising. It let her have total independence and all the time with Joey she wanted.

"Wow. Strong words."

"I don't mean them to be strong. My mother is the best. And she made sure that I never wanted for anything. And I don't. I didn't need a dad to teach me to throw a ball."

"Your mom taught you?"

"No. She told me if I wanted to learn something I ought to find someone who was good at it and ask them. I got hauled out of Globe Life Park trying to get one of the Rangers to show me how to throw a ball. The baseball player made the security guard bring me back to the field and he showed me. I learned."

He stared at her, and she continued. "I don't know how to fix tractors. At least not tractors this old. But I don't think my dad could've helped me with that anyway. I also don't think he would have taught his daughter to fix a tractor. My grandpa certainly never did."

"Your grandpa is Jack Hathaway?" he said.

"Yes. This is Jack Hathaway's land."

"Yeah. But I'm connecting all of the relationships," he said. "You buying this place?"

"I'd like to inherit it. Not like we're waiting for Grandpa Jack to die—we don't want Grandpa Jack to die—but we were hoping that he would parcel off a piece for us, because it's too much for him to take care of. Understand?"

"Vaguely," he said.

"Good.

"These are the tractors," she said.

"I gathered that. Judging by the fact that they're tractors."

"Sure. But you didn't get that I was a woman."

"Entirely different," he said.

"How?"

"A woman isn't a tractor."

For some reason, she tried to ponder that.

He wandered around and cast an eye over all the machinery. "You want all this fixed?"

"Yes."

"Just running?"

"I mean, what are my options?"

He arched a dark brow and her stomach did a corresponding swoop. "I can be as thorough as you like."

"Indeed. Well. How about a bid?"

"I can do that, just give me a few."

It took more than a few, and Joey stood back and watched as he went over the equipment. Thoroughly. She found herself staring at his hands. She didn't quite know what was wrong with her.

"I've got two figures for you, the mechanics, and mechanics and restoration, which honestly..." He went over to the old, faded green John Deere. "I'd only bother with this one." And then he went over to a red baler. "And this one."

"Okay, give me the figure for that."

He did, and she sputtered. But she knew that they had the money in the farm fund. They'd all contributed fairly equally to the fund, as they were able, but they were wedded enough to the joint venture that they were all open to doing more, paying more, whatever needed to be done to make it right. Still, they had to consult each other on all things. "I'll have to get back to you after Sister Sunday to confirm."

"Sister Sunday?"

"Yes," she said. "Sister Sunday. We have a sister day every Sunday, where we have themed meals. We each choose a different one every— Well, you don't care about that. But we'll need to discuss the logistics of this."

He nodded slowly. "Okay."

They walked out of the barn together and she was thankful for the glare of the sun, which shocked her eyeballs enough that she had a reprieve from the intensity of his handsome maleness. Male handsomeness. All of it.

"What the hell is that?" He stopped in his tracks, and gestured toward the vehicle in which she'd come.

"The doohickey," she said, as if he was stupid.

"Did you want me to restore that too?"

She blinked and looked at the absurd vehicle, and all of its ribbons. "Don't be silly. We already did."

And then she climbed back into the truck and drove away, doing her best not to look back at Hollis Logan.

CHAPTER TWO

HOLLIS COULDN'T GET the image of Joey Hathaway out of his head. It was her eyes. Violet eyes. Who had ever heard of such a thing. But then, the fact that he had expected a person named Joey Hathaway to be a man—as any sensible human being would—had thrown him off a bit too. Though, if it hadn't been for her eyes he might've been able to get his bearings a bit better.

He couldn't remember the last time a woman had impacted him quite so much. The degree where his house—filled with the solitude he normally welcomed—felt unpleasantly empty.

He walked over to the fridge and cracked open a beer. Then he went back to his chair and sat. Honestly, most days he didn't really notice the picture that hung on the back wall. Not because he didn't care, but because like his grief it was simply there. It wasn't sharp or cruel. It was a piece of who he was now. A scar from a wound, faded by time.

But he noticed the picture tonight. That young couple happy and hopeful for the future, laughing and smiling, completely unaware of the road that lay up ahead. Right on the edge of the frame was a tiny bundle of flowers. Faded now like his memories. But it was the piece of her bouquet she'd handed to him at the end, and he never could part with it.

Even though when he looked at the man in the picture

he didn't even think of it as him. Not anymore. It was some stranger standing there in a tuxedo, clutching a woman in white. Maybe that was just wishful thinking, because if he stared too long, he knew it was him. Yes, if he stared too long he knew. And he remembered.

Well, either way, he wasn't that young fool anymore who couldn't fathom all the ways in which the world would cut him open, gut him and turn him inside out. It wasn't that there hadn't been women. There had been.

It had been eleven years, after all.

It was just that they didn't usually surprise him. But then, he didn't usually see them again, either. And he was committed to doing this job for Joey Hathaway. And so there that whole thing was. He sighed. He hadn't exactly wanted to, he never wanted to. It made him wonder if he should take the picture down.

Then, that would be a whole lot like not his own skin. But there was something about Joey Hathaway's eyes that made him feel different. And he chastised himself for that, because he was old enough to know better, and several steps too cynical to get caught up in that.

But there were some things he wouldn't mind getting caught up in.

He shook his head. No. He had a job to do. He didn't mix business with pleasure. He didn't mix pleasure with any personal aspect of his life. There was a reason he didn't stay in Jasper Creek when he felt the urge to find a woman. It would make things complicated.

And he didn't want that.

He'd left the place he'd called home with his wife years ago.

There were ghosts on every street corner, not to mention members of his late wife's family. Plus single women lining up to make him pity casseroles and all manner of other things he just didn't want to deal with. And so he'd left.

Found something new. Found something simple.

And one of his goals had been to never make Jasper Creek complicated. He'd managed it so far. He wasn't going to go messing things up because of a pair of violet eyes and a ridiculous name. Nope. He was going to fix her tractors and make some money and that was all. Yep. That was all.

IT WAS HER very first Sister Sunday, and since she had to pitch the idea of spending an awful lot of money to repair and restore some of the tractors, she felt like it needed to be particularly spectacular. Thankfully, the starts that she had carted in her truck all the way from Texas were finally beginning to bear fruit—quite literally—in the greenhouse, and she had a plethora of nice things to help set the table. And soon, enough for the roadside stand, and then the farm store.

Granted, she needed Georgie's expertise to turn fruit from a healthy snack to something that people *wanted* to eat. She knew that Elliot would enjoy a bowl of raspberries, and that Teddy would try anything, smiling bravely and claiming her love of nature, but she would want something sweet. Georgie most definitely would want sweet, as sweet was her entire wheelhouse. Well, when it came to food. Not so much when it came to her personality.

And Joey meant that with a deep and abiding amount of love. She adored her sister's prickly personality. Truly. But she was going to have to cultivate her goodwill in order to get a spectacular table spread for tonight. She came in with a large basket of raspberries, and another of strawberries and approached Georgie with a wide grin on her face. Georgie was standing over a bowl with some dough and scowling. She didn't like to interrupt her sister when she was scowling over dough. It was dangerous.

"Did your dough not rise?"

Georgie looked up. "My dough always rises. But one of Teddy's chickens has walked across the dough."

"Oh no," Joey said. "Teddy's going to feel really bad…"

Georgie wiped her hand over her brow. "I know," she said. "I know. And it is impossible to be mad at Teddy. But it is not impossible to be mad at these chickens, Joey. It is in fact, very, very possible."

"What are you going to…do to them?"

She had sudden visions of chicken for Sunday night dinner.

"You know that Teddy has a hard stance against eating chickens that she knows."

Georgie scowled. "I also have a hard stance against eating animals I know, but that doesn't rule out violence."

"What are you going to do?"

"I bought a water pistol."

"Oh, Teddy won't like that."

Georgie flung her arms wide, her sweatshirt—massively oversize—giving her the appearance of a flying squirrel. "I don't like chickens in my bread dough."

She knew she was taking a risk in asking for Georgie's help right now when she was so cross, but Joey had always felt there was value in a calculated risk.

"Georgie," Joey said. "Dear, Georgie."

Georgie eyed the berries, and her gaze went narrow. "What?"

"Would you make pastry for my lovely berries?"

"I'm having a dough disaster." She sighed. "What did you want me to make out of the berries?"

"I don't know. I thought you could come up with something better than I could."

"That is not the point of Sister Sunday," Georgie said crisply.

"Are you really going to be a stickler for rules?" Joey asked. "I never thought you would be the type."

"Only insomuch as I am forced to follow the rules, and therefore you must too."

"She's right," came a singsong voice from the next room. "You have to follow the rules." They both turned as Teddy walked into the kitchen, followed by Elliot. Elliot hadn't commented, but was merely observing.

"What are the rules, Teddy? Explicitly. Do I have to make everything?"

"Of course not," Teddy said. "Contributions from all are part of it, but it is supposed to be your week."

"My theme would hardly be welcome," Joey said, rolling her eyes. "Nobody wants to have a hoedown on Sister Sunday."

"Sure we do," Elliot said, her expression totally deadpan.

Joey narrowed her eyes. "No you don't."

And the thing was, she wasn't even sure she wanted to have a hoedown on Sister Sunday. She kind of liked it when it was fancy, though she would never admit it. It was just that she wouldn't be able to think of how to do fancy. Teddy had done something truly extraordinary only last week, and it had been like a fairy wonderland.

"Part of the point of Sister Sunday is the celebration of what makes us all unique," Elliot said.

"And eating our weight in pastries," Georgie added.

Joey sighed. "Fine. Make me something country, please, Georgie."

"Sure," Georgie said. Then she turned her focus to Teddy. "Teddy. Henrietta was in my dough."

"How do you know it was Henrietta?" Teddy asked.

"Because Henrietta is a pest. She's infatuated with my kitchen."

"I don't know what to tell you," Teddy said. "She's like a cat. She senses that you don't like her and so she wants to spend more time with you."

"That is absurd. The chicken is not like a cat. The chicken is just a nuisance."

"That's very rude, Georgie."

"She isn't even in here," Georgie said.

"All right," Joey said. "Get your overalls, sisters. It's a hoedown night."

Actually, it was fitting that they have a hoedown to talk about tractor repair. And to get started talking about her plans for the old barn. Because they was going to make a farm store out of it, with fresh produce from her garden, from her greenhouse, flowers and baked goods by Georgie, eggs and honey by Teddy, and ceramics by Elliot.

They were already doing it small scale at the stand, but the store was the ultimate goal.

"Excellent," Elliot said. "A hoedown it is."

CHAPTER THREE

THE HAY BALES had been perhaps a little bit much, but Joey actually thought it looked pretty nice. She had stacked them all in a big semicircle that went around the long table they had set up in the front yard. She had Mason jars set out on the table, and she had even found a little plaid handkerchief for Henrietta. Joey was wearing a pair of denim overalls, and she had a very accomplished playlist going in the background. If she said so herself.

She had also fired up the grill, deciding that meat would go nicely for dinner with her hoedown.

Anyway, it was something she could do.

Her mother was something of a grill master, and she had passed her knowledge on to Joey.

She had also rounded up a couple of cowboy hats, and some wide-brimmed straw hats, in case anyone wanted them for added accessorizing.

One thing she had learned about her sisters was that they were all fond of an accessory.

Georgie came out of the kitchen a moment later, rolling a tray with her baked goods sitting on it. The berries shining bright like jewels.

Georgie herself was wearing an extremely oversize pair of linen overalls that looked more like a flower sack.

Elliot arrived with handmade vases with flower arrangements tucked into them. She had on a pair of much more fitted, waxed canvas overalls that she had cuffed cleverly down at the ankle. Joey admired that about Elliot. Her attention to detail. It was something that Joey herself didn't have the patience for.

And then Teddy came with jars of honey, her red hair like a ginger halo around her head, and a grin on her face. She was not wearing overalls. She was wearing a white dress with thin straps that had a little knot in them. She had put a white T-shirt on underneath it. And the dress itself was white with pink rosebuds.

"You are in violation of the dress code," Georgie said.

"I don't wear pants," Teddy said.

"Well, I don't wear dresses, but I put one on when asked," Joey said.

Teddy patted her arm. "And I honor your decision."

"Well I don't honor yours."

Teddy made an amused sound. "But I honor it. And in the end, Joey, that's what matters the most. That you come to a peace with your own choices."

Joey grumbled, and they sat down at the table, everybody beginning to excitedly dish their food.

"I have a proposition," Joey said.

"Yes?"

"I know it's going to cost a lot of money, but I would like to fully restore all of the antique vehicles in the barn. Then we can move them out, use some of them as decoration, use some of them practically, but in general, they'll make a nice attraction for the store."

"Ah, the store," Elliot said.

"Yes," Joey said. "The store."

"I'm excited about the store," Elliot said. "It's just that there are not a lot of details to it and I feel in my heart of hearts that these are not details that resonate with my spirit."

"Indeed," Teddy said.

"All fine for you to say," Joey said. "But without the store, I don't have income. You have your ceramics, Elliot. And Teddy has her bee removal. I'm selling things at the stand but my fruit isn't coming in robustly just yet and I can only sell so many bushels of rhubarb. And Georgie needs a storefront."

"It's true," Georgie said. "I want to transition into doing baking full-time, but I need a commercial kitchen. And that's part of the farm store."

"I know," Elliot said. "I was teasing. I will obviously take on any tasks that you would like to assign to me."

In truth, she didn't actually want to assign anything to Elliot. Not because she didn't love her sister. Not because her sister wasn't wholly and completely capable. But because Joey was a control freak. She liked to do all the things. Hell, something she thought she might need to do all things.

"What exactly is going on here?"

Joey turned to look at the same time as all of her sisters. And was surprised to see Grandpa Jack standing there, dressed in an old flannel shirt, his hands stuffed into the pockets of his jeans.

"It's a hoedown," Joey said.

"It might actually be more of a hootenanny," Teddy said matter-of-factly.

"Doesn't look like either such thing to me. But I smelled barbecue."

Joey suddenly felt shy. Which was silly. They had come to this place because of their grandfather. Because they cared about him. It was just that they didn't really know him. Not deeply. They wanted to.

And Joey realized it was easier to think of it in terms of they. The sisters. Not so much her.

Her mother had always been so profoundly okay with the way things were, and as a result Joey had tried to feel the same. What she wanted was to be completely fine with the way everything had gone down. Her mother and father had had a quick fling, her mother had gotten pregnant. Her father hadn't wanted kids. It was fine. She didn't need a dad who wasn't all that jazzed to have her. Not when she had a mother who was so happy about it. And as for her grandfather… Her mother had never been opposed to her knowing him. And he had always been prickly, vaguely difficult.

She was sad sometimes that she really hadn't gotten to know her grandmother, Mary, well as she'd died years ago. But of course…they weren't her mother's family. And her mother didn't know them at all. So. It made sense.

And it was fine.

Suddenly, though, she felt a familiar deep yearning in her chest, one that she often tried to ignore.

"Why don't you eat, Grandpa?" Georgie asked, happy to take the bull by the horns, clearly.

"As long as I'm not intruding," he said, sounding both prickly and polite all at once, and she wondered if that was where Georgie got that particular skill from.

"If you come inside with me, you can look at the drink selection," Elliot said.

"I don't need to go inside," he said, his voice firm. "I'll sit out here. Tell me about your plans."

"How are you feeling?" Teddy said.

"Strong as an ox," Grandpa Jack said.

"Very good to hear," Teddy said, reaching out and patting his arm.

Joey momentarily envied Teddy's ease.

Joey wasn't as open about certain things as Teddy was. Up until last week, Teddy had never been on a date, and she had been completely honest about that—and her overall lack of experience—with everyone. It had made Joey deeply uncomfortable. She was about as big of a virgin as they came. And she wasn't ashamed of it or anything. Teddy seemed completely fine with her own virginal status. Joey just…didn't want to talk about it.

Meanwhile, Elliot was lusting after the neighbor, and she wasn't shy about that either. Joey felt deeply uncomfortable about most things. Most feelings. She shifted slightly. And she tried very hard not to think about Hollis Logan, and just how handsome he was.

Good grief. While she was sitting there thinking about her relationship with her grandfather?

Their grandfather stayed a while, and then the girls migrated into the kitchen to do dishes.

"Are you going out with Beau again, Teddy?" Elliot asked.

"Yes," Teddy said, looking serenely pleased.

"We do have a store to open," Joey pointed out.

"My dates are not preventing me from helping with anything. And if they do, all you have to do is tell me, Joey. Of course I'll make time."

That was the problem with Teddy. She was endlessly accommodating. So you could never be irritated at her. And truly, the only thing that was sort of scratching at her was that there was all this… Stuff going on around her that she couldn't be a part of.

She had always wanted sisters.

Her deep secret dream. When she had been living on the farm surrounded by men, and her mother, she had dreamed about having sisters, and then it had turned out she had them, and then she had met them and they were wonderful.

But there was this… This whole other language they were speaking around her.

This language of men and crushes and sex.

Well, not that Teddy had said anything about that. Elliot would likely laugh at her for thinking it was possible Teddy's relationship wasn't…carnal. But Elliot was very knowledgable about such things.

Elliot was perfectly calm when it came to her entanglements with men. She got what she wanted, and moved on.

That was what Joey wanted, in theory. And why not? After all, her own mother had had sort of something like that with Joey's father. She had been undented in the end, she had just ended up having a child.

Well, the thought of that gave Joey a full body recoil. She did not want to have children. Not yet anyway. Honestly, she hadn't given any thought to that sort of thing.

And she wasn't thinking about it now.

"All right then," she said. "I'll get in touch with Hollis tomorrow. He can get the tractors out of the barn, and set up a makeshift spot to work on them. I can start on the farm store… Everything is going according to plan."

"And you can delegate if you want to," Teddy pointed out.

"I will," Joey said.

"There's nothing wrong with wanting help, Joey," Elliot added.

"I had Georgie baking things for me earlier. I don't have any problem asking for help."

Her three sisters exchanged a glance.

"Unjust," Joey said.

"We just know you," Teddy said shrugging. "That's all." And she couldn't be mad after her sister said that. Because there was something pretty special about feeling understood, especially when you had problems talking about how you felt.

HOLLIS WAS BACK at the Hathaway property a couple of days later, to get started on the tractors. Joey had sent him a text on Sunday night saying that her sisters had agreed to the expense of the restoration project. And hell… He'd been… anticipating coming back here ever since. He didn't know what it was about her. She was an intriguing little thing. Sort of prickly, a lot pretty. Though, not the kind of pretty he usually went in for. The thing about living life the way he did was that he didn't have time for subtle. He liked obvious. Because it was simple. He liked a flashy sort of beauty that sparkled from across the room. Joey was something else entirely.

He walked up to the front door and knocked, and the door jerked open. A woman in an apron was standing there looking at him, and in the background, another woman in a baggy sweatshirt was chasing what looked like a chicken across the room, as she fired a squirt gun in its direction. As that was happening, a woman in a flowing dress carrying another chicken came down the stairs.

"Oh, please don't do that," the dress woman shouted.

"Henrietta needs to stay out of my kitchen," said the squirt-gun-wielding woman.

And just then, Joey came down the stairs herself, *not* holding a chicken.

All of the women stopped and looked at him, and he was

pinned to the spot for a moment by four sets of extremely unusual violet eyes.

And just up at the top of the stairs he saw a third chicken, peering around the corner, before she quickly tucked herself away, out of sight.

He chose to ignore that.

"Good morning," he said. "I'm here to see Joey."

"Really," the one in the dress said, as if she had forgotten her anger in her intrigue.

Joey clearly wasn't interested in intrigue.

"This is Hollis," Joey said, coming down the stairs at a faster pace now. "You know. Tractor mechanic." She gestured to the others. "Georgie. Teddy. Elliot."

"Nice to meet you," he said, following her fingers as she pointed to each of them and named them.

"Nice to meet you too," the one named Teddy called, but then Joey was out the front door, and closing it behind them.

"All right," she said. "Let's head out to the barn."

She was walking toward that ridiculous vehicle that he'd seen her in that first day. With the ribbons.

"Why don't we drive my truck over?" he said.

"Well, all right," she said. "Suit yourself."

She hauled herself up into his truck before he could go and open the door for her and offer any kind of assistance. "Let's go," she said.

He shook his head and got into the driver's side, starting the engine.

"Thanks for taking on the job," Joey said. "I appreciate it. It's important to find good laborers. I learned that from my mom."

He chuckled. "I don't consider myself a laborer."

Of course, when it came to discussions of his life, it was all complicated. And he didn't particularly want to have a complicated discussion with this woman who was pretty much a stranger.

"Sorry," she said. "Though there's nothing dishonorable about labor."

"I didn't say there was. I'm just saying."

"Right," she said. "My mom has a ranch back in Texas."

That explained her accent.

He hadn't recalled hearing a drawl on any of her sisters. But then, she had mentioned that they were half sisters.

"Is that right?"

"Yes," she said. "Hundred acres. And she's got a couple guys that have worked there for a long time. Good crew. I grew up surrounded by all of it. And I'm bringing my general farm expertise here. In terms of growing produce and flowers and…trying to manage and oversee maintenance and repairs," she said.

"Really?"

"Yes," she said. "I'm going to sell all of my sister's goods from a new farm shop. There's a commercial kitchen in the back of the barn from when the ranch was a huge operation that had a hundred ranch hands to feed. It just needs a little bit of restoration and then Georgie is going to use it."

"Sounds good to me. Exactly like the kind of thing I would enjoy."

She looked at him, and he felt something shift low inside of him, and unfortunately, he was familiar with the feeling. He was attracted to her. But that was a might too complicated for where he was at in his life. She was too complicated for where he would ever be at in his life. There had been a time when things had been different.

When he was younger, he'd assumed that love and marriage were in his future.

But now they were in his past. And that changed everything.

"Really?" She looked at him critically. "You don't seem like a farmer's market kind of guy."

"What does a farmer's market guy look like?"

"Skinny jeans," she said.

"You seem to have a lot of opinions, Joey Hathaway."

"Oh, I'm full of opinions," she said, stepping out of the truck now that he had parked.

She flung open the barn doors, and started to pace around the big space. He thought it best not to comment on how much work the restoration was going to be. The floor in the place was nicely intact, but there was quite a bit of finish work that would need to be done.

"You know," he said, before he could stop himself. "I don't just work on tractors."

"Really?"

"Yeah. I… I can take a look at some of this too."

"I'd have to check with the girls."

"Were you going to Sheetrock and drywall all on your own?"

"Yeah, you can buy the supplies for it down at the feed store."

"And you were going to…watch a video about it on the internet?"

"No. I figured I'd talk to somebody who knew."

"Right."

"A person can take care of most anything by themselves. And if it's complicated, like tractor mechanics, there is no shame in hiring someone. Getting an expert involved." She looked around critically. "But sometimes, it's just a matter of putting in the appropriate elbow grease yourself."

She stared at him for a moment, her expression shifting.

And he was struck again by the color of her eyes. She was a pretty little thing, with a stubborn-looking chin, and he didn't know why the hell that seemed appealing.

"Well, I can be your expert."

"You have experiencing fixing things up?"

"Yes," he said. "I remodeled the place I live in now." It wasn't the first place he'd remodeled either. But he didn't want to get into that.

"Well, if you don't mind. I'd appreciate it. I don't know that I have the budget to hire you to do it, but you could show me."

"Sure."

He hadn't met…well, very many people who just wanted to learn something and jump right in. It was a strange thing, coming from a singularly odd little woman. Joey.

And then suddenly she was across the barn, climbing up the ladder, and his eyes were drawn to the way her pants stretched over her tight little behind.

Lust he was used to. That was commonplace. It was the fascination that struck him as strange.

"And what are you doing now?"

"I've been meaning to go up here and look for tools. Pay me no mind. You're welcome to just get started on the tractors."

"And you're just going to…work here?"

"Yes, Hollis, I have things to do."

She vanished up into the loft and he found himself just… staring.

He shook his head and turned to the first tractor. He'd already ordered all the parts he'd need, so now it was a matter of getting going. It made sense given the scale of the project to do as much as possible on-site.

Which meant he was going to be working around a purple-eyed temptress.

As he lined all the tools out, he had to wonder if she was the kind of woman men normally found…tempting.

She was pretty in a corn-fed, whole-milk kind of way. Right now it appealed to him more than anything in recent memory, but he couldn't quite say why.

He didn't suppose he had to.

What he had to do was fix the tractor.

JOEY SCURRIED AROUND the loft, going through the boxes, trying to find the tools her grandpa Jack had sworn up and down were up there.

She had a small pile of them by the time she sneaked a peek down at Hollis.

He was bent over a tractor, his hand up on the top of the hood hinge, and she couldn't help but notice the very pleasing way his bicep flexed.

Experts…

When she wanted to know about something, she asked an expert.

The thought made her face break out into bonfire.

Yeah, that applied to drywall, not men.

But Teddy had been lately consumed with Beau and it had really gotten Joey thinking. And she wished she didn't have such a hard time talking to her sisters about things like this. She was usually all right going to someone and admitting she needed some help, as she didn't like sitting and marinating in her ignorance.

Two different things.

You don't even know if he's an expert on…sex.

Oh, great. She couldn't even think the word…*sex* without putting a pause in front of it. There was no way she was actually thinking about it in context with the man down there.

Except she was. And it was making her warm.

She pulled a wrench out of a box in the back and added it to her pile. "Found them!" she shouted, mostly to break the tension in herself.

There was a bang, and Hollis cussed.

She peered over the edge of the loft. "You okay?"

"I don't need surprises when I've got my head in an engine," he said, looking up at her as he rubbed the back of his head.

"Sorry," she said, her heart thudding hard.

She collected the tools and did a one-handed climb down the ladder, the box under her arm.

"You got your drywall tools?"

"I'm not really sure," she said. "Some of them might be."

He moved away from the tractor and came to peer into the box. "You've got a trowel in there."

"And I need that?"

He looked at her, all blue eyes and heat she'd never felt before. "Yes."

She wanted to kiss him. And she'd never felt that before. Not in twenty-five years. She'd known a lot of men, a lot of cowboys. She'd never known or seen anyone like him before.

And Joey Hathaway's mother hadn't raised her to sit on what she wanted, nor had she raised her to indulge in embarrassment. If you wanted something and you didn't ask for it, you couldn't go blaming anyone else for your disappointment.

"So. Um. You're happy to give me some pointers? For Sheetrock? And…mud and the like."

"Yes."

"I don't guess you give pointers on anything else?" Her throat felt scratchy.

"Such as?"

He smelled like hay and hard work, and she'd always liked the smell of both. But there was something underpinning that. Something she wasn't familiar with and it made her want to lean right in.

The thing was, if you wanted to learn to throw a ball and you weren't willing to sneak into a professional baseball stadium you just didn't want it all that bad.

And the worst that could happen is security escorted you out. And she knew from personal experience it wasn't all *that* bad.

There was no security here, either. So really, it was fine.

She cleared her throat. "Well, I was actually wondering if you would be open to giving me some kissing lessons."

CHAPTER FOUR

FOR A SECOND, Hollis thought he'd hit his head harder on that tractor than he'd originally given himself credit for.

Not because women didn't want to kiss him—they did, and often.

But none had ever asked him for...kissing lessons.

With the most earnest eyes he'd ever seen, and all that bravado and... Hell, he'd been right. It was a stubborn chin.

"You offering to pay an hourly rate?" he asked.

A crease appeared between her brows. "Do you think it might take more than an hour?"

"Oh...hell, Joey. You don't even know me." What a damned hypocrite he was. He hadn't known any of the women he'd kissed in the past eleven years, and consequently, they hadn't known him. And he hadn't cared, not one bit.

But this woman...

"Should I know you, Hollis?"

"Girl, if you need to ask for kissing lessons, you probably ought to know the man."

"My mama did not know my daddy," she said. And she wrinkled her nose. "Not that I'm suggesting you ought to become my baby daddy."

"Right."

For some reason, those words twisted something up inside of him.

He had no intention of having children. But he had at one time. At one time, he had every kind of normal hope and dream. Those things you just took for granted because all of the important people in your life before you had done them.

Falling in love. Getting married. Having children.

Normal.

There were all these other dreams out there in the world, accumulating wealth and becoming successful in careers, fame and whatever other shit people aspired to.

But it seemed to him that those everyday things, that crushing suburban mundanity, or however people tended to see it... Those were the things people just assumed they could get.

Assumed they could keep.

And Hollis knew better. And he knew that it was a precious thing. Something that you could never hope to buy, hope to manipulate your way into. It was a gift of fate. And people just didn't realize it. God knew he hadn't.

And he hadn't thought about all that in a long time.

"Shit," Joey said. "I think we ought to just kiss already."

And with that, she launched her athletic frame toward him, and he caught her in his arms.

Her eyes.

Damn, her eyes.

And he should probably say no. Because she was betraying a lack of experience that ought to send him running in the other direction. She was demonstrating—quite handily—that she was a disaster in cowgirl boots, and the type of calamity he ought to avoid.

But she was soft.

And there was something about her eyes.

He thought, when he was younger, and the world had some possibility in it, he would've said yes to this moment.

To kissing the improbable girl who flung herself right into his arms. And in that wild, violet second, he wanted to do it.

And so he did.

He lowered his head, angled his mouth, and pressed his lips down to hers.

JOEY DID NOT FEEL adequately warned.

Teddy had been fluttering about for a while now, obsessed with Beau Riley, Elliot was a woman of experience, who often waved her hand when speaking of men and earthly pleasures. She suspected Georgie had about as much experience as Joey did, but they would never speak of it.

And as for her mother…

Nothing to fuss about.

Men are awfully fond of their penises, but if you ask me, it's all a bit overrated.

All the good press out there about men is spread by them, remember that.

Never any heat in her words, just a kind of mild amusement.

But that was her mother. Practical. Unaffected.

She didn't get wound up about emotions. She didn't worry about things. If there was a problem, and she could fix it, she did.

If there was a problem and she couldn't fix it, she found the person who could. And if it was an unfixable problem she threw her hands up and said: *well, dammit all to hell.*

But then she got on with things.

And that was exactly what Joey aspired to be like. No, that wasn't even right. It was just how Joey figured she was.

Her mother had raised her, after all. And when it came to getting overexcited and all that kind of stuff, she didn't figure that her father was prone to such things, given that the man had walked out on his daughters and all of that. Not that he could have reasonably stayed with all of…

Hollis parted his lips, and hers along with them, and suddenly his tongue touched her teeth, and that erased every thought in her mind.

She gasped, and he took it as an invitation to go deeper, and suddenly, his tongue was sliding against hers.

Her knees straight up gave out on her, and if his arm hadn't been wrapped around her like a steel band, she'd have gone straight to the barn floor.

She had not been expecting that.

She was shaking. The center between her thighs was molten hot and aching.

She wanted to climb up his big, hard body and…she didn't even know. She just wanted to rub herself up against him.

Like their cat Jasper Junie.

Well, that was the most unflattering comparison she could have ever thought of.

But then, she felt about as tetchy as a barn cat, so it was fair enough.

She pushed her fingers through his hair, and then let them run down his back. He was all muscle. So big and broad.

And she realized she didn't know anything about him. How old he was, why he lived here, where the rest of his family was. If he was married.

A lot of men didn't care about things like that.

Another thing her mother had told her matter-of-factly.

Because if her father had been married, he wouldn't have given a thought to cheating on a wife. He had four women pregnant at basically the same time.

And she had…she had just asked Hollis to teach her how to kiss.

And he'd said that she didn't know him.

But suddenly, all of those red flags were swimming around in her head with the desire that was building between her thighs and spreading outward, making her limbs weak, and she just couldn't sort through it all.

Liar. You don't want to.

For the first time in her life, she didn't want to take it apart and see if she could put it back together. For the first time in her life, she didn't want to know how something worked. She just wanted to be in the magic.

His mouth was magic.

And suddenly, she wanted to tell her sisters that. She really did.

Except the very idea of it made her face go all hot, and sweaty.

And she wanted to hide it. As much as she wanted to share it. Wanted to keep it all for herself, like it was the kind of magic that would vanish if anyone else saw it.

His hands were big, and they moved with certainty down her back, cupping her rear. Her head fell back, a gasp of pleasure escaping her mouth as she arched her hips forward and felt his very, very hard…self.

And she wanted to make a note to let her mother know that it was entirely possible some men *did* have magical penises.

She just hadn't seen one.

Not that Joey had.

Yet.

Then they parted, and they were both breathing hard.

"No charge for that," he said, his voice rougher than it had been before the kiss.

Which meant maybe that he was affected by it too. In ways other than physical, that was. She understood how men's bodies worked. In the strictest sense.

But she had never heard that arousal could affect the way you talked. She didn't know that it could make you breathe different. Make your heart beat different. Make you feel like you might be different.

"Well," she said. "Are you sure about that? Because I'd pay pretty good for it."

"Joey," he said, his tone a warning.

Like he knew her.

Did kissing like that mean they knew each other?

Except she looked at him, and while she saw a man who was strangely familiar in some ways, she still saw a whole lot that she didn't know. But his face felt more like hers, and his eyes now seemed personal. The downturn of his lips, and the way his skin creased right there as he frowned…

Well, now, that seemed like it was for her. She got up on her tiptoes and kissed him again. Just quickly.

"And what was that?"

"I wanted to taste your frown," she said, and immediately she was assaulted by a rush of embarrassed heat.

"And?" he asked, the lips now turning upward into a lopsided grin.

"Well now I have to give that a taste too." She kissed him again.

"Indulge me, Joey," he said. "Was that your first kiss?"

"I would've thought that was pretty clear."

"Why would that be clear?"

"Because of…" She took a step back and spread her arms. "All this?"

"You're damned pretty."

"Oh," she said.

She could honestly say that she had never given it a lot of thought. She had never needed to.

"I don't care about that," she said. Except that she found she did. And she felt a little bit like he'd picked a flower and handed it to her.

"Then what exactly do you mean?"

"I've been busy," she said. "And I'm obviously not the kind of woman that runs around looking for things like this. Also, if I had been kissed before I would know how to do it."

"Is that right?"

"Yes. I wouldn't have had to ask for a lesson from you, because I would've already had one."

"Pretty confident in your ability to learn quick?"

"Yes," she said, except something wobbled in her chest, and she wasn't accustomed to that kind of insecurity.

"I like that about you," he said.

"Good. I'm all right with it. Which is nice, because I do think that you have to arrive at a place of comfort with yourself."

"Yeah," he said, his eyes getting a faraway look. "That is true."

"Well, since you are charging me for the tractors, I'll let you get back to that," she said.

"That's it?"

"Thanks," she said.

And suddenly, she couldn't get away from him fast enough, and she didn't know what the hell had happened. She just felt...she just felt strange and awkward. And like she wanted more, but the very idea terrified her.

She couldn't very well ask the man to teach her how to have sex.

Couldn't she?
And that question scared her even more.
Because she wanted the answer to be yes.

CHAPTER FIVE

WHEN HOLLIS GOT BACK to his place that night, he felt a strange sort of heaviness in his chest.

He was preoccupied. By...by everything. It wasn't that he had kissed a woman. He had kissed any number of women in the years since...

He didn't feel any guilt about that.

But there was something different about Joey. And it wasn't guilt that sat with him now. But something else.

He walked over to the picture frame, but he wasn't really looking at the picture. He was looking at the flowers.

He brushed his fingers over the bluebonnets.

That color felt burned into him right now.

He had a drink, had some dinner. Went to bed.

But he could only think about Joey. And when he finally did drift off to sleep, it was just that same dream.

He'd had it for eleven years. Starting when Samantha died, and coming back to visit now and again. No rhyme or reason.

He was standing in a field, looking all around him. The sun was shining, and the sky was clear. And somehow, he didn't feel sad.

It was impossible to feel sad.

Because he was surrounded by an entire field of bluebonnets.

TEDDY HAD A date with Beau. But it wasn't just any date, because according to the house gossip, which obviously spread quickly and easily because there were only four of them and none of them were really all that adept at keeping secrets, it seemed as if this date was significant and Joey felt a kick of protection as Teddy skirted the issue of whether or not she was going to have sex with Beau.

It was strange. She didn't feel protective of her own self in quite the same way. Even though she and Teddy were the same when it came to experience. It was just that Teddy was so *soft*. And she worried that if someone wasn't careful, they could easily crush Teddy.

Teddy with her chickens and honey and bees. Teddy with her pretty dresses and easy smile.

She didn't have the same sophistication and philosophical nature as Elliot. Elliot seemed to be able to take hard things—no matter how hard—and find a place for them. A meaning. Joey supposed that was the artist in her. Forming answers out of clay, when before it had been nothing but a shapeless lump.

Georgie was spiky and definitely had the air of someone who would and did protect themselves.

Teddy seemed defenseless, and it hit Joey in a strange place right now.

It's because you feel defenseless, you dope. Because he kissed you. Because you understand why Teddy wants to have sex with Beau, and you also understand that if it feels like it could be dangerous to you it could devastate Teddy.

She didn't want to feel in danger. She didn't even know Hollis. It wasn't the same. Teddy was in uncharted territory. Teddy was dating a man. Joey had just kissed one in a barn.

It was feelings that were tricky, at least Joey imagined.

Kissing and sex and all of that… That seemed like it could be pretty straightforward.

"You're going out with him again tonight?" Joey asked.

"Yes. We had fun last night." Teddy was practically shimmering with joy, and it was almost painful to look at. Joey didn't know why. "Besides, it's just a horseback ride."

"Do we need to have 'the talk' with you, Teddy?" Elliot asked.

"Don't be silly," Teddy said, waving Elliot away. "My mother has been having 'the talk' with me since I could walk. I've been on the pill since I was in high school. If there's a mother who prepared her daughter for all the consequences of sex, it is mine."

"Maybe that's why you haven't *had* sex," Elliot said.

A fair point. Joey's mother had played sex off as the same kind of thing as falling off a bike, or falling out of a tree…

Well, maybe not.

There was no falling involved at all in her mother's retelling.

"Well, maybe," Teddy agreed. "But I'm not planning on having any tonight. Probably."

Joey was a virgin and even she knew that was the ultimate in famous last words.

"Moving a bit fast," Georgie said, her tone imbued with concern.

"It doesn't feel that way," Teddy assured her.

"Maybe he should come to something on Sister Sunday," Joey said. "So we can give him the once-over."

She'd feel better if she had a chance to evaluate the guy.

"You gave him the once-over last night when he picked me up. You said he passed the test."

"Sure, the date test. Not the is-he-good-enough-to-have-sex-with-you test," Elliot replied.

"That is not a real test," Teddy replied, giving what Joey was certain she thought was a stern look, but what was actually the smallest crinkle in her smooth brow. "Certainly not one you'd ever subject anyone who you wanted to have sex with to."

"You have no idea what I'd do," Elliot replied, sniffing. "I am unknowable."

Unknowable. Right.

"I know you can't stop drooling over Colt West," Joey said, before she could stop herself.

But honestly.

Elliot's fascination with the single-dad-cowboy next door was not subtle.

"Drooling and sex are two very different things," Elliot returned. "Besides, his physical form is infinitely droolworthy. From an artistic standpoint. Perhaps, though you aren't an artist, you've noticed Hollis's *physical form*."

Joey frowned, but said nothing.

"Your body is your own," Elliot said, to Teddy. "And he should see to your pleasure first. If he doesn't, he isn't worth a thing."

It made Joey think about that kiss. She hadn't really thought a kiss could be so…pleasurable. But it had been…

It made her want to fan herself.

And the irony of her having just accused Elliot of not being subtle.

She was probably lit up like a beacon.

"Well, of course," Teddy agreed.

Teddy went all crimson then, and given this afternoon's activities… Joey really wanted to know why.

"What are you blushing about, Teddy?" Joey asked.

"I'm guessing it has to do with something *sizable* or *massive*," Elliot said.

Teddy frowned deeply. "I'm not thinking about bee colonies."

"I wasn't suggesting you were."

Joey thought of Hollis. He was big. Like in the general sense, as a man.

She wondered how big the rest of him was.

It was supposed to be a good thing? But like...surely there had to be a limit.

"How *can* you tell if a guy is massive?" Joey asked. "I'd hate to get his pants off and then be like...accosted by a tree trunk."

Teddy made a choking noise, while Elliot howled with laughter and Georgie fell into a coughing fit.

Joey was appalled at her own lack of self-control. She shouldn't be running off at the mouth. She flung her hands in the air. "It's a fair question."

It *was*.

"Trust me, far worse to get his pants off and find a toothpick instead."

The image made Joey feel dry and dead inside.

So maybe tree trunks were preferable.

"I have to go," Teddy said, extracting herself from Elliot.

"Make sure to call us if you won't be home," Elliot called after her.

"I'm the only one who ever answers the landline," Teddy called from halfway down the stairs.

"Call anyway," Georgie shouted back.

Once Teddy was ushered out of the house, Georgie, Joey and Elliot all sat on the couches downstairs.

One of the chickens wandered through the living room

and Georgie's gaze followed her meanly. But she didn't do anything.

"Do you think she's going to be okay?" Joey asked.

"She's going to be fine," Elliot said. "Beau seems like a good guy. More than that, he seems like the sort of man who cares about a woman's pleasure. And if Teddy is going to have experiences, they ought to be mutually beneficial."

"And if he breaks her heart?" Georgie asked.

"I'll peel him like a grape," Elliot said cheerfully.

"That's descriptive," Georgie said. "I like it."

Elliot looked between the two of them. "Are you both worried because you don't have any experience with this kind of thing?"

And Joey wanted to gag and die, because this was something she had avoided explicitly sharing. Georgie shrugged. "I'm not overly excited by men. There's no…no mystery in it. I was raised by my brother and his best friend, and… what is there to say? Sweaty, dirty towels left all over the place. Who can be bothered. I have other things to do. And if I decide I ever want one of those things to be a man, then rest assured I will. But… I'm not worried about it."

Joey found that she was actually quite worried about it. And that made her feel weird and small, because she had always thought that she identified more with Georgie, or Elliot, who had rather unbothered airs about them. Like her mother.

"Joey," Elliot pressed gently.

"You know, they've done all these studies about movies and shit, where girls sit around and all they do is talk about boys," Joey said. "And it's not feminist. Just so you know."

"Who cares if it's feminist? It's what's happening in your life," Elliot said. "This is not a movie, this is a moment. What's the purpose of dishonesty so we can pass some hypothetical test?"

"I kissed Hollis," Joey said, the words just kind of falling out of her mouth and laying there on the floor.

"You did what?" Elliot asked.

"I kissed him. Well, I asked him to teach me how to kiss. So, all right, I guess that answers your other question."

"*Joey,*" Elliot said grinning. "Are you a virgin?"

"I thought you didn't believe in that as a concept," Joey said. "Didn't you call it a construct one time?"

Elliot shrugged. "Sure. Again, I'm all about these kinds of discussions in a theoretical sense, but sometimes when they become personal it's a bit different."

"I have never... No. So I haven't... It's just that I haven't...haven't found anyone I wanted to ask to show me how. I like an expert. And when I looked at Hollis, and his hands, I thought he might be an expert."

"Oh my," Elliot said. "Were you going to ask him to teach you how to do other things too?"

"Maybe," Joey said. "I mean...if Teddy is going to have sex, and then..."

"Who cares what Teddy's doing?" Elliot asked. "The question is, what do *you* want."

"I would like to..." Except she couldn't make it about concepts right now. She could just think about him. And what Elliot had said about the personal suddenly felt much more relevant. "I feel like I want to be closer to him." And that admission made her feel dizzy.

"Then you should be. You don't have to think of it as a before and after. You don't have to think of it as losing anything. That is where you can ditch societal ideas if you want. Unless it feels momentous to you. Then have a ceremony."

"What about me makes you think I want to have a ceremony over such a thing," Joey said.

And Georgie laughed. Laughed harder than Joey had ever heard her laugh. "I'm sorry," she said. "I'm just trying to imagine it. Sister Sunday. And we're celebrating Teddy and Joey becoming women."

"I *am* a *woman*," Joey scowled. "A penis isn't going to change that."

Well. *Well.* They knew what she meant.

"With flower crowns," Georgie said. "I'll bake a cake. Congratulations on—"

"I beg you not to finish that sentence, Georgie Hathaway. Or I will put Henrietta in your bed."

Georgie sobered. "I don't want that."

"I know you don't."

"You know, Joey," Elliot said. "The big thing is not everything has to be a proclamation or a project. You could just see what happens with him."

"I guess."

But the idea made her feel like she was free-falling, and she didn't like it.

BUT IT WAS all surprisingly easy, since he was doing a lot of his work in a separate area to her, and her gardening and everything that took precedence over the other aspects of the ranch kept him at a distance.

And then, Beau broke Teddy's heart.

Absolutely smashed it, and all sisters had to have their hands on deck for threats of violence and triage for the poor damaged Teddy.

But then just as quickly, Beau professed his love for her, and it was like the sun had come out from behind the clouds, and Teddy shone brighter than she ever had, love doing a sort of magical, brilliant thing to her that made Joey's chest feel strange.

And Elliot started sleeping with Colt.

She waved her hand about it, and talked about female pleasure, but there was something about the little smile on her face that made Joey worry. And Colt had a daughter, a daughter that Elliot was giving pottery lessons to, and she was only getting more and more attached to the little girl. Hell, Joey even felt attached to the kid.

And Joey didn't even like kids that much.

She felt like she and Georgie were holding down the maiden spinster fort.

And those were words she never thought she would apply to herself.

"They're boy crazy," Georgie said one day, scooping a bit of homemade lavender ice cream into a dish for Joey.

"It's stunning," Joey said, taking a bite of the ice cream. "I meant our sisters' preoccupations. But also this ice cream."

"Thank you," she said, inclining her head.

"It's true."

"It's not worth it," Georgie said.

"What's not?"

"All the drama."

"I thought you were…"

"I am. But…that doesn't mean I haven't… That doesn't mean there isn't…" Georgie seemed to bristle, then deflate slightly. "It's complicated."

But before she could finish the story, Henrietta peeked her head around the corner into the kitchen.

"Out," Georgie shouted, and she went for the water pistol, which sent Henrietta scrambling back out.

"She needs to take the chicken with her when she moves in with Beau," Georgie muttered.

"Oh," Joey said, suddenly feeling sad. "She is going to move in with Beau, isn't she?"

"Of course she is. And if Elliot and Colt…"

"They're just indulging their physical chemistry," Joey said, trying to imitate her sister's philosophical tone.

"Sure," Georgie said. "Sure."

"It's possible," Joey said. "My mom wasn't bothered by her relationship with my dad at all. She just…she said it was no big deal. Just a little fling that resulted in a pregnancy. Then she figured… It was a good time in her life to try the motherhood thing. To go on another adventure. She was always just willing to kind of see where life would take her next."

"Yeah," Georgie said. "My mother is not."

She knew that Georgie's mother had never gotten over their father. And that she had most definitely punished Georgie for it.

"She's full of sharks," Joey said darkly.

"True."

Full of sharks was an autocorrect from a text conversation they'd all been having once a few months ago. It had been an attempt to say that Georgie's mother was *full of shit*, but had been altered to *sharks*, and all things considered the girls had thought it a reasonable descriptor.

Full of teeth and bad intent.

And now it applied to all those who were untrustworthy and pointy.

"I will never let a man make me full of sharks," Joey declared.

"Me either," said Georgie, grabbing a spoon and sticking it into Joey's ice cream and stealing a bite. "This is good."

"I told you it was. I might let a man do other things to me, though," said Joey, thinking about that breathless kiss. Because she had thought of little else.

"Great," Georgie said. "Leaving me behind?"

"Never," Joey said. "And in fact, even if Teddy does leave, she's not leaving us behind. She's expanding the circle."

And they both smiled at that, and ate more ice cream.

CHAPTER SIX

SHE WAS AVOIDING HIM, and he had been content to let it happen.

He didn't know what he thought about the kiss.

Well, he did.

When he didn't have dreams of standing in fields of bluebonnets, he dreamed of Joey. He dreamed of stripping those no-nonsense T-shirts away from her body, and exposing her sweet athletic curves. He dreamed of kissing down her collarbone, to her small, round breasts, down her stomach, to the waistband of her jeans and...

His dreams got pretty graphic from there.

He could not recall the last time he'd been so hot and bothered for a woman. Least of all one with no experience.

Why her? Well, he could name a dozen things about her that he found compelling. Her boldness, her openness. The name *Joey*, and that initial shock he'd felt when he'd first seen her. Like a bolt of lightning striking him from on high.

But, he was just working on tractors.

When he showed up at the barn that morning, the doo-hickey was already out front, the streamers blowing merrily in the wind. There was an addition to the vehicle, he noticed. A little bundle of violets.

Dangling from the mirror.

He looked at the little red tractor he was in the process of restoring. The paint job that he'd done the other day was looking great. It was one clear coat away from being done. And all the sanding and elbow grease had been worth it.

He loved restoring old things. Because there was something gratifying about it. Taking what was lost and bringing it back to somewhere new.

In life you couldn't really do that. When things were gone they were gone.

And that was just how it was.

But when you restored something, you gave it new life.

A beautiful metaphor he didn't much believe in for anything other than tractors.

He heard a crash coming from inside the barn, and he leapt forward, opening the door. Because he knew it was Joey. Because he knew she had done something grand and silly, and epically Joey.

Because he knew she tasted like sunshine, and he had only kissed her the one time.

And he shouldn't be thinking of it.

When he walked in, she was kicking a bucket off to the side, looking angry. She was wearing a pair of oversize overalls covered in white splotches, which looked nothing like anything he'd ever seen her in before.

"Well, it's not going well," she said, waving a trowel.

"This is a job for an outfit with several men," he said. "Or women, Joey, don't look at me that way. But you can't go mudding the place all by yourself."

"But I should be able to," she said. "Seemed easy enough on YouTube."

"There's a reason people train for this," he said.

"I just want to get it finished."

"You silly girl."

"I am not a silly girl," she said angrily. "I am a woman, thank you very much. And one who has watched enough videos to know the technique to do all of this, and it would've worked if I hadn't tripped. In fact, it'll still work. It's just I had a little bit of a rage explosion. It happens."

She was wearing long sleeves and work gloves, clutching a trowel tightly. Her hair had fallen partway out of its ponytail, and she had flecks of plaster all over her. And she was the most beautiful thing he'd ever seen in his life.

"Joey," he said. "I'm going to kiss you again. Because I haven't been able to think about any other damn thing for five weeks now."

And her eyes went round. "Really?"

But he swallowed the tail end of that question as his mouth touched hers. And it was like an explosion of the warmth that he only ever felt when he stood in that field in his dream.

That dream that had become his vision of heaven when Samantha had slipped from the world.

But the heat changed, burned into something else, and he felt like he was exploding with it.

Like it was tearing down walls built up inside him and leaving him exposed. Open to all kinds of things.

Things he hadn't even believed were possible.

He growled and backed her up against the wall, and she returned his kiss with equal parts enthusiasm and inexperience. He arched his hips against hers, let her feel the evidence of his desire. "Is that okay?"

"Oh hell yeah," she said, grabbing his face and kissing him harder, and it was the strangest thing, the bubble of joy that expanded inside of his chest, because Joey's enthusiasm, Joey's wonder at all these things reminded him of something he hadn't even really remembered existed. That joy in possibility. And what could be.

That had all been extinguished in him so long ago.

Because somewhere along the way, he'd had to learn to live with acceptance. And he knew what it was to exist in a space where hope and acceptance lived alongside each other. Where you wanted that miracle but had to find a way to accept the way the world would be if it didn't happen. But he had forgotten hope somewhere along that road. He had forgotten what it felt like, because he had had to let it dim. Had to let that spark all but die so that he could give his wife the end that she deserved. Because when someone was trying to go with grace it was a piss-poor tribute to kick and scream and rail against fate like it was a monster.

When someone was handing you pieces of wedding bouquet and smiling, and thanking you for being the fulfillment of their dreams it felt wrong to stand around and yell: *what about mine?*

So he had put hope down because when it burned too bright it made him want to demand things, miracles and second chances and restoration.

But it was like it had flared back to life with all the force of a wildfire now.

Because of Joey's wonder.

Because of Joey's joy. And all that warmth she made him feel was like the sun on a field of bluebonnets, and it was the deepest, strangest feeling he'd had in a long while.

"Have mercy," she whispered when they parted, her Texas drawl more pronounced.

And he kissed her again.

"Why did you do that?" she asked.

"I had to taste that sweet accent of yours."

"I don't have an accent, darlin'," she said, playing it up just a little bit, and he'd been certain he couldn't get any harder, but he had.

And it was the lightness of it all mixed with those previ-

ous revelations that surprised him most of all. Because he
didn't feel upset or sad or anything of the kind. He felt…
different. New.

Or maybe old again.

Like that tractor out front.

Like he'd got in a shiny coat of paint, and he'd just been
thinking how that kind of shit wasn't possible.

"I tell you what," he said. "Why don't I help you with
this?"

"Okay," she whispered.

"And then…"

"I like the sound of and then."

"Joey…"

And he opened his mouth to tell her all the things he
could never give her. But he didn't want to. He found he
just didn't want to, because of that feeling. Burning at the
center of his chest where before there had been nothing. Or
at least, for a long damned while there had been nothing.

So he didn't tell her anything. Because he wasn't going
to think past tonight. Because something in him felt vibrant
with the promise of all the things he'd forgotten existed.

All the things he'd forgotten to feel.

And he didn't actually know if he could make a proclamation about a damn thing. So he didn't. Instead, he
touched her face. And took a step back.

And set about to teaching Joey Hathaway how to texture a wall.

CHAPTER SEVEN

BY THE TIME they were finished, Joey's body ached. But she felt satisfied with a job well done. That was one of her favorite things in the entire world. The satisfaction of a job well done. Learning something new and excelling at it.

A little zip of pleasure went through her body.

Was that what was going to happen today? Was it what was going to happen with him?

And then she looked down at herself and realized she was absolutely covered in drywall mud.

She wrinkled her nose. "This has been a pretty messy business."

"It has."

"Let's go down to the creek and clean up."

He lifted an eyebrow slowly.

"I wasn't propositioning you," she said. "If I was, you would know."

"Somehow, I don't doubt that at all."

"Are you disappointed?"

"Disappointed with what?"

"The fact that I wasn't propositioning you."

He didn't say anything, but a slow smile crossed his face, and if she could read it even half as well as she thought, she was pretty sure the subtext was "you will be by the time this is said and done."

And she didn't doubt it.

She squirmed slightly, and then jumped into the doo-hickey. "Climb on in," she said.

"Are you kidding me? You expect me to get into that thing?"

"The doohickey is my preferred mode of transportation on the ranch, Hollis. A rejection of the doohickey is rejection of me."

"I think we both know that isn't true."

"You don't know what I know."

"No I do not," he said.

But he got into the doohickey, and she turned the engine over and started to putter down the bumpy dirt road that led to a swimming hole out on the edge of the property.

"Well, I know how to throw a ball," she said.

"That I know."

"I know how to hunt, fish, shoot—guns and a bow and arrow—I can make a pretty mean trap, I can start a fire, I can put on eyeliner." She sneaked a sideways glance to see if that surprised him. If it did, he didn't show it. "Elliot taught me that. I know how to make macaroni and cheese. The blue box. I can thread a needle and do some basic mending if need be. I also know how to texture a wall, and I know how to kiss." She looked at him, and was almost embarrassingly satisfied by the small amount of awe he saw on his face.

"That's a lot of things."

"Yeah. It is."

"What *don't* you know how to do?"

A harder question, but then, if Joey didn't know how to do something it was usually because she didn't care to learn.

"I can't craft worth shit. I get glitter all over the place, it just makes me mad. I end up with glue on my hands, and I hate that. I would much rather have the remnants of a fish all over my hands than glue. That's just a fact. I won't run unless I have to. Running for heart health? No thanks. I'll run away from a bear, that's it. I don't know how to sing. And I guess I don't know how to have sex."

She felt uncharacteristically embarrassed. Because this was just a list of things, and the sex thing was true, and it shouldn't really embarrass her. Especially because he already knew since he was the person who had taught her how to kiss. But he didn't look at her like she should be ashamed. He just nodded.

"All right."

"How about you. List your skills, Hollis Logan."

"Why? So you know what all you can ask me?"

"Yes," she said.

"Okay. I know how to fix a tractor. That's a given. Hell, I can fix just about any kind of engine. You got a problem with your doohickey, I could fix that too. I know how to thread a needle also. Can also do some basic mending. I'm a halfway decent cook, you put a recipe in front of me and I can probably figure it out. I have an all-right singing voice. I know how to hunt, fish and start a fire."

"Useless to me," she said. "I already know how to do that."

"Let me finish. I can tan a hide, which let me tell you is a pretty useful skill at the end of the day. I can build a basic survival shelter. I know how to introduce myself to new people. And I know how to say goodbye." He paused for a moment. "I also know how to have sex."

Her heart slammed against her breastbone. And her breath started to come in short, sharp bursts. "I... Oh. Well. That is...that is interesting. And... I figured you did."

"I wondered what you thought. If I was a candidate for

your particular brand of liking to learn. If I passed your bar for expertise."

"So far."

She pulled the doohickey up to the creek, and got out.

And suddenly she felt shy, because she hadn't really thought this through. Because somewhere in her mind she had imagined stripping off in front of him and getting into the water, but everything had gone hazy after that. She had been serious when she said she wasn't propositioning him, because…

Because part of her couldn't think that far ahead. But she wanted him. And it was crazy, because she didn't really know him.

Does it matter?

No, it shouldn't matter. This was just…the sex stuff. That was all.

And like he'd said… He knew how.

She took a deep breath.

And like when she'd been standing in front of the stadium when she was a kid, she just needed to do it.

Just hop the damn fence, Joey. Don't be a coward.

"I *might* be propositioning you now."

She undid the hook on one side of the overalls that Georgie had given her for today. An oversize pair that she said she didn't want. And then she undid the other side, and let it drop down. She pulled off her work gloves, and jerked the long-sleeved shirt up over her head, leaving her standing there in nothing but a sports bra and a pair of plain underwear.

"Are you?" His voice had gone all rough again.

"Yes."

And suddenly his eyes seemed to catch on her arm. And stay there. Which was a strange thing, considering she was standing there in her underwear. She would've thought that that would be the defining characteristic of the moment.

But no. He was staring at her arm.

"What is that?"

He walked over to her, and ran his finger along the tattoo on the inside of her forearm.

"Bluebonnets." She smiled. "I'm from Texas."

"Bluebonnets," he said, something in his eyes going intense. "I'll be damned."

"It's just a flower."

"Yeah," he said. "Yeah."

He took a step back, and he jerked his own shirt up over his head, and her mouth went dry at the sight of his body.

It was perfection. Muscles and the perfect amount of dark hair sprinkled over them.

Her heart started thundering so hard she thought she might pass out.

He took off the rest of his clothes, and he was standing there naked in front of her. And aroused.

And Joey suddenly felt stupid. Because this wasn't sneaking into a baseball stadium. It wasn't the same as asking somebody to teach you to throw.

And she didn't know why she knew that all of a sudden staring at the reality of his naked body, only that she did.

And *what a time to figure it out*. It was sort of too little too late there on the revelation front.

"Oh," she said.

"Joey," he said, his voice low and serious.

He crossed the space between them, and he gripped the edge of her sports bra, running his finger beneath the edge of it, his fingers skimming the sensitive spot just beside her nipple.

"Nothing has to happen if you don't want it to. It's a lot to go from a kiss to this so fast."

"You usually take more time?"

He lowered his head. Then he lifted it again, his eyes meeting hers. "No. Usually I meet a woman in a bar, and we kiss, and once that happens, I know she wants to go home. So I take her to a motel. And we both scratch the itch. And then I leave."

"So, why does now feel fast then?"

"Because you've never done this before. I mean it's fast for you."

"Maybe it's not," she said. "Maybe after this, this is how I'll do it. And maybe it'll be slow, because you know technically we kissed a few weeks ago."

"Yeah," he said. "But I don't think so."

"Right. But you don't know."

"We never do," he said, suddenly, his voice grave.

"Well. I'm just saying. I'm a virgin now. But I'm thinking pretty soon I won't be. And maybe that's when…maybe that's when I'll decide that I really like sex and I'll just want to have it all the time. I wasn't allowed to have sugary cereal when I lived with my mom, and now that I live on my own, I've tried all of it, and I decided that I really like Lucky Charms. So sometimes I just have it for dinner. Because I can. So maybe I'll just have sex because I can."

But when he looked at her she trembled. And she felt stupid for reducing that feeling to something like cereal. Which you could buy for a couple of dollars. When she knew that you couldn't just buy a feeling like this.

She swallowed hard, and he lowered his head and kissed her. And immediately, she was swept away again. Just like she had been before. Maybe they wouldn't even make it into the water.

She didn't care. Oh, she didn't care. Because this was just so lovely. And perfect, and it could never just be a lesson. He had just taught her one, and it was nothing like this. Never would be. It was something real and deep and raw, and for Joey, who had experienced a lot of a little, a lot of more surface things, it was like nothing else she'd ever known.

And she had just thought it was how she was. Because it seemed like it was how her mother was. Like all the people around her had these easy, simple attachments.

Her mother had had this thing with her father, and it had been a strange bump in the road, little bit of a laugh, and nothing more.

But this wasn't funny.

And it didn't feel like an instruction manual.

It felt like he had reached down inside of her soul and touched something she hadn't even known was there.

He took her bra off, her underwear, and it was all so fast and smooth, she hadn't even seen it coming.

"There's a blanket in the back of the doohickey," she said.

And he laughed. He laughed against her mouth.

"That is one of the most ridiculous sentences anyone has ever said to me, let alone a woman that I've got naked and pressed up against me."

"It is not my fault that you can't accept the doohickey," she said.

"I will. I will if I have to. If it means getting to hold you."

He released his hold on her then, and went to the back of the doohickey, grabbed hold of a blanket and laid it down on the sandy shore of the river.

He laid her down there too. Kissing her and touching her, stroking her until she felt like she was on fire. He put his hands in places she never even imagined somebody might touch, and she was alight with a need she hadn't realized existed.

And she was thankful that he had all kinds of presence of mind that she just didn't, because he managed to get a condom and put it on, then put his hand back between her thighs, murmuring words to her that were both impossibly sweet and impossibly dirty all at once.

And then she combusted. She rolled her hips against his hands as her pleasure overtook her. As wave after wave of desire swept over the top of her.

She just hadn't known. She really hadn't.

Because this wasn't a simple meeting of skin on skin. This wasn't an easy, leisurely lark. A funny story to tell later.

This was the moment. This was the magic.

She was still shaking with the aftereffects of her orgasm when he positioned himself between her thighs, and the blunt head of his arousal was right there. Stretching her. And she arched against him as he filled her, as he kissed her, swallowing her cry of pain mingled with pleasure. It was perfect. So was he. And then he was inside of her. He was inside of her. And nothing had prepared her for this.

Nothing.

Nothing that her mother had told her about men and their penises and the high regard they held them in. Nothing in what Elliot had said about owning your pleasure and your body.

Nothing.

Because in this moment he owned her.

In this moment, she was closer to him than she had ever been to another human being. Closer to him than she ever could be to another person. It was… It was terrify-

ing and wonderful all at once. It was something altogether
unexpected. That made her feel strong and fragile, like
she might be able to win a war, or like she might fall apart
just as easily.

She regretted it. She regretted it, and she wanted it to
never end. She wanted to never do this again, and she
wanted to do it forever.

And she couldn't explain it to herself let alone to anyone else.

But then he began to move, and her need, her desire,
eclipsed everything else. How had she gotten here. To this
moment, to this man.

But she was here. And he was making her feel things,
deep things. Raw things, that made it so she couldn't
breathe. And then he looked down at her face, and their
eyes met and held, and his hands traced the trail from her
collarbone down her arm, down to the bluebonnet tattoo
there, and the expression of wonder on his face took her
breath away. Because when had anybody ever looked at
her like that?

She didn't understand it. She didn't understand how she
could make him make that face.

Not when she felt those very same things looking up
at him.

But he was beautiful. And he was…

She lost her ability to think. Her desire rolled through
her like a tide, all thunderous and uncontainable.

And when she cried out her pleasure, it came from the
deepest part of her, and then he thrust into her one last
time, and shook with it, his climax like an earthquake she
hadn't been prepared for, that set off another shock wave
inside of her. And then they lay there together, on a blanket

on the shore, and he picked her up and carried her down into the water.

"Cold," she said, clinging to him, pressing herself against his broad chest.

Then she watched her hand, watched as it drifted down his chest, down his stomach. And she forgot the cold water, and was lost in the heat of his skin.

"Are you propositioning me now, Joey?"

"Maybe," she said. "I can't really think right now, I'll get back to you when I figure it all out."

"Well, that's good to hear. You're coming back to my place tonight?"

"Tomorrow is Sunday," she pointed out.

"That's all right. I can have you back bright and early."

"Sister Sunday is very important," she said.

"I'm sure that it is."

"It really is."

"You won't miss it."

"I will have to tell them that I'm staying the night elsewhere."

"That's fine by me."

"I grew up without them. We didn't have each other until we were thirteen, and even then, opportunities to spend time together were so few and far between. This is our chance to be a family."

"We get to make family in all kinds of ways," he said, and he suddenly looked sad.

"Do you have a family?"

It seemed like such a stupid question.

"Yeah. I mean... I lost my parents."

"You mentioned."

"I have a brother," he said. "He lives up north."

"I see. Is that where you're from?"

"Washington," he said.

"Oh. Why did you come to Jasper Creek?"

"I drove all around, for a while, doing repairs. Out of all the places I saw I liked this one best."

"What made you want to leave home?"

His expression went very serious. "When home doesn't have all the people you care about anymore, it's not home. It changes. I think a place can hold your heart, but mostly it's the people. Mine were gone."

"I see."

"How about you?" He was tracing down to the bluebonnets again. "Is it Texas that has your heart? Or is it here?"

"I thought I'd miss Texas more than I do. My mom is still there. I love my mom. But she's…she's an independent woman. I respect it. I do. An awful lot. But…you know, it would be nice to be needed. I'm a little closer to that with the girls."

She sounded so wistful. So sad.

"Forget I said that," she said. "I dunno what's wrong with me. I'm a little emotional."

"Sex will do that to you sometimes."

"Not all the time, right?"

"No," he said. "Not all the time."

"Your normal bar hookups don't make you emotional?" she asked.

She'd meant it to lighten the mood, but he looked at her like the answer to that might be complicated. "Not really."

"I would be happy to take you back to the farmhouse to…"

"I would rather not be in the house with your sisters and the chickens."

"Right," she said. "There really would be no escaping Henrietta."

But she hesitated.

"What's wrong, Joey? You gotta be able to tell me."

"I don't want to go to a motel," she said.

It was small and foolish, perhaps. That she was betraying the fact she didn't want to be like his other women. It was silly. Who cared if she was like his other women. Seriously. Who cared?

She didn't want to be. She wanted to be Joey. And she wanted to be special.

Because he would always be Hollis to her. And special.

Because he would always be her first.

And she hadn't really thought about that in the grand scheme of things. Because, constructs and all that.

Except, on that score Elliot was correct. Constructs were only constructs when they were theoretical. And they became something else entirely when they were moved into the realm of the personal.

"Give me directions to your house," she said. "I'll drive up."

"In the doohickey?" he asked.

"No," she said. "Of course not in the doohickey. I have a truck."

"And you choose to drive that thing anyway."

"Yes," she said. "I do."

"You're a strange woman, Joey Hathaway."

"Yes," she said. "I am."

CHAPTER EIGHT

JOEY SCURRIED IGNOMINIOUSLY into the farmhouse, hoping that she wasn't boldly proclaiming what had just happened down by the river with…all the everything about her. Of course, her hair was wet.

"What are you doing?" Teddy asked, the minute that she was in her room pulling out a bag to pack some overnight things.

"I am…preparing for an overnight trip."

Those seemed to be the magic words that summoned Elliot and Georgie.

"An overnight trip?" Elliot asked.

"Yes," Joey sniffed. "I'm spending the night with Hollis, if you must know."

"And lo, I alone remain," said Georgie, her tone unreadable.

"It is not… It is not a thing," Joey said. "I'm boldly owning my womanhood. Or something. Now go away, I have to change."

They disappeared behind the door like a flock of chickens, and Joey changed into her nicest pair of jeans and a gray T-shirt she had always thought enhanced her bustline, such as it was.

Then she opened the door again.

"Oh, Joey," Teddy said. "Is that what you're wearing?"

"Yes."

"Is the theme of your sex life also a hoedown?" Georgie asked with amusement sparkling in her eyes.

"Yes," Joey responded, stuffing a pair of pajamas into her bag. "There are any number of opportunities to do-si-do in the sack. I have heard."

"Really?" Teddy asked.

"So, when did this development occur?" Elliot asked.

Joey looked up at the ceiling. "A time."

"Today," Georgie said, looking at her intently. "It was today."

"Well. I… You know, does it never bother you that we are not really any better than our mothers? I mean, I love my mother, but I didn't ever think that I was going to be weak for a cowboy."

"Too bad," Teddy said. "I am weak. On that score, I will own it."

"Weak," Elliot said.

"Standing firm," Georgie said.

"Well. Your mother is full of sharks," Elliot said pragmatically.

"Full of sharks," Teddy agreed.

As if that gave the excuse for Georgie to not be carrying the weakness for cowboys.

"My mother is not *actually* weak for cowboys," Joey pointed out.

Georgie and Elliot shared a glance.

"I think your mother's not weak for men," Elliot said.

Joey blinked. "Huh?"

Elliot looked at her blandly. "Do you think she prefers women, Joey?"

It would make a lot of sense. Just in general. And actually explained quite a few things from her life. "Well.

Maybe. I guess… I guess the weakness for men thing is just…a flaw in my wiring."

"It's not a flaw to enjoy sex," Elliot said. "Honestly."

"No, it's not that it's just… He has 'temporary' written all over him."

"Do you want permanent?" Teddy asked, looking worried.

"No," Joey said, ignoring the feelings that had come up inside of her earlier. Ignoring that feeling she'd had about wanting to be needed. Ignoring the extreme closeness she'd felt to him down by the river.

"Then there's nothing wrong with it," Teddy said cheerily.

"Nothing at all," Elliot said.

"Not even I judge you," Georgie said.

But Joey thought she was lying. In fact, she was absolutely certain that Georgie judged her a little bit. And she couldn't blame her. She judged herself a little bit too. So much for the solidarity that she had promised to stand in with her sister.

"I'll be back for Sister Sunday."

"Are you going to bring him?" Teddy asked hopefully.

"What's the theme?"

Teddy grinned. Broad and wicked in a way that was not like Teddy at all. *"Chickens."*

HOLLIS WAS HALF THINKING she might not come. But hell, he couldn't really blame her.

He'd taken her down by the river with absolutely no finesse and no patience.

But the bluebonnets…

That had stunned the hell out of him. And he had no idea what to make of it.

Bluebonnets.

He had not been a man who believed in signs and symbols, not once upon a time. But he began to look for those things, to reach beyond all that you could see when you lost the people you cared about.

And bluebonnets had been… Well, they'd been a sign to him, of things to come probably or maybe even a vision of the next life.

Bluebonnets had meant something for a while. It just seemed… It seemed so desperately random that Joey would have them on her arm.

But then, she was from Texas. He supposed it could be chalked up to being all kinds of a coincidence.

But he looked up at the picture on his wall, at the dried-out bluebonnets that he'd taped there. Just a piece of his wife's wedding bouquet, and the thing that he had often credited with triggering his dreams about the bluebonnets.

It was the damnedest thing.

He heard an engine then, tires on the gravel, and in spite of himself, a strange sort of exhilaration raced through him.

It was Joey. She had come. She'd really come.

He hadn't felt this way in… Well, it was that same thing that he'd felt out in the barn.

The strange sort of excitement, a possibility that he had forgotten about a long time ago.

And it made everything feel new.

And there was a fair amount of old in this place, in his house, this place that he'd never had a woman in, but it didn't feel old. It didn't feel old in the sense that it wasn't needed, or in the sense that it didn't serve him. It felt like pieces of who he was. And he stared at those bluebonnets, and he had to wonder what that really meant.

There was a stout knock at the door, and he was amused

by the forcefulness of Joey's knock, as much as he was by the fact that she had come.

He went over to the door and opened it. She was wearing jeans and a T-shirt, a duffel bag slung over her shoulder.

He wanted to know what was in it. He desperately wanted to know what Joey Hathaway thought she needed in an overnight bag for an evening of sex.

But he wanted to know everything about her. That was just the bottom line. He…

He hadn't seen this coming. Not even in a million years.

He had been convinced for the past eleven years that he had this singular thing that he could never recapture.

And the fact of the matter was, he wasn't recapturing it with Joey. She was new. And so was he. He was eleven years further down the road than Samantha ever would be. He had gone through hell losing her.

He had emerged somebody else.

But he had to wonder if Joey Hathaway was part of who he had always been meant to be. If that first pain that he'd gone through had been in part for this moment.

It wasn't all a terrible mistake, but the way life was meant to go.

He could remember what Samantha had said when she handed him those bluebonnets.

She had thanked him.

For making her feel like her life wasn't unfinished.

She'd been sick as a child, and they'd hoped that the disease wouldn't return. But it had. He married her anyway. It was why they'd gotten married so young.

And he'd hoped. He'd prayed for a miracle. He'd also understood it was unlikely.

So had she.

And he had gotten down to the business of just focusing on loving her, because he didn't want her life to turn into a vigil.

And she'd said she'd gotten what she wanted. Even if it wasn't for all the time she wished she had.

His life was longer. He didn't know how long. Nobody did.

But the bluebonnets had always been there.

Maybe Joey had always been there.

Maybe Joey had always been what was down that road.

He kissed her. And she sighed. And then he took her hand and led her into the living room.

She looked around the cabin.

And he tried to see it through her eyes.

It wasn't grand. But he had fixed up and restored every piece of it. This old nineteen-twenties property with big logs and brightly painted shutters. He had restored the floors and replaced the roof. Had made sure to replace any structural pieces that hadn't withstood the test of all these years.

He had done it all by hand, and he had done it all himself.

He'd finished only recently.

And he looked at her and he wondered if he had been finishing it for her.

This whole time.

"This is great," she said, her face lighting up.

And something in him lit up too.

"Glad you think so."

"Yeah, I really love it."

And he saw the moment that her eyes stopped on the picture frame at the back of the room.

He had considered taking it down. Because why have a conversation. He was just teaching her the ropes, right?

Except…he knew that he wasn't. He knew that he wanted

the conversation. He knew that he wanted all the conversations. Easy or hard. He knew that he wanted to see this thing through.

He'd been in love before. But this was nothing like it.

And it made him want to smile.

It really did.

"Oh," she said, as if she couldn't help herself. She looked from the picture to him.

"That's my wedding," he said. "She's been gone eleven years, Joey."

"Gone as in she…"

"She died."

A strange expression went over her face, color creeping into her cheeks. "Oh. Hollis…"

"I'm the same person I was before you knew that. It's not fresh. Not anymore. But… It's me. It doesn't come up in conversation, you know?"

"Yes," she said. "I… I understand that."

He could see that she had questions.

"Do you want to do this now?"

Why not? It was only an interruption if they were only doing this temporarily. Otherwise, this was an important conversation they needed to have about who he was and why.

"Do you want to tell me?"

He nodded slowly. "Her name was Samantha. She was my high school sweetheart. We were nineteen when we got married. Twenty when she died. It wasn't unexpected. She was sick. She was sick before I knew her, and then after the wedding…it came back. Then… You know, we could see how it was going."

"You loved her."

"Yes. I hoped… I married her hoping I'd get my lifetime. But I didn't. She got hers, though. And I'm grateful for that."

It was something he'd wrestled with for a long time, but she'd told him she was satisfied with their life. And he felt like believing her was essential.

If it did something to help the ache in his chest, all the better.

"And now you do motel hookups." Her eyes widened. "I didn't mean it to sound like that. Like she wouldn't be… Like she would…"

He laughed. "She would. That's why I said… When you asked me if I had feelings after my hookups, I told you it was complicated. Because at first I did. Look, she was the first girl I was ever with. So anything after that… It was somebody else. And it was different. It wasn't being in love."

She looked wounded. And he could understand why. But he had never talked to anybody about this before. And he wanted to talk to her.

"So at first, yeah. I thought about what she would think about taking what we shared and turning it into… I don't know. Whatever the hell it was at the time. A coping mechanism. Not a very good one. It felt like trying to get distance at first. And then it got simple. Because time has a way of changing things. Of making the past feel less real."

She had moved closer to the picture. "Are those…"

"Bluebonnets. Just one of the flowers she had in her wedding bouquet."

"That's why you kept looking at my tattoo."

"One reason."

"Hollis, I don't know what to say. I didn't… I feel like I misjudged you? I thought I could just…"

"You figured you could use me to learn a thing or two.

And I was happy to let you, Joey. Because hookups are old hat for me now. Easy enough. But I want you to know, this was never only that to me. I thought it, for a moment. But… in the end, it wasn't that." She shifted and looked down. "That's why I had you come here."

And he let her sit with that for a second. Because he let her come here and he hadn't hidden away the details of his past. He was willing to answer her questions.

"I quit bargaining with fate a long time ago," he said. "I quit asking for signs. I quit… I quit thinking that there were any out there for me. You know your eyes really are more like bluebonnets than violets."

He didn't know when he'd moved closer to her. But he had.

And then he kissed her, and she kissed him, wrapping her arms around his neck and arching against him. He picked her up, her and her duffel bag, and carried her out of the living room into his bedroom.

She set the bag down on the floor, and he laid her down on the mattress, stripping her slowly, kissing every inch of her body.

And in that moment, he felt blessedly free of the implications of the past. There was nothing old between them. A funny realization, considering he had just told her that story.

But it was just him and Joey.

In this, they were all that mattered.

After he had kissed her everywhere she stripped him naked, and took her turn. And she was bold, adventurous, every bit as glorious as he'd known she would be.

And when they came together, it was an explosion.

One that rocked him down to his core.

One that left him in no doubt of what he wanted.

And Joey never opened her overnight bag, because they made love until they fell asleep. And he had that dream again.

Standing in that field of bluebonnets.

But he wasn't alone.

Joey was standing with him.

CHAPTER NINE

JOEY FELT TENDER the next morning, not just physically but emotionally. She woke up in Hollis's bed, in his beautiful, lovingly restored cabin.

And she woke up before he did.

Scrounged around for coffee after she put on her pajamas, and stood for a moment, staring at that wedding picture.

He had been married.

He had been in love.

She wasn't jealous.

It was just that she felt...inadequate.

She didn't know how to love.

And she suddenly remembered what he'd said to her yesterday.

He knew how to meet new people. And he knew how to say goodbye.

He had said such a hard goodbye.

And she hadn't realized that's what he was telling her.

That he knew how to do this big, deep, impossible thing that she couldn't even fathom.

She blinked hard, and took a step closer to the picture.

She was a pretty woman. She looked soft. She was blonde.

And Hollis looked so young. He hardly looked like himself.

Just a kid, who didn't know what was up ahead.

And she wondered... If he would choose it again knowing.

It made her want to cry. And she could feel tears pushing at her eyes.

This wasn't simple. It was complicated. So complicated.

She heard footsteps behind her, and felt guilty staring at this window into his life. Even though he had told her all about it.

"Good morning," he said.

She turned around, and there he was standing in only a pair of low-slung jeans, his chest broad and bare and so sexy her mouth went dry.

"Good morning."

"When do we head over for Sister Sunday?"

"Soon," she said. "Maybe...maybe you can come for dinner. And I will do the morning stuff. The theme is chickens, and it's Teddy," she said apologetically. "And I really don't know what that means."

There you go. Throw Teddy under the bus because you can't cope.

Honestly, though, what were sisters for but ironclad excuses when you needed them?

He walked over to her and kissed her on the mouth. "Whatever you need."

WHATEVER SHE NEEDED?

She turned that over the whole drive back to the ranch, and when she arrived, her sisters were out on the porch already, all of them wearing frilly, Teddy-inspired dresses.

And there were chickens all over the lawn. Wearing aprons.

Frilly little aprons.

"Oh Teddy, how long have you been working on those?" Joey asked as she walked up.

"A while," she said cheerfully.

Beau came out of the kitchen holding a tray of deviled eggs.

"Eggs," Joey said. "Really?"

Teddy shrugged and took an egg off the tray, munching on it cheerfully.

"It is time for the man to become scarce," Elliot said.

"No problem," Beau said, nodding.

And he vanished as quickly as he'd appeared. And Joey couldn't help but wonder what that was like. Beau and Teddy understood each other. Shared a life. He participated in their Sunday ritual, and then they went back to a bed they shared. Every night. Without question.

"So," Elliot said. "How are things?"

"Good," she said vaguely. "I mean, very good. I..."

This was silly, her inability to share this. They were adults. There was no embarrassment.

Except she did feel like a child right now. A child who didn't quite know what she wanted, or what she was doing.

And it wasn't embarrassment stopping her from speaking. It was something else. Something more. Something bigger.

Something that lodged in her chest, bright and radiant and terrifying.

"He's a generous and thoughtful lover?" Elliot asked.

Joey's face caught fire. "He's...good at it. Though I don't have anything to compare it to. But I know when I'm having fun."

Fun.

What a dumb, inane word for what was happening between them.

And today it couldn't possibly feel less fun.

"I'm so pleased for you, Joey," Teddy said. "Good sex, and he didn't even have to answer a questionnaire!"

"Indeed," Joey said, sitting in the chair and availing herself of some deviled eggs. When in... Chicken Rome and all of that.

"Is he coming over later?" Georgie asked.

"Yes," she said. "He'll be here for dinner."

THE DAY PASSED QUICKLY, most of it spent sitting on the porch eating snacks and Joey did take the opportunity to mention to her sisters that Hollis had been married before. And while they were sympathetic to his loss, she didn't know if they understood what she was feeling. Which was really inconvenient, because Joey didn't understand what she was feeling, and she was kind of hoping that Elliot would just tell her.

Elliot was so calm and realistic about feelings, and when she had explained things to Joey in the past, they had made clear and wonderful sense.

But, she didn't offer that up this time, and Joey was not wanting to ask, because that sounded stupid. "Tell me what I feel about all this." Yeah, that was not overly realistic.

When it was time to set the table, it was an extremely Teddy affair with fairy lights and papier-mâché lanterns, flowers and adorable, ornate, nonmatching silverware with chickens and bees.

"I don't really see how this is chicken themed," Georgie commented.

Teddy winked. "Chickens are always the theme."

And then Hollis drove up.

He was wearing a button-up shirt, and a dark pair of jeans. He had on a white Stetson, and he was holding a bouquet of flowers, and Joey had never seen anything quite so attractive in all her life.

She swallowed hard, and tried to get a hold of her fluttery breath.

"I'm glad you could make it. Girls, you remember Hollis," she said. "And this is Beau. Beau Riley. He's… Teddy's…"

Hollis stuck his hand out. "Nice to meet you formally. I think I've seen you around."

Beau nodded. "I expect so."

It was all very macho and alpha. They sat down at the table, and oohed and aahed when an elaborate spread of food was placed before them, including the most beautiful, pastel cake that even Joey had to admit was a marvel. It was so delicate and girly, with pink meringue and lovely berries from Joey's garden.

"That is the most glorious cake I've ever seen," said Elliot.

Georgie visibly brightened. "It's terribly sweet," she said. "But I made it with Teddy's honey, and there's little bits of honeycomb on the top too. It has Joey's berries, and of course is on one of Elliot's platters. I'm thinking of calling it the Sweet Home Cake. You know, when we sell it in the store."

"I like that," Elliot said smiling. "And I can't wait to eat it."

"Dinner first," said Teddy brightly.

It was a vegetarian affair, because apparently Teddy's hard limit was eggs when it was a chicken themed meal, but neither Beau nor Hollis complained. And really, they were all grateful for the lighter dinner when Georgie's desserts were served, particularly the cake, which Joey knew would become a signature of their farm shop when it opened up.

And while they were eating, she lifted her gaze and met Hollis's eyes, and something in her stomach turned over.

She had invited him to Sister Sunday, and she didn't quite know what she had been thinking. That was something more. Something different than a simple sex lesson.

She had brought him to meet her sisters. She had…

She suddenly felt slightly panicky, and she didn't think she could finish the glorious cake.

Teddy was explaining the bee removal process to Hollis, with animated hand gestures, and he was listening intently, and she was grateful for the opportunity to simply sink into her feelings for a second, and tried to figure out exactly what was going on.

She had been so confident that this would be easy, because her mother had made her feel certain that it could be.

She had always done things the way that her mother had.

But there was something different inside of her, and she didn't know what it was or why. And she didn't… She didn't like it.

And when they were all done, Hollis stood up from the table and took her hand. "Am I allowed to take you for a walk on Sister Sunday?"

"Just a walk," Teddy called.

"No funny business," added Georgie.

"Do what you want," Elliot added.

Joey rolled her eyes.

But she took Hollis's hand, and the two of them began to walk down a path that led from the farmhouse out into one of the fields.

"When do you think you're going to get your store open?"

"I'm hoping by the start of June," she said. "I know that seems lofty, but I'll have ample berries by then, and nothing inside is going to be terribly fancy. Just finished. But I have all the electrical and plumbing in place. So mostly, it's just a matter of getting the shelves and all that."

"That's exciting," he said.

And she felt like he meant it. Like he actually cared a whole hell of a lot about this project of hers.

Like he would be around to see it happen. Like he wasn't just fixing tractors.

And it made a note of disquiet go off in her chest.

"Joey, I really enjoyed spending time with your family tonight."

"Oh. That's…"

"I would have never thought I'd say that to somebody. I would have never thought that I would mean it. I don't know if you understand… When I say that my grief isn't sharp like it used to be, I'm telling the truth. But there are some things that I accepted along the way about my life and what it could be, what it looked like…that I don't think are true anymore. Something changed when I met you. And I don't know how best to describe it. I just know that it did. I had all these ideas about the world. All these ideas about the chances we get… Joey, I love you."

Joey's heart stopped. Her breathing stopped. Everything stopped.

"You don't know me," she said.

"I don't know you as well as I would like. I'd like to know more. I'd like to know everything. I find you an endless source of fascination. I think you're brilliant. Beautiful. Incredible. I think you're something I never knew I wanted. Never knew I needed."

"Well, you did know you wanted this." Her heart started to pound. "Back when you got married."

"No. I knew that I wanted her, and whatever that life

looked like. At the time, that's what I knew. And I couldn't imagine ever wanting to fall in love again, but I was picturing something so much the same to what I had before. But this… It isn't. You aren't the same. And neither am I. Joey…" His voice went rough. "When she died I dreamed that I was standing in a field of bluebonnets, and I didn't know what that meant. Bluebonnets. I thought it was because she handed me the piece of her bouquet. I was alone, but I thought maybe it was…a vision of heaven, because I felt peaceful. I felt happy. And in that moment, I knew that whether it was here or there I would feel happy again. But it was you. That happiness, that piece…that moment. It was you. You're the bluebonnets, Joey, and you were always there. We were always meant to be. From the beginning. I can't explain it, but I know it's true. It was a sign, that…that that life that I had from before was preparing me for you. There was a piece of you there even then. I was meant to be here with you. And it's all bluebonnets now, Joey. And I'm all here for you."

"We barely know each other," Joey said.

"It doesn't matter. People can know each other their whole lives and not really know each other. But I know you. You are determined, and you… I love the way that you just decide that you're going to do something and you do it. I love the way that you make me feel. I hope that I make you feel good. I really do."

"I…"

"You don't need to answer me right now," he said. "I promise, I can wait. I've waited a long time for this. For you. And I can wait… I can wait longer. I'm not in a hurry. Just—"

"Hollis," she said, and her heart was breaking, but she just couldn't. She couldn't do this. She didn't want to be like Georgie's mom, and go off leaving her children behind because some man had damaged her. And she wasn't her mother, God knew.

Maybe she was her father. She didn't know. She didn't know the man.

And she…she didn't know what to do with any of this. Because no one had taught her. No one had prepared her.

She wanted to go back to being who she was, because that girl had felt simple. And she felt much closer to being toothy and filled with sharks now than she ever had before in her life.

And she didn't want that.

She didn't want it at all.

Because she didn't want to need in this endless, awful way that changed who you were. She hated the…the idea she might need someone she couldn't keep forever.

Grandpa Jack.

Her own father.

She didn't want to care about him.

She wanted to stand on her own and be happy about it. She didn't want to ache.

"Joey, don't be afraid of me. I know… I know how big this is. Believe me."

"I just wanted to learn how to have sex," she said. "That's all I wanted, Hollis. I wanted to have a little bit of fun and I…"

"Then why did you ask me to Sister Sunday? And why did you go back to my house? And why did you care whether or not we went to a motel? Why did you want to be different then, Joey?"

"Who doesn't want to be different?"

"Why?"

"Hollis…"

"Joey," he said, his voice firm. "This is real. We are real. We are meant to be together and I'd—"

"Does anybody fall for that line? We are meant to be together? A woman doesn't need a man, Hollis. No one needs anyone. We just… We figure out how to get along. We can all stand on our own."

"Are you trying to tell me that we can be an island? Because I'm pretty sure there is a saying that says otherwise."

"Yeah, there's also some saying about weasels going pop, and they don't actually do that. So… I don't trust a cliché to figure out how to run my life."

"Joey…"

"No. I know how to get by. I know how to get by on my own. I can build what I need to. I can set up a farm store. I can grow my own food. I can…"

"You can't let anybody love you, though, can you? Not real, not deep, because you can't reduce that down to something easy."

"Maybe not," she said. "I'm sorry, Hollis. Because Lord knows you've been through enough. But I'm not going to be the thing that fixes you."

He looked at her, long and hard. "Joey, I never asked you to. You're the one who thinks I'm broken. I'm trying to tell you that I'm fixed. That I understand why I went through what I did."

"No."

"You're the one who doesn't understand," he said. "And that's okay. But you're not going to be able to learn this from watching a video, or asking an expert. You're going to have to dig down in your heart and contend with the sharp things in there. And when you're ready, I'll be there. I'm not going anywhere. I've waited eleven years. I'll wait a while longer."

And as Hollis walked away, Joey wanted to call him back. Because she suddenly felt her knees wobbling.

And she didn't think she could stand without him.

Which was all the more reason to let him go.

She couldn't do this.

Not to herself.

She just couldn't.

CHAPTER TEN

MAYBE HE'D BEEN WRONG. Maybe he'd been wrong about the bluebonnets. Wrong about fate. Maybe he hadn't understood any of it, and it was just wishful thinking. Looking for healing where it didn't exist.

Except as he sat there in his truck in front of his cabin, he knew for certain that he wasn't.

He loved Joey. Apart from anything else.

He just felt like the universe had given him a whole set of signs because it didn't trust him. And that was fair enough. He was hardheaded, and he knew it well.

And he felt...

He felt heartbroken.

A smile curved his lips.

"I'll be damned."

He was heartbroken over Joey Hathaway, because his heart worked. Because he could love. Because he did love her.

In a new, brilliant, singular way. Because pieces of who he'd been had found their way back to him, but they were part of the man he'd become.

Because the man he was needed Joey, and wanted her. Two different things, and feeling both was a glorious revelation.

Even as he sat there feeling like he was being stabbed.

Even the pain felt new. Even the pain was brilliant.

Even the pain was welcome.

But under all that was hope.

Bright and brilliant as if it had never been doused before.

He hoped. And no part of him accepted that it was done.

It was all glittering gold and burning inside of him.

They were meant to be.

She was supposed to be his.

And it was terrifying, scalding, to hope.

But it was also the brightest, clearest thing he'd ever felt in his life.

WHEN JOEY RETURNED to the farmhouse, she was reduced.

And she couldn't figure out quite how to hide it.

Teddy came running across the yard immediately, her arms windmilling, her hair flying behind her.

Georgie and Elliot were not far behind.

"What happened?" Georgie asked.

"I…"

"What did he do?" Teddy asked. "I'll claw his eyes out."

"My thoughts are too dark," Elliot said. "I will not subject you to them. But I promise, I *vow*, the man will know endless pain."

"I'm with Elliot," Georgie said.

"It wasn't him," Joey wailed. Standing out in the yard, shouting, her voice echoing off the mountains around them. "It was me. He said that he loved me and I told him no. I told him that I couldn't. I don't… I don't want to. I don't want to love anybody."

"Even us?" Teddy asked.

"No. I can love you. That's fine. I can love my mom. I… I don't like this. I don't understand it. I want it to stop. I want it to… I want it to go away."

Teddy looked suddenly sympathetic. "Oh, oh Joey, it doesn't go away."

"It can. I don't love him. That's a him problem. It's not a me problem. I just wanted sex. And I got it. But sex isn't love, and he's just confused."

"I don't know that he is," Georgie said, very delicately for Georgie.

"It's terrible!"

"It is," Teddy agreed. "But you know, you did exactly to him what Beau did to me."

"No. That was different. Beau was scared because—"

"You're scared," Teddy said.

"No I'm… I'm reasonable. I'm realistic. I've known the man for a few weeks. We barely just started sleeping together and…"

"And he loves you. Even though you are spiky and difficult."

"I'm not," Joey said.

Her sisters looked at each other. "You are wonderful," Elliot said. "We all are. But we are ourselves. And if you can find someone who is up for all that…"

"You aren't supposed to need anybody," Joey said. "None of us are. You're supposed to be able to figure out how to get on with things in—"

"I know that's how your mom feels," Georgie said. "But that doesn't mean that's how things are."

"You need us," Teddy said. "Is it so bad?"

"It's not that it's bad… It isn't. It's just… You can't… make people keep on loving you, can you?" She blinked back tears. "And if you can't make them then what's protecting you if they decide they don't want you after all?"

"Do you mean our dad?" Georgie asked.

"Our dad. Your mom."

"What about your mom?" Elliot asked. "And my mom and Teddy's mom? And Beau. And Grandpa Jack?"

"I don't… I don't…"

"Joey, it's okay," Elliot said. "You know you don't have to know the answer right away. You don't have to figure it out."

But that was the most ridiculous thing that Joey had ever heard. Because she obviously did need to know. Immediately. Right now. Because the alternative was sitting in these awful, uncomfortable feelings, and she hated that. Couldn't deal with it.

"I just need… I need to be by myself," Joey said.

And she found herself walking down the same road she'd come.

When she looked up, she saw a solitary, familiar figure.

Grandpa Jack, walking slowly with his hands in his pockets, Jasper Junie the barn cat trotting along beside him. He was looking down at the animal with some seriousness, as if they were having an intense conversation.

Then he saw Joey.

"Well, howdy there," he said. "You don't look like you're dressed for a hoedown today."

She looked down at the ridiculous dress she was wearing. "No. No hoedowns."

"You look upset, Joey."

It was the greatest insult Joey had ever endured. That she was showing her emotions so easily.

"It's no big deal," she said.

"I see. Do I have to threaten some other knucklehead? You girls are causing some trouble. I had sons…"

"Yeah, and one of them is terrible," Joey said flatly. "So you could hardly get mad at us for sleeping with one cowboy apiece." She felt a little bit guilty bundling Georgie into this all things considered. But, it was for effect.

"Well now," he said sternly. "You make a good point, but I would rather not have any details."

"None are on offer."

"But really. Do I need to shoot him?"

"No," Joey said. "I broke things off. It's not the right time. It... You know, I just think that this kind of stuff isn't for me." The back of her throat lifted, and she could feel herself trying to hold back emotion, tears, and all of it made her voice sound tight.

"Why is that, Joey?" he asked.

And she hadn't expected that. Hadn't expected Grandpa Jack of all people to ask about her feelings.

"Because it's awful," she said. "Because I can't control it. Or make it a system, or plan it, or anything of the kind. And I just want to be able to learn something, and then be done with the hard part. Be done with the thing that makes it difficult. I just want to get a lesson and then go on to being good at it."

"Well, I hate to break it to you, but that isn't how this works."

"What?"

"Life," he said. "You never know what the hell you're doing. Not if you're doing something appropriately big enough or challenging enough. It will always feel a little bit hard, and you might always feel a little bit lost. I ought to know, because I'm very good at avoiding these things. I've avoided taking my son to task, and I've avoided getting to know you girls as well as I should, because it's a reminder. A reminder of those difficult things. Of what I didn't do. But Joey... We gotta face them eventually. When I had my heart attack...and you girls were there, I realized that I wanted it to be different. I don't know how to make it different. But I'm working on it. It's okay to just be working on something. You don't have to be an expert to try."

He looked at her, and she saw herself in his eyes. Bluebonnets. Hurt, and a little bit of lonely.

He was there. He was there, and her dad wasn't. But that didn't mean she didn't have love.

Just like her mom had always been there.

"Grandpa…"

"You're a good girl, Joey. No man is ever going to make you weaker. The right one might help you be stronger, though." He smiled. "Love can hurt. I've had my share of hurts with it. I'm not proud of Mickey, not for the way he treated his girls or the women in his life. I'd have taken forty more years with your grandmother if I'd had my way. But I'd never trade the love I gave, just like I treasure all the love I ever got. Because it's what makes all of this worth anything."

And then he and Jasper Junie continued on down the road. And in the middle of all that was broken, Joey felt something in her soul begin to mend.

Did she really not need to figure it all out?

She had a hard time with that.

She called her mother, and she thought it was funny that she had avoided talking about her feelings all this time, and now she seemed to be making the rounds to spill them on everybody. "Well," Joey said. "You're a liar," she said.

"Am I?" Her mother's voice was as calm as it ever was.

"I tried the whole sex thing. And I'm not… I'm not okay. It's not easy. He is magic, and I don't know what the hell I'm supposed to do with that?"

"Oh darlin'," her mother said. "It just wasn't magic for me. That doesn't mean it's not magic."

"But I—"

"Joey, I wasn't in love with your father. So it didn't matter to me that it ended."

"I'm not in love," Joey said. "That's stupid. It would be stupid."

"People are stupid," her mother said, as matter-of-factly as she said everything else.

"Not you."

"Yes," she said. "Me. I've been stupid, I've been wrong. I've been wrong in my personal life, I've been wrong when it came to raising you. I've done wrong things as a ranch boss. We are all stupid sometimes."

"But you always seem so... Like you know what you're doing."

"Joey, you're my child. I don't show you when I struggle."

That was a revelation. One Joey hadn't been expecting, but it seemed so obvious when you put it like that.

"Well now I'm struggling," Joey said. "I don't know how to—"

"You just have to sit in it."

"I don't want to do that."

"No one does."

"I want to be independent," Joey said, sniffing. "I never wanted to want a father who didn't want me or..."

"Let me stop you there, Joey. Just because I didn't want him, doesn't mean you don't have to miss him. Or at least miss a father figure, if not Mickey specifically. I did the best I could do, but the fact is, there's a man out there who is your father. And he let you down. You're allowed to feel something about it."

"But it hurts," Joey said. "Wanting love you can't have hurts."

"Joey Hathaway, does it hurt to put in a hard day's work?"

"Well, yeah…"

"Do you do it anyway?"

"Yes."

"Is it what makes life worth it?"

"Yeah."

Her mom took everything and made it sound so simple. Except it had taken everything and turned on its head.

Everybody was stupid. Everybody struggled.

And you couldn't make the bad feelings go away or control them.

And if Grandpa Jack was to be believed, you weren't even supposed to when things were big and complicated.

After that, Joey went back to the house and sat in her room for a long time, pacing around and watering her plants. And she tried to imagine her life going forward. The farm store, being here with her sisters…

They were going to move on. They were going to find people.

But it just didn't feel exciting the way that it had before. Because something in her had changed fundamentally. It was the part of her that wanted Hollis. The part of her that…

She loved him.

She really did. She loved him, and she wanted her life to be shaped around that. She wanted her life to be different now. She didn't just want the farm store, and the little family that she and her sisters had dreamed of.

She wanted to expand that family. She wanted to expand what her life could be.

And no, she wasn't going to be able to learn it in an afternoon. She might make mistakes.

But suddenly, all of that seemed better than not having Hollis in her life.

And she was going to do whatever she had to to get them back.

She was going to have to share. She was going to have to be willing to make a fool out of herself. She was going to have to be willing to be wrong.

And she realized she was.

And it made her laugh.

CHAPTER ELEVEN

HOLLIS FINISHED DOING the rearranging in his living room and looked around. He had moved the picture. Not to hide it, not to pretend like it had never happened, just because the position that it held in his life had changed.

It would always be part of him. Part of his journey. But it was different now. He was different now.

He was so absorbed in taking in the new shape of things, that he didn't hear a truck come up his driveway. And he didn't hear anything at all until there was a knock on the door. He went over there, and he opened it.

It was Joey.

She had Band-Aids on her hands, and her hair was a mess, and her eyes were red.

"Joey," he said.

"I've been building shelves," she said. "Because I had some thinking to do. Not maybe the thinking that you think I might have had to do but, just some more thinking. And it turns out that I'm not very good at building shelves. And I hurt myself a bunch of times. I've hit my thumb with a hammer at least six times. I don't like it."

"I wouldn't think," he said.

"Well, it's just a big pain in the butt, in general. But, I might get better at it. Just because I'm not good at it today doesn't mean I won't be. You know what I mean?"

"Not really."

"I like knowing how to do things. I like being in control. I don't like having to learn how to do something. I don't want to take time. I think mostly I don't want to be hurt. Well. I'm hurt. I'm really, really hurt."

Tears started to fill her eyes.

"And I want to figure out how to do better. How to be better. But I'm going to have to learn. And it's going to take some time. And I'm learning… I'm learning how to love you. And how to let you love me. And I want to learn how to share a life. I want to learn how to be together."

"Oh Joey," he said, and he pulled her into his arms.

Because he had known that she would come. He had known, but that didn't make this less sweet.

Because he didn't take anything for granted. Not now. It wasn't money, a career, a cabin, that mattered. The greatest gift in life was this right here. Finding that person who could share your life—whatever it looked like—with you.

This was the prize. This was that field of bluebonnets.

This was what mattered.

"I love you," he said.

"I love you too. I guess maybe you will be my baby daddy," she said.

"Only if you want me to be," he said. "I want whatever future you see."

"Really?"

"Yes. Because my future is sweetest for having you in it."

"Well, I think we should get married and have kids and in general be really sappy and ridiculous. And love wildly. No matter what."

"That sounds like it could be dangerous," he said.

"I know. But I'm up for it. I'm not afraid. Well. I am. I am quite afraid. And I don't know what I'm doing. But I'm here anyway."

And he knew that from Joey, that was the strongest declaration a man could ever get.

"And when our kids want to learn to throw a ball, are you going to have them go to a professional ball field?"

"No. I'm going to have you teach them. And maybe... Maybe they won't be very good at it. Because maybe you aren't the best. But you'll teach them with love. And maybe that matters more."

He looked down into those bluebonnet eyes, and he knew that for the rest of his life, his world would be that color purple.

"I think it does, Joey. I think it does."

* * * * *

GEORGIE

Jackie Ashenden

We'll all meet again…some sunny day.

CHAPTER ONE

THERE WAS A chicken on the counter again.

Damn.

Georgie Hathaway grabbed the water pistol she'd positioned within easy reach, carefully sighted the chicken clucking around far too close to the Japanese milk bread she had hopefully rising. And fired.

The stream of water caught the chicken's tail feathers, making the bird squawk angrily and flutter off onto the kitchen floor.

Pleased, Georgie ceremonially raised the water pistol and blew nonexistent smoke from the barrel.

Mission accomplished.

"Georgie!"

Georgie turned to find Teddy, the fluffiest and most warm-hearted of her three sisters, coming into the kitchen and hurrying over to the disgruntled chicken.

"What?" she demanded. "The chickens aren't allowed inside."

"You've upset Henrietta." Teddy gathered the chicken into her arms and gave Georgie a chiding look. "She doesn't know she's not allowed inside."

Georgie, who was a diva about her yeast and had no patience for wildlife near her baking, scowled. "That's not my problem. That's Henrietta's. She shouldn't have got near my dough."

Teddy frowned. Her violet eyes, the same violet all the Hathaway half sisters shared, were slightly accusing. "You could just pick her up or gently usher her out. You don't need to fire guns at her."

"It's not a gun, it's a water pistol. And I'm not touching that bird." She knew she was being overly grumpy, but then grumpy was kind of her thing. As was being prickly. Most especially when she was baking.

And most especially, especially when she was baking for Sister Sunday.

She and her three half sisters, Teddy, Elliot and Joey, all lived in the run-down farmhouse owned by their grandfather. They'd promised to renovate the place so Grandpa Jack wouldn't sell either the house or the land, and had all done quite a bit of work to make it livable. Now as spring edged into summer, it was looking pretty good.

Sister Sunday happened every Sunday, where each of the sisters would host a day for the others, where they could all be together in a way they hadn't when they were growing up.

It was Georgie's turn tomorrow and she was quietly planning a sumptuous high tea consisting of each of the others' favorite pastries, plus some sandwiches. Joey wanted a raspberry Danish, Elliot perfect scones, excellent clotted cream and homemade jam. While Teddy, irritatingly, had said that she didn't mind, only that it was chocolate based in some fashion.

It was just the kind of challenge that Georgie liked with her baking, but it wasn't going to happen with random chickens clucking around and getting into her test loaves.

Teddy smiled down at Henrietta. "She's lovely when you get used to her. Anyway. I was just coming to tell you that there's a man at the door."

Georgie frowned. "Man? What man?" She wasn't expecting any visitors at the farmhouse today. In fact, even
in the little house in Jasper Creek that she normally lived
in with her half brother Felix—or had up until she and the
others had moved in to do up Grandpa Jack's farmhouse—
she'd actively discouraged visitors, male or otherwise.

It wasn't so much that she was an introvert, she just
didn't like people all that much. People excluding her sisters, of course.

Having been brought up by her half brother, she'd had
nothing but testosterone shoved in her face since she was
ten years old and though she loved her half brother very
much, she also loved the feminine energy her half sisters
brought with them.

Cheerful, fluffy Teddy. Intense, creative Elliot. Straight-
up, honest Joey.

The three of them had lived in different parts of the
country and normally Georgie only got to see them a couple of times a year, but since Grandpa Jack had given the
farm to the four of them to run, Teddy had suggested they
all come and live there for a bit.

Georgie had thought that was a great idea, especially
since Felix had recently been tossing up whether or not to
sell the ranch and move elsewhere.

She hadn't wanted to leave Jasper Creek, so here she
was, living with her sisters the way she'd always dreamed.
Except with more chickens.

Anyway, bottom line was she was spending quality time
with her sisters and she absolutely did not want to be dis-
turbed, especially not by some random dude.

Admittedly it had been nearly two months since she'd
moved into the farmhouse with the others, and maybe she

was getting a little bit sistered-out, but still. It was mainly Teddy's chickens she didn't like.

She was even starting to think that maybe the others were launching chickens into her pristine kitchen accidentally on purpose.

"A tall man," Teddy said. "Could be said to be drop-dead gorgeous by some."

"Okay, great. A tall, gorgeous man." Georgie made a circling motion with her hand. "Can we hurry it up and get to the point?"

Teddy's violet gaze turned very interested all of a sudden. "He said he's here for you."

"For me," she repeated stupidly.

"Yes. He said…" Teddy's voice dropped into a terrible imitation of a man's baritone. "'I'm here for Georgie. I owe her some chores.'"

There was a sinking feeling in Georgie's stomach.

Oh, great. So it was *that* man. What the hell was *he* doing here?

"Um, okay." She moved over to where the bread stood on the counter and lifted the edge of the cloth that covered it. "Can you tell him that I'm a bit busy today? He can come back tomorrow." At least the bread hadn't been affected by Henrietta. It seemed to be rising nicely.

But Teddy was already turning to the door that led from the kitchen to the yard outside, with Henrietta luckily. "You're big enough to tell him yourself," she called over her shoulder. "I have a hive I need to check on."

Georgie bit her lip, scowled at her bread a bit more, then flipped back the cloth, turned around and leaned back against the kitchen counter.

The kitchen was her domain and the others very kindly let her have her little diva fits about it. It was a pretty, rustic space with big windows that let in lots of light and a scrubbed wooden floor. The counters were wood, the white walls full of open wooden shelving.

Wood had been Grandpa Jack's aesthetic of choice apparently.

Joey's specialty was growing things and her houseplants overflowed from the shelves on the wall and the top of the big dresser that held crockery, some of Elliot's beautifully turned bowls, plus neatly folded linens, and Georgie had to admit, the plants did give the place a certain…charm.

Still, she liked the counters to be clean, the big stainless steel sink to be empty, and the giant gas cooker to be free of clutter.

Her pride and joy, the retro-looking cake mixer that was the only thing allowed to "clutter" up the countertop, stood at one end, all ready to start mixing up the chocolate cake batter she was going to make for dessert tonight.

She really wanted to talk to that man like she wanted another hole in her head, but all the wanting in the world wasn't going to change things.

Con Stone was a damn stubborn cuss and if he was here then neither hell nor high water would move him.

Fantastic.

It was that stupid poker game Felix had roped her into, that was the issue. He'd been all "let's remember the good old days," AKA her childhood, which was being looked after by Felix in Jasper Creek after her mother had given up pining over Georgie's father and left.

Well, looked after by Felix *and* Con, since Con was Felix's best friend and had been at the house more or less constantly when Georgie was a kid.

He and Felix had played poker every Wednesday night

and Georgie had insisted on being dealt in once she'd gotten old enough.

Stupid her.

Because last Wednesday—after Felix had relentlessly nagged her—she'd joined him and Con in a game for old time's sake, and since she'd refused to play for money since all the money she'd saved from working in the café in Jasper Creek was going into the farmhouse, Con had suggested she play for chores.

She hadn't really wanted to do that either, since the idea of having to do chores for Con, or indeed anything for Con, made her feel hot. But her competitive streak wouldn't let her refuse and so she'd played. And since she was good at poker, she'd won.

She'd won Con doing any chore she cared to name for two whole weeks.

He hadn't seemed to mind—in fact he'd been disturbingly okay with it—and now clearly he was here to make good on her winnings.

Except she didn't want him.

He not only made her feel hot, but restless and edgy, and he had for a while now.

Ever since she'd gone up to look at the horse ranch Con had once worked at and now owned after the previous owner—an old guy with no other family—had left it to Con in his will.

That had been six months ago and Con hadn't been doing anything out of the ordinary. Just dealing with some ornery gelding and she'd found herself mesmerized by the way he'd talked to the horse so quietly, soothing the animal with his low, deep voice. Then the way, when the horse had finally been ready, he'd swung himself into the saddle, effortlessly commanding the animal as if he was part horse himself.

Tell it like it is, fool. He was sexy. That's why you're uncomfortable.

Yes, okay, sexy was exactly what he'd been and that was the problem. For so many years he'd been like a brother to her and that had been great. She knew brothers. They were irritating and familiar and most of all, safe.

But sexy was not. Sexy was dangerous and complicated and it made her feel things. Georgie did not like to feel things.

Then a month ago she'd done something stupid and she'd been avoiding him ever since.

Anyway, sadly there was no help for it. She was going to have to not only let him in, but have him in the house and be generally around, completing chores in front of her sisters which was going to be…annoying.

But what else could she do? She didn't want him to know that she had a problem with it, because then he'd ask questions and once he started asking questions, he'd eventually get the truth out of her. Which would be embarrassing to say the least.

Better if he didn't know she had a problem at all.

Still, she didn't have to make this pleasant, did she? In fact, she could make this extremely *un*pleasant. And maybe if it was unpleasant enough, he'd take himself and his disturbing presence away before the two weeks was up.

Yes, that was a good idea. No, that was a *great* idea.

Decision made, Georgie girded her loins and strode out of the kitchen, going down the bright, airy hallway of the farmhouse.

The front door was already open and of course, there he was, all six foot three of him, standing there with his muscular arms folded, staring at her with a peculiar kind of intensity.

Georgie's heart gave a little kick.

Come on. He's gorgeous and sexy and you like it.

She really wished she could ignore that thought, but she couldn't.

He was in a plain old dark green T-shirt and plain old worn jeans, with a plain old black cowboy hat on his head—his usual uniform in other words—but there was nothing "plain old" about Con.

His hair was black and cut short, his eyes hazel bordering on gold, his features fierce and compelling. She'd never thought of him as handsome or even good-looking, because he was basically always Con.

But since that day a month ago, when she'd done that stupid thing, he'd never be "just Con" to her ever again.

And no, she did *not* like it.

Coming to a stop in the doorway, she glared at him. "Today? Really?"

"I told you I would." His familiar voice was deep and gritty, and he did not smile. "Debts need to be paid, kiddo."

Con watched the annoyance wash over Georgie's pretty face at the nickname she'd suddenly randomly disliked all of six months ago without explanation.

He probably shouldn't have used it, but hell, he'd known her since she was ten and he was eighteen, and she'd always be kiddo to him.

Not that he saw her as an actual kid, mind. He'd stopped seeing her that way at least five years ago. Things were different now, at least they were for him. Ever since that day a month earlier when she'd suddenly started avoiding him like the plague.

Didn't take a genius to work out why.

He'd been waiting patiently for Georgie Hathaway to

make up her mind about him, and he'd been beginning to think that maybe she might not ever see him the way he saw her.

Until last month when she'd kissed him.

Losing a poker game didn't take a lot of skill, but losing a poker game while at the same time giving the winner a run for their money *and also* making them feel like they'd outplayed you brilliantly was much harder.

Still, he'd managed it. Georgie wouldn't be pleased if and when she found out he'd lost on purpose, but hey, if she'd answered his texts or his emails or his calls, or had stayed at home whenever he happened to come by instead of going out, then maybe he wouldn't have had to.

He could have asked her out on a date that maybe she'd have refused, or maybe she'd have said yes to. Either way, they could then have had a proper conversation like normal adults.

Sadly, he was dealing with Georgie, who was more skittish horse than normal adult, and so he had to act accordingly. Luckily, he had plenty of experience with skittish horses of all kinds, plus he was extraordinarily patient.

He'd been waiting for Georgie Hathaway to become aware of his existence as a man for the past five years, after all.

Georgie glared at him like she was six-four and not the five-two she actually was, her downright beautiful violet eyes glittering angrily. Long blond hair the color of clover honey had been gathered into a very messy ponytail at her nape, and the oversize blue sweatshirt she wore had flour dusting the front of it. Her jeans hung loosely, hems rolled and she had on her favorite scuffed tennis shoes.

She was tiny and the oversize clothing only emphasized her delicate femininity, even if it annoyingly hid her curves.

And she had curves, he knew that. In fact, he knew exactly how many times he'd seen those curves on display. When she'd been wearing a tank top instead of the baggy T-shirts or men's button-ups, and hell yeah, he'd looked, because he wasn't made of stone.

But of course, she wasn't only curves.

No, Georgie Hathaway had a hell of a lot more to her than that.

"How about tomorrow?" she said crossly. "I'm too busy today."

He ignored this, since it was clear that if he wanted to have any sort of discussion with her he was going to have to, and looked past her small figure and into the farmhouse hallway.

It was a ramshackle old place and while obviously a lot of work had been done, he could no doubt rustle up some things that needed fixing.

"If you're too busy, I could help," he said. "Check out your wiring, take a look at your plumbing."

"I don't need help, Con," Georgie insisted. "And please stop calling me kiddo. I'm twenty-five for God's sake."

Con looked at her. "If you don't need help, then I can't pay my debts. And I always pay them. I'm a man of my word. You wouldn't want me not to be a man of my word now would you? Also, you like it when I call you kiddo."

"I do not." She sniffed. "Plus, I don't care about your word. Come back tomorrow."

So that's how it was going to be, was it? Well, if there was one thing he knew it was that while Georgie Hathaway might be stubborn, he was even more so. Especially when he was on a mission.

"Fine," he said mildly, leaning against the door frame. "I guess I'll just wait out here on the doorstep until then."

Georgie scowled. "What? Seriously?"

He shrugged. "I don't have anything better to do." Which was a total lie. He had a thousand better things to do, but this was important.

Georgie Hathaway was important.

"You've got a sad life in that case," she muttered.

At that point, another woman in clay-stained overalls came into view. She had dark hair, the same violet eyes as Georgie, and an intense look about her.

"Did someone say something about wiring?" She gave him an up and down look, then narrowed her gaze. "Don't listen to Georgie. She doesn't know what she's talking about. I've got a light in my bedroom that's randomly stopped working and it's annoying." She gave Georgie a sidelong glance, stepped in toward him, and said quietly, "I'll pay you double if you fix my light first."

Georgie rolled her eyes. "Oh for God's sake, Elliot. He's not a handyman. He's Felix's best friend."

Amused, Con held out his hand. "I'm Con."

Elliot, who was not one whit fazed about her mistake, gave him a blinding smile and shook his hand firmly. "Elliot. And the offer still stands."

"Well," he said. "I'll keep that in mind."

"See that you do." Elliot gave her sister one last look, then disappeared back down the hallway.

Con raised an eyebrow. "Shall I start with the light in the bedroom then?"

Georgie let out a long breath, radiating annoyance like an irritated cat, and silently Con thanked Elliot for her well-timed appearance. Georgie was fiercely competitive, even though she tried to hide it, and Elliot's suggestion re doing the light first had clearly kicked Georgie's competitiveness into high gear.

"Definitely not," she said. "You can start in the kitchen."

It wouldn't do to smile, since that would only irritate her more, which wasn't ideal when he was here to talk to her, not annoy her.

So all he did was merely tip his hat and step inside.

He wasn't going to broach his topic quite yet. He'd take things slowly, carefully. Soothe her. Get her used to him, maybe feed her a metaphorical sugar lump or two.

Because she was going to marry him.

She just didn't know it yet.

CHAPTER TWO

GEORGIE WAS VERY CONSCIOUS of Con's tall figure following her down the hallway. She was very conscious of Con, period.

She wished she wasn't. She wished he was still Felix's annoying friend who'd used to sneak her candy, let her watch gory movies, and had taught her to ride back when she'd been a kid. Who'd been more of a big brother to her than her own brother had been, and sometimes even her partner in crime.

But he wasn't any of those things, not anymore.

"Nice place," Con said from behind her.

He wasn't walking particularly close but even so she felt his presence like a kind of pressure. An awareness of his height and the broad expanse of his chest. Of his stare, because she could feel that too.

It made her feel hot and restless, and even more grumpy than she normally was.

Men weren't something she'd ever thought about particularly, at least not in relation to herself. After her mother had realized that the feckless charmer that was Georgie's father would never see the light and declare undying love, she'd decided to ditch Jasper Creek, leaving a ten-year-old Georgie in the care of her much older half brother Felix. He'd been a good brother and had brought her up in a practical, no-nonsense way, but subsequently men weren't a mystery to her. They left towels on the floor, made a mess of her kitchen, thought ordinary bodily functions were hilarious, and were generally idiots. Who wanted to deal with that nonsense? Georgie didn't.

Plus, it didn't help that the male population of Jasper Creek was sparse in terms of hot men, or at least hot men who were unattached. She supposed Teddy had chosen well when it came to Beau, and she could kind of understand Elliott's current fixation with Colt West, not to mention Joey's obsession with Hollis, but really, those guys were just darn lucky that her sisters had deigned to notice them.

She herself hadn't been compelled by anyone, and so she'd largely ignored dating, preferring instead to work as many shifts as she could at June's Kitchen, one of Jasper Creek's most successful cafés, while practicing her baking so it was good enough to supply the café. Baking full-time had been a dream of hers for a while now and she was hoping to do more of it.

She hadn't missed dating because you couldn't miss something you'd never experienced. Or at least she hadn't until last month and Con and that stupid, extremely ill-advised kiss.

And now she couldn't stop thinking about him.

Him and his chest, and his intense face, and the gold flecks in his hazel eyes, and the way his mouth curved and oh man, she was such a mess.

Con coughed ostentatiously behind her. "I said, nice place."

"I heard you. And it's not a nice place. It's a dump."

"A dump you've been very happily living in for nearly two months. At least according to Felix."

Of course, her brother had been discussing her behind

her back. Geez, couldn't he keep his mouth shut for two seconds? Why did he have to go talking about her to Con?

"Yeah, well, women are much nicer to live with than men," Georgie muttered with some irritation, as she stepped into the kitchen. "At least I don't have to worry about idiots leaving the toilet seat up all the time."

"Well, sure," Con said, sounding amused. "I guess that's fair."

Georgie ignored him, going over to the peg on the wall that held her collection of aprons, because if he was going to turn up randomly where it was clear he wasn't wanted, then she was going to make it as difficult for him as she possibly could.

She sorted through them, found the one she wanted, which had roosters all over it, grabbed it and turned.

And her breath caught.

He'd taken his hat off and placed on the counter, and was now standing in the middle of the kitchen, his hands in the pockets of his jeans, looking around her domain with a great deal of interest. The late spring sunshine coming through the window bathed him in glory, glossing his black hair and highlighting the exquisite bone structure of his face. The gold in his eyes glowed like small fractured sunbeams…

He looked at her and finally gave her the slow-burning, warm Con smile that she knew so well, which wasn't the charming, easygoing one he gave everyone else, but the one he saved just for her.

It made her heart turn over in her chest.

Girl, you've got it bad.

No, she did not. Whatever that feeling was, was an aberration, nothing more.

She thrust out the apron jerkily. "Put this on, please."

He didn't even look at it. "You've been avoiding me, kiddo. Don't think I haven't noticed."

Oh no, they weren't having *that* conversation, not now and especially not here. Her kitchen was sacrosanct. The only thing that could be discussed was baking.

Georgie shook the apron at him with wordless authority.

He glanced at it then back at her, his expression relaxing into what looked like amusement mixed with something warmer, almost tender, causing her heart to give another of those little kicks. "An apron? Really?"

She ignored her heart. Her heart was stupid. "If you're going to be in my kitchen, you have to wear an apron."

"Except, you're not wearing one."

Fool man. Why did he think he could argue with her? He was only here on sufferance and that sufferance was wearing thin.

"No, idiot," she said, because she could and because he *was* an idiot. "I don't have to. It's my kitchen." She shook the apron at him again. "You want to do chores to pay your debt? Then you wear the apron. I'm the boss. You have to do what I say."

He held up his hands, amusement still dancing in his eyes. "Okay, okay. You win. I'll wear the apron." He took it from her then looked down at it. "Roosters. That seems appropriate."

"Don't," Georgie said warningly.

He lifted one black brow in a way she'd never found particularly wicked before, but she certainly did now. "Don't what?"

"Don't make jokes about the…uh…content of the apron." She knew men's minds. She knew what he'd be thinking. Certainly her brother would have made some dumb joke about roosters.

"The content of the apron," he echoed, looking down at it again. "Well, I could point out that—"

"Con."

He grinned. "Getting prim in your old age, kiddo?"

Oh, that grin. He'd always had a particularly infectious smile and he always used it to good effect on the women of Jasper Creek. The man was the very definition of a laid-back, easygoing cowboy, and that combined with his charm and good looks made him virtually irresistible.

Georgie used to find his effect on women mystifying back when she was a kid. He'd already been living in an old cabin down the back of the property when she'd first come to live with Felix—her half brother took in a lot of strays—and the number of women who'd used to traipse down the path to Con's cabin had always been puzzling. What did they do in there? Play computer games? Do jigsaw puzzles? Play poker?

As she'd gotten older, she'd figured it out, because she wasn't stupid, but she'd still used to find it weird. To her he was just like Felix. Another annoyingly protective older brother.

Until he wasn't. Until she'd suddenly realized exactly what it was about his grin that made women's heart flutter.

Sure, he was sexy, but there was definitely no fluttering happening anywhere about her person.

"Getting prim?" She folded her arms over her chest to quell any traitorous unsettled feelings and gave him what she hoped was a stern look. "No, just bored of dumb male jokes. Put it on, go on."

Still grinning, he looped the top strap over his head then turned around so his back was to her. "Can you do me up?"

She blinked. "Uh…what?"

"The ties." There was unmistakable humor in his voice. "I can't quite reach."

He was teasing her, the asshole. But then that was nothing new. Con always did like to tease her. He'd never been cruel or mean with it, more a gentle poking fun and done with a certain amount of affection. Like a brother with a very young sister. She'd always liked it, because Felix was so serious and he never smiled, but she didn't like it today and she wasn't sure why.

You kissed him, that's why. And he's still treating you like a little kid.

Yeah, but wasn't that a good thing? She didn't want him to treat her differently, and she didn't want that kiss to have changed anything between them.

And actually, what she *really* wanted was to have never accepted his offer of a day's riding, which meant that kiss would never have happened at all, and then she wouldn't be standing here overthinking every little thing.

"Fine," she muttered, letting out a breath and coming over to where he stood. She grabbed at the ties. "Is this a man thing? Can men not tie their own apron?"

"Hurt my shoulder getting a new mare settled. Can't quite reach behind me."

It sure sounded like a plausible explanation, but that note in his voice was there again, warm and just a little too playful... He didn't sound like normal Con annoying her. He sounded like...

He sounds like he does when he's flirting with a woman.

A flush of heat caught her and she almost dropped the ties. No, she was being ridiculous. He didn't sound like that. And anyway, why would he be flirting with her? Sure, she'd kissed him, but his response had been...

Well, she hadn't waited around to see. And since she'd

been avoiding him for weeks, she still didn't know what he'd thought about it. Not that she wanted to know, to be honest, but what she did know was that he wasn't flirting with her, definitely not. Because after all, it was *her*.

Annoyed both with herself and him, she gripped the apron strings and pulled them hard around his narrow waist.

He gave a slight grunt of what she hoped was discomfort.

"Too tight?" she asked sweetly.

"Nope."

"Good." She tied them as tight as she could, trying to ignore the powerful expanse of his back and how the cotton of his green tee stretched over his wide shoulders. He was very warm and he smelled of faintly of horse, hay, and sunshine.

Her mouth dried. Oh, she liked that scent. It was familiar, comforting. Reminding her of times when Felix had gone out on some errand or other, and Con had helped out babysitting her. He'd make popcorn, then they'd sit on the couch watching a movie that was usually far too old for her, something with car chases and things blowing up, and bad language that he'd tell her not to listen to, that she of course listened to even more closely.

She'd loved those times. Felix worked hard on the ranch he owned so he wasn't often around, and there was her dad…

Georgie had tried on and off to build a relationship with him—much to her sisters' collective disgust—mainly because while he might have treated her mom badly, he was still her dad. But Mickey had never been all that interested in spending time with her. These days she didn't try as hard as she once had, but still called him every couple of months just to say hi.

"So, what's the deal?" Con asked over his shoulder.

Georgie gritted her teeth and tried to ignore the effect his physical presence had on her, tying an extra big bow at the small of his back. "What deal?"

"You not replying to a single email, text or phone call. Oh yeah, and also accidentally being out every time I visit."

"I've been busy." Georgie stepped back, putting some space between them. "I've moved into the farmhouse here and I've had my sisters around. Plus, we're wanting to get this farm stand idea off the ground so Grandpa Jack won't sell this place out from under us, so yeah. Busy."

It didn't sound like a whole raft of excuses. It really didn't.

Con turned around, suddenly looming very large in front of her. He should have looked ridiculous in an apron covered in roosters, but the sad fact was that she didn't even notice the roosters. Or the apron.

All she could see was the sunbeams caught in his eyes.

"Georgie," he said very gently. "We need to talk about that kiss."

SHE STOOD THERE very still, looking completely adorable in her overly large sweatshirt, her blond hair in its messy ponytail over one shoulder, her stunning violet eyes going very round. Her perfect little mouth opened. Then shut.

Then she gave him her furious Georgie-scowl that he'd always found so endearing given that it hid the sweetest, warmest heart in Jasper Creek.

Ignoring him completely, she turned and strode over to where a wooden-handled broom stood leaning against the counter, picked it up and strode back to him, presenting him with it in much the same way as she'd presented him with the apron, which was aggressively.

"You can sweep the floor first," she ordered.

Perhaps he shouldn't have teased her with tying his apron. He'd only wanted to see what would happen if she got close to him, which was apparently her getting even more grumpy.

That was a damn good thing, since Georgie always got grumpy when she was having a feeling.

In which case, he hoped that feeling was what he thought it was and that kiss she'd laid on him the weekend they'd gone riding together had been the precursor to something more, rather than an aberration.

Shit, he hoped it wasn't an aberration.

Then again, that's why he was here. To figure out exactly what it was, what she felt for him, and what they were going to do about it.

And they did have to do something about it, because he was sick of pussyfooting around. Felix was thinking of selling the ranch, which would leave Georgie on her own in Jasper Creek, and although she did have her sisters—no one would ever dare say the words *half sisters*—Con didn't know what plans those sisters had. Sure, he'd heard that Beau Riley had hooked up with one of them and apparently there were rumors about Colt West too, but who knew how those things would pan out? Plans changed, people left, and then Georgie would be on her own, and he hated that thought.

He'd waited long enough and now it was time to make his move.

Except it was clear she was *not* ready to talk about it.

Well, that was fine. He'd give her a bit more time to come to terms with the fact that *he* was going to talk whether she was ready for it or not, but if she thought she could avoid him forever she was wrong.

"You don't have to talk about it now if you don't want

to." He gave her a very direct look as he took the broom from her. "But we *will* talk about it."

She scowled back then turned sharply around and marched back to the counter, but not before he'd caught a glimpse of the blush that had washed through her cheeks.

No wonder she was grumpy in that case. Feelings were definitely happening from the looks of things, which was very satisfying. Especially given that a blush could only mean one thing.

Georgie didn't say anything, bending instead to look at whatever was in the large blue pottery bowl covered by a white cloth, her ponytail drifting over one shoulder like a streak of sunlight.

Goddamn, she was pretty.

He'd started to notice it over the past couple of years, just slowly. First it had been about the color of her hair and how it reminded him of pale honey. Then he'd started taking note of how the gleaming gold of her eyelashes really set off the unusual and beautiful color of her eyes. From there, he'd started thinking that her face didn't have that kid roundness any more, her features precise and delicate, and now that he'd noticed, quite lovely. And then it was just a short step to suddenly realizing that on the rare occasions when she wasn't wearing anything oversize, she had the most delectable curves.

Yeah, it had been a slow dawning thing and he'd fought it at first, because she'd still been Felix's little half sister to him. And then she wasn't Felix's little half sister.

Then she was beautiful Georgie, whom he'd fallen for, hook, line and sinker.

Con gripped the broom and began to sweep the worn wooden floor. It was already clean, though oddly enough there were a couple of what looked to be chicken feathers lying around.

"You don't talk much about your sisters," he said conversationally, because they were going to talk about something, dammit. "You've got three, right? And if that was Elliot, what about the other two? I heard one of them had hooked up with Beau Riley."

"That's Teddy and she hasn't 'hooked up' as you so charmingly put it," Georgie said crossly, still with her back to him. "She's in a relationship."

"A relationship. Right." He swept the chicken feathers into a pile.

"I don't know where Joey is." Georgie had moved over to where the shelves were and was standing there with her head tilted back, looking up at the recipe books on them. "Digging in the dirt probably."

As Con watched, she went up on her tiptoes, reaching for one of the books on the shelf. Her fingertips only just grazed the spine; obviously she wasn't tall enough to grab it.

"Dammit," she muttered.

Con briefly debated standing there and watching her try and reach for the book, since it was cute, but his better self told him not to be such a dick, so he rested the broom handle against the table, and walked over to where Georgie stood. Then he reached for the book she wanted himself, took it off the shelf for her.

Not being less of a dick, sorry.

Probably not, considering he made sure he was standing close so he could get a hit of her sweet scent and feel her soft warmth. He made no apologies for it though; being close to her was one of his life's joys and he took it where he could. Since old Frank had left the horse ranch to him and he'd started living there, having her around was one of the things he'd missed.

Hell, it was the *only* thing he'd missed.

He hadn't let a lot of people into his life—after a childhood spent moving around from state to state, his friendships had been very much of the surface variety—but she was one of the few he had and her absence had left a hole.

"This what you're after?" he murmured, putting the book down on the counter in front of her.

She'd gone quite still again and he could see the curve of her cheek. It was a pretty, dusky pink.

Apparently, she wasn't indifferent to him after all.

For a second, he debated staying where he was, just to see what she'd do. Perhaps turn around and kiss him again or more likely move away. But then he dismissed the idea. Georgie wasn't exactly experienced with all of this and if he wanted things to go his way then it would be best to take it slow.

So, he put some distance between them, taking a step to the side.

"Thank you," she said tightly. "But I could have gotten it myself."

He grinned, because he was pretty sure he knew where her grumpiness was coming from this time and it had everything to do with his nearness and that pretty blush in her cheeks. "Of course you could," he said. "Just trying to be helpful."

"Sweeping the floor would be more helpful." She didn't look at him, opening the book and ostentatiously leafing through the pages.

"The floor's already pretty clean." He leaned a hip against the counter, watching her. "Looking for a recipe?"

"No, I'm looking for instructions on how to fix the toilet."

Oh, he was definitely getting to her. How satisfying.

"Well, you won't find instructions in there," he said easily. "I, on the other hand, have fixed many toilets in my time."

"Go away, Con," Georgie growled, shooting him a very annoyed glance. "Go do that rewiring thing or something. Just stop…hovering."

He smiled, which he knew wouldn't make her any less annoyed, but he couldn't help it. Her violet eyes were glittering with irritation, her skin was pink, there was a little bit of flour on her cheeks, and she was the most adorable thing he'd seen in weeks.

No, make that years.

"But you wanted me to start in the kitchen first," he said. "And I've got my apron on and everything."

The glitter in her eyes became even more pronounced. "You are *so* annoying."

"So I've heard. Do you want to talk about it?"

"No," she snapped. "What I want to do is find a recipe, so why don't you stop bugging me and let me do that."

"I'll stop bugging you when you stop avoiding talking to me," he said calmly, folding his arms. "I can do this all day, kiddo, and you know I will."

CHAPTER THREE

GEORGIE FELT LIKE throwing an extremely inappropriate adolescent tantrum.

Con was standing beside her, his muscular arms crossed over his broad chest, his hazel gaze fixed on her, being the most Con, which consisted of him being maddeningly easygoing while letting all of her grumpiness just wash over him.

It was their usual dynamic and yet there was nothing usual about the intense, physical awareness of him that prickled all over her skin. When he'd come up behind her to grab that book, part of her had wanted to jump away like a scalded cat, while another part had wanted to lean back into the seductive warmth of his body. To surround herself in the scent of sunshine and hay and Con.

This whole crush thing was ridiculous—because obviously it was a crush—and it made her so mad. She didn't want to feel that way about him, especially when she had no idea how he felt about her. Not that she wanted to know. In fact, she could quite happily spend the rest of her life not knowing.

But what if he feels the same way about you that you feel about him?

A peculiar rush of heat went through her, which did *not* help her temper. If he did feel the same way, well, she'd probably have to do something about it, which if she was being really honest with herself, scared her. Because it would change their relationship, turn it into something different, and she wasn't sure she wanted that. No, she was sure she *didn't* want that.

She was happy with him being more a big brother, her crush on him notwithstanding. That was safe, that was familiar, and crushes…well, they went away didn't they?

Your mother's didn't.

It was true, her mother had stuck around Jasper Creek for years hoping that Georgie's father would finally see the light and fall madly in love with her. He never had though, leaving her mother heartbroken.

Yeah, she wasn't going to be like that, hanging around mooning futilely over some guy. Ignoring the crush was the fastest way to get rid of it, she'd thought, so that's what she fully intended on doing.

Kissing him probably didn't help.

And that was a thought that she didn't need in her head. The less she thought about that kiss the better.

"I haven't got time to talk about that." She tried not to snap and failed. "I've got more important things to do."

Con raised one black brow. "Such as?"

"Sister Sunday is tomorrow and I'm doing a high tea. And before you ask, Sister Sunday is a day hosted by one of us for the other sisters, where we get to be together in a way we never got to in our childhoods. Anyway, the others have requested specific food, but Teddy said she didn't mind what I made her, as long as it included chocolate."

"That sounds good," he said, looking interested. And then, obviously taking in her expression, added, "It's not good?"

She shouldn't rant to him about Teddy's request, but it

had been bugging her and since he was here, adding to her being bugged load, he was going to get an earful.

"No," she said. "No, it is *not* good. I wanted to do something spectacular for her, and it's so much easier to be told what someone wants than to have to figure it out yourself."

"But she said she didn't mind, right?"

Georgie frowned. Did she really have to explain? "Yes, but what if I make her something she doesn't like?"

"So?" He looked supremely unbothered. "She didn't specify what she wanted, that it was your choice, so if she ends up not liking it, that's not your fault."

Okay, he was kind of right. Actually, he *was* right, she supposed. But still…

"I want her to like it. I want them all to like it."

Con's expression was still relaxed, his mouth curved in that half smile that lent his face so much warmth and charm. But his gaze, like the falcon he'd been named for, had a sharp edge to it. "They mean a lot to you, don't they? Your sisters, I mean."

How to explain what being with her sisters meant? It was a question she didn't particularly want to answer, because she'd always found it difficult to articulate what she felt without sounding awkward. Yet not answering it felt like a disservice and she didn't feel right about that either.

"They do," she said after a moment. "With them I feel like I'm part of something, you know? Like I belong somewhere."

An expression she couldn't name flickered over his face and was gone. "Ah, okay," he said. "Girl power, huh?"

She frowned, caught suddenly by the odd note in his deep voice. "Something wrong with that?"

"Not at all." He was smiling now, that odd note gone.

"It's only that you didn't get this worried when you baked something for me and Felix."

Georgie stared at him, forgetting completely about her crush and the whole kiss drama. If she didn't know any better, she would have said that he was...jealous maybe?

But no, that was silly. Why would he be jealous of her sisters?

"That's because you're men and will eat anything." She paused, wanting to reassure him, because whatever happened between them, he was an important part of her life and always would be. "You know you and Felix are my family too, right? I love my sisters, but you guys were home."

Sunlight caught the gold flecks in his eyes, making them glitter, and all of a sudden his smile vanished, leaving his expression taut and intense. "And are we still home to you, Georgie? What if Felix sells up and leaves? Where will home be then?"

He was asking her something important, she knew it, and maybe a braver woman would have asked him exactly what he meant. But she wasn't a braver woman. All she wanted was for things to stay the way they were.

She tore her gaze from his and looked back down at her recipe book. "Then it'll be here with Teddy, Joey and Elliot," she said.

It wasn't the right thing to say and she knew it, but she also didn't know what else she could say. He wasn't her home now. He had his own life to lead and that wouldn't include her.

Which was fine. She had her sisters finally here in Jasper Creek after so many years, her little dream come true.

She'd been the only female in the house growing up and no matter how good a brother Felix was, she couldn't help but feel the lack of female company. She'd been a girl, different from Felix and Con. But not here with Elliot, Teddy and Joey. Here, she was the same.

Same father. Same eye color. Same kind of masculine-sounding name. Same kind of creative, home and hearth interests.

Here, she belonged.

There was a moment's tense silence then Con said, "Chocolate soufflé."

Georgie blinked and glanced back at him. "Um, what?"

The taut expression had vanished as if it had never been, and he was grinning again. "You always make them for me on my birthday. They're delicious. They'll blow your sisters' minds."

An odd feeling she couldn't quite place wound through her.

Chocolate soufflé had always been Con's treat. She'd first made them for his twenty-first birthday, back when she'd been thirteen.

She'd wanted to make something special for him, something challenging and difficult, but also delicious and impressive, because yes, back then, she'd wanted desperately to impress him.

In the end she'd decided on a chocolate soufflé and sure enough, it had been a challenge. She'd burned two batches and a third had come out of the oven pancake flat, but she'd persevered, eventually coming out with the perfect soufflé, light, chocolatey and delicious.

Since then she'd made one every year for his birthday and they'd always come out perfect. They weren't difficult for her, not anymore, but still, they were…his and she couldn't deny that she felt weird about making them for her sisters.

Except weren't you just thinking that your sisters were where you belonged?

Yeah, sure, but Con was special. He was—

No. She wasn't going there. No more thinking about how special Con was.

"Are you sure?" she asked instead. "That's kind of yours."

"I don't mind." His gaze was very direct. "It's delicious, simple and you make it really well."

She could feel heat steal over her cheeks, which was silly. She knew Con loved her baking. She didn't need his praise.

You like to hear it anyway though, right?

She looked back down at the recipe book on the counter, hoping he wouldn't see her blushing like an idiot. "That feels like cheating."

"Or it could be just showing off your signature dish."

He wasn't wrong. And she did make very good soufflés. Really, it was a great idea all round, so she wasn't sure why she was even arguing with him.

"Okay," she muttered. "They don't take that long to make, which only leaves me making pastry for the Danish and doing the clotted cream Elliot wanted." Elliot had also requested homemade jam, which luckily she already had since she'd made a whole batch last summer from the raspberries out the back of Felix's ranch.

"Excellent." Con pushed himself away from the counter with a suspiciously determined air. "And now we've got that sorted out we can have our little discussion."

Georgie's heart suddenly began to beat faster. "Oh, but I—"

"Now, kiddo. I'm tired of waiting."

HE THOUGHT SHE might change the subject yet again, because she had that startled rabbit look to her. She was staring down at the damn recipe book like it had the answers to every mystery of the universe, her brow deeply furrowed.

She really needed to look at him that way, because he had some answers, as it happened. And to questions she probably didn't even realize she had yet.

He really wished she'd start realizing those questions, even if they weren't going to be in his favor, because as he'd just told her, he *was* tired of waiting.

She'd told him she was home to her, but was he really? Now she was here in this run-down farmhouse with her sisters around her? It was obvious that the other girls were important to her and he got that, but he didn't like feeling as if he wasn't. Especially when he knew that wasn't true, but still…

It's almost as if you're jealous.

Hell no, he wasn't jealous. He'd never want to get in the way of her connecting with her family. He just wanted to know where he stood so that he could start making plans. Plans that he hoped would include her, but if she wasn't into that, he'd deal the way he always did.

Things were getting good for him and he really hoped she'd want to be part of that. He'd worked hard at old Frank's ranch ever since he'd been eighteen and at first it had just been for the money. Then he'd discovered he had a gift for horses and that he loved working with them and he'd decided that was what he'd wanted to do. Frank had liked him a whole lot, but no one had been more surprised than Con when the old guy—who'd had no children—had left his ranch to him after he'd died.

Con wanted to do the old man proud so he'd worked hard at building up the place, boarding horses mainly, but also offering a sanctuary to mistreated animals too.

The business side of it was going well, and so now was

the time to start looking at what else he wanted. And that was a family.

His own childhood had been a shiftless existence, just him and his mom and she never liked to stay in one place for long. A month here, a month there, living in trailers, the floors of friends, and motel rooms, there had never been anything permanent, never anything stable.

Since then he'd craved a place of his own, a place he could put down roots and never have to leave. A home and a woman to share that home with. A woman to share his life with.

A woman who was always going to be Georgie Hathaway.

Eventually she lifted her head, staring hard at the shelves in front of her for a second. Then very purposefully, she turned and looked at him. "So, okay. I kissed you. It was a mistake and I shouldn't have done it, and I'm sorry."

He might have been disappointed about that if he hadn't known she'd been avoiding him for weeks. If she hadn't blushed when he'd gotten close to her, and if she wasn't as grumpy with him now as she'd ever been.

But she had been avoiding him and she definitely had blushed, and she was certainly *very* grumpy, all of which added up to that kiss meaning more to her than she was letting on.

Which was excellent and very much on the right track as far as he was concerned.

"Oh yes," she added, her pale brows drawing down. "And stop calling me kiddo. It's weird and creepy in this context."

He laughed, unable to help himself. "Okay, fair enough. But it's only creepy if I get off on it and to be clear, I do *not* get off on it."

"Well, good, because that's—"

"I do get off on you, though."

Her eyes got very wide and very round, the expression on her face shocked. "I'm sorry, what?"

That pleased him rather more than it should have.

"You kissed me, Georgie Hathaway," he said, holding her gaze. "And what I'm saying is that I liked it."

Georgie blinked. "I… You… But we… What?"

Maybe he should have been angry at her shock, especially considering how long he'd waited for her to make any kind of move on him, for her to even show him that she was interested. But he wasn't.

He hadn't made his feelings known so of course she had no idea of his thoughts on the subject. Then again, if she'd waited around after that kiss, she would have found out exactly how he'd felt, but she hadn't.

She'd pressed her mouth to his after he'd helped her off her horse, given him one shocked look, then turned and left before he'd had a chance to say a word. And afterward had steadfastly refused to speak to him.

Little idiot.

He knew it had meant something to her otherwise why would she have avoided him? And why would she be looking at him right now like he'd grown another head?

Avoiding him wasn't the answer and wasn't good for either of them, because his feelings weren't going to go away any time soon. He wasn't a man who waited around once he'd decided he wanted something, he generally just up and took it. But Georgie was different and she was worth being patient for and so he'd gotten a grip on himself and been patient.

But he was done with that now. He was ready to look

to his future and he wanted her to be part of it, and if she didn't want that then he had to know.

"Believe me," he said. "I'm well aware of what we did. Or rather, what you did."

"Well then I'm sorry," she burst out. "I didn't mean to and I shouldn't have done it and it was a—"

"Don't be sorry," he interrupted, wanting to shut that bullshit down as quickly as he could. "And you absolutely should have done it, and in fact, I wouldn't mind if you wanted to do it again."

Her mouth opened. Closed. She'd gone very pink, a delightful contrast to her gorgeous violet eyes. "Con…"

"What?" He didn't look away. "You think I didn't enjoy every second of it? Because if so, you'd be wrong."

"Oh," she said, blinking rapidly. "Oh."

Okay, had she really not picked up on any of his feelings for her over the years?

Come on, this is Georgie, remember? She's very good at not seeing stuff she doesn't want to see.

That was true. She'd doggedly kept contact with her no-good dipshit of a father, even though he ghosted her at every opportunity. And once she'd refused to even acknowledge one of Felix's girlfriends because she didn't like her.

She didn't like your girlfriends either, remember?

Oh yeah, that was true. He'd thought she was just being Georgie at the time, but maybe not. Maybe there'd been a reason. Just like there was a reason she was so shocked now.

A reason he might be pleased about.

He lifted a brow. "That all you got for me? Just 'oh'?"

Instantly her gaze narrowed, scanning his face in a suspicious fashion. "You can't have *wanted* me to kiss you, come on."

"And why would I not have wanted you to kiss me?"

She blinked again, looking incredulous. "Why not? Because I'm me, Con. I'm like a little sister to you, right?"

He didn't move. Just looked at her. Time for the truth.

"Hate to break it to you, Georgie, but you haven't been a little sister to me for a couple of years."

"A couple of years," she echoed blankly.

Perhaps he should have been more sympathetic about laying all of this on her. Then again, she couldn't keep her head in the sand about everything and certainly not about him. He wasn't here for it.

"A couple of years," he confirmed. "There wasn't a specific day. I just started noticing things about you."

"Things?" Her voice had become sharper. "What things?"

He smiled, which he probably shouldn't have done, but hell, it was satisfying to put her so off balance like this. Especially when she'd done the same to him for years.

"Oh, things like your pretty hair and your gorgeous eyes. The way you smell of sugar and vanilla and cinnamon. Your smile." He didn't look away, letting her see the truth in his gaze. "It wasn't immediate. It wasn't a bolt from the blue or anything like that. Over time I realized that all the things I was noticing about you meant something and what it meant was that I wanted you."

Georgie said nothing, staring at him, her cheeks gone a blazing red.

So, he kept going.

"I didn't want to say anything, because I didn't want to make things difficult between us. And you showed no sign you felt the same way about me. So for two years I locked it down. Then you kissed me, Georgie. Right out of the blue. And so I reckoned it was time to say something."

She was silent, still as a statue.

"You're killing me, kiddo," Con said, because he was at the end of his patience and things had to change between them. "And I need to know how you feel, because if you don't want what I do, then I'm going to have to make some decisions."

CHAPTER FOUR

GEORGIE FELT FROZEN, shock bouncing around inside her and resounding like an echo.

He wanted her. Con Stone, her brother's best friend and the man she'd been crushing on for quite some time now, wanted her.

He'd wanted her *for years*.

She had no idea what to say, while he stood there, so tall and gorgeous despite the stupid apron she'd made him wear, looking at her steadily and calmly as if he hadn't just upended her entire world.

Isn't this what you always secretly wanted, though? That he would finally realize you were a woman?

No. No, she *didn't* want that. That would change what they had, take their relationship into uncharted territory and that had never been what she'd wanted. What she wanted was for him to stay being the big-brother figure he'd always been, while she nursed a secret crush that would forever stay unrequited.

That was safe. That was familiar. That was controllable.

But this wasn't. This wasn't controllable or safe or familiar and she didn't like it one bit.

She tore her gaze away and looked fixedly down at the recipe book on the counter, her cheeks feeling like they were on fire.

He said nothing.

Come on, stop being a coward.

It was true, she *was* being a coward. She'd done nothing but avoid, avoid, avoid, while he'd been up-front and honest.

Then again, talking about this kind of thing had never been easy for her.

Feelings were hard. The intensity of her own mother's longing for her father and the misery she'd projected after he'd told her that there would never be any possibility of a relationship between them had seemed so painful that Georgie never wanted to experience it for herself. Or even talk about it.

Marianne had moped around while they'd lived in Jasper Creek, cycling between pining and being furious. She'd forbidden Georgie to visit him, but her mother's sadness had only made Georgie more curious, and she'd gone to see him anyway.

Mickey had been friendly, but he'd also made it very clear that he didn't want any kind of relationship with her or to forge any sort of bond. Which was fine since he wasn't exactly the world's greatest guy.

But she didn't like the thought that she might have accidentally fallen into the same pattern as her mother, pining for a man who wouldn't ever reciprocate her feelings.

Not that she was pining. She might have had the odd physical feeling or two about him—okay, maybe more than two and maybe she'd even fantasized a few times about what it would be like to kiss him, but nothing more than that.

She'd just…never expected for him to see her in the same way.

"What?" Con murmured. "Got nothing to say?"

She swallowed and fussed with the book. "I don't know what decisions you're talking about."

"Decisions about what to do if you don't feel the same way."

Oh, boy.

Georgie stared hard at the picture of the chocolate cake on the page she had open. Its icing was glossy and delicious looking, and she wanted to eat the whole thing in one go and hopefully drown all these horrible feelings inside her in sweetness.

"It was just a stupid kiss," she said grumpily. "It wasn't a big deal."

"Yeah, it was." His voice had gone quiet, a thread of something intense weaving through it. "It was a big deal to me."

Georgie shut her eyes.

She still didn't know why she'd done it. Why she'd kissed him.

Con had taken her out riding on one of the trails behind his property and they'd had the most perfect day. With a picnic and a visit to the secret waterfall they'd both discovered a couple of months earlier.

She'd been so happy. The weather had been beautiful and she was living with her sisters. And she was with Con, basically her favorite person in the whole world.

At the end of the ride, he'd helped her down off the horse and she'd slid right into his arms. And he'd smiled at her, as if he was pleased to find her there, and it felt like his smile was the icing on the cake of the greatest day ever.

Her heart had given one hard beat and she'd found herself rising up on her tiptoes to kiss him before she could stop herself.

If only it had been a terrible kiss, like the one she'd given Kevin Robert back when she was thirteen as an experiment. All clashing teeth and saliva and tongues, and it had completely grossed her out.

Kissing Con had not grossed her out. Kissing Con had been the opposite.

That kiss had been warm and firm and exciting. Making her knees weak, changing her blood into sparkling champagne, and turning her completely inside out in the best way.

"Why?" she asked into the heavy silence, still staring at the picture of the chocolate cake. "It was only me."

He gave a soft laugh, but there was no amusement in it. "Only you? Georgie, sweetheart, I've been fantasizing about kissing you for years. That's what wanting you means."

You can't minimize this. You can't make it mean nothing.

Her heart was beating way too fast and her palms were getting sweaty.

He wanted her, he really did, and if he hadn't sounded so serious about it, she would have turned around and flung herself at him. But he did sound serious. This meant something to him and now she didn't know what to do, because she hadn't planned on that.

She hadn't planned on anything at all.

Still, she couldn't stand here continuing to give him nothing. This was Con and he was important to her. And he'd been honest so she had to be honest with him.

Taking a breath, she very deliberately closed the recipe book then turned around to face him.

He was still standing there with his arms folded, the material of his T-shirt pulling tight around the hard muscle of his biceps, his steady hazel gaze on hers. He wasn't smiling anymore and she regretted that.

She loved his smile.

"So, what do you want to do?" She tried to make her voice sound level.

"Oh, lots of things. I'd like to take you out on a date and hold your hand. And then I'd like to take you home and kiss you again." Gold glimmered in his eyes. "And then I'd like to take you to bed and make you feel good. And I'd like to keep doing that for as long as we both can stand it."

Heat swept through her and it was all she could do to hold his gaze.

A date. A kiss. Bed. You want that. You want all *of that.*

"But that all depends on you," Con went on in the same tone. "If you don't want me like that then I'm going to have to figure out what to do with myself, because things can't keep going on the way they have."

She swallowed, her mouth dry. She had a feeling she wasn't going to like this. "What do you mean?"

"I mean, I'm going to need some distance." He paused and then added, as if it wasn't obvious. "Some distance from you."

Her stomach dropped away. He could *not* be saying what she thought he was saying. He just couldn't.

"What?" she snapped. "So if I won't sleep with you, you won't see me anymore? Is that what you're saying?"

For the first time his gaze flickered and he looked away. Then he muttered a curse under his breath and abruptly shoved a hand through his hair. "No, shit, that's not what I meant," he said, a hint of a growl in his voice. "I'm not trying to force you into doing something you don't want or manipulate you. Hell, kiddo, that's the last thing I want to do." His hand dropped. "But the last two years have been… difficult. I can handle being told no, but you have to respect that I'm going to have some feelings about it and that I might not be able to see you for a while, okay?"

No, it wasn't okay. None of this was okay.

She didn't want him to have feelings about her and she didn't want to have feelings about him, but most of all, she didn't want him to stop seeing her.

Too late. Things are changing and there's nothing you can do to stop them.

It was true, she couldn't. Just like she couldn't tell herself that all of this was *entirely* unwelcome. Because if it had been unwelcome, she wouldn't be feeling so weird and nervous and afraid about it. She'd just tell him she didn't feel the same way and to handle himself.

But it wasn't unwelcome and she wasn't indifferent. It was the opposite in fact. She'd had…thoughts about him. Kissing thoughts. One might even go so far as to say there had been fantasies about more than kissing, that she never thought about during the day because they felt kind of wrong and certainly just a bit…dirty.

Stop being so damn missish.

God. Yes. Okay. She'd had dirty thoughts about Con. So sue her.

"Georgie." Con's gaze burned with something that made her heart skip a beat. "Give me something here."

She opened her mouth, to say what she didn't know, then the door to the yard opened all of a sudden and Joey stuck her head around it. She scanned around the room, oblivious to the tension filling it, then her violet eyes lit up as she saw Con.

Georgie had never talked about Con to her sisters. When she'd been a kid, that had been because he'd felt private to her and special, and she hadn't wanted to share him with anyone. Then, as they'd grown into adults, there had been other reasons she hadn't mentioned him. Reasons that were mostly to do with not wanting to be teased about him.

"Oh hey, Teddy said there was a man here. Can I borrow you for a sec?"

Con shifted, the tension draining from his face and he turned, giving Joey his trademark charming smile. "Sure, what do you need?"

Joey came into the kitchen, holding out her hand. "I'm Joey by the way. Yes, another sister."

"I figured." Con took Joey's hand and gave it a shake. "I'm Con. Friend of Georgie's."

"Oh, a 'friend'?" Joey glanced meaningfully at Georgie and Georgie could just about see the quotation marks Joey had put around the word. "Good to know. Nice apron by the way."

"Thanks." Con's smile was easy, but his voice wasn't. "Georgie insisted."

Joey, still oblivious to his tone or maybe just ignoring it, dropped his hand. "Yeah, she's like that. So there's a rock out in the yard I need help moving. If you could just shift it out of the way, I'd be grateful."

"A rock, huh?"

"Yep." Joey's smile was way too big to be natural, which meant she was planning something. "A big-ass one. Getting in the way of my beans."

"Beans," Con echoed, his gaze narrowing slightly. "Right. And where is this rock?"

"Head out that door and look to the left. I've got a vegetable garden there and the rock's sitting in the middle of it. You can't miss it."

As she spoke, Jasper Junie, the little stray cat that the sisters had adopted, made a beeline for Con and began winding herself around his legs as if he was some long-lost friend she'd been pining away for.

The cat knows what's up.

Bah. The cat was a cat. It didn't know anything. And she sure as hell was not *pining*.

Con gave her a glance, his gaze opaque. "Are cats allowed in the kitchen?"

"No," Georgie said, which was a total lie because she allowed Jasper Junie liberties she didn't allow Teddy's chickens. But she wasn't in the mood right now for disobedient avians or traitorous felines.

Con bent and scooped the cat up in his arms. "Fine. I'll take her out and go deal with this rock."

He gave the cat a quick stroke, then strode out of the kitchen as if he couldn't wait to leave.

Oh hell. She'd really made a mess of the whole situation, hadn't she?

Then again, if he hadn't come in here with his dumb confession, then the only mess she'd have to deal with was an excess of chicken feathers.

He only said it because you kissed him.

Ugh. She really had to stop thinking about that kiss.

Georgie folded her arms over her strangely aching heart and pinned her sister with a suspicious look. "Moving a rock, huh?"

Joey held up her hands. "Hey, there actually is a rock, okay? But also, I wanted to check out the dude."

Of course she did.

"He's just a friend."

"Sure." Joey nodded knowingly. "That's why you gave me a filthy look when I shook his hand. Because he's 'just a friend.'"

Georgie blushed, which was aggravating. "I did not."

Her sister only grinned. "You were a little jealous, admit it. You don't like anyone stepping to your man."

"First of all," Georgie waved a finger in the air, "he's not my man and second, no one is stepping anywhere."

"Well, if he isn't, then he should be," Joey said in her usual blunt way. "How come you never mentioned him before? He's hot."

She's not wrong.

No, she wasn't. Con was hot. Very hot. Scalding hot even. Except something inside her found it difficult to admit it out loud, so she turned away, busying herself with her recipe book yet again.

"I never mentioned him because the subject never came up." She turned the page of the book with a little more briskness than strictly necessary. "And I guess he's okay. If you like that sort of thing."

Joey came over to the counter and stood beside her, looking down at the recipe book for a second. Then she murmured, "I kind of like that sort of thing."

The page Georgie was in the process of turning ripped nearly clean through.

"Men," her sister said sympathetically and with some amusement. "You know I'm only teasing you. I'm all about Hollis at the moment."

Of course, Joey was all about Hollis. She couldn't say a sentence at the moment without mention the damn man, and fair enough, Hollis was a good-looking guy. For a cowboy.

You like a cowboy.

She shut her eyes. This was ridiculous. *She* was ridiculous. She had to get a handle on herself and start dealing with this situation, because it wasn't going to go away no matter how hard she wished it did.

"You want to talk about it?" Joey asked.

Georgie's heart felt tight. She wasn't used to having other women to talk to about stuff like this, especially stuff that concerned men, but if she was going to start dealing, then she needed some advice. And Joey was, after all, no longer a maiden spinster.

She let out a breath and turned to face her sister. "Con's my brother's best friend and he's kind of been around for most of my life. And I... I kissed him a few weeks back. I didn't mean to, it just happened. And I guess I've been avoiding him ever since."

Joey gave her a grin full of warm sympathy. "Who wouldn't?"

"Yeah, well, he's here because apparently he's tired of me avoiding him and wants to talk about the whole kiss thing."

Joey leaned her hip against the counter. "I guess he was into it then?"

You're killing me, kiddo...

"Yes." Her voice sounded hoarse. "At least he said he was."

"That's a good start. What about you? Do you want him?"

Georgie sighed, the strange knotted lump of feelings sitting like a stone inside her. Emotions were difficult, but her physical feelings about Con were not. In fact, they were pretty simple.

"Yes," she said slowly, trying it out for size, because she hadn't ever said it aloud to anyone before. "I...think I do."

It felt like a dangerous thing to say, the words sitting heavily in the quiet kitchen air.

Joey only grinned and gave her a little punch on the arm. "Hey, you said it. Go you."

"Gee thanks," Georgie muttered.

"Okay, so now my suggestion would be to sleep with him," Joey went on, holding up a hand as if she expected

Georgie to protest. "It's really the best solution. Take it from me."

A scalding rush of heat went through her and she blinked at the countertop, her heart beating very fast. "What do you mean sleep with him?"

"Georgie, when a man and a woman love each other very much—"

"I don't love him!" she squawked, the heat inside her climbing higher. "And that's not what I meant."

"Okay, Okay. Seriously, he wants you and you want him, so what's stopping you from uh…trying before you buy?"

Georgie just about spontaneously combusted at the thought of "trying before you buy," her brain helpfully providing her with a couple of interesting images to go along with Joey's suggestion.

She's got a point. You could totally do that.

Her skin got all prickly, her breath getting short.

Well…she could, couldn't she? He wanted her, he'd been very clear about that, and she *did* want him. And sure, it would be changing things, but hadn't they changed already? She'd kissed him. That had crossed a line and it was obvious that it wasn't a line she could cross back over again. Con wasn't going to let her.

If you're going to go, go big and go hard.

A shiver swept through her. Con was certainly big and she'd bet her favorite mixer that he'd be hard also.

"I moved the rock." Con's voice came from the kitchen doorway. "Let me know if there are any more you need moving."

"Think about it," Joey murmured, before pushing herself away from the counter.

Oh, she was thinking about it. She was definitely thinking about it.

"Hey, thanks," Joey said from behind her, obviously to Con. "I appreciate it."

"No problem."

Slowly, Georgie closed the book, hiding evidence of the ripped page as she turned Joey's suggestion over in her head.

Really, it came down to two choices. Either she followed up on this attraction between them, or she didn't. And if she didn't…what? Con wouldn't come around so much, which would be one way of dealing with their attraction. But then she wouldn't see him as often and having too much Con in her life was one thing, but not having him at all? Yeah, she wasn't sure that was any better. In fact, she was pretty sure it was worse.

"Hey, what's out in that barn?" Con asked.

"An old commercial kitchen that used to serve the farmhands here," Georgie said absently, still turning the idea of sleeping with Con around in her head. "Joey thinks it could be a good place to start baking properly."

"That sounds great. You need a bigger space if you want to make baking your business." He paused. "You still want to do that, right?"

"Of course." Thoughts in her head whirled. She needed to talk to him, tell him that she might want to bypass the whole dating scenario and get straight to the good bits. Because really, did they need to date? She knew him already and he knew her.

One thing was for sure. She couldn't talk to him here, not with her sisters popping in every time they needed something or just to eavesdrop.

They needed some privacy.

Georgie thought for a moment, glancing toward the

kitchen range that was adequate but really needed a double oven.

The kitchen at Con's house had a double oven.

Her heart began to beat even faster, adrenaline pumping through her. Crossing this line was the hardest part, but hey, if it didn't work out they could go back to being friends, right? It wasn't irrevocable. She didn't know much about sex, it was true, or at least she knew all about it, just had no personal experience. But Joey had said it like it was no biggie so maybe it wasn't.

Con was looking at her, frowning slightly. "You look like you want to announce something."

"I do." Georgie stepped away from the counter. "Can I use the kitchen at your place to do some baking? It's got a great double oven."

A look of surprise crossed his face. "You want to go to my place?"

"Yes." Georgie folded her arms and gave him a very direct look. "And then we can continue this discussion. Uninterrupted."

CON STARED BACK, his body already starting to celebrate because that determined look in her violet eyes could only mean one thing: if she wanted uninterrupted time to "continue this discussion" then it was likely because she wasn't completely indifferent to him.

However, that was quite the change of mind, especially when before he'd gone out to move that dumb rock—which had turned out to be not all that big and definitely something Joey could have moved herself—she'd been shocked and kind of upset.

Which he understood, since he'd basically given her an ultimatum.

But what the hell else was he supposed to do? Pretend she meant nothing to him? That being around her wasn't difficult and he didn't feel a thing?

That wasn't happening. If she didn't want him then he had to know so he could deal with himself and his recalcitrant heart. And that had to be away from her. It didn't mean he'd never see her again, it was just that he'd need some distance.

Still wasn't entirely fair on her.

Too bad. He wasn't feeling entirely fair. He'd been wrestling with these feelings for a couple of years now and he was over it.

If she didn't want him, that was fine, but she had to respect that he wasn't going to be happy about it.

"What changed?" He tried not to sound too belligerent about it since he really did want her to come back to his place. "You didn't seem that interested in talking about it before."

"Yes, well, I'm interested now."

He gave her a narrow look. "Because I told you I might need some space if you don't feel the same way?"

"I don't like ultimatums as a rule and that was definitely an ultimatum. But I get it. And I do respect it, even if I don't like it." She sniffed. "That's not why I changed my mind though."

That was something.

"Then why?"

"I'll tell you later." She lifted a brow. "Are we going to your house or not?"

Why are you arguing? Wasn't this what you wanted?

Yeah, it was. And since it was obvious she wasn't going to talk to him here, getting her back to his place ASAP could only be in his interests.

Besides, he liked her being at his house. It had been quite run-down when he'd inherited it and he'd put a lot of time and money into doing the place up. And yes, he'd probably spent more money than was strictly necessary on his kitchen, mostly in the hope it would lure Georgie up to the ranch more.

A kitchen you don't even use, you damn idiot.

Cooking and baking weren't his forte. He could feed himself—he wasn't that much of an idiot—but he couldn't do what Georgie did. And he couldn't lie to himself. When he was doing up his kitchen, he'd pictured her in it, small and blonde and wearing an apron. Filling his house with the warm scent of sugar and cinnamon, or baking bread. Making a mess of his countertops and spilling flour on his floor. Giving him one of her rare, precious smiles when she presented the products of her labor.

Food was caring for Georgie and he'd always known that. It was how she took care of people, the way the first thing she did when she'd met him was to bake him cookies to take home with him, even though he didn't have a home.

His mother had barely cooked meals let alone baked anything, and as far as taking care of him was concerned, the extent of her care was clothing him in hand-me-downs from friends, enrolling him haphazardly in school when she remembered, and sometimes letting him play at a playground if he was lucky.

It wasn't until Georgie that he'd even known what being cared for meant.

She'd never said it out loud, because Georgie and feelings didn't mix, but every time he'd come around, she had something to give him. Cookies. Cinnamon rolls. Cake. Soufflés…

Her baking had gotten better and better after that first batch of cookies, until she wasn't baking treats for him any longer, but putting together her own recipes and using him to taste test her experiments, as if his opinion mattered to her. He'd never had that before either. His mother certainly hadn't wanted to know what he thought when she'd taken off to Portland, leaving him on the side of the road with only a duffel full of clothes and her cell number in case of emergencies, her duty as a mother done.

They both knew that she didn't want him to call and that he wouldn't call even if there was an emergency.

And he hadn't called. Not once in the fifteen years she'd been gone. She'd called him a couple of times, but that was it.

So no, the only person who'd ever been interested in his opinion had been Georgie. Even though he'd known nothing about baking or how things were supposed to taste, Georgie still asked him, as if his words had weight and meaning to her.

So of course when he'd designed his kitchen, he'd done it with her in mind. And was he going to refuse her when she asked to bake in it?

Hell no.

"Okay," he said mildly. "You want this discussion in private, then let's get us some privacy. Bring your stuff and let's go."

Georgie frowned. "I'll need to bring Matilda."

"Matilda?" Con took a surreptitious glance around in case she was talking about yet another animal.

"My cake mixer," she clarified. "Oh, and I'll need all my ingredients."

Ah, well, that he could do.

"Okay, not a problem."

"And some of my favorite bowls."

"Fine."

"And I've got a spoon that I like to use, and my baking scales."

Con raised an eyebrow. "Anything else? I'm not sure I have room in my truck." He had plenty of room in his truck. He just wanted to tease her.

On cue, she gave him a scowl then moved over to where she had the dough rising on the counter and grabbed the bowl. "We'll need a box to put everything in."

A box was found and ten minutes later, the ingredients loaded, including her precious implements. There was a moment of indecision where Georgie fussed around with Matilda the mixer because she was cradling her dough and wanted to be sure Matilda would make the trip okay. The tray of the truck was *not* adequate.

But then he managed to secure it in the footwell in the cab.

Her sisters came out and watched them interestedly, but Georgie ignored them as she climbed into the cab.

"What are they all looking at?" he asked as she closed the door.

"Probably you." She awkwardly clutched at her bowl as she put her seat belt on.

"Why me?"

"Because they're nosy parkers who want to know what's going on." She clicked her belt on and threw one last look at the assembled sisters. "Come on. Let's go before one of them says something dumb."

"Good luck!" Joey called out as the truck pulled away, giving a thumbs-up.

"Too late," Georgie muttered.

Con eyed her. "Good luck with what?"

Her chin jutted in that stubborn way she had and she was clutching her bowl like it was a small animal. She didn't look at him. "I'll tell you when we get there."

CHAPTER FIVE

CON'S RANCH WAS about twenty minutes out of Jasper Creek and consisted of a cute little wooden farmhouse with a pointed red roof and wide porches set in the middle of rolling green pastures. It was a down-to-earth house, nothing fancy, but practical and solid, and Georgie had always felt comfortable there, even before Con had restored it.

It got a lot of sun and there was a peace to the place, a sense of calm and Georgie could never figure out whether it was the property or had more to do with the man who owned it.

Either way, she liked it.

Especially the kitchen.

It had a fancy new range with a double oven and lots of counter space. The windows looked out over the pastures, so there was lots of light and even a view. A fabulous place to bake in.

Except it was difficult to think of baking as Con helped her unload her stuff from the truck, especially when they were about to have a discussion that would change everything.

She put her bowl of dough down on the gleaming wooden counters in Con's kitchen, very conscious of his tall figure as he carried Matilda in and put the mixer down on another counter nearby.

Okay, so how to approach this? Should she try seducing

him? Then again, she'd never seduced anyone before and had no idea how to go about it, so perhaps not. Perhaps she should come right out and say it.

Joey certainly would. Elliot too was very confident about men—or so she kept saying—so she'd likely have some idea. Even Teddy, who'd been about as experienced as she was, knew more than she did now, considering Beau.

Meh. She should have played around more, gone out and gotten some experience with a starter dude instead of moving straight into the big leagues.

Because Con was definitely the big leagues. He was older, more experienced, hotter than the sun, and really, what was she even thinking?

He wants you, don't forget that. He said you were killing him.

A pulse of heat went through her, making her feel breathless. That was true. He *did* want her. He hadn't been lying when he'd said those things, he genuinely did. Which meant she wasn't exactly starting from scratch here. She did have an advantage.

Con finished with Matilda and turned around to lean back against the counter, watching her speculatively. He was still wearing that stupid apron and he still looked good enough to eat.

His gaze was all golden and he was frowning just a touch, his black brows giving him a slightly hawkish look.

He's looking at you like you're a particularly succulent rabbit.

A shiver went through her as she recognized the heat in his eyes. Or rather, let herself recognize it. Had he looked at her that way before and she'd just never seen? Or had she known exactly but hadn't let herself be aware of it?

Whatever the case was, it made her breath catch.

"So," he said, his voice low. "You wanted to have this discussion without interruptions."

She swallowed. "Yes."

He folded his arms, the look on his face impenetrable. "Then, I've said my piece. The rest of it is up to you."

She wasn't sure why she was so nervous, especially when he'd been very clear about what he'd felt. It was all to do with how things would change, because they would. Once she said it out loud, there would be no going back.

Georgie grabbed her courage and held on tight. "Okay. So, I guess it's my turn then."

He said nothing, just watched her with those hawk eyes of his.

"I am a-attracted to you," she began, stumbling over the words, much to her annoyance. "I mean, that's why I kissed you. So… I was wondering…uh…maybe we could see where that took us?"

His expression had gone even more impassive, giving her no clue at all what he was thinking. "You need to be more explicit, kiddo."

Of course, he'd want her to say it out loud, damn him.

"Okay, fine." She shoved herself away from the counter, her heart beating way too fast for comfort. "I'd like to sleep with you. That explicit enough?"

The gold in his eyes abruptly gleamed bright, like flames, and she could feel an answering heat in herself begin to burn.

Yet he didn't move.

"You'd like to sleep with me," he repeated slowly, as if tasting the words.

"Yes." She lifted her chin. "That a problem for you?"

He shifted against the counter, his expression once again impassive. "Yeah, actually it is."

Oh, for God's sake. Seriously? She'd scraped up all her courage to tell him that and now it was a problem?

She scowled. "Excuse me? What happened to the whole 'you're killing me, kiddo' thing?"

He didn't look away, his stare becoming even more intense. "I don't want you to sleep with me just to keep me from leaving, because if that's the case then thanks, I'll pass."

Okay, it was fair that he'd think that. She'd been avoidant, desperate not to have this particular conversation, and so this would probably seem like an abrupt change of heart.

She gave him a narrow look. "Do you seriously think I'd sleep with you just to get you to stick around?"

"I don't know," he shot back. "Would you?"

"No," she snapped. "I wouldn't."

"Don't get mad at me, kiddo." His stare was uncompromising. "I tell you I can't be around you and suddenly you're offering to sleep with me? Did you really expect me to take the offer?"

Georgie took a step toward him, the thread of annoyance inside her winding tight, which wasn't quite fair of her. Not when she hadn't explained herself completely. "I don't want to sleep with you just to get you to stick around, idiot," she said flatly. "I want to sleep with you, because yes, there's a reason I kissed you and no, it wasn't nothing to me either." She met his fierce gaze. Held it. "I want you too, Con. I know it seems like it's sudden, but believe me it's not. I think I've wanted you for a while, I just…didn't want to admit it. Not even to myself."

The flames in his eyes blazed higher, yet still he didn't move.

"What?" Georgie demanded, getting even more annoyed now, because this was not the reception she'd been hoping for. She'd expected him to maybe look relieved or even close the distance between them and take her in his arms.

She did not expect him to stand there and stare at her.

"Well?" she demanded again. "Aren't you going to say anything? I thought you wanted me."

"And I do." His gaze glittered, something intense there that she hadn't seen before. Something that scared her. "But I don't want to just sleep with you, Georgie. That was never the end goal."

It didn't make any sense. What more did he want?

"What do you mean, the 'end goal'? What the hell is the 'end goal'?"

Con's gaze never moved from her face. He looked hard and uncompromising and fierce. "I want to marry you, kiddo. I want you to be my wife."

IT TOOK ALL his considerable willpower to stay where he was and not close the distance between them. to not drag her into his arms.

Finally, after all these years she'd said the words he'd hoped and dreamed she'd say.

But he couldn't give in, not yet. Because the end goal had never been just sex and it wasn't fair on her to let her assume that it was.

He loved her. He wanted to make her his wife and she had to know that was what his intentions were. Even if it meant her turning around and walking away.

"Your wife?" she repeated, as if the word was strange to her and she had no idea what it meant, her violet eyes darkening into amethyst and going very round.

Maybe he shouldn't have said it so bluntly. Then again, how else could he say it except bluntly? This was important to him, this was vital, because he'd never been a half-measures type of guy.

If he wanted something he wanted *all* of it or he didn't want it at all.

And he wanted all of her. He wanted a family with her, he wanted a home.

Sex was fun and pleasurable, easy come, easy go, but he was tired of it. Sure, he finally had a place of his own, but he was tired of it being empty too.

He was tired of being alone.

He'd never been able to make lasting friendships due to his mother's rootless existence, or even do things normal kids his age would do. Consequently, he was always the new kid, always the outsider.

It had been hard and lonely, and even though Felix had taken him in and given him as much of a family as he'd ever had, he'd never been able to shake the feeling that none of it was his. The house had been Felix's just like Georgie had been Felix's and Con wanted something of his own.

He wanted a home, a place where he belonged, and a family he belonged to, and he wasn't going to accept anything less.

"Yes, that's right," he said. "Sex is great and believe me, if that's all I'd wanted you'd be flat on your back in my bed right now. But that's not all I want. I want something more permanent."

"But…but a wife…" She stopped, her violet eyes still full of shock. "Why?"

A fair question, especially given that his life so far had been more about living in the moment than planning for the future. He was the go-to guy for a good time not a long time, and he was well aware.

But everyone was allowed to change their mind, including him.

"Because I'm sick of coming home to an empty house and an empty bed," he said. "And I'm tired of being alone. I want a family. You and Felix were that for me for a long time and you'll never know how much I appreciated that. But with Felix thinking about leaving Jasper Creek and you making connections with your sisters, I have to think about my own future." He gestured at the house around them. "I have this place and that's a start, but now I want to make it a home, and that means a wife and kids."

Georgie was scowling—so far, so Georgie. "Is this because of Felix? Is this something you two cooked up between you to protect me or something, because if so—"

"No," he interrupted before she could get going, because while he could understand why she thought that since Felix was protective of her, that wasn't the reason. "No, this is my idea. I haven't talked to Felix yet obviously. I wanted to talk to you first."

She was not happy, that was clear, and maybe he'd shot himself in the foot with the whole wife and family thing, but shit, he had to be honest with her before they started anything.

She had to understand he wasn't going to settle for half measures.

"Why me?" she asked after a moment's silence. "Why am I the one you want? You could have any woman, Con. You know all you have to do is snap your fingers and they come running."

In the spirit of staying honest, he should tell her the truth, that he wanted her because he loved her, but she'd had a lot of shocks already and declaring his undying love right now might be a bridge too far.

So all he said was, "I don't want just any woman. I want you."

"Why?" She took another couple of steps toward him. "Because I'm Felix's sister?"

"No. That's not—"

"You just said you wanted a home and a family, and because Felix is leaving you want to create your own. But that's not about me, though, is it?"

Seriously? Did she really think this was more about him creating a family than it was about her?

Isn't it though? If this was really about her, you'd take the time to do this properly.

Con shoved that thought away. He *was* doing this properly. He was being honest with her about what he wanted, and if she wanted to know how much this was about her then he'd tell her.

"It is about you," he said into the sudden silence that had fallen "I love you, Georgie."

Her eyes went very round. "You…love me?"

Con held her gaze, letting her see the truth. "You think this was just about me wanting you? Well, it's not. I've loved you for years, Georgie Hathaway. And I can't think of another woman I want more to be my wife than you."

There was another long silence as she stared at him. "Oh," she breathed after a moment. "Oh…"

"I know," he said, because he had to say something and he wasn't exactly happy about the astonished look on her face no matter what he'd told himself about what he expected. "This is probably kind of a shock. But you have to know this isn't just me randomly deciding to start a family with you because you're the closest available woman."

She looked away at that, folding her arms in what looked

like a protective gesture. Almost as if she wanted to protect herself from him.

He didn't like that one bit. He'd never hurt her, never, and all of this honesty was supposed to prevent that.

His mother hadn't given him any warning when she'd dumped him on the side of the road. He hadn't had any idea what she was planning. She'd taken him out for breakfast and they'd had a nice time, then the next minute he was standing in the street holding his duffel bag and watching her car drive away.

He couldn't do that to Georgie. He couldn't let her think things were okay one minute only to find out the next that they weren't okay in the slightest. She wasn't a person who liked change and he knew that, so it was better she knew everything right from the get-go.

"I'm not telling you this to hurt you," he said into the silence, hating the tension her small figure was radiating. "You know about my childhood and about how my mom left me, without even one goddamn warning. I just wanted to be honest with you."

She said nothing, her attention now on the floor, and rubbed her brow with a hand that shook slightly.

He wanted to close the distance between them, take her in his arms, tell her it was okay, she didn't have to be afraid, he'd take care of everything and spend the rest of his life making her happy.

But he had the feeling she wouldn't welcome that right now so he stayed where he was.

"This is a lot, Con," she said faintly at last. "I was only just trying to figure out why you suddenly want to marry me and now—"

"It's not suddenly," he felt compelled to point out. "I've felt this way for a long time."

"What? The whole love thing?"

A flicker of amusement went through him at the look on her face, which was part shock, part deep suspicion, which was fair. And at least it wasn't absolute horror.

"Yes," he said, "the whole love thing. I wanted you and then I realized that sleeping with you, treating you like just another one-night stand wasn't going to work for me. That it had to be more, because *you* were more. And then I started thinking about what more I wanted and that's when I realized I wanted a family. And I wanted one with you."

Georgie dropped her hand from her brow and looked at him for a long moment, her expression guarded. Then abruptly, she lifted her chin. "Okay, well, since you've been honest with me, I'll be honest with you. I don't know how I feel about this, Con. I haven't thought about families and whatever. I haven't thought about marriage. What I have thought about, though, is you. So what I'm saying is…" She waved her hand in a vague gesture. "Can't we try before we buy so to speak?"

Right, so that wasn't a no. He'd take it.

"Have sex you mean?"

"Yeah." A bit of color tinged her cheeks. "Wouldn't that be okay? I mean, we might not be compatible or something."

Heat gripped him, the memory of that kiss floating through his head. Her perfect mouth, so sweet and hot on his, the warmth and softness of her body melting against him, her arms around his neck…

"We're compatible," he said shortly, trying to stop his body from throwing a celebratory party. "Believe me, I know."

"You might, but I don't." She shoved her hands into her

pockets, looking uncomfortable. "It's not like I've had a lot of experience in that area."

And it's not like he hadn't known that either. Part of him had always been glad that Georgie hadn't shown any interest in anyone. And not just glad, but savagely satisfied by it.

You could be her first. Wouldn't you like that?

The heat inside him deepened, gripping him tighter. Oh yes, he couldn't deny it. He'd love to be her first. He'd love to be the one who showed her what physical pleasure was and how good he could make her feel. And if she hadn't been who she was, he wouldn't have waited two days let alone two years.

But he'd waited this long and he wasn't going to give in just to have sex. He wanted all of it. He wanted everything.

"I could show you," he said quietly. "But I'm not settling for one night and that's all. Not even a couple of nights, or a week, or a month. I want forever, Georgie. That's what I waited for and that's what I want."

She didn't say anything to that, just stood there staring at him.

He knew that this was going to be hard. That she might not be ready. But someone had to make that first move, to break this stalemate that they'd been in, otherwise all there'd be was yet more years of waiting and hoping and wanting.

He'd be in the same place he was back when he'd been a kid and he'd used to watch families at the mall or by a motel pool or in a restaurant. Laughing with each other, the dad ruffling his kids' hair and the mom wiping their faces. Or in a park, having a picnic together, tossing a baseball and playing with the dog.

He'd been so jealous. All he'd wanted was a taste of that kind of stability, that kind of affection. But stability had been a foreign concept to his mom and she'd never been very interested in what he'd wanted.

She'd never been very interested in him period.

Well, he was tired of that and he was tired of waiting. He wanted certainty for his future one way or another.

"I need to go check on a mare in the barn," he said. "Give you some time to think."

Then he turned and left her to it.

CHAPTER SIX

AFTER CON HAD GONE, Georgie was seized by the sudden urge to do something, so she went through the motions of getting her dough out and punching it down. Giving it a bit more of a knead and then finding the tin to put the bread in for its next rise. She greased it then shaped the dough, laying it in the tin. Then she put a cloth over the top so it could rise again.

There were other things she needed to do, like getting the cream ready for the clotting process, not to mention making a start on the pastry for the Danish since it required at least two refrigerations. Everything would have to be timed well in order to be ready at the same time for maximum freshness.

She wanted this to be perfect for her sisters.

Except stupid Con and his stupid marriage idea and his stupid declaration of love was threatening to derail everything.

How could she concentrate on her baking when he'd told her he wanted to marry her, start a family with her? When he'd told her he loved her for God's sake.

Asshole.

Georgie kicked the door of one of the cupboards with the heel of her tennis shoe, allowing herself some very real anger.

She hadn't asked for him to love her, just like she hadn't

asked him to want to make her his wife. And now he was going around making all these…proclamations. Just what did he expect her to do with that? Fall into his arms immediately? Because if so, she kind of had. Except he hadn't wanted "just sex."

What man ever refused "just sex"? Wasn't that the kind they preferred? Certainly all the years she'd known him, that had seemed to be his preference when it came to women.

Apparently, he's changed his mind. Apparently, he now wants you.

Okay, so if she thought about it, she understood why. He'd been on his own ever since his mom had driven off and from what he'd told her about his rootless childhood it made sense that he'd want a family of his own.

Even from the day she'd first met him, when Felix had introduced him and later told her that he'd been left behind by his mother as well, she'd felt a kind of kinship with him. They'd both been abandoned by their parents and she knew what that felt like. So, she'd baked for him, hoping that would make him feel better because baking did that for her.

Ever since then they'd looked out for one another, but was it really her that he loved or was it more that he loved the idea of having a wife and kids?

He'd never known his father after all, and while her own father was a feckless dick, she at least knew who he was and had had at least some contact with him. Her mother called her a couple of times a month at least, while Con was lucky if he spoke to his even twice a year.

So maybe it wasn't so much about her as it was about him tired of being on his own and wanting some permanence and stability in his life.

Why are you so sure it's not because he really does love you?

Why would it be? She'd always been like a little sister to him and while she could kind of handle him wanting her, him being in love with her was a step too far. Oh, she didn't doubt that he loved her in his own way, but it wasn't *love* love. It was more friend/brother type stuff, because she was familiar, because he knew her.

Seriously, he could have any woman in the entire world, so why would he pick her? She was grumpy and prickly and not much interested in anything beyond baking and hanging out with her sisters.

What would she know about being a wife and mother anyway? Her own mom had taken off, abandoning her and Felix, so she had no way of knowing what being a good mom was all about. And as for being a wife…she had no experience with relationships at all and it wasn't as if the relationships she did have were stellar. Her father hadn't been interested in her and even Felix, whom she knew loved her, wanted to leave.

Face it, you're hardly good wife and mother material are you?

There was a tightness in her chest but she ignored it as she glanced out one of the kitchen windows toward the barn where he'd disappeared. Giving her time to think, he'd said. But think about what? Her own shortcomings?

She'd already decided she wanted to sleep with him. It was the marriage thing she was having difficulties with.

The tightness in her chest became an ache, as if her heart didn't agree with that assessment, which was dumb. What did her stupid heart know anyway?

Her heart had thought making contact with her dad was a good idea and it still kept insisting on her calling her mom, even though those conversations tended to always be about Marianne rather than Georgie. She was in Florida now, because it was warm and she'd found some guy who had a nice place "near the beach." It was always "some guy" and it never lasted.

Georgie hadn't wanted to end up like her. Why would you waste your life chasing some guy around? Or even multiple guys? She hadn't gotten it and she still didn't. Love was painful and turned you into a cringing mess, and she wanted no part of that.

So yeah, her heart could stay right out of it. Felix was leaving, it was true, but she wasn't alone. Not now she had her sisters.

But Teddy has Beau and Joey has Hollis. What about if Elliot finds someone? What if you're the only person who doesn't have anyone?

Georgie rubbed absently at her right wrist, where the little tattoo of a rose with a thorny stem was inked. She and her sisters all had a flower there as a declaration of their sisterhood back when they'd turned eighteen. She'd chosen a rose because though roses were beautiful and delicate, they also had thorns, and after all, she *was* rather prickly.

Maybe she should have gotten a hedgehog instead of a flower...

Whatever, she certainly wasn't going to marry Con or anything else just to stop herself from ending up alone. That was a terrible idea.

But still, why did it have to be all or nothing? Why couldn't they have sex and see how it went? He'd mentioned wanting to take her out on a date so what was wrong with that? After all, it wasn't as if she didn't want him or anything, she really did. It was just that going from big brother's best friend to husband was a big leap.

She gave her wrist one last rub then looked out the window again at the barn.

He'd wanted to leave her time to think and now she'd thought. Time to go share those thoughts with him whether he liked it or not.

Georgie went out of the kitchen and out of the house, striding over the field to where the barn stood.

It was traditional looking and painted red, and when she opened the door, the smell of hay and horses greeted her, reminding her of him. Reminding her of all the good things she associated with him. Of warmth and safety and laughter. Of an affection she'd never had to ask for, that had always been given to her and never once been denied.

This is what life could be like with him.

For a second she imagined it, her baking in the commercial kitchen she and her sisters were hopefully going to get going, and him working on the ranch during the day. And then in the afternoon she'd come home and go into the barn to find him with a batch of fresh muffins all wrapped up in a clean dishcloth. He'd smile at her, tell her she was amazing, and then he'd take her in his arms…

Her heart gave a little kick, though she tried to ignore it.

Con was standing over by some stalls, feeding one of the mares an apple. He had his hand on the horse's neck, stroking gently and he was speaking in a low, deep voice, soothing words that washed over Georgie as well.

The mare's head came up sharply as she spotted Georgie, prompting Con to put a gentling hand on her nose. He murmured another couple of words and then turned from the stall.

He didn't say anything, his hazel eyes now more green than gold, and he didn't smile. "What have you decided?" he asked.

Irrationally annoyed at the question, Georgie said, "I've decided you're an ass. You can't lay all this stuff on me and expect me to make a snap decision about the entire course of my life in, like, five minutes. Seriously, Con. You're asking me to respect your feelings, but you're sure as hell not respecting mine."

His brows twitched. Murmuring one last thing to the mare, he stepped away from the stall, that hawkish look settling over his features. "And how am I not respecting your feelings exactly?"

"I told you what I wanted and you said no." She lifted her chin. "Not 'sure, let's talk about it.' Not 'let's have a discussion.' It was just a flat-out no."

His frown turned into a scowl. "I'm not interested in casual, Georgie. I told you that."

"Yeah, I know. But you don't have to be so…absolute about it. Haven't you ever thought of a compromise? It's always your way or the highway."

Con shoved his hands in his pockets. "It's not my way or the highway. I just know what I want."

"Well, I know what I want, too. But *I'm* willing to talk about a compromise."

Con stared at her a long moment, his gaze narrowing. Then eventually, he asked, "What kind of compromise?"

That was unexpected. She hadn't thought he'd even want to discuss it. In which case it was a pity she hadn't actually come up with any options.

Georgie shifted on her feet, trying to come up with something that wasn't giving in entirely, but wasn't dismissing everything he wanted either. "Uh…well, I don't see why we can't…um…at least try getting…you know… physical. You said we were compatible, but I don't know that. I mean if we have…um…sex, maybe afterward you might change your mind about marrying me."

Con's expression was impenetrable. "I'm not going to change my mind. But you might."

"Change my mind about what? You?"

A muscle jumped in the side of his jaw. "You haven't done this before, kiddo. And sex changes things."

"I know that, Con. I'm not stupid."

"I didn't say you were. But it will change our relationship. We won't be able to go back to the way it was before."

This time it was her turn to frown. "Our relationship has already changed. I don't see how sex could change it even more."

Unexpectedly, what looked like reluctant amusement rippled over his features. "Says the virgin…"

Georgie ignored that. "What are you afraid of?"

One corner of his mouth turned up and before she could move, he'd reached out to brush a lock of her hair behind her ear, his fingertips lightly brushing her skin.

The touch made her shiver.

"Maybe I'm afraid of losing you," he said quietly. "Of losing what we have entirely."

Her heart twisted at the wistfulness in his voice, while heat spiraled through her from the effect of his touch. "You won't lose me. Let's just…see what happens."

He didn't move, but tension gathered around him.

So, she closed the last couple of inches between them, tilting her head back so she could look up into his face. He was so tall, so broad, and so very warm. He smelled of sunlight and hay and Con, and she was suddenly desperate for him.

"I don't want to hurt you, Georgie." His voice had taken on a rough edge. "I don't ever want to hurt you."

Her chest felt tight, because that was Con all up. He was strong and protective and he cared, and she'd always loved that about him.

"I know you don't." She lifted her hand and after a second's hesitation, she put her palm on his broad chest, feeling the solidity of hard muscle and the warmth of his skin rising from beneath the cotton. It made her mouth go dry. "And you won't. I promise. I'm stronger than I look."

He was still a moment longer, then he put one hand over hers where it rested on his chest. The heat of his palm on her skin shocked her, but in a really good way. His other hand lifted and cupped her cheek. "What if this is a mistake?"

"But what if it isn't?"

His mouth curved. "You have an answer for everything, don't you?"

"Yes. And I learned that from some asshole cowboy who thinks he knows everything." Her gaze seemed to have gotten stuck on his mouth, on the full curve of his lower lip. She remembered how he'd tasted… "Con," she whispered. "Why don't you stop talking and kiss me?"

He held out a few seconds longer. Then slowly he slid his fingers into her hair, drawing her head back gently, and bent, covering her mouth with his.

IT WAS GOING to be a mistake, Con knew that in his bones. But he could no more have resisted her than he could have resisted breathing.

Her mouth was just the way he remembered from that fleeting kiss weeks ago, warm and sweet. Honey and vanilla and the indefinable, delicious taste that was all Georgie.

He could feel something inside him relax, even at the same time as he felt something else get tight and hot. All the blood in his body had rushed to settle behind the fly of his jeans, an ache that seemed to permeate every part of him.

He closed his hand into a fist, gathering all her hair into it so that she was held, gently still, but more firmly, and then he deepened the kiss, pushing his tongue into her mouth, exploring the heady, intoxicating flavor of her.

She gave a soft moan, her body abruptly melting against him like it had the time before, all soft curves and warmth and sweet, female heat.

He couldn't remember the last time a kiss had managed to get him this hot, this fast.

He couldn't even remember the last time he'd kissed a woman at all.

All those memories, all those other women were gone, vanished beneath Georgie's taste and the feel of her in his arms. Beneath the heat of her body against his and the way she pressed herself against him. The way she kissed him back, inexperienced yet no less demanding.

She might be a virgin but there was no hesitation to her, no holding back either. And this was the heart of her, wasn't it? Not grumpy or prickly, but sweet and warm and generous.

Oh, he wasn't going to be able to hold himself back. Not now.

He hadn't wanted casual and she wasn't wrong, usually it *was* his way or the highway. But she'd been perceptive when she'd asked him what he was afraid of, because it had made him see that no matter what he told himself about stalemates and holding patterns, he *was* afraid. Afraid of breaking things irretrievably between them, of losing the relationship they already had.

Except, she'd been persuasive, his Georgie. He knew it wasn't fair he'd confessed all these things to her and then expected her to have an immediate answer about the direction for the rest of her life. And it was true, if he didn't at least meet her halfway then neither of them would get what they wanted.

That all sounds good. But you were just looking for an excuse to get her into bed.

Sadly, that was also true. Certain parts of his anatomy had decided they were tired of waiting and were steadfastly ignoring what his brain and his logic were trying to tell them.

He'd decided he was going to ignore them too.

Letting go of her hair, he gripped her hips and pulled her harder against him, fitting the soft heat between her thighs to the hard length between his, molding her against him so he could feel the whole of her pressed to him.

She made a hungry sound into his mouth, wriggling against him, making his breath catch hard as desire gripped him by the throat.

"Georgie," he murmured against her mouth, "if you keep doing that I'll have you right here in the hay. And that's not happening."

"I don't mind some hay."

He lifted his head and looked down at her, deeply satisfied by the dazed, almost drunk look on her face. Yeah, he'd put that there. That was all him.

What about this being a mistake?

It probably would be. But that was too late now.

Her face had gone the most delightful shade of pink, her eyes almost dark purple, like pansies. "What's wrong? Did I do something I shouldn't?" Her brow creased. "You better not have changed your mind, Falcon Stone, otherwise I'll be very, very annoyed."

Shit, when she called him Falcon it meant he was in big trouble.

He slid a hand beneath her chin and gripped it, dropping a kiss on her mouth. "No, I haven't changed my mind. But your first time should not be in a barn with the horses."

Georgie gave him a shy smile. "I don't mind."

"Yes, but I do." He let her go only to then sweep her up in his arms and hold her fast against his chest. "I want you in my bedroom, where you belong."

She'd settled against him, her head on his shoulder, and he was very conscious of how right she felt lying there.

You can't let her go after this, and you know it.

The feeling was so strong, so powerful, he was afraid he wouldn't be able to fight it when the time came. Then again, that time wasn't now. Now, he got to hold her as long as he wanted. His arms around her tightened in reaction, keeping her close.

She gave a sigh and relaxed, looking up at him. She didn't speak, but she gave him a smile as if she knew that this was where she belonged too.

Con's heart gave the strangest kick, but he ignored it.

And strode with her out of the barn and toward the house.

CHAPTER SEVEN

GEORGIE HAD NEVER been inside Con's bedroom and she couldn't deny that right now, held in his arms against the hard strength and heat of his chest as he kicked the door shut behind them, she was pretty damn curious.

It was very tidy since Con had always been something of a neat freak, unlike Felix who loathed doing cleaning of any kind.

The room itself sat under the eaves of the house with the giant bed drawn up beneath the windows, the low ceiling giving it a cozy look. There were lots of pillows and a thick comforter in dark blue. The bed frame looked hand-carved out of rustic timber.

Sturdy. Able to withstand any kind of sexy shenanigans.

A quiver of excitement and nervousness wound through her at the thought. Her body felt heavy, a dragging kind of ache between her thighs, and her mouth was tingling from the effects of Con's kiss, the rich flavor of him lying on her tongue.

She caught her breath, risking a glance up at the carved planes and angles of his face. He wasn't smiling now, no longer the easygoing Con she knew. His features had gone hard, tight, as if he was holding himself under the most iron control.

That was her, wasn't it? That was her doing this to him.

Wiping away that easy smile, bringing out the more serious part of his nature. The hungry part...

She shivered. She never thought she'd be thrilled about that, but she was. It made her feel good, made her feel powerful. She hadn't realized how intoxicating it would be to make a man want her like that.

Not just any man. Him.

It felt as if something tolled inside her, like a bell being struck, vibrating through her entire body. A knowledge she'd been running from for a long time, even though a part of her already knew.

There was a reason she hadn't wanted anyone else. Had never looked at anyone. Never even thought about anyone else. And the reason was him.

It was only him. It had *always* been only him.

He's right, sex does change things.

The knowledge crept down through her, a slow growing understanding. This would make things different between them, it would change things irrevocably and she knew it.

She didn't quite know how yet, but it would.

Perhaps you should stop this then.

The thought came as Con deposited her beside the bed then reached for the hem of her sweatshirt. Then it went as he drew it up and over her head. Because she wasn't going to stop this. She couldn't. She didn't want to.

She wanted to know what would happen if they came together in this way. They'd been together through everything else, when she'd had another disappointing meeting with her father and had been sad, when he'd had a pointless call with his mother. Sitting on the couch watching movies and eating popcorn. Playing poker. Feeding him her latest recipe for chocolate cake...

But they'd never done this.

This is the piece of him you've always been missing.

She shivered again at the look in his eyes as he pulled the sweatshirt off and then reached for her T-shirt. And it was true, this was the part of him she'd never seen, the part that he'd never shown her.

The part she hadn't known she'd even wanted until now.

"Wait," she whispered and caught his hands.

He stilled immediately, his gaze pinned to her face. "What? Did I hurt you? Did I frighten you? Georgie—"

"No, it's okay. I just…" She reached for him this time, her hands going to his T-shirt. "I want to do this for you. Can I?"

He was silent a moment, then he let out a shaky sounding breath. "Okay." And then, like a gift, he smiled. "I can't guarantee I'll be able to keep my hands off you before you're finished though."

A little pulse of pleasure went through her at that. She liked the idea of him not being able to hold himself back. She liked it very much.

"I guess I'll have to be fast then," she murmured, gripping the soft cotton hard and then tugging it up.

His eyes had darkened as he lifted his arms, letting her pull the T-shirt up and over his head, though he had to help her since she wasn't that tall.

But then it was done and there was nothing but the expanse of smooth, golden skin stretched over muscle carved by hard, physical work.

Her breath caught. She hadn't realized, not completely, how beautiful he was.

She lifted her hands and touched him, feeling his muscles tense as she let her fingers run over his skin. He was smooth and satiny, and so hot. She swallowed and looked up at him, her fingers drifting down to the cut lines of his abs.

He held himself so still, the tension pouring off him, the sunlight in his eyes darkening into flames.

He looked on edge and very, very hungry.

Thrilled with the effect she was having on him, Georgie rose on her tiptoes and kissed him, letting her hands drift down lower to the buttons on his jeans.

Con made a deep growling sound and suddenly her clothes were somehow lying on the floor along with his, and she was being pressed down on the bed, his naked body settling on hers.

The weight of him was a delicious anchor, the slide of his bare skin on hers, exciting her in a way she hadn't thought possible.

She looked up into his eyes, a taut expression on his face. He was worried for her, she could see that. Concerned as he always was, that she was okay.

Her heart thumped hard in her chest at that concern and she appreciated it. But she didn't need it. Because this was exactly where she wanted to be, she realized. Naked. Beneath him. Surrounded by him and his warmth, by the scent of hay and sunshine and Con. Protected and cared for, because he'd always represented that for her.

That and unconditional acceptance.

Maybe you can do this. Maybe it doesn't matter that you don't know how to be a mother or a wife. He's never walked away from you, not once. Not like your parents did...

It was true. He hadn't. Con had always been there for her no matter what.

"I'm okay," she whispered, since she knew he'd be worried. And then, so he knew, "I want you." And she lifted her arms and wound them around his neck, and brought his mouth down on hers.

The kiss was warm and sweet and it went on for a long

time. Then he groaned and his mouth moved to explore her, his hands stroking, touching.

Pleasure bloomed inside her, beautiful, intricate, and she gasped as he built it, stoking it like it was a fire. His gaze held her fast, so full of heat and hunger, as if she was the only thing in the world worth looking at.

She loved how it made her feel. She loved how *he* made her feel.

He's right, it will change things.

Yes, she knew that now. She understood. And as he dealt with the protection and spread her thighs, settling himself between them, she became aware that it wasn't simply going to change things, it was going to shift the very foundations of who she was.

This magic they were creating between them was the missing piece of herself. The missing piece of their relationship.

He cupped her face between his palms as his weight settled firmly onto her and watched her as he pushed inside her, going slowly, carefully. But it didn't hurt. There was a moment of discomfort and strangeness, but then there was just the feeling of Con inside her. Around her. Everywhere.

She looked into the heat of his gaze, into the gold of his eyes and lost herself as he began to move. As the pleasure became deeper, wider, and there was glory all around.

She couldn't look anywhere but at him. He was her entire world, and he always had been. She'd started baking because of him, he'd given her that gift and he now he was giving her this too.

So she gave it back to him, wrapping her thighs around his waist, moving with him the way he showed her, staring up into his beautiful eyes, letting him see the pleasure he was creating inside her and how amazing it was.

How amazing he was.

"Georgie," he whispered. "Oh, my sweet Georgie."

And then his mouth covered hers and things became a little desperate and feverish, their movements faster, harder. And then finally, he touched her gently where they were joined and everything exploded in a glory of light, pleasure overwhelming her in a great, glorious rush.

And she was lost to it.

Lost to everything but him and the feeling inside her.

The feeling she couldn't run from anymore.

A COUPLE OF hours later, after Con had showed her a few more interesting things in bed, Georgie remembered that she still had some bread dough rising. She gave a little squawk and leapt out of bed, pausing only to fling on his T-shirt as she dashed downstairs to deal with her dough.

Amused, he pulled on his jeans and followed her down to the kitchen, watching as she bustled around turning on the oven and brushing the top of the dough with some milk, before examining the shape of the loaf in the tin.

It was restful, reminding him of all the times he'd done this same thing in the kitchen at her and Felix's house, watching her as she moved around the kitchen, creating magic with sugar and butter.

It felt familiar. It felt like home.

A sense of well-being, of calm had settled down in him and he went over to the fridge and got out a beer. Then he sat down on one of the stools and pulled the tab, taking a sip as he watched her.

This was it. This was what he wanted. Her in his kitchen doing her thing. Filling it with the warm scent of bread. Her, being grumpy and prickly and tutting over her baking. Her, giving him one of her rare and precious smiles.

Her in his bed, holding him inside her, giving him the gift of her warmth and her presence. Drowning him in heat and softness and those rare, deep violet eyes.

She might not feel the same.

The sense of well-being rippled slightly, but he ignored the thought. She hadn't run screaming for the hills yet, a good sign the sex hadn't broken things irretrievably, which was what he'd feared.

In fact, he might go so far as to say she seemed very happy with how things had unfolded up in his bedroom, and that surely had to be positive.

Anyway, right now he was just going to watch her bustle about his kitchen, basking in the pleasant afterglow of the best sex he'd ever had.

Oh, she had been worth the wait. Every second of what had happened between them upstairs in his bed had.

"Do I get to eat any of that?" he asked as she fiddled with the timer on the range.

She flashed him a serious look. "No, that's for my sisters."

He smiled. "You're very serious about your sisters."

"Of course I'm serious about them. I get a little tired of testosterone."

"You didn't seem to be very tired of it just now," he murmured, because he could. Because teasing Georgie was one of his favorite things.

She flushed. "No, but you still can't have any of that bread. It's for Sister Sunday."

Con took another sip of his beer, studying her face. "That's important to you, isn't it?"

She straightened and turned around. "They're my sisters. They're important to me."

"And you're important to them." He put the beer down

on the counter. "You don't have to get everything absolutely perfect, kiddo. You know that, right?"

"I know. But they're worth making an effort for." She gave him a glance, the look in her eyes turning smoky. "I can make you something if you want. Or we could just..."

"We could just what?" He pretended to look puzzled, purely to mess with her.

She obliged by turning pink. "Go back up to bed."

You could keep doing this. You could keep having this. But the more you have of her the more you want, and what if she doesn't want what you do? What if she decides to leave?

A cold feeling wound through him, disturbing the peace of the moment.

He could tell her yes, gather her close again and carry her back up to bed. He could forget about what he promised himself, lose himself instead in exploring every inch of her delectable body. And then maybe come morning she'd decide that one night was enough, that she didn't want more. That she wanted to remain friends.

Then he'd be left with the taste of her in his mouth, the feel of her against his skin, the memory of her heat surrounding him and that's all.

He'd have to let her go and he would, because if she didn't want him that way, he had no choice. But it would hurt. And he was tired of hurting. Tired of always being that kid on the outside with his nose pressed against the glass, looking longingly at all the things he couldn't have.

If she was going to do that to him then it was easier not to have her.

All or nothing. That's the only thing he could do.

"We could," he said quietly. "But—"

"But you want an answer," she interrupted unexpectedly, her violet gaze open and very direct.

He stared at her, a little surprised she'd managed to read him so easily. Then again, why he should be surprised he had no idea, not when she knew him better than just about anyone else alive.

"Yeah," he admitted. "I need to know, Georgie. I told you sex changed things and it does, and I can't—"

"I know," she interrupted for a second time. "Believe me, Con, I know. And you're right, sex does change things. And since you wanted an answer, well, here it is." Her pretty mouth curved in one of her smiles, shy and sweet. "I think… I mean I'm pretty sure that I wouldn't mind being your wife."

Con went very still, a hot, powerful emotion seizing him all of a sudden. Like a fist closing around his chest, squeezing all the air from his lungs. "You will?"

She shifted on her feet, another wave of pink washing over her face, but she didn't look away. "I know it seems like a sudden change of heart, but… Being with you upstairs changed things for me. Like…that was the missing piece of the puzzle and now I can see what the picture is supposed to be." Her smile deepened. "Or maybe like a dough that won't rise until you put some sugar with the yeast to activate it. And then it suddenly rises and you have a beautiful, perfect loaf."

Warmth flooded through him and before he knew what he was doing, he'd put down his beer, crossed the space between them and hauled her into his arms. "Are you really comparing our relationship to a loaf of bread?"

She leaned into him, her palms on his chest. "Hey, I'm a baker so of course. But yes, why not? You've got a great kitchen—"

"That's one word for it."

She hit him on the arm. "Stop that. You know what I

mean. And I do love your house, plus…other things." This time her gaze was very meaningful and even smokier than before.

The hot feeling was spreading through him, making him feel possessive and a little wild. Beneath he could feel the faintest sliver of doubt, but he ignored it, because what was there to be doubtful about? Georgie was here in his arms, agreeing to be his wife and that's what he wanted.

That's exactly what he wanted.

"What other things?" He gathered her close. "Tell me."

"I can do better than that." She gave him a sultry look. "Take me upstairs and I'll show you."

CHAPTER EIGHT

GEORGIE NEARLY BURNED her bread because Con distracted her so much. But she eventually remembered the timer and dragged him with her back downstairs again so she could get the bread out of the oven. It was looking pretty good, despite having left it far too long for its second prove, and she was pleased.

Con sat with her in the kitchen the way he had before, sipping a beer that he shared with her while she went about the process of making the clotted cream.

It was a good feeling to have him here, watching her.

It was a good feeling to know that she'd said yes to him.

Perhaps it was a sudden change of heart for her, but it didn't feel sudden.

Being in his arms had changed things. Had made her aware of what he'd been to her over the years and how the fears she'd had, had never really been about him, but about herself. About whether she had what it took to be what he wanted. Her parents had never seemed like they wanted her, but Con always had. He'd never turned her away. So how could she turn away from him?

Because she did want to be his wife. And now that was not only a likelihood but a certainty, she realized she'd never wanted to be anyone else's, but his.

Felix might have something to say about it since her brother was nothing if not protective of her and always had been, but she wasn't a kid anymore. She was an adult and she could make her own choices.

Con was her choice.

"I'll tell Felix," Con said as she fussed with the cream, obviously reading her mind. "I'll call him tonight."

A burst of warmth went through her. Felix mattered to her and Con wanting to speak to him personally about his intentions felt as if he was respecting both the relationship she had with her brother and the one he had with her.

"Are you sure?" she asked shyly. "I can do it, if you like. He's my brother."

"I'm sure. As his sister you're important to him and I want him to know that you're important to me too."

She blushed. "I suppose if you'd like to, you can do that."

Con grinned, the way he always did when he was teasing her. "Would you be horrified if I asked for his permission?"

A smile tugged at the corners of her mouth too, though she tried not to let it loose. "No."

"Good. Though if he doesn't give it, I'm warning you right now that I'll put you over the back of my horse and ride off with you."

She laughed. "Are you going to ask my sisters too?"

He lifted a shoulder. "Sure, why not? Seems only fair."

"I'd pay good money to see that."

"That can be arranged." His smile faded and he put down his beer, sitting on the stool he'd been lounging on. "Come here," he said quietly.

She walked over to him.

He dug around in the pocket of his jeans and brought out a small box. Then, looking very serious, he opened it with a certain amount of ceremony.

Inside was a delicate ring with the most gorgeous purple stone glittering in it.

Georgie's heart tightened, her throat closing. The ring was the most beautiful thing she'd ever seen.

"It's not a diamond," Con said, reaching for her hand. "But I could get you one if you wanted. I just thought the amethyst was the same color as your eyes and I liked it." With gentle movements, he slid the ring onto her finger.

It fit perfectly.

Tears filmed her vision and she had to blink them away hard. She didn't have any jewelry as a rule—she'd never thought of buying any, truth be told, and she certainly hadn't received any as gifts.

Her brother was great when it came to remembering to get her birthday and Christmas gifts, but they'd always been relentlessly practical.

Con, on the other hand, would get her stuff that wasn't practical in the slightest. Feminine things she secretly loved. Girly candles or bath salts or chocolate.

And apparently amethyst engagement rings the color of her eyes.

She swallowed, trying to find her voice. "I love it. When did you get it?"

"A year ago." He gave her a rueful smile. "I was being optimistic." He brought her knuckles to his mouth and pressed a kiss there. "Are you sure you don't want a diamond? I can afford one, just FYI."

She shook her head. "No. This is perfect." And it was perfect, the gem glittering beautifully on her hand, set off by the platinum band.

"Now it's official," he said softly. "You're mine."

But is he yours?

The thought tugged at the back of her mind, and it seemed ridiculous because of course he was hers. He would be her husband, wouldn't he? And he said he wanted a family, wanted a home. Said that he loved her. That didn't indicate a man who didn't know what he wanted and might take off at any moment.

He might though. If you end up not being what he wanted. After all, your mother left you for a reason...

Georgie shoved that thought aside hard. Her mother left her behind because her mother wanted something that Georgie couldn't give her. She wanted someone to take care of her, to ease whatever pain was in her heart. The mother-daughter bond hadn't been enough, but that wasn't Georgie's fault. That was her mother's. Her mother only wanted what she wanted, she hadn't cared at all about Georgie, but that was okay.

What she and Con had wasn't the same thing. They had a relationship built on mutual respect and a shared history. On friendship.

And most of all, on love.

It had taken her a little while to get there because she'd been running from it a long time. But her days of running were over.

She knew what she wanted now and that was him.

"And you're mine," she murmured back. And kissed him on the mouth, sealing the deal.

CON OFFERED TO make dinner that night, but Georgie wouldn't hear of it, bustling about with the fixings of one of his favorite pasta meals. Since arguing with her was about as successful as arguing with a bull, he left her to it, going out to stand on his porch and call Felix.

His friend wouldn't be thrilled, since he was fiercely protective of his sister and Con's reputation with the ladies was well earned. Still, it had to be done and he certainly wasn't going to let Georgie do it.

He turned to face the pastures where the horses grazed—his horses, his pastures—and allowed himself some satisfaction and contentment. This was going to be good. His mother had done nothing but the bare minimum when it came to bringing him up, feeding him and clothing him, and mostly giving him a roof over his head, even if it was never the same roof. And he'd always had the feeling she resented him in some way, though what he'd done to deserve it, she'd never said and he'd never asked. Nothing he'd done had ever seemed to change her opinion of him though, and eventually he'd given up trying.

By the time she'd left him, her job of bringing him up done, he'd given up trying at everything.

Then he'd met Felix and then Georgie, and both of them had made him realize over the years that there were some things worth trying for.

This place for example. And her.

Always her.

Con reached into his pocket, dug out his phone and called his friend.

"Hey," Felix answered, ever laconic. "What's up?"

"I've got news," Con said. "And you probably won't like it."

"Well, shit. That's a helluva way to announce something."

"Just warning you." He looked out over his pastures. "I'm going to marry Georgie."

There was a silence and Con let it hang there. He wasn't going to make any excuses or overexplain or try to justify. He was going to marry her. The end.

"What?" Felix's voice held no expression whatsoever. "I think you just said that you were going to marry my sister. My baby sister."

"I did," Con said. "I've wanted to marry her for a couple of years now. And before you say anything," he added, because he could hear Felix take a breath to rant. "No, I didn't take advantage of her and I didn't force her into anything. I asked her if she wanted to be my wife and she said she would."

Yeah, you told her what you wanted. But did you ever ask her what she wanted? She'll make you the most wonderful wife, but did you ever think about what kind of husband you'll be for her?

Doubt flickered through him, but he ignored it. The kind of husband he'd be would be the kind that made her happy, bottom line.

"So, what? Do you love her?" Felix demanded.

"Yes," he said without hesitation. "I've been in love with her for years."

"And does she love you?"

Con shifted on his feet, uncomfortable all of a sudden. It was true that she'd never said anything about love, but he knew she loved him. She did. She wouldn't have agreed to marry him otherwise.

"She said yes to my proposal," he said. "She wouldn't have done that if she didn't feel anything for me."

"Right. So, she hasn't said it to you."

He hated he had to admit that. "Not in so many words, no."

"So, she could only be marrying you because she feels she has to." Felix's voice was uncompromising. "You know Georgie, Con. She likes taking care of people and she's always liked taking caring of you."

A cold feeling shifted in Con's gut. She'd said that the sex had been the missing piece of the puzzle, that now she could see the whole picture. And that picture included her being his wife. But she'd never mentioned love.

You didn't ask her either. You just assumed.

The cold doubt deepened. Felix wasn't wrong. Georgie was a caregiver and she'd been caring for him in her own way ever since they'd met. Even those evenings when he'd babysat her, or helped her with her homework, or sneaked her candy from the store, those had been her taking care of him in a way, letting him take care of her because he'd needed someone to look after.

Then there was the care and effort she put into her preparations for her sisters, not to mention the dogged attempts to keep communicating with her no-good parents.

She was loyal and she never gave up on someone.

So was her agreeing to be his wife because she loved him and wanted to be with him? Or was this just another example of her caregiving?

Why would she want to be with you? No one else has...

The doubt became an icy lick of frost deep in his heart.

His father—whoever he was—hadn't bothered to stick around and his mother had made her feelings about him very clear. She'd been biding her time as he'd grown up, waiting for the moment he was a legal adult so she could dump him by the roadside like a piece of trash.

Georgie will never do that, you know it. She'll stick by you forever. Even when you fail to make her happy, which you will because when have you ever made anyone happy?

He tried to ignore the thought. "I know that," he said roughly. "Which is why it's my turn. I'm going to spend my life taking care of her."

"I hope so." Felix's skepticism was clear. "But I don't think that's how it's going to play out, Con."

He gripped his phone hard. "Look, you're thinking about

leaving Jasper Creek, and once you do that, she'll have no one. And I don't want her to be alone. I've got a house, I've got the makings of a successful business, and I want a family. I think—"

"What? You're only marrying her because you don't want her to be alone?"

"Shit, that's not what I'm saying."

"Does she love you?" Felix's voice was hard and flat. "Yes or no."

Something in his chest twisted.

"I don't know," he said at last, unable to give his friend anything but the truth. "I think she does, but—"

"Then you can't marry her," Felix said shortly. "And no, you don't have my blessing."

Con scowled at the pastures he'd been so pleased about not a second before. "I've been in love with her for years, Felix. I don't need your permission to do a single damn thing."

"Then why the hell did you call me?"

Dammit. He had no answer to that so he said nothing.

There was a silence, then Felix said, his voice softening slightly. "Don't make it about you, Con. This is about her and what she wants, not what she thinks would help you. She needs to come first. Our mother didn't give a shit about her, and neither did her father, and she really, really deserves to have someone who does."

"Hey, I give a shit." Yet his voice sounded strangely hollow. He adjusted it. "I'll make sure she never wants for anything. I'll make sure she's happy."

"You know what'll make her happy, Con."

Yeah, he did. Him.

Yet after the phone call had ended and he stood on the

porch, watching the last rays of the sun disappear behind the hills, he couldn't shake that doubt.

Damn Felix and his questions. And damn his own doubts too.

Are you sure this is what she wants? Are you sure you can take care of her the way she should be? Are you sure you can make her happy?

Something inside him clenched hard, all his satisfaction draining away.

Oh, he could make a woman happy. For a pleasant couple of hours. He could give her some satisfaction, make her smile. He was the "here for a good time not a long time" guy. But marriage was forever—or at least the kind of marriage he wanted was—and did he really have what it took to keep a woman happy for the rest of her life? He'd tried with his mother, he really had. By being a good boy and doing what he was told. Always smiling, always happy. But it never mattered what he did. In the end she'd left him on the side of the road.

You'll always be left on the side of the road in the end.

No, shit, this wasn't about him. This was about Georgie and what was best for her.

A soft footstep came from behind him and warm arms snaked around his waist, holding him. "What are you doing out here?"

For some reason, her embrace almost hurt so he gently unwrapped her arms from around him and turned.

She stood behind him, still only dressed in one of his T-shirts, her blond hair hanging over her shoulders. She was smiling, her delicate face full of warmth, making him ache.

"I called Felix," he said, his voice sounding harsh in the night.

Georgie blinked at his tone. "I take it he wasn't impressed?"

"No."

She shrugged. "Well, too bad, right? Like I just told you, I'm an adult. I don't care what he says."

"You might not," Con said, his voice getting rough. "But I do."

She frowned. "You do?"

He couldn't do it, could he? He couldn't let her tie herself to a man even his own best friend had doubted. A man whose own father couldn't even be bothered sticking around for him and whose mother couldn't wait to be rid of him.

How could a man like that make her happy? How could a man like that love her the way she needed to be loved?

Felix was right. He *was* making this all about him. He'd been the one to drag her into this, to sleep with her, demand for her to be his wife, and because she was Georgie and caring, she'd yes to it all.

And that wasn't fair. That wasn't about what she needed. It was all about him.

"He asked me if I loved you," he said roughly. "And I said I did. Then he asked me if you loved me and I didn't have an answer."

Instantly her expression cleared. "Is that all? Of course, I love you, Con. Surely you know that?"

"And are you marrying me because you love me?"

She smiled. "You know I am, you big idiot."

He should have found that a relief, he should have been happy. But he wasn't. Because all he could think about was how this was all about what *he* wanted and *his* dream. He'd never asked her about hers. He'd never thought about whether she wanted to marry a horse rancher and live on a farm. He'd never asked her whether she even wanted to have kids.

And now he was assuming he had the ability to make her happy, when he'd never made anyone happy in his entire life.

At his silence, Georgie's smile disappeared. "Con? What's all this about?"

Tension crawled through him, the need to grab her and not let her go gripping him. But he couldn't.

"Do I make you happy?" he asked instead.

She frowned. "What? Of course you do."

"And is this what you wanted? What you really wanted? Marrying me and living here? Having kids? A family?"

"Yes, absolutely." She took one step forward and lifted a hand, touching his cheek gently, searching his face. "What's going on? Where is all this coming from?"

Her touch burned for some reason and he had to turn away from it. "I don't know if I can do this, kiddo." He had to force the words out. "I don't know if I've got what it takes to make you a good husband."

Her hand dropped away, her expression darkening. "What? That's ridiculous, Con. Why do you think that? Was it something my stupid brother said?"

"No, I just…" He paused, staring into her dark, violet eyes. "All this time I've been thinking about what I want and what I need. But I never stopped to think about what you need."

"That's easy." She reached for him again. "What I need is you."

But he avoided her hand. "Kiddo, listen. You deserve so much. Especially after all the crap you put up with from your mom and your dad. You deserve someone who can make you happy and for the rest of your life, and I…just don't think I can do that."

Her pale brows drew into an abrupt and furious Georgie-scowl. "What on earth are you talking about, Falcon Stone? Of course, you can make me happy. And you have. Ever since I met you."

"But what about in a year? Or two? Or ten? What about in twenty?"

"Con…"

"You take care of so many people, Georgie. And you're so loyal. And you deserve to get something back for that, you deserve someone who can make you happy and not just for a few hours in bed, but forever."

"What?" She'd gone pale. "What are you saying?"

"I think you know." He took a breath. "I can't give that to you. I'm not a guy who can make any woman happy let alone you."

Shock rippled over her face. "Why on earth would you say that? It's crap."

"Really? Then ask my mother how happy I made her. Ask my dad who never even bothered to show up, not even when I was born."

"Your mother was an idiot," Georgie said suddenly, fiercely. "I don't know what was up with her, but it wasn't your fault. And your father didn't deserve you."

"Didn't he though?" Con shot back. "Or did he just decide I wasn't worth the effort?"

"Con—"

"I'm sorry," he said flatly, feeling something in his chest tear straight in two. "I can't marry you, kiddo."

She went even paler. "Why not?"

"Because I'm not husband material. Not for you. You deserve better."

"Better than what?" Anger flared to life in her eyes. "Don't be stupid. You're an amazing man and I love you. I always have. Are you really going to let your parents' bad choices dictate the course of your life?"

"It's not about me, Georgie," he said, unable to hide the edge of bitterness in his voice. "It's about you. It's about you waking up one day wondering what on earth you're doing here with me. And you won't leave, because you're not a quitter. You'll stay, because you're you, and how is that a recipe for anyone's happiness let alone yours? How is that putting you first?"

Her face had gone the color of newly fallen snow. "But Con—"

"I need to go." There was no point playing this scene out any longer than it needed to be. He was done. "I'll see you round, kiddo."

Then he turned on his heel and left.

CHAPTER NINE

GEORGIE WAITED FOR HIM, but he didn't come back.

Her heart ached, everything ached.

He loved her, he'd said, and she believed him. But he hadn't believed her when she'd told him the same thing. He'd thought he couldn't make her happy.

And the worst part of that was she could understand why.

His mother had done a real number on him, and he'd never known his father at all, so no wonder he had doubts.

A pity it was all nonsense.

He was a man who knew what he wanted and went out and got it, and she'd always admired that in him. It was that determination that had gotten him from living in the cabin at her and Felix's to having a horse ranch of his own. Sure, he was a stubborn cuss at times, but this thinking that he'd never make her a good husband was ridiculous.

Hell, if he thought he could treat her like a kid with all that bullshit about her happiness, then he had another think coming.

So, she waited for him. And then she waited more. But after a couple of hours, after the bread had come out of the oven and the cream was chilling in the fridge, she realized that waiting for him wasn't going to work. That he wasn't going to come back at all.

The damn man was probably afraid—men always said self-denying, noble crap when it came to getting out of something they were afraid of doing, and because they didn't want to admit they were afraid. And the stuff Con had spouted at her was definitely a prime example of Grade A self-denying, noble crap.

He wasn't afraid he couldn't make her happy, especially when he knew damn well he'd given her nothing but happiness since the day they'd met.

No, this was fear talking. Cold feet at finally having the future he'd always wanted. She got it though—hell, she was afraid too. Then again, she'd spent years being afraid of what was right in front of her and she was done with that. She'd embraced it so why couldn't he? Why was he hiding it from her?

She wondered if she should go after him, but then decided against it. She was too angry. And so the only choices she had were to wait here at his house until he'd finished having his mantrum, or go home to the farmhouse and her sisters.

It wasn't even a choice.

She called Joey who came in her truck, and didn't ask questions as Georgie loaded in all her gear—at least not until they were back on the road.

"Sooo," Joey said at last, "the sex thing didn't work out?"

Georgie turned her head to the side and looked out the window, trying to hold onto her anger and not the pain inside her, ignoring the tear that ran down the side of her cheek. "No. It didn't."

"Why not? Was he crap in bed?"

If only that were true. Sadly, it wasn't.

"No, the opposite. He... I..." She stopped and cleared her throat. "It's a long story."

Joey was silent a moment. "Do you want to talk about it now?"

"No." Georgie cleared her throat yet again and tried harder to hold on to her anger. "No, I don't."

Her sister put her hand on her thigh and patted her gently. And was silent the rest of the way back to the farmhouse.

Georgie didn't sleep that night. She spent a long time staring at the ceiling in her bedroom before finally getting up and going down into the kitchen, and getting rid of some of her heartache and anger by losing herself in an orgy of baking.

When morning came, her sisters left her alone to bake in peace. No chickens dared to cross the threshold of the kitchen.

She determinedly didn't think of Con as she pulled together the most magnificent high tea ever. She decorated the scrubbed outside table under the pergola with napkins and silverware and the most beautiful teapots and cups. The weather was amazing, with lots of sun but just enough cool in the air to be fresh.

There were raspberry Danishes and scones and homemade raspberry jam, and clotted cream. Exquisite sandwiches and mini quiches. And the chocolate soufflés. Those she ended up weeping over, because of course they reminded her of Con.

Her sisters were gratifyingly amazed when the time came for them all to sit down. Elliot praised the scones and clotted cream lavishly, while Joey pronounced the Danishes excellent. Teddy went into raptures over her soufflés and told Georgie they were the most amazing things she'd ever eaten.

Which of course made Georgie burst into tears yet again.

Instantly her sisters were there and they didn't ask questions or press her for answers. Teddy gave her a comforting hug, while Elliott patted her shoulder and Joey poured her another cup of tea.

"Men," Joey said after a while. "Because it's always a man, isn't it?"

"Oh, not the helpful one," Elliot said in some disgust. "He had good energy I thought."

"He does," Georgie wept, all her anger vanishing and turning into pain. "He does have good energy. He asked me to marry him and I said yes, and then he changed his mind, because he thought he couldn't make me happy and didn't believe I wanted to marry him because I loved him."

"Idiot," muttered Teddy. "That makes exactly zero sense."

"Oh no," Georgie sniffed, wanting to defend said idiot even if he had broken her heart. "If you knew his past, it does make sense. I just don't know how I'm supposed to make him believe it."

"Why should you have to make him believe anything?" There was a look of extreme disapproval on Elliot's face. "If he didn't believe you, that's on him."

Georgie swallowed and wiped her eyes. "I should have gone after him."

"Absolutely not," Joey said definitely. "I'm with Elliot on this. If he wants you, he has to come crawling back like the worm he is."

"Agreed." Teddy looked absurdly fierce and warlike despite her floaty dress. "Of course, he'll have to get through us first."

Georgie sighed. "He's afraid, I think. And I… It's just… He might decide that being afraid is preferable to being with me."

"Look," Joey said, putting another Danish on her plate. "If he doesn't, we'll rope him like an ornery colt and drag him here to make him grovel whether he wants to or not. And then we'll set the chickens on him."

Georgie couldn't help laughing at that, if only in a watery fashion. "You really think I shouldn't go after him?"

"No," Elliot said with some firmness. "Give him a day and then if he doesn't show his face, I say we do what Joey says. And then get Grandpa Jack to threaten him with the shotgun."

"I like the bit with the chickens," Teddy added.

"Me too." Elliott spread some cream on a scone and put it on Georgie's plate. "In the meantime, let's eat more."

So they did. And if her day wasn't exactly what she'd hoped it would be, Georgie knew one thing. Whatever stupid Con decided, it was good to know she wasn't alone. And that she had her sisters and they were here for her no matter what.

CON RODE HIS favorite stallion into the dark, into the hills around his farmhouse. Trying not to think of Georgie. Trying not to think of the bleak look in her eyes as he'd told her he'd changed his mind.

He'd made the right decision, he knew he had. It might not be better for him, but it was certainly better for her. And sure, she might think she was upset now, but she'd soon figure out that she'd had a lucky escape.

She deserved all the happiness in the world and she'd find that happiness eventually. It just wouldn't be with him.

Eventually, he tired out the horse so he rode back and rubbed him down and put him away for the night.

Then he went back to the farmhouse and into the kitchen to get himself a glass of water.

And stopped.

The air was full of the smell of baking bread, but there

was no mixer on the counter. No bowl full of rising dough. No small woman wearing his T-shirt.

No Georgie in his life.

No Georgie anywhere.

That's what you wanted, though. That's what you decided.

Sure, but it wasn't what he wanted. He loved her and he wanted her to be his wife, he just didn't have it in him to make her a good husband.

Yeah and she told you that wasn't the case. That she loved you. So why didn't you believe her?

The doubt he'd felt earlier that evening wrapped around him, gripping him tight, and he didn't know why it was there, because he'd made the decision not to marry her after all and he was fine with that decision.

Putting her happiness first was the most important thing.

But isn't that yet another thing you *decided? Weird how you get to make all the decisions while she gets to make none of them.*

A dull anger burned in his gut, an anger at himself. Yeah, well, he was just trying to look out for her. He had to protect her somehow.

Are you really protecting her? Or is it just yourself?

Con shoved the thought away hard and then went to bed.

HE DIDN'T SLEEP and in the morning the smell of baking bread was still lingering in his kitchen, just as the pain of Georgie's absence was lingering in his heart.

And as he stood there in the kitchen, downing his third cup of coffee in as many hours, he suddenly knew one thing.

That changing his mind hadn't made him feel better. And it hadn't done a damn thing for her, either. In fact, he'd probably made her feel worse. Which seemed a poor reward for everything she'd done for him.

He'd promised Felix he'd put her first, but he hadn't. All he'd done was protect himself at the cost of hurting her.

Because that was true what he'd thought last night. He *was* protecting himself. He'd told himself he didn't have the ability to make her happy based on what? His mother? His absent father?

"Are you really going to let your parents' bad choices dictate the course of your life?"

She'd flung that at him the night before and he hadn't taken it in then, but he was taking it in now. And she was right, that was exactly what he was doing. He was letting their actions and the doubts they'd seeded in him make his choices for him.

Which made this basically about his own fear. His fear that he wasn't enough for her, the way he hadn't been for his mother.

But Georgie was different. She'd never made him feel like he wasn't enough. She made him feel as if he was important and valued, so why would he trust the opinion of two people who'd never made him feel anything but unwanted over that of a woman who'd always made him feel as if he was the most important thing in the world?

A woman who made him feel loved.

He couldn't. And believing anything else made him a coward.

So why are you standing around *here thinking about it? Go after her, you damn idiot.*

He left the remains of his coffee on the counter and he drove his truck at speed straight to the run-down Hathaway farmhouse.

Chickens squawked at him as he followed the sound of

voices around the side of the house to where the patio and pergola were, and there were Georgie and her sisters, along with the remains of her high tea.

She was sitting there with the little cat curled on her lap and a pile of scones in front of her, a sister to the right and left of her. And she was smiling.

He would have thought she might not need him at all, except that her eyes were red.

At the sound of his footstep, four pairs of violet eyes looked in his direction, and silence reigned.

The temperature plunged.

He'd been a tad worried about telling Felix, but now he knew he should have been more worried about telling Georgie's sisters.

Con cleared his throat. "Georgie, can I talk to you?"

She lifted her chin. "No."

"Ready the chickens, Teddy," Joey murmured, not taking her eyes off him. "They can peck his eyes out."

Okay, so they were going to do this her way were they? Good, he was fine with that since clearly his way was a complete and utter failure.

"I'm sorry," he said, not taking his eyes off her. "I was wrong. I treated you really badly last night and I...put a lot of my own stuff onto you. I should have believed you and I'm sorry I didn't. I was afraid, kiddo. I guess... I'm afraid I'm not going to be able to make you happy the way you deserve to be."

"Well, this is awkward," Elliot said. "Shall we leave you guys to have some alone time? Or shall we get Grandpa Jack?"

Georgie looked at him a long moment, then she put the cat down and got to her feet. "I think we need some alone time."

The others melted away, Joey slightly reluctantly, until it was just him and Georgie.

There was a long silence and Con bore it, because hell, he deserved it.

"I love you, Con," she said at last, fiercely, angrily. "You do understand that, don't you?"

"Yes," he forced out. "I do."

"And you know what that means, right? It means I'm going to be here for you through everything." Her violet eyes glowed. "Even when you're being a dick and pushing me away."

"Georgie—"

"Because even if you don't believe in yourself, I do, Falcon Stone."

His heart gave one hard, painful beat.

She was brave, this woman. Brave to put herself out there for him. How could he do any less for her?

"You were right," he said baldly. "About me letting my parents' bad choices dictate my life for me. I told myself a lot of crap about how I couldn't be the husband you deserved, how I couldn't make you happy, but…like I said, I was afraid. Afraid I wouldn't be the husband you need me to be."

She scowled at him. "You're an idiot. I don't need you to be anything but who you already are. You made me happy the day I met you and you have every day since. And yes, it's taken me some time to come around to it, because you're not the only one who was afraid." Her chin lifted in that inimitable Georgie way, challenging him. "But I'm not afraid anymore."

His chest tightened. "Georgie…"

"You're the man who cared for me and made me feel safe." Her scowl disappeared, her violet eyes were full of the warmth and love that was the very heart of her. "You're the man who always accepted me, who always made me feel loved, and what I want is you in my life and you at my side."

His heart kicked before a feeling of pure joy swept through him.

"Then that's where I'll be," he said simply.

Then he walked over to the table, took her in his arms. "Did I tell you how happy you make me, Georgie Hathaway?" he murmured, just before he kissed her.

"No," she said, smiling up at him. "Tell me."

So he did, with a kiss.

And every day after that, for the rest of their lives.

* * * * *

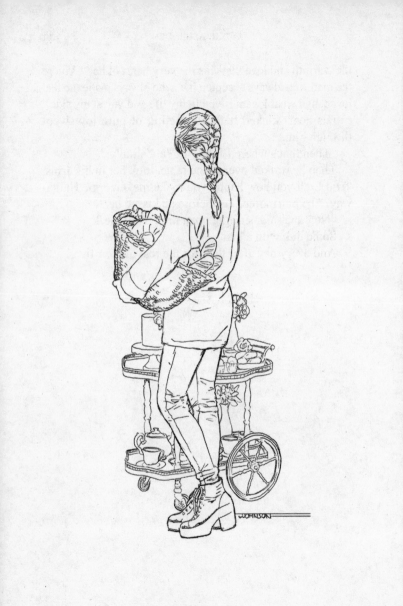

ELLIOT

Caitlin Crews

For Peggy, who should still be here, with all my love.
You are forever missed.

CHAPTER ONE

THE COWBOY NEXT DOOR was pounding on his fences again.

Sadly not a euphemism.

Elliot Hathaway was beginning to think he was doing it *at* her.

She blew out a breath and tried to center herself the way she always did. Clay. Her hands. Whatever the wheel before her brought into being—

But the pounding got loud. Again.

Elliot had been doing her best to ignore it. But every day that the racket went on, she lost a little more of her center. And her cool. And she *hated* losing either—it reminded her a little too strongly of her chaotic childhood. Still, she did not intend to take this kind of daily provocation lying down when her only sin was being a granddaughter of crusty old Jack Hathaway and thus entitled to the land her brand-new pottery studio sat upon.

The land everyone knew Grandpa Jack's too-cowboy-to-live neighbor had been planning to buy himself.

If the remarkably grumpy Colt West wanted a war, well. Elliot was prepared to wade right in, guns blazing.

"Not real guns," she corrected herself out loud, because she didn't need to put that kind of negative energy out there. "Obviously."

She blew an errant strand of her dark hair out of her face as she worked the clay on the wheel before her, her gaze trained out the window on the gorgeous Oregon field that stretched out toward hills bright with spring green. Promising a serenity she wanted very much to feel.

Despite the endless pounding.

Elliot tried to focus on the pretty view. This part of Oregon was very different from Portland, up north, which she supposed was more her home than anywhere else. She'd not only gone to school there but had kept what few things that didn't travel with her in a storage unit on the outskirts of the city after graduation. She'd spent the three years since wandering. Crisscrossing the country from craft fair to kiln seminar to communities of clay enthusiasts, wherever her trusty van could take her.

She'd seen a great many of the country's most beautiful places, but she thought this particular view was her favorite. This sweeping view from this particular spread of land, because it was hers. Or close enough. She and her sisters, all raised apart from each other by their respective mothers— or, in Georgie's case, her half brother—had finally gathered in one place the way they'd dreamed since the day they'd finally met. *This* place, deep green everywhere, with forests on the mountains and fields of rich, fertile earth. Sweeping lines of cherry and plum trees, blossoming pink and white this time of year, marking the one-lane roads that chased clear blue rivers through the valley of pear orchards, vineyards, and meandering fields. Graceful lilacs and plucky jasmine grew everywhere, spilling their sweetness into air that always seemed washed clean and blue.

This was the home Elliot had always secretly wanted.

She'd known it the moment she'd seen it on the first trip her fiercely protective mother had allowed her to take here, to meet her grandfather with the half sisters she'd only just met the previous summer. She'd dreamed of it ever since.

And when she and her sisters had vowed to move here and take over the parts of the land their crotchety old grandfather couldn't handle any longer, she'd been sure that when she drove herself and all her things here, she would *know* that she was home at last.

And she had. That sparkling sense of homecoming had been confirmed when she'd driven down these familiar country roads in the van that had been her world, towing her life and her kiln toward the ramshackle buildings that were hers now. Theirs.

Hers and her sisters' at last.

The old main house might have been falling down, but they'd patched it up with love—and the hands-on craftsmanship they all possessed in their own ways. The barn they'd made the center of their new farm stand business had been a mess before they'd got it into good enough shape to open, but they were still making it prettier and more inviting by the day. And when Elliot wasn't working on the communal projects that made up the heart and soul of Four Sisters Farm, she'd set up her own pottery studio in one of the outbuildings.

Her very first pottery studio. Not mobile. Not removable. A roof overhead and four walls, all hers.

Home sweet home, she liked to think—a lot—every time she looked around at what they'd made here this glorious spring, because it was perfect.

Except for the ornery cowboy right in the middle of it all, hammering away up and down the length of the property line all the freaking time.

And he wasn't very good at whatever he was doing, obviously, because he seemed to need to keep on doing it. All day every day.

Elliot knew the moment the damp mound of clay between her palms surrendered to her mood. It caved in on one side and she took her foot off the pedal of her pottery wheel, sighing.

That was what she got for letting her mind wander instead of connecting to the clay.

She took her time getting up, washing off her hands, and cleaning up her workspace. When she finished, she made herself a huge mug of coffee in her tiny kitchenette, because it might be midafternoon but she'd barely been up for two hours.

She could get up at the crack of dawn like her sisters, but mostly she let her body tell her what it wanted. And she was an artist, meaning she was often a night owl. A slave to the muse—

But the hammering kicked in again then, making her grit her teeth and grip her mug—one she'd made herself, with a pretty blue glaze that reminded her of a few sweet weeks near Chesapeake Bay. She set it down before she crushed it.

Elliot had been ignoring the cowboy problem. Hoping he would go off and do other cowboy things, whatever those were. She had complained about him. She had reenacted various disruptions for her sisters' amusement, but had always claimed it wasn't worth a confrontation.

It felt worth it today.

She wanted to call in the cavalry—because everything was better with her sisters—but the farm existed in a cell service black hole. If she wanted backup she would have to go collect it, and she was ready to deal with Colt West *now*.

And Elliot lived her life to the beat of her instincts, always.

So she didn't dither. She didn't change out of her clay-spattered overalls, pay any attention to the mismatched patterned socks and Birkenstock combo she was rocking, or do anything to the wildly untamed hair that was mostly tied back in one of her ancient bandannas.

She marched out the door of her studio and headed straight for the fences.

It was a lovely early April afternoon outside. And as she walked toward the property line, it was tempting to forget her mission. The birds were singing as if they were competing with each other, the competition somehow creating a chorus that rose and fell with the sunshine, spinning around and around on the breeze. Elliot wanted to sing along with them.

She tilted her face back as she moved, happy to feel the grass beneath her feet and the warmth on her face, as if she was a part of that blue sky.

But as she drew closer to the edge of her grandfather's property, the noise grew louder. There was the usual, ubiquitous pickup parked at an angle beneath the canopy of a leafy tree on the other side of the fence line, but her foe wasn't in it. She scanned the area until she saw the figure responsible for the ruckus.

The cowboy in question had his back to her as she approached, and Elliot came very close to tripping over nothing as she registered what she was looking at.

Colt West, the grumpiest neighbor of all time, was stripped down to his Wranglers.

Elliot about swallowed her tongue.

She had seen Colt before, but it had always been from a distance. Scowling from beneath his Stetson. Cantering about on one of his horses. Peering suspiciously out the windows of his pickup if they passed each other on the same dirt road that led to both their homes.

And somehow, in all those distant not-quite-interactions,

Elliot had somehow missed the fact that the man was smoking hot.

Maybe there was something to all this carrying on with the fences. Someone ought to alert the CrossFit community, because the man was...mouthwatering.

She drifted closer, coming to a stop only when she reached the end of Hathaway land. And she knew it was the end of their land because there was nothing subtle about the fences Colt spent so much time working on.

And then Elliot...just stood there, not sure what her plan was. Maybe she was in shock. It suddenly felt a lot more like summer. That hot. That breathless.

She wondered why, in her lifelong pursuit of the most sublime intersection of form and function, she'd never more closely considered the glory of a male back. Acres of faintly golden skin stretched over an array of hard, long muscles. The way it all seemed to shimmer on its way down to narrow hips, a very fine backside, strong legs, and cowboy boots.

Oh my.

Elliot felt the urge to giggle, and wished her sisters were here with every part of her, so they could partake in this particular moment of awe and wonder.

And sure, if the situations were reversed, she might not take kindly to looking up from her business to find some man gaping at her. Then again, if it was *this* man, she might take to it just fine. She had the sense that Colt West, apparently built rangy and tough and *delicious*, could take it. So she stood there while her heart did profoundly silly things in her chest, taking note of the fact that it appeared her neighbor spent a whole lot of time wandering around shirtless, because he had no farmer's tan to speak of. It seemed critically important that she know this information.

She felt compelled to fan herself, but restrained the urge.

"I told him he was making too much noise," came a voice, and Elliot felt a streak of something it took her a beat to realize was embarrassment. "He always makes too much noise."

Elliot felt exposed then, and looked around a little bit wildly until she found the speaker.

A young girl was sitting in the shadowed pickup truck. She must have watched Elliot walk toward her. And had obviously then also seen Elliot stop still and stare at Colt.

She didn't really believe in embarrassment, because she was opposed to shame, but there was no pretending her cheeks weren't a little red as she gazed at the girl who'd seemingly appeared from nowhere to hang out the rolled-down window of the truck. Elliot decided to blame Colt for that unwelcome response too.

"He spends too much time alone," the girl continued with a measure of stern authority that made Elliot's lips twitch. "I keep telling him that makes him unfit for being around other humans."

The girl leaned out the window, and Elliot revised her initial impression of perhaps a ten-year-old upward to something a little more firmly preteen. Adolescence was clearly coming for this girl, all awkward limbs, dark hair in braids, and a spray of freckles across cheeks still rounded with youth. Everything about her, from her sulky mouth to her intent gaze screamed that she was *on the cusp.* Elliot wanted to sketch her immediately. She reached into the deep pocket of her overalls to pull out her pad. She fished out her favorite pencil from where she'd used it to spear her hair into a messy bun behind the bandanna, and shook the fall of it back as she quickly got her pencil dancing across the paper.

"What you doing?" the girl asked.

"Sketching you."

"...why?"

Elliot looked up to find the girl staring back at her, something like apprehension on her face. But she could see it was mixed in with a painful sort of hope.

And her heart thumped so hard it hurt, because Elliot could remember what that felt like. Poised there between girlhood and womanhood, awkward and unsure, and so desperate to *be something*.

She knew that if she told this girl the truth, that she was absolutely gorgeous in every possible way, the girl would scoff at it. And think Elliot was a liar, which, as she recalled, was the worst thing a person could be when she'd been this girl's age.

"You have a fascinating face," she said instead, matter-of-factly. She leaned onto the fence—noting, despite herself, that it really was expertly constructed because it wasn't flimsy in the least—and turned the pad around so the girl could see it. "See?"

And as she watched, the suspicious look on the girl's face melted away to something like wonder. "That looks like me."

"You have good lines," Elliot told her briskly. "You're lucky, of course. Not everybody does."

It was only when the girl's face cracked wide open into a smile, and Elliot returned it, that she realized something had changed.

It took her moment to work out what.

She could hear the birdsong go straight up toward the sky. She could hear the rustle of the breeze high up in the tree.

There was no noise. No hammering.

And for some reason, a sense of deep foreboding swept

over her, as if the sun had dipped behind a cloud. But Elliot could see that the sky was as bright and blue as ever, stretching from one green mountain range on one side of the valley to the higher, still whitecapped range on the other.

She turned, very slowly, and sure enough, Colt West was staring right at her.

From all of five feet away.

And nothing could possibly have prepared her for the man at close range.

Because he tipped back his Stetson and there was that *chest*, and she felt as if she was tumbling, head over heels, from some great height. When she could feel perfectly well that her feet were on the ground and she was leaning against the fence he'd built. It didn't seem to make a difference.

He was beautiful.

His eyes were dark, his mouth was firm, and she thought she could *feel* his cheekbones beneath her hands like ridges in clay. Or maybe she had never wanted to feel anything quite so badly in her life. And she was famously tactile.

She thought: *this is a man.*

To be distinguished from the great many males of the species she had observed in her time. None of them had claimed their space like Colt West did, as if he was as much a part of the land as the tree that arched above them or the mountains in the distance. He held himself as if he knew exactly who he was and exactly where he stood in the grand sweep of the universe, and looking at him made Elliot feel something like flustered.

Or maybe reckless.

Like he was a different kind of homecoming.

And Elliot had the distinct impression, a lot like a kick to the stomach except much, much hotter, that she would never be the same again.

CHAPTER TWO

THE WOMAN LEANING over the fence waving sketches at his twelve-year-old daughter lived up to every single one of Colt West's dire expectations about the situation next door.

And then some.

He'd known the Hathaways his whole life. Old Jack was a local treasure, though the same could not be said for his son, who had long been notorious in Jasper Creek for his inability to hold his liquor. That he'd also gone to the trouble to impregnate four separate women in the same year, then abandoned them all before all his babies were born, was just insult piled on top of injury. Especially when Colt knew that he, by God, would have done things differently.

Because he had.

Still, there had always been an unspoken agreement that when Jack couldn't handle his land anymore, Colt would take it over. Not only because he was the oldest of the West brothers and would run the family ranch one day. But because Hathaway land ran alongside the part of the West ranch that Colt had claimed as his own when he turned eighteen, so it made sense.

He'd expected it was possible that Jack's no-good son might turn up the way he did sometimes, putting bad pennies to shame. Colt had been prepared for that.

What he had not been prepared for was the influx of the purple-eyed Hathaway sisters—half sisters, but word was they didn't like it when anyone called them *halves*—and all their…ideas. Ideas and a farm stand and enough enthusiasm to stretch the length of the Oregon coast. Twice.

But not a lot of experience. How could there be? They couldn't be a day over twenty-five.

Colt was all for creative approaches to living in rural areas. There were only so many cash crops, after all. His brother Remy's wife worked in town part-time when she wasn't working the spread her grandmother had left for her and Remy to handle, having started with her own coffee cart. Because there was never enough coffee in the Pacific Northwest. His brother Browning's girlfriend and her friends had taken over an otherwise derelict strip of shops right there on Main Street and had made them into sweet little boutiques. Colt might have personally represented old Jasper Creek—all ranching and land, cowboys and country songs—but he wasn't his parents. He knew that the more small businesses around the valley, the better for everyone involved, and he was the very definition of involved, locally speaking.

But he was too much of a rancher not to think that good land ought to stay in the hands of those who would use it properly. And not fall victim to what his mother, the always brusque and to-the-point Annette, like to call *those silly internet fantasies*.

This was Oregon. There was always a little too much eclectic flair in places that would likely benefit from some experience. He supposed it was a good thing that the Hathaway sisters were clearing out that old house that Jack had up and walked away from. Just moved into a smaller house on the property and left the big house to rot. And last Colt had heard tell in town, rumor was the sisters planned to make the equally decrepit old barn into some kind of farm shop—to go along with the roadside stand that had actually had a line of cars in front of it the last time he'd driven that way.

It wasn't that he objected to those things, in and of themselves. It was that he had serious doubts that a bunch of city girls from God knew where, plus one local girl who liked to bake, had the wherewithal to do much more than lounge around taking pictures of things and hash-tagging them—a practice he would happily know nothing about if it weren't for his kid.

The good news about the Hathaway sister in front of him was that Katy seemed more interested in her sketchpad than her cell phone, for once.

That was where the good news stopped, because otherwise, the woman leaning against his fence embodied each and every one of his worst fears.

Colt couldn't remember the last time he'd seen a grown person wearing overalls when not engaged, waist-deep, in farm work. And hers were something. They were white, for one thing, and she looked like she'd rolled around in mud, so there were smears of it everywhere. Even though the overalls were baggy, they swooped down low on the sides, so he could see entirely too much of a sleek, slender body that he wanted to dismiss as weak. But couldn't, because for all his impression of her had been that she was skinny, she wasn't. She was…smooth. Interestingly muscled, not skinny at all.

And he had the disturbing urge to go over and put his hands on the place where the little T-shirt she wore rode up and he could see a swathe of her skin before the waistband of whatever else she was wearing under there.

Settle down, he ordered himself.

And was dimly horrified that he was having this kind

of reaction in the presence of his child. Still, he didn't look over at Katy's enraptured face.

Because he was still too busy looking at the Hathaway sister before him. There was the overalls and the skin on display. Her dark hair was in careless waves down to her shoulders, and as the father of a girl, he was certain that the only brush it had seen of late was her fingers. Something that did not impress him when it was his daughter's head, but which he found…kind of delightfully bohemian on this woman.

Maybe it was because, up close, the punch of those purple eyes was something else.

Colt rubbed a hand over his face and when he looked again—no matter how he tried to concentrate on what appeared to be more mud on her cheek, the bandanna she wore like a hippie headband, and all the other indications that she was pretty much anathema to him in every way—he was caught up in the unsettling sensation that her angular face…clicked into place inside him.

He had no idea what the hell that was, so he turned his gaze on Katy instead.

"What did I tell you about talking to strangers?" he asked, then bit back his grin at his daughter's look of outrage. "Every day since your birth?"

"She's not a stranger, *Dad*," Katy said, in that tone of deep suffering and total outrage that only twelve-year-old girls could produce. "She's a Hathaway."

"Guilty as charged," the woman said, her mouth curving into an edgy sort of shape that he wanted to call a smirk. But it wasn't that. Not quite. Not on such a generous mouth. On her it made her…edible. "I'm Elliot."

"That's a boy's name," Katy told her.

"Clearly not." Colt lifted a brow at his daughter. "Pretty sure I didn't raise you to be rude."

Katy had the grace to look shamed, for all of three seconds. Then she rolled her eyes. "Well, it is."

And Colt bit back a number of responses he wanted to make about his daughter's brand-new attitude this week, courtesy of her mother. As always. Kaylene hadn't set foot in Oregon in twelve years, preferring to spread her brand of misery over the phone the way she had this week, and she retained her title as the biggest mistake of his life. The only mistake, he liked to think. And yet the result of that mistake was Katy, so how could he regret it?

He was used to that particular roller coaster that led exactly nowhere, so he shoved it aside.

Elliot was smiling at his surly preteen as if she was made of unicorns and fairy dust, the way he'd imagined a little girl baby would be while he was nervously awaiting her arrival. He'd since learned that unicorn horns were pointy and fairy dust could be used as a weapon. "It's a fair question," she said. "All of my sisters and I have traditionally male names. I think our mothers felt giving us boys' names was a way of giving us little talismans that could be part of us forever. Everybody can use a little magic, can't they?"

Colt didn't believe in magic. He believed in hard work. Responsibility. Long days filled with necessary labor and commitment, because that was the only thing that brought results. He went to great lengths to instill his beliefs in Katy without treating her the way his father had treated him and his brothers as kids—like indentured servants, on a good day, because Flint West was a hard man and that wasn't even getting into his mother's never-tender touch. But when he looked at his daughter, what he saw was the dawning of unmistakable hero worship.

Stars in her eyes as she gazed at this Elliot of the overalls.

And that was the last thing Katy needed. She already had a mother who had signed away her parental rights at birth, and popped up only once every blue moon to make promises over the phone that she'd then break. The last thing Katy needed was to hero-worship some city girl playing cute little #farmlife games who would only disappear on her when she got bored.

"Come on, cricket," he said, sounding more gruff than he should have. "We still have chores to do."

He, for one, was looking forward to a few more hours of Saturday chores, because he needed to do something to deal with the fever kicking around inside him. He didn't understand it. He took care of his needs pretty regularly, with a few good friends who had as little interest in anything more as he did. He didn't know what to do with the bizarre sensation washing through him at the sight of Elliot that hadn't faded any. Too hot. Too wild. Too…needy.

Edgy and angular, he thought, like that mobile face before him. Violet-eyed and exactly the kind of clever he didn't want in a woman. He was a man who worked with his hands. He liked his women soft. Yielding.

And not covered head-to-toe in mud.

"Are you an artist?" Katy asked Elliot, only the stubborn set of her jaw indicating she'd heard her father at all.

Elliot sent a laughing sort of gaze his way, and Colt hated to admit that speared right through him, all that violet heat. "Not exactly. Or not the way you mean, I think. I'm a ceramicist." But she smiled wide when Katy only stared back at her. "I make pottery." She waved a hand over the front of her overalls. "It's messy. You end up with clay everywhere. But then, if you're lucky and the kiln is kind, a little bit of art, too. The best kind of art, in my opinion. The kind you can use."

"That's my favorite kind too," said Katy, who, to Colt's knowledge, had never expressed a single opinion on the subject of art in her entire twelve years on this planet.

But he loved his kid, even when she was sucking up. So he kept that to himself.

"Do you sell pots and mugs and things in your little farm stand?" he asked, trying to be neighborly. It was harder to do than it should have been, he could admit. Because he didn't have the same driving urge to get any of his other neighbors naked.

That violet gaze flashed and Colt, who went out of his way to avoid drama at every turn, felt it as if she'd scraped her claws down his chest.

Felt it and liked it.

"Our little farm stand," she repeated. "You don't think much of us, do you? You haven't even introduced yourself, but don't let that keep you from minimizing our undertaking over here."

Her voice was light. Friendly, even. Somehow, that made the slap of it worse.

"I'm Katy West," his daughter announced with that great authority she wore with increasing ease and had since she was all of three. "That's my dad. His name is Colt. Because everyone in his family, all my uncles, are named after guns. Welcome to Oregon. Ore-*gun*-ians are everywhere, like pears and Dutch Bros coffee."

Colt shook his head at his daughter. Who ignored him.

"Guns," Elliot said. The way people always did. That violet gaze found his, and he liked it more than he wanted to admit that her eyes seem to be dancing again. "I guess that fits."

"Colt. Smith. Remington. Browning. Parker." Katy listed them all off. Like it was evidence.

"I would have said there weren't that many gun names, so that shows you what I know."

"I didn't realize that everybody went around naming their children thematically," Katy said, frowning. "All I get is Katy. Not short for anything. Just Katy. How boring is that?"

She wasn't asking Colt. He opened his mouth to defend the name her mother had put on her birth certificate in her single maternal act—not that he could now imagine his daughter with any other name—but Elliot was leveling that steady purple gaze of hers on Katy instead.

"It's distinctive," she pronounced. "A woman with a fascinating face needs a distinctive name. Don't you think?"

It was like he didn't exist. And Colt might not have been the kind of ladies' man his brother Browning had notoriously been in his pre-Kit years, but that was definitely not the reaction most women had to him.

Meaning most women actually had a reaction to him.

"Um." Katy was gazing at Elliot, utterly starstruck. "Yes. I do think."

"I agree with you." Elliot straightened from the fence, then sent a flashing sort of smile Colt's way. "Are you going to keep on hammering? All day long, as far as I can tell?"

"Well, I could stop," he drawled. "But you might want to think about whether or not you're really interested in experiencing an actual bull in your china shop. I'm betting not."

There was something about the way she looked at him, then. As if she'd latched on and could see deep inside him, deep into every last corner of his soul. He told himself he was unnerved, but that wasn't the whole story.

Because as far as his sex was concerned, that might as well have been foreplay.

God help him. He was standing in front of his *child*.

"I'm not used to practical reasons for a racket," she was saying. "How interesting."

He believed that she really did find that interesting. "I guess you don't get much of that in…whatever city you came from."

Colt watched as laughter transformed her angular face, taking it from striking to so pretty, it made his chest go tight. "Mostly Portland, though that was years ago. Full-time, I mean. Mostly I travel."

"I love to travel," announced Katy, in a worldly tone, which was pretty rich for a girl who'd never been out of the county.

But Colt was so dazed by Elliot Hathaway he didn't comment on it.

"I have a little van," Elliot told her. "And a cute little trailer. They're both bright green with daffodils painted all over them." She held out one arm so Katy—and he—could see the sprig of daffodils tattooed there, happy and bright. "Like this. I spent the past few years going wherever the wind takes me."

And that was the kick in the face Colt needed. A hard little jolt back to reality, no matter how pretty Elliot was. No matter what *clicked into place* when he looked at her.

He was a West, and so was his daughter. Generations of his family's sweat and tears soaked this land. It wasn't so much that they had roots here—they were simply part of it. A part of the seasons. The green of the spring, the wild blue of summer, the rich brown of fall, the mist and frost of winter. The world turned at will, but the Wests remained.

And Colt didn't consider himself overprotective, but one

thing was for sure. He was not going to let another female mess around with his daughter's heart. He couldn't do much about Hurricane Kaylene, who he knew had no intention of ever coming back to meet the amazing child she'd made. But he certainly didn't need to let his little girl get involved with a substitute version when it was obvious to him the whole thing would end in disappointment.

Because he knew the Hathaway sister experiment was not going to last.

"I'll make an effort not to disturb you any further," he told Elliot, trying to sound as even as he could. "I'm sure your farm stand will continue to be a big hit. Even though it doesn't look like you're doing any farming."

Elliot blinked. "We have bees. And honey. A thousand vegetables. And, not that you deserve it, the best baked goods in the west."

"Sounds great," he said. And he tried real hard to sound like he meant that.

It was harder than it should have been to turn his back on her, toss his tools into the bed of his pickup, then swing behind the wheel. He ignored his daughter's look of outrage as he tipped his hat to his edgy little potter, who aimed that not-quite-a-smirk in his direction, and said nothing.

And still, he felt like she'd said a whole lot with that steady, intense gaze of hers.

So much, in fact, it seemed like her voice followed them all the way home across the fields.

Like the wind that had carried her here, and would take her away again, the very moment she got bored.

The way Colt knew she would.

CHAPTER THREE

THE ANCIENT, YET delightfully *inhabited* kitchen of the main house was buzzing when Elliot tossed open the door and threw herself inside. Her three sisters were already there. Georgie was fussing at the big, oversize antique stove, muttering at her pies. Teddy was talking animatedly, mostly with her hands, to Jasper Junie, the little gray fluff of a cat who'd adopted them. The cat appeared to be replying, which didn't surprise Elliot. Cats were old souls. At the wide, farm-style kitchen table, made of the kind of wood that could tell tales, Joey was frowning down at a tray of starts—tiny little plants in their individual little pots like an egg carton of green things.

Elliot breathed out the way she always did at sights like this, because no matter how involved in their different pursuits they might have been, the Hathaway sisters *belonged*. With each other, if nowhere else. That had been true when they'd met at summer camp at thirteen. It was even truer now that they'd finally made themselves a home.

The kitchen was the heart of things, bright and happy with the spring sunshine pouring in. There was cheerful mismatched pottery everywhere, from the mugs hanging on pegs to the stacks of colorful plates, a showcase of Elliot's favorite blazes from years back. Looking at them all, a march of her memories that she could hold in her hands and make into table settings to feed people she loved, made her glad. Deeply, brightly *glad*.

There were plants everywhere, here in the kitchen and all throughout the house, which fulfilled a need Elliot hadn't even known she'd had. Her thumbs were as black as they came, and she'd never managed to keep a plant alive for more than a few days—no, not even succulents—but that was the beauty of moving in with her sisters. Joey could keep the plants alive. Elliot could enjoy them.

The house always smelled of butter and sugar, thanks to Georgie, who grew crabbier the sweeter the baked goods she produced, which made the rest of them laugh and wonder—to her face—if she hid all her personal sweetness in her cakes.

What I hide in my cakes is arsenic, she'd said once. *For all you know.*

Worth it, Joey had retorted, wolfing down the last slice.

And Teddy was the family's Snow White. First she'd taken in Jasper Junie. Then had come the house chickens. And Teddy was such a ray of light that it was hard to draw any lines when she was so clearly *in love* with every creature that gravitated to her.

Though Elliot felt a line should be drawn at house chickens, plural. To say nothing of the cowboy Teddy had also brought home to Sister Sunday a while back.

But that reminded her of her own cowboy dilemma.

"I just had a run-in with Colt West," she announced, flinging herself into a chair at the table as punctuation.

"With your van, I hope," Georgie muttered from the stove, doing something with a fork to the crust of whatever she was baking.

"He has a fractured energy," Teddy said airily.

"I don't know what that means," Joey said. She looked up from her tray of baby plants. *Starts*, Elliot corrected herself, the way Joey had many times already. "That seems like a lot of words for...he's hot."

"I was tired of all the hammering and fencing nonsense," Elliot told them. "So I went over to ask him to stop. And was confronted with a whole lot of shirtless cowboy."

She was suddenly greeted with what was possibly her most favorite view of all time: three pairs of eyes just like her own, looking back at her. *Purple power*, she liked to call it.

"How shirtless?" Georgie asked.

Joey looked considering. "Are there degrees of shirtlessness?"

"Shirtlessness is less fractured," Teddy agreed.

"Apparently all that hammering has a sculpting effect." Elliot waved a hand as if that could encompass the singular glory of Colt's chest. "I almost swooned."

She'd never felt the slightest bit *swoony* in her life. She'd only said it because it was a hilarious word, in her opinion, and clearly dramatic—except now that she thought about it, she really had felt nothing short of dizzy when she'd looked at that man.

Left to her own devices, she could have looked at him forever.

"Please tell me you did." Teddy clutched Jasper Junie to her chest and the cat purred along, encouraging her. "Please tell me you collapsed in a dead faint but he caught you in his sculpted arms and *carried you away*, waking you only to ravish you with a single, perfect kiss."

"Can a single kiss be ravishing?" Georgie asked.

"I feel sorry for you that you have to ask that question," Teddy retorted.

"Feel free to linger on the sculpted part," Joey said from across the table, a smudge of potting soil on her cheek.

"You all have your heads in the gutter, and frankly, I'm embarrassed," Elliot said loftily, and laughed when Georgie threw a dish towel at her. "I am obviously entirely too mature for swooning ravishment of any kind. I simply had a remarkably adult conversation with our neighbor, that's all. Who happened to be shirtless. And kind of...*gleaming* in the sunshine."

"I would've said he was too grumpy to gleam." Joey sounded almost philosophical. "He's always scowling, isn't he? At us, anyway."

And strangely enough, Elliot, who agreed with this assessment of their neighbor or she wouldn't have stormed over there to confront him, felt the oddest sort of surge inside her at that. Almost as if she wanted to protect the man.

But why would Colt West need protection? Much less from her sisters?

"Is he mean?" Teddy asked, and it was difficult to tell if she found the prospect alarming or exciting. Jasper Junie meowed. "In my head he's like a troll under a bridge, except without a bridge."

"A cowboy troll?" Georgie asked from the stove, with a laugh.

And the very notion of a cowboy troll was so ridiculous that before she even knew it, Elliot had her sketchbook in her hands. She flipped it open so she could sketch out exactly what she thought a cowboy troll should look like. Preferably on a mug. A novelty mug, she thought, Colt's deep voice in her head. For their little stand.

"Who's that?" Joey asked, looking at the picture she'd sketched of Katy West on the facing page.

"His daughter," Elliot said.

Teddy sighed. "That makes any troll tendencies less amusing."

Because they all knew what it was like to have a troll for a father.

"He seemed more cowboy than troll to me," Elliot told them. "And a lot more…normal."

All her sisters nodded with great seriousness, as if any of them had the slightest idea what normal was. And as if Colt West even fit that bill.

It wasn't Sunday, so dinner wasn't one of their sister pageants, the family days they took turns hosting and put on out beneath the wisteria and the fairy lights, because they could. Because they got to decide what their family was, and so far, it was everything Elliot could ever have dreamed. And had dreamed as a lonely only child, forever moving place to place.

Rituals and weekly pageants. Secret languages, projects, and three best friends she happened to be related to, building a life that made them all happy. *Purple power* in every possible way.

And okay, sure, she felt guilty about that. Because it was exactly the opposite kind of life to the one her mother had always wanted for her. Elliot felt a twinge as she sat there, doodling in her sketchbook as Joey told them about the latest improvements she'd made to the doohickey, the funny little vehicle that looked silly, but ran like a dream, thanks to Joey. Festooned with garlands though it might have been. It was a familiar ache, but that didn't make it hurt any less.

Elliot wished that she could be more the daughter her mother had tried so hard to make her. Christine Placer had been, by her telling, a profoundly foolish recent college graduate when she'd met Mickey Hathaway. Met him and succumbed to him in what she had never shied away from calling an unfortunate bout of intense chemistry, so intense that she'd entirely failed to insist upon protection.

Use chemistry for your own ends, Christine had always told her. *Never let it use you.*

I won't, Elliot had vowed, though she'd been all of eight and hadn't the slightest idea what her mother had meant. She thought of her first sight of Colt West and sighed a little. She knew better now.

Christine's parents, having paid for her college education, had taken a dim view of their daughter's determination to keep her baby—which, Elliot's mother was always the first to acknowledge, might have been the determining factor in her doing just that.

Because they didn't approve, Christine had furthermore decided that she would do it all herself.

I won't say that wasn't a foolishness all its own, she had told Elliot more than once. *But at least it was a foolishness born of determination, not idiocy.*

Elliot had always been fiercely committed to determination.

Christine had treated her daughter like they were partners. Friends. She had been honest about everything— sometimes too honest, Elliot reflected, remembering the overly frank discussions her mother had insisted they have when she was young. Christine hadn't believed in *the talk*. She believed in telling her daughter everything she wished she'd known. In detail.

Everything that might have saved her from her own foolishness, that was.

Elliot had taken great pleasure in therefore becoming a great authority on all matters that most girls were years away from learning. She'd used it like currency, every time they moved.

And they always moved. Christine followed work wherever she could find it. Over time, she and her parents had softened towards each other, which had made holidays nicer, but it hadn't changed Christine's take on things any. Elliot had been raised to be wildly independent, captain of her own destiny, and never tied down to the expectations of others.

When Elliot had entered college—paid for entirely by scholarships despite her grandparents' offers of help because, her mother had told her, it was important Elliot understand what a privilege an education was, and more, never feel beholden to others in the getting of it—Christine had decreed her essential duties done. She had spent the past seven years wandering about the world as the mood took her. She ran her own consulting business, was capable of working from anywhere, and delighted in sending Elliot pictures of the many gorgeous destinations she found—not to mention the many lovers she took along the way.

If Elliot was as forthright as she pretended to be—as she aspired to be—she knew she would have made it a little more clear to her mother that as far as she was concerned, she and her sisters were settling down here in Jasper Creek. Not for a season, as Christine seemed to think. Not because Grandpa Jack had health issues. But for good.

But she hadn't. Because she knew Christine wouldn't understand. Not when she'd dedicated the whole of her life to convincing her daughter that roots were chains, settling was sadness, and a person could only be free if she was unfettered by such things as houses, property, or even a hometown.

Christine would pretend otherwise, but Elliot knew that her mother would find her choices not just baffling, but a betrayal.

After dinner, they all sat around the pretty old living room, each of them attending to their favorite craft projects.

Teddy was attempting to actually weave baskets. Georgie was crocheting furiously. Joey was frowning down at a selection of beads as if she could scowl them into earrings.

Elliot was sketching absently, thinking vaguely of what she would work on when she went back into the studio tonight. Cowboy trolls, no doubt. She liked to head back out there when it was late. When the dark seemed to press in all around the outbuildings she'd claimed, thick and deep. Often she would stand outside for some time before she went in to get started, because the stars seem to shine their way inside her. There were so many of them, scattered across the night sky. She'd spent a lot of time lying on the roof of her van in this or that campground, studying constellations, but they were different here. Brighter, somehow.

Privately, Elliot thought the stars knew she was home, and liked to put on a little show for her to make sure she knew it too. No matter what her mother might think of her choices.

She looked down at her pad and flushed, because she hadn't been doodling. Or even drawing one of her sisters, which she liked to do.

Instead, she'd drawn the unmistakable symphony of muscle that was Colt West's back.

She closed her sketchpad.

"I think we should go out," she announced.

"I'm in," Teddy said at once.

Because Teddy's enthusiasm for pretty much anything and everything was one of the many delightful things about her. She would've been equally excited by literally anything else. A card game. A hike. Everything except, maybe, the basket-weaving project before her that looked like a pile of reeds.

"You mean, like, where there are people?" Georgie asked. Grumpily. "*Groups* of people?"

"Not all of us sleep all day," Joey said loftily from where she was shoving piles of brightly-colored beads around. "Some of us have stuff to do and rise at a reasonable hour."

"I let my body decide when I wake up." Elliot shrugged. "Not an alarm."

"Or the sun," Joey retorted. "The thing that rises every day."

"Or when it's afternoon already," Georgie agreed.

"In fairness," Teddy said loyally, "it rains a lot here."

"It's a peak sister thing to go shot for shot, make foolish decisions, and stagger about drunkenly in a group. With lots of fried food and possibly tears over unworthy gentlemen in bathrooms. These are the things dreams and memories are made of." She looked around the room, and three sets of violet eyes looked right back at her. Elliot smiled. "I'll even drive."

And that was how they all ended up piling into her sweet little van not long after. Elliot blared songs they'd used to sing when they were kids who never saw enough of each other, only camp and New Year's back then, careening down unlit country roads in the dark. Elliot sang as loudly she could, her sisters belting out the words along with her like this really, truly was their fight song. Like they were seventeen all over again.

She didn't stop singing as they drove into the actual town part of Jasper Creek, looking extra pretty with all the streetlights on. There was still the faintest bit of blue far above, easing its way out of the sky, but that only made the sweet little town of old brick look that much more perfect.

The main street of town looked like it belonged on a woodcutting. It was an Old West fantasy come to life, with all the preserved brick buildings, graceful facades that whispered of pioneer pasts, while Oregon's soft hills rose all around. Elliot parked the van down by the feed store with a goat statue in front. Then they all piled out and walked up along the street. The restaurants were still open and there were people strolling up and down the sidewalks, taking in the warm spring evening.

The Hathaways walked two by two, as if they'd grown up together and had always walked around like this, linking elbows and telling each other stories. Forever engaged in this conversation of theirs that never ended. And yet Elliot hadn't spent time with her sisters until she was thirteen— which seemed impossible now. If she tried, she was sure she could conjure up memories-that-should-have-been of them all as babies together.

Tonight as they laughed their way down the street, while Teddy told them all stories of beekeeping adventures, Elliot found herself thinking about Colt's daughter. Who was almost the same age she'd been when she'd met these women. Her best friends. Her family. Maybe that was why she remembered so well what it felt like to be Katy's age. Glimmering there in between so many *almosts* it had been difficult to breathe some days.

All along, this had been the dream. All of this time together. Days upon days, with no end in sight. The freedom to truly marinate in each other, at last. And the ability to make up for lost time along the way.

With the added benefit of being grown, which meant they could walk into the Rusty Nail Saloon and order themselves as many rounds of shots as they liked.

Which was exactly one. Just enough tequila to get silly, but not sloppy. Just enough to get them dancing. Well. Not really dancing, because the Hathaway sisters were many things, but coordinated wasn't one of them. The jukebox was playing country music and they claimed their spot on the Saturday night dance floor, laughing almost louder than the music as they swayed in a loose circle, singing along with the lyrics, pretending to try out ridiculous dance moves none of them knew, and generally having a glorious time.

Elliot felt like sunshine by the time she made her way off the dance floor, got herself a glass of water, and found her way to a little space on one wall. She waved at her sisters to indicate she was okay and not in need of any company, and she drank her water while she took in the Saturday night scene.

Daydreaming of sculpted backs and glorious chests all the while.

And when Colt West appeared before her, tragically shirted this time, she didn't react.

Not because he wasn't hot—he was. Oh, he really was. She couldn't say if he was more or less hot than earlier, because he was wearing a button-down plaid shirt, a different pair of jeans, and had foregone his cowboy hat, which meant there was no impediment whatsoever to gazing upon that beautiful face of his.

But it took her a moment to be sure she wasn't just imagining him.

"Struck dumb, are you?" he asked. "I have that effect on women."

And as she watched, he first grinned, then let that grin fade as if it had been chased away.

"I thought I made you up," Elliot confided, feeling sunshiney, and maybe a little bit sparkling, and she knew that she'd danced too much for it to be the tequila.

Colt looked...disarmed. "What?"

"Not in general." Elliot waved a hand. "Generally, I'm aware you exist. But right now it's as if I conjured you from midair."

"I have no idea what you're talking about."

But he didn't say that sternly, as if he thought she was teasing him. Or as if he found her off-putting and strange. Both reactions she would have found perfectly reasonable. Instead, Colt came and leaned against the wall next to her, so he was staring right at her, face-to-face.

Making the whole saloon, twangy music and laughter, fade away.

Elliot had the strangest notion that he wasn't entirely certain why he was there.

"It's okay," Elliot said, trying to sound soothing. "It's different for me. I'm used to the pull of a force greater than me."

"Do you mean…aliens? The Lord? Or are we back to conjuring things, whatever the hell that means?"

Elliot thought of Teddy's lists of questions for the men who asked her out, then. Because a simple litmus test that she'd always had was that no man should treat her as silly. Not what she said, not what she did. And yes, she was perfectly aware that many of the things she did might very naturally be considered silly out here in this world filled with depressingly practical people who had never felt called to rise from their beds in the middle of the night to dance in the light of a harvest moon, simply because it was there.

And because it felt good.

She lived her life by that one rule, and so far, had no regrets.

But it had never occurred to her that a cowboy might come along and look at her with all that laughter dancing in his dark eyes, as if he found her silly in every possible way—but liked it.

The extraordinary thing was that instead of putting her off, that look in his gaze made her want to test it. Pull him outside this bar, here and now, and see what the moonlight might make her do. And better still, what seeing her dance for the sheer pleasure of it might make him do.

And she only realized that she'd lapsed off into a fairly detailed daydream about those things when the way he was looking at her changed.

His gaze went hot. So molten hot she felt her breath catch.

"Listen," he said, and his voice sounded darker. Rougher. "I have a question to ask you, that's all."

"Yes," she replied.

He blinked. "You don't know what I want to ask you."

"I feel like my answer is going to be yes."

Colt looked almost as if that pained him. Maybe it really did, because he straightened from the wall. And though he didn't actually step away from her, it still felt as if he'd suddenly put a whole lot of space between them.

"My daughter likes you," he said, almost stiffly. "A lot."

Elliot nodded sagely. "I'm the kind of woman who inspires a strong reaction. You're either taken with me, or you take against me, usually quite violently." She tipped her head slightly to one side as she regarded him. "Which is it for you?"

"I prefer not to make snap judgments," he said, in what she assumed was a very fatherly tone of voice, all chiding and masculine.

"I'm like cilantro." She lifted a shoulder. "There's no middle ground. You either want to put it on everything or you think it tastes like soap."

"Katy is a good kid," Colt said with a frown. He did not share his feelings on cilantro, the herb of dichotomy and decision. "She's had a rough road. She doesn't have a mother."

And it shocked Elliot straight through to realize that it hadn't even occurred to her to think about the fact that Colt West might very well be married. There she'd been, ogling the man and having a conversation with his preteen daughter, and it had never once crossed her mind to think about the woman who must be involved in that scenario in some form or another. She made a note to complain to Georgie, who surely should have given her more biographical details about Colt than simply his interest in the Hathaway land. And his bad temper.

"I'm so sorry," she said, genuinely, because she honestly couldn't imagine not having her mother. That would be like talking about a world without a sun.

Colt's face set in that way that told her this was a topic he was very used to discussing, and more, had built up a set of rote responses to any possible comments that came his way. She knew that look. She did something similar when talking about her father. Or not talking about him, as the case might be.

"No need to be sorry," Colt told her. Very matter-of-factly. "Her mother's never been around. It was an accidental pregnancy that she carried for me, then she signed over her rights and took off. But every now and again, she likes to call and stir things up. I know she's never going to come back here, but, you know. Katy wants a mother."

"Or," Elliot suggested softly, "she wants to know what's so deficient in her that forced her mother to do something so monstrous as abandon her at birth."

Colt jerked. Then scowled. "She doesn't think that. I

work hard every day of her life to make sure she doesn't think that."

Elliot reached out before she thought it through and took his hands in hers.

She would have reached out to anyone, because she'd inadvertently hurt him and she wanted to offer comfort. It was that simple when she reached out. But then his hands... They were rough and hard. Solid.

And even though she knew that he wasn't particularly hot, temperature-wise, the grip she took of his hands seem to rebound, flashing through her like a lightning storm.

She almost dropped his hands at the shock of it. But she didn't.

Still, she was so taken aback that it took her a moment to get her bearings. And while she tried, his gaze dropped down—incredulous—to where they were touching. Where *she* was touching *him*.

And then rose to hers again, with a whole lot of that lightning back in his eyes.

But she couldn't focus on that. Not yet.

"I can tell how loved she is," Elliot told him, urgently. "It's obvious in how comfortable she is around you. Comfortable enough to act up a little, without any worry about your reaction. You should be proud of that. But I'm guessing you have both of your parents." When he nodded, barely, she smiled. "It's perfectly natural to wonder what it is you did that made a parent go against every natural instinct humans are supposed to have. It's perfectly natural to assume that it must be something in you. And no amount of love in the world can keep you from worrying about those things. Because it's not about who else is loving you. It's that deep down inside you're not sure if you should love yourself, if your own parent couldn't."

"Thanks for that sucker punch," Colt gritted out after a moment, and his hands tightened beneath hers, so that Elliot wasn't entirely sure if he meant the way they were touching, or what she'd said. Or maybe both, she revised, when his dark gaze found hers again. "I don't really want to hear that. Which probably means it's true."

The Elliot Hathaway story, she thought, maybe a little ruefully. But she kept going. "My mother always made it safe, emotionally, for me to feel whatever I wanted to feel about my father. Which is how, over time, what I felt was that it was his loss. She never told me not to feel all those gross things inside me, that really, are nothing more and nothing less than grief. That was a gift."

Colt looked almost stunned, as if she really had punched him. When she'd never laid hands on another person with violent intent in her life. Elliot watched the strong column of his throat as he swallowed, hard. Then he pulled his hands away from hers.

And she had to curl her fingers up tight to keep from reaching out to him again.

"I don't know if you give pottery lessons," he said, and there was that distance again, but she was caught up in all the heat and torment in his gaze. And he was standing like he was facing a firing squad that was all her. "But I'm hoping you do and that you'll teach her. Maybe…not just how to make a mug."

Elliot felt her heart seemed to slip out of place in her chest. "I already told you my answer. Send her over after school someday, and we'll get started."

"Thank you," Colt West said. Almost formally. But he didn't go. He stood there, and Elliot had the distinct impression that he was wrestling with himself. She waited, holding her breath. "What did you think I was going to ask you?"

All the sunshine inside Elliot was threaded through with more complicated weather, now, but still. She could only smile at him. And she made no attempt whatsoever to hide her silliness, or to disguise the things she wanted, fully aware that they were probably written all over her.

"If you want to know that," she said, holding his gaze steadily, because that was who she was, "you can stop by the studio yourself. Not so much after school. More the middle of the night, because that's when I do my best work."

And then she pushed herself away from the wall and walked away from him without looking back.

While she still could.

CHAPTER FOUR

SATURDAY NIGHTS WERE, barring any events or parties or other unforeseen social events, the nights Katy spent with her grandparents. Officially. Unofficially, she slept over there whenever she felt like it. Because when Colt had manned up, sat down with his parents, and told them that he was expecting a baby with a woman who didn't want much to do with him—and better yet, that he intended to raise the baby on his own—they'd told him that family was family and while they didn't intend to raise his daughter for him, they would pitch in.

They'd been true to their word from the start.

Colt knew that Flint had been a hard-ass, growing up. He knew his brothers had different opinions on that and what it had meant for them. But he and Smith were the oldest, and he didn't think it was a coincidence that the two of them had given their lives over to various forms of duty. The ranch, of course. But Smith had spent years in the service. And Colt had thrown himself head over heels into fatherhood.

A duty that might have been hard work, but work he loved. Because he'd taken one look at the tiny little creature the nurses had brought him and fallen madly, wildly, irrevocably in love with her right there. Maybe part of that had been some single-father panic, but who cared? Katy had been his from her first breath, so he made sure that he was hers, too. In every way that mattered.

So maybe he wasn't quite as sympathetic to the plight of his younger brothers as he could have been because of that. Remy had taken himself off when, way back, he and Keira had broken up after she'd finished college. Colt hadn't much seen the point of Remy dramatically cutting off the family to go work old Grandma June Gable's land before she'd died. He'd told Remy that, as often as he could. Browning had alley-catted around most of the state of Oregon, and it was possible Colt might have been a little too hard on him, too. Possibly because his brother's carefree social life had never been available to him. A point Browning's girlfriend Kit had taken upon herself to make to him. More than once. Even the baby of the family, Parker, got away with murder as far as Colt was concerned. He couldn't possibly know what it was like to grow up with the pressures that Colt had shouldered as the eldest son, not to mention the pressures he'd taken upon himself by doing the right thing by his daughter.

Though I feel like I know, Parker liked to say to him. *Since you tell me about it all the freaking time.*

And tonight, he was wide awake at two in the morning when he knew better—a man with a ranch never slept in when there were chores that needed doing—thinking about duty and responsibility and his family not because he wanted to, really. But because the only thing he *wanted* to do was go find Elliot Hathaway.

With those impossible purple eyes of hers that he couldn't get enough of. That little curve in the corner of her lips that he wanted, very badly, to taste.

And the invitation she'd offered that he should not, under any circumstances, be considering.

Yet he couldn't seem to put her out of his head the way he should. Colt never messed around with women. It wasn't worth it. He had no intention of having any kind of serious relationship, because he already had one. With his daughter. Katy came first, always and forever, and the only women he ever got close to not only understood that—after the extensive conversations he had with them on the topic— they tended to have kids of their own. And often complicated exes they needed to work around, meaning they didn't want another man in their lives either. Those were the only women Colt could be sure wouldn't get the wrong idea.

He never dropped by unannounced. There were no surprises, no wild, two a.m. *what-ifs*.

Kaylene had put an end to that. His life was the opposite of messy these days, by design, and he went to great lengths to keep it that way.

There was absolutely no reason he should have found himself driving out across his field in the middle of the night, bumping along the old dirt road, lying to himself about what he was doing.

Just out for a drive, he'd told himself, as if that was a thing he did when he had to be up before dawn.

As if that was a thing he did…ever.

He told himself that he'd misinterpreted what Elliot had said to him in the bar. That it hadn't been an invitation, and even if it was, she didn't mean *tonight*. He told himself that when he drove over, just out here on this random drive with no particular destination, he would find the outbuilding where she did her pottery thing as dark as everything else ought to have been at this hour.

But when he got to the property line, he could see that there were lights blazing. And when he accidentally stopped his pickup, and climbed out of it, he could hear the music.

He told himself he was going to stand here for moment,

that was all. He was going to congratulate himself on his self-control, then head back home to bed.

But he didn't do that.

Colt made his way over to the fence and took a moment to curse himself, because if he hadn't spent quite so much time shoring up the fencing here it would have been a little bit easier to pretend he didn't know what the hell he was doing.

Instead, he had to jump it, like he was still a teenager, and there was no pretending he was doing anything at all but that.

But something changed when he was midair, jumping a fence so he could get near a girl.

Maybe it was the music, floating on the night air. Maybe it was the way she'd looked at him earlier. Too much violet while her hands on his were surprisingly strong and capable.

If asked, Colt would've delivered a lecture on the topic of how he liked softness, but he didn't think he'd ever felt anything as erotic as Elliot Hathaway's callused palms and hands he already knew made pretty things. Whimsical things. As if the best kind of soft was the kind that only came around after hard work.

He told himself to think of Katy, but the truth was, in the twelve years of her existence on this earth, he had never thought about her less than he did just then. Because he knew she was safe. And this was about him.

Colt drew close to those brightly-lit windows, flung open to the night so that anyone happening by could look in— though, to do that, they would have to be deep on Hathaway and West land and that would be pretty foolish—and saw Elliot inside.

She was dancing.

And the half-assed attempt he'd made to shame himself into turning around, going back home, thinking about his daughter and his duties as a father, faded away.

Because the only thing he felt when he looked Elliot Hathaway was heat.

And the fact that he was here, as if she'd called to him so that he could come and witness her spinning around and around inside her studio as if she were made of light, made him feel like a man.

Not that he'd ever considered himself anything else, but there were a lot of things that went before that. Father, first and foremost. Dutiful son. Rancher. Older brother. Local businessman. And on and on and on.

For once he just felt like *Colt*.

Inside her studio she pumped out music and spun around, artless and inelegant, and yet somehow the most graceful, beautiful thing he'd ever seen. Her head was tipped back, her eyes shut, and her arms were high above her head. She was singing along to a song he'd never heard before and she wasn't wearing those overalls. He could see them, tossed aside on one of her pottery wheels. She was barefoot, wearing little boy shorts low on her hips and the kind of bralette that was all about show and not support.

He could see every inch of Elliot Hathaway's sleek, supple form. And he'd been absolutely right about those curves, smooth and muscled, because he could see the definition in those muscles as she moved. He could see the faint roundness of her belly, the swell of her hips. The roundness of her breasts.

Colt understood full well that this was simply who she was. The kind of woman who turned the music up loud and danced for her own pleasure, something he found so unbearably hot that it wasn't clear to him, for a moment, if he'd be able to control the wild heat that flooded straight to his sex.

That little smile was on her face when she wasn't belting out the lyrics. Her hair tumbled all around her, looking dark and wild and begging for him to get his hands in there, deep.

One moment he was watching her, out there in the dark, and the next he was filling up the door frame of the little studio, having thrown the door open like she was already his.

She spun around, and he found himself caught up in all that dizzy, dazzling purple.

The song she was listening to was fading out, and Colt was aware of the heaviness of his own breath. The way his chest heaved. And he thought, *this is a terrible mistake*.

But then Elliot's face cracked wide open with a smile so bright it was as if he'd never seen a shine before. Anywhere.

"You're here," she said, with an unmistakable delight.

Then she ran straight for him, and jumped.

Straight into his arms.

Colt had no choice but to catch her, no choice and no earthly desire but that.

His hands were filled with her then, all that silken glory as she wrapped her arms around his neck and her legs around his waist. And he would never know if she kissed him first, or he kissed her.

Who cared? It was slick, wild.

She tasted like sunshine and wonder, with a touch of sweet, hot woman beneath.

So he dug his hands deep into all that soft, wild hair, took the step or two necessary to get further inside, and then kicked the door shut behind him so he could turn her around, prop her up, and get serious.

Because serious was what Colt did best.

He tugged her hands from his neck and stretched them up over her head, pinning her to the door behind her. Then laughed when she arched against him, pressing her breasts to his chest.

"Is this funny?" she asked, but her eyes danced with laughter, and the way she moved her hips against his made him think that funny or not, this might kill him.

"Only in the way all near-death experiences are funny."

The look she leveled on him then was serious, even if her lips were curved. "Don't worry, Colt. I'll be on my best behavior."

He found himself grinning despite himself. "God, I hope not."

And when he kissed her then, he slowed it down and took his time.

Colt kissed her until she writhed against him, and then he kissed her some more, until she was limp in his arms. Only then did he tear himself away from all that heat and need, like the finest shot of whiskey he'd ever had with a sweet little chaser that made him feel as close to dizzy as he ever had.

He looked around and was delighted to find a little couch against one wall. He carried her over there and tipped them both down, catching himself on his arm so he could hold himself above her. Then he just looked down at her for a minute. The tousled hair, the hot purple gaze. That mouth of hers, swollen from his, and already grinning again. Her hair in its usual tousled state, but now he knew it was all messed up from his fingers, which was another spike of heat straight through him.

"Clay is the way?" he asked.

She frowned at him as if he wasn't speaking her language, then followed the jut of his chin to look down at the T-shirt she had obviously discarded at some point, lying there beside the couch with those words emblazoned across the front.

Elliot nodded. Seriously. "That is my mantra."

"The way to what?"

As he watched, braced there above her, she smiled. It was another one of those heartbreaking, brand-new-dawn sort of smiles that made everything in him turn inside out.

"Everything," Elliot said softly, reaching up to trace patterns along his chest. "There are two kinds of ceramicists. Some like molds and make things that fit them, again and again. Others let the clay become what it wants to become. No molds. No plans. Just the peculiar magic of hands, dirt, and water."

He didn't need to ask what sort of ceramicist she was.

"Sounds like planting," he said. "But it's not magic, Elliot. It's hard work. Ask any farmer."

"That's the thing about magic, isn't it?" Her fingers danced over his jaw, then found his hair. "It's not supposed to be easy. It's always hard work. Or it wouldn't feel like magic, would it?"

And he was gripped by something he couldn't explain. He couldn't understand what was happening to him. Magic was the only thing that made sense.

"There's absolutely no room in my life for this," he told her, maybe too harshly. "For you."

He expected her to stiffen. To recoil, but all Elliot Hathaway did was smile wider, and if anything, melt more beneath him. "Okay."

"Okay?" he repeated, feeling faintly outraged.

Elliot shrugged, and then, as he stared down at her, began to…wriggle.

For a moment, all he could do was marvel at her, how unselfconscious she was, how sure of herself. But then he realized what she was doing.

By the time he realized he really should stop it, it was too late.

She was naked.

"Do you think you can…change anything by getting naked?" he managed to ask.

She only smiled at him and stretched beneath him, like a deeply satisfied cat. "I do, Colt. I truly do."

And she was right.

Because she was like quicksilver and moonlight beneath him. And he was only a man. He bent his head to taste her breast before he knew he meant to move.

And one taste wasn't nearly enough.

Elliot was a marvel. Everything between them was electric and wild, and he would've thought that she was simply like that, that she could have chemistry with the doorknob if she wanted, but he could see she looked just as dazed as he felt.

And that only made it better.

"By the way," he managed to say, his mouth against her neck. "I love cilantro."

Elliot's laugh was pure joy. "I thought you might."

Her hands were greedy and impatient, tugging on the T-shirt he'd thrown on when he'd left the house and then tossing it, not even watching it as it went because her hands were all over his chest. Then her mouth followed, and Colt was a grown, adult man and still, she made him feel like he was almost a kid again.

He felt that reckless and glorious. That washed through with need.

Colt sat up, pulling her over his lap, so he could watch

her and make sure his hands found every part of her. He traced the indentation of her spine, cupped her firm behind, and then entertained himself with that sweet center of her, hotter and greedier than the rest.

He made her shatter that way with his hand—once, then again.

And when he took her back down to the couch and settled himself between her legs, he was finally naked too.

It seemed the most natural thing in the world to let her sheath him with protection, then guide him where she wanted him. It felt preordained, somehow, and that was before he thrust deep inside her. And held himself still as she shattered once again, arching up against him, the most beautiful thing he thought he'd ever seen as pleasure had its way with her.

And then he followed that driving need inside him, and set a rhythm that made them both sigh, then groan, then lose track of everything but the sweet, hot glory of it.

The next time she broke apart, he went with her.

Colt didn't know how long they lay there, tangled up with each other as if they were puzzle pieces finally snapped together.

He couldn't say he liked that sensation.

But he didn't do anything about it. He flipped them around so she was stretched out on his chest, and the sweet weight of her sleek body against his, still breathing hard, felt like a gift.

Elliot stirred, opening sleepy violet eyes and smiling up at him. Colt surprised himself by kissing her, then running a hand down the length of her back, finding her lithe. Warm.

His.

And when she drifted off to sleep again, he told himself to leave. To disappear the way he'd come, in the dark of night, so he could maybe convince himself it had all been a dream.

But instead he held her much longer than he should have.

And the faint hint of dawn was beginning to stain the sky outside when he finally, carefully, rolled her gently to one side and covered her with the brightly colored shawl that hung on the back of the little couch.

He stared down at her longer than he should, even after he dressed again, as if he could make sense of her. Of the complication that he'd just indulged in, wholeheartedly, when he prided himself on a life without such things.

Colt stood there, waiting to feel regret. Self-disgust. Something.

Anything but what moved in him despite himself.

Possessiveness.

Longing.

And the craziest little inkling that this thing that never should have happened, and could obviously never happen again, was only the beginning.

CHAPTER FIVE

"You look entirely too pleased with yourself," Joey observed when Elliot came dancing into the bright, happy kitchen that morning, fresh from a shower. Because who needed sleep when Colt West existed in the world in all his delicious *Coltness*?

"I am pleased with myself," Elliot replied. She stretched her arms up over her head, skirting a selection of Teddy's house chickens and a stream of water from Georgie's anti-chicken water pistol. "But if I'm honest, Joey, I'm often pleased with myself. *Usually*, in fact. I've never understood why that phrase is bandied about like an insult. Surely it's a good thing to be pleased with yourself. After all, you can't expect anyone else will be, can you? It has to start at home."

"I saw you talking to Colt West last night." Georgie had put down her water pistol, ignoring Teddy's look of betrayal, and was now whisking something in a big, red bowl that Elliot had made for her years ago. She paused, narrowing her eyes. "Elliot Hathaway. Did you have carnal relations with the neighbor?"

Elliot danced her way to the coffee machine and poured herself a big mug of coffee, then dosed it with the lavender honey that was one of the first Hathaway sister joint projects. "I did. I absolutely, one-hundred-percent did."

Georgie sighed. Joey grinned. The house chickens clucked. And Teddy...blinked.

"How do you do that?" she asked. She wrinkled her nose. "I don't mean the act itself. I mean, how do you talk to the man in a bar and then just...*do* it?"

Elliot could have made the expected flippant remark. But instead she studied Teddy over the rim of her mug. Her hair was still wet, lying damply against her neck. Her body was pleasantly humming, keeping her happily aware and in tune with all the glorious ways she'd used it last night. And there was something else inside her, a lot like a wave drawing near shore.

She didn't feel flippant, it turned out. "One of the things our unusual upbringings gave us is the ability to set ourselves outside the boxes everyone else lives in. Sometimes that might make us feel like aliens, sure. But other times, it means we get to do exactly what we want, when we want, without having to worry about the silly things that inhibit everyone else. It's a gift."

Teddy look dubious. "Is that an us thing? I think maybe that's a you thing."

Elliot felt something brush her legs and looked down to see Jasper Junie figure-eighting her, rubbing her cheeks as she went. "If every woman did exactly as she pleased, to suit nothing and no one but herself like this cat right here, the world would be a far better place."

"Or it would be overrun by female sociopaths," Joey said. She looked up at the silence that followed that remark. "What? I can't be the only one who has nightmares about sociopaths, right?"

"I don't have nightmares," Teddy said, frowning at her.

Elliot shrugged. "I only really have lucid dreams." And she grinned when Joey rolled her eyes at that.

"If we can get back to Colt West," Georgie said, plunking her mixing bowl down, her gaze on Elliot. "It's not as if there aren't lines of women who would like to have carnal knowledge of the man. But he doesn't do that. He likes widows and divorced women who don't live in town, and he doesn't do relationships. Ever."

Elliot felt the unusual urge to…get tense. She repressed it. "It's funny how you have all this information about Colt, yet failed to mention that he has a twelve-year-old daughter whose mother abandoned her at birth."

"Wow," Teddy breathed. She was now clutching one of the chickens to her chest.

Joey was shooing the other one away from the table, but her violet gaze was as riveted to Georgie's as Elliot's was.

"It never occurred to me that Colt West's private life would be relevant," Georgie said, sounding defensive instead of grumpy, for once. "Had I known you would jump the man, I would have made sure to share his biography sooner."

"Literally," Elliot said, and smiled serenely when all three pairs of purple eyes swung to her. "I *literally* jumped him."

She took a big swig of her coffee, but that almost-tense feeling was still in there, kicking around.

"So are you and he…?" Joey asked.

"I didn't ask," Elliot replied.

With more serenity than she felt. And what was *that?*

"Meaning he took off?" Georgie asked, with a raised brow.

"Georgie. You know I'm about the moment. Not all the drama."

Georgie snorted. "I'll take that as a yes."

And the funny thing was that Elliot wasn't kidding. She didn't get hung up on the things other people seemed to. She wasn't about expectations. She rarely knew what day it

was or what time it was, so she never cared much if someone called.

It occurred to her, suddenly and not so pleasantly, that
maybe it wasn't that she was so *chill* and *evolved*, as she'd
always imagined. But that she hadn't actually cared all
that much before.

She couldn't say she liked the revelation.

"I'm supposed to give his daughter pottery lessons," she
said, and she was sure that her sisters could all see right
through her studied casualness, but if they did, no one said
anything. "I feel pretty certain I'll see him again. Plus, there
are all those fences."

The conversation moved on to chicken house rules and
the llamas down the road that Teddy wanted to add to her
zoo.

"Llamas are mean," Georgie said. "They spit."

Joey shrugged. "They're cute."

"The mama llama's name is *Traci*," Teddy said. Raptur-
ously. "And she is *wonderful*."

Elliot laughed, but she wasn't really listening. She was
too busy dealing with the fact that, for the first time in her
entire life, she really did feel a twinge of something she
was very much afraid was...

Uncertainty. About a man.

It was new. She told herself it was a gift.

And Elliot was not one to waste a gift. Even if she
couldn't see its use at present, she was certain she'd find
it. Sooner or later.

Even if it made her feel too much...*stuff.*

Because she was up so early, which happened rarely,
she spent her morning tending to the livestock with Teddy,
which included a little too much beekeeping time for her
tastes.

"Bees don't want to hurt you," Teddy told her when she noticed Elliot standing there, looking frozen solid in panic, she assumed. Because it was that or scream as they all buzzed around her. Teddy, naturally, acted like they were confetti. "They're fuzzy and cute and make delicious honey."

"I like honey," Elliot muttered, moving as little as possible. While also breaking out in a sweat. "Things that can sting me, on the other hand, I've made a concerted effort to keep away from me."

Her sister looked over at her, her expression wise. "You can't have one without the other, you know. Not even you, Elliot. That's life."

And Elliot chose to think of that as a gift, too.

She spent the afternoon with Joey on her doohickey, bouncing around the property with streamers flapping in the wind. They waved at Grandpa Jack up on his porch, scowling at them in what they all accepted was his love language, and then she acquainted herself with Joey's extensive gardens. They picked up Teddy and made their way back to their sweet little falling-down house—that really wasn't falling down any longer, but they'd all tacitly agreed that an enchanted cottage *should* look charmingly run-down on the outside or what fairy tale were they even in?—and cajoled Georgie into icing them some cupcakes. Then all four of them ate too many iced cupcakes outside in the breeze until there was nothing left but crumbs and a communal sugar high.

And only when Elliot thought life couldn't possibly feel any better than it did just then—full up on Colt West, sisterly love in all of its forms, and the sweet love of perfect cupcakes—she took herself off to her studio to see if she felt like the pieces that had presented themselves to her this week were ready for firing. She felt, deep in her bones, that she might want to play around with some salt glazing experience, but she'd historically preferred to experiment like that in a ceramics community.

So it seemed like fate when she looked out the window sometime later, realizing she'd spent a long while busy carving intricate patterns into clay she'd already shaped, to see Katy coming over the fence. Then running full out toward her studio, her braids behind her like a cape. The sight made her heart glad, and begged for a sketch.

But she didn't pull out her sketchbook. Because she looked past Katy and seemed to…flip end-to-end, then go hot, when she caught the eye of the cowboy behind the wheel of the pickup that had dropped Katy off. Right there on the other side of the fence he'd built.

Colt nodded. Elliot nodded back, when she would not have said that was her primary form of communication.

Still, when he drove away, she knew she'd see him again that night.

And then she pushed him out of her mind and went to the door of the studio, throwing it open to welcome the girl who stopped running when she saw Elliot. Katy coughed. Then assumed an air of studied indifference.

"I guess I'm supposed to do some pottery lessons," she mumbled, her eyes somewhere on Elliot's overalls.

"I guess." Elliot leaned against the doorjamb. "You'll probably hate it."

Katy stared back at her, all freckles and a stubborn chin. "Why?"

Elliot shrugged. "Everyone thinks that pottery must be easy, because they use it all the time. And people look down on things that feel familiar. They always think that if they had a free weekend, they could make six bowls and a set of mugs. They don't understand that the easier something looks or seems, the harder it is to do. I can teach anyone to make a bowl. But real pottery? Art that you can use? That takes a different kind of person altogether."

"Is this reverse psychology?" Katy asked. "My dad tries that with the chores. It doesn't work. I still don't like mucking out stalls."

"I'm not your parent," Elliot said as the girl inched closer, so they were both standing more or less in the doorway of the studio. "He is, so it's his job to show you that sometimes, we all have to do things for the greater good."

Katy huffed at that. "I don't see why everyone but me gets to decide what the greater good is when I'm the one who has to *do* it. Forever. I just want to make my own decisions."

"What do you want to decide?"

Katy sighed. Melodramatically, of course. "Literally anything."

"Then you've come to the right place," Elliot said. "You can make all the decisions you want in here."

She took Katy inside and gave her a quick tour of the studio. She offered an overview of how things worked, then set Katy up at a pottery wheel with a hunk of clay to play with.

Then she sat down with her and showed her how to hold her hands, how to use the pedal at her feet to keep the wheel moving, and how to play with thickness and thinness, width and height.

And when it was time, she let Katy do her own thing. She sat at the wheel next to her, pretending not to notice the girl's increasing frustration.

"This isn't working," Katy declared after a while.

Elliot looked over and smiled. "What did you decide to make?"

Katy glared at her wheel. "A bowl."

"It looks like you made a bowl. It's bowl-shaped and everything."

"But…it doesn't look like yours. At all."

Elliot let her foot off the pedal and the soup bowl she was working on shimmered to a stop. "Why would it?"

Katy sighed. "That's what I wanted it to look like."

"Well, there's your mistake. The clay in your hands isn't the same clay in mine." She went and crouched down next to the girl, her gaze on the wheel before them. "Let's look at what you actually made. It's a bowl. You can put things in it. It looks like it will hold water. I would call this first time at the wheel a success."

"It's not pretty, though," Katy said after a moment, still staring at her wheel.

Elliot shifted around to look at her. "You only think that because it doesn't look the way you want it to. That's not the bowl's fault, that's all you. And it doesn't mean the bowl isn't pretty. It just means you haven't learned how to see what is, instead of what you want."

And she bit back her smile when Katy's eyes seemed to soften, and took on that gleam of wonder that Elliot recognized. It meant the clay was doing its job.

When she heard the faintest sound, she looked up and saw that the light had changed. It was growing dark outside, not that she would have noticed. But Colt was standing there in her tiny studio, watching her talk to his daughter.

With an expression his face that looked, almost, like pain.

It made her heart lurch around inside her chest.

"What time is it?" Elliot asked. "I don't know why I'm asking. I don't really care. But you look like we're late."

"Katy has school tomorrow," Colt said.

Forbiddingly, Elliot thought.

"I'm staying at Grandma and Grandpa's," Katy told him, rolling her eyes, clearly unfazed by the forbidding tone. "Grandma has to go into town tomorrow morning and she said she'd drive me. So I might as well just stay there."

"Be careful what you wish for," Colt told her. "You know your grandmother takes homework more seriously than I do."

Katy looked Elliot. "He's obsessed with homework."

And Elliot had a lot of thoughts and feelings about homework, and how unnecessary it all was when a child could be doing art instead, but she didn't share that. Not with the glowering father looking on.

"Why don't you get going," she suggested. "I'll put everything away and show you how to do it next time."

"Is there going to be a next time?" Colt asked.

And he was asking his daughter. Of course he was. Elliot knew that. But his gaze was on her and she felt something like breathless.

"I didn't learn enough in one lesson," Katy said. "So." Colt turned that steady gaze of his on her and she shifted, all awkward preteen. "I mean, yeah. I want to come back."

"Go on and get in the truck," Colt told her. "I'll settle up."

And Elliot felt that surge of what she'd thought was uncertainty earlier today as the door closed behind Katy, leaving her alone once again with Colt.

She understood now that it wasn't uncertainty. It was only that she wasn't sure she'd ever wanted anything as much as she wanted him. She believed in indulging herself, whether it was dessert for lunch or sleeping until noon. But this man was her greatest indulgence yet.

Elliot wanted more.

"Are we settling on more pottery lessons for your daughter?" And she couldn't keep herself from smiling at him, because she wasn't the sort to play games. Why not let him see what she felt? "Or do you want to set up another date?"

"Is that we we're calling it?" he asked, though the look in his eyes was hot. So hot it made her shake a little bit.

"The best kind of date," she said, smiling even wider. "All business."

"The thing is, Elliot," he said, as if the words cost him. "I don't date."

"Then I guess it's a good thing that you didn't consider last night a date. That would have been so confronting."

She saw the storm cloud move over his face, then seem to settle in there. She laughed as she crossed to him, gripping his wrist and steering him to a spot against the wall that couldn't be seen through the window. Just in case a twelve-year-old was watching.

"Settle down, Colt. I'm not asking you for anything scary. That's not how I operate."

But the storm didn't lessen any. He reached over and ran his hand over her cheek, as if he couldn't keep himself from touching her. "I believe you. But that doesn't make it any better."

"I don't understand."

Colt sighed. "How could you? I have a kid. A kid I love more than anything else on this earth, and who I will always put first. I don't make mistakes with women anymore, Elliot. Once was enough."

"I have good news for you," Elliot said. She drifted closer, reaching up to put her hands on his face. She kept her gaze steady, and loved feeling the heat of him against her palms, the hint of stubble, the *Coltness* of it all. "I'm a

singularity, Colt. And I'm not going to beg you to recon-
sider. If you want what I want, you know where to find me."

And for moment, she thought he would simply storm
out, taking that tight line of his mouth and all his strong
words with him.

But instead, he caught one of her hands with his. He kept
it there against his cheek, but turned his mouth to her palm.

For one beat of her heart. Then another.

And he didn't look back when he left.

Elliot told herself she had no doubt, no uncertainty. She
told herself that she knew he'd be back—and not because
she was cocky. But because she threw herself, body and
soul, into the things she felt. That was how she lived her
life, and she was very rarely wrong. It was how she made
art and better yet, lived off it. It was how she always knew
when to move on. It was how she'd known, when she'd
gathered here with her sisters after Grandpa Jack's hospi-
talization, that it was time to come home.

She always knew.

And she might not have worn a watch, but she could tell
the time that mattered by that knowing.

But the truth of the matter was, she didn't really breathe
easy until the moon was high. There was a knock on the
studio door and when she threw it wide open, Colt was
there.

Right where he belonged.

So she welcomed him back the way she'd been dreaming about all day, right there on her knees in the doorway,
until he groaned out her name.

And then Elliot pulled him inside, and got serious.

CHAPTER SIX

FOR A PURPLE-EYED singularity who was almost certainly a land mine of one kind or another, it was amazing how well Elliot just…slid into Colt's life as if she belonged there. As if he'd gone ahead and arranged his whole life over all these years just to fit her when she finally showed up.

He dismissed that notion as ridiculous, but it didn't stop him thinking it.

Katy wanted to spend every spare moment she had in the pottery studio, and even though Elliot waved her hand in that way of hers and claimed payment wasn't necessary, Colt wasn't comfortable with that. So every time he came to pick Katy up, he put what he considered an appropriate amount of money in a little green jar by the door.

A jar she never seemed to empty, he noticed, but that didn't stop him doing it.

Because if he hadn't done that, he would have to believe that he was taking advantage of her. And that was the last way he wanted to feel on all the nights he showed up at that same door, without Katy, to sink himself deep into every last contour of the singularity that was Elliot Hathaway.

He figured he'd get his fill of her, and soon, but *soon* never seemed to show up. One week became two. Then another few weeks slid by. And he still wasn't anything near *full*. Elliot could sit naked on his lap and talk to him seriously about pottery facts, for hours, and he was riveted.

Like how ceramicist types were often ejected from museums because they couldn't seem to keep themselves from touching the ancient pottery. *It goes with the territory*, she would say, with that laugh of hers that seemed to carve out its own space in his chest. She was inventive. Imaginative. She moved her hands over his body as if he was nothing more and nothing less than more clay for her to shape, and there was no doubt that she was a master.

And Colt, in his turn, took a significant pleasure in turning her inside out.

As many times as possible, every time he saw her.

Almost as if, something in him liked to whisper when he was staggering around through his early morning chores after another night with Elliot, *you're afraid every night with her might be the last.*

The trouble was, he looked forward to getting back to her. Always. No matter how many nights a week Katy stayed with her grandparents, it was never enough. In the past, Colt had always been grateful he had his kid as a handy excuse, whenever necessary.

This was the first time, ever, he didn't want to use Katy as any kind of excuse.

Especially because Katy's love for Elliot was far more uncomplicated.

He couldn't count the number of times Katy would quote her in the course of a day. An hour. *Elliot says* was how just about every sentence seemed to start these days, and what Colt couldn't figure out was when all the typical warning flags and alarms had turned into some kind of delightful little chorus inside of him. Making him want more.

Instead of what they were supposed to do, which was make him head in the opposite direction. Fast.

"Elliot says this, Elliot says that," his brother Browning

said one afternoon. They were down at the ranch complex with Smith that day, loading up Colt's pickup with a new side-by-side so they could take it up to Flint in one of the upper pastures. "You know, I thought our Katy had herself a crush. But it turns out, Elliot isn't a boy. She's one of those Hathaway sisters."

"My favorite part about your whole thing with Kit," Colt drawled, "is how it's really honed your observational skills. Had to figure that all her smarts might wear off on you."

And he knew he'd scored a point when Smith *almost* let his lips curve.

"See, I said you were just doing that fatherly thing you do, setting your girl up with some extracurriculars." Browning leaned back against the side of the pickup, smiling broadly. "Smith argued, like he does. But now I think there's more to it."

"More to a pottery class?" Colt didn't comment on the possibility of their brother Smith actually arguing about anything. That would require a whole lot more talking than Smith liked to do. He *might* have lifted a brow. "I think you'll find it's pretty simple. Clay. Heat. Art, if you're lucky. Otherwise, a collection of mismatched mugs."

"All these deflections, Colt." Browning shook his head in mock amazement. "Why, it's almost like you don't want me to talk about the Elliot Hathaway of it all."

"You can talk about Elliot Hathaway all you like," Colt said as if he couldn't care less about such things. And it cost him. Because he didn't want Browning to talk about her. For the simple reason that he wanted to keep Elliot Hathaway all to himself. Possibly forever. "Hell, Browning, you should think about taking a pottery class yourself. Who knows? Maybe you'd really take to it, what with your heretofore unknown artistic side."

"I might just do that, Colt," Browning replied with his trademark broad grin. "If only to have a chat about my up-tight older brother. Just to see what Elliot says on the subject, since as far as I can tell from your daughter, she's the expert on everything."

"She's an expert on pottery, not me, and not Katy," Colt retorted.

He regretted it at once. Because he'd showed too much heat. Might as well turn over and show his belly while he was at it.

And a couple years back, Browning would've gone in for the kill. But this was the new Browning. The Browning who lived with his woman in the apartment above her bookshop, and was happily settled in a way Colt would have said was impossible. For anyone, but specifically for Browning. Settled and happier with it by the day.

It was an infection going round the West family of late. Even Remy, once a dependable source of misery, was so happy with Keira that he was unrecognizable. Colt was almost tempted to wonder if something was wrong with him.

But not while Browning was studying him. "You know," he said quietly, "you did the right thing. That always seems to get lost in translation. You stepped up. Why are you still punishing yourself for that?"

"I'm not punishing myself."

It was Smith who turned then, his dark gaze arresting. "You've been paying penance for twelve years." His voice always sounded gruff and rusty, but that was only part of why it hit Colt like a blow. "Penance is what you pay for sins, Colt. Not gifts like Katy."

Then he slammed his way into the cab of the pickup, leaving Colt and Browning to stare at each other in amazement, the way everyone always did when Smith stirred himself to use his words.

"Well," Browning drawled after a minute. "If Smith says it, you know it must be true."

And Colt had more time to think about that than he wanted. Three more nights before he could get over to Elliot's again, and he told himself he had no idea why it was he drove so fast across the fields after taking Katy to his parents' and suffering through an overly-long dinner with them. Why he couldn't seem to catch a breath. He was thinking about gifts and penance, mistakes and land mines.

You need to stop this, he told himself. *This is crazy and you don't do crazy.*

But as he walked toward the studio he thought that really, he was going to have to build a gate in that fence.

It was a cool night. The air was thick, letting him know it could rain at any moment. Maybe it already was. But Colt couldn't care about the weather when Elliot Hathaway pushed her way out of her studio and came across the field to meet him.

"It's been too long," he heard himself say, to his horror.

"An eternity," she whispered in agreement.

And he didn't know when the rain started to fall, only that it made it all that much better. Because he was far too wrapped up in the glory that was Elliot. She was a wonder. A marvel like the stars above he couldn't see tonight. Unselfconscious and wholly herself as she wrapped her body around his, right there in the field with only the Oregon sky as witness.

When he moved in her at last, it felt sacred.

Like the vows he could not make.

But he could press them into her skin with his mouth, his hands. He could make them real, bright and hot between them. He could do absolutely everything except speak them aloud, even here, out in the thick night where no one would hear.

And later, she lay beside him on a blanket of their discarded clothes. She tipped her face up to the rain and laughed as it fell.

Carving that space for herself inside him again. It was beginning to feel as if that space would always be there. As if she was the only thing that could ever fit.

And Colt knew what it was, that dawning understanding that made him feel as if the world was tipping him straight off its surface, sending him hurtling off into the dark.

He might not have felt it before, but he knew it all the same.

But he also knew that he was as tied to this land as she was lit up by the stars above, and sooner or later, the stars would take her back again.

He knew one thing as well as he knew the other.

Colt gathered her close and carried her inside. He dried her off, then laid her out on that little couch and started all over again—vow after vow, flame upon flame—until the only thing she could say was his name.

Like it was as much a part of her as she was of him, now.

Something to remember him by, he thought. Long after she was gone. And the following evening, he braced himself when he went to pick Katy up from pottery, because he'd spent the whole day feeling raw. But there was no time for his feelings, because Katy came dancing toward him, covered head to toe with smears of dirt.

"Did you know that every Sunday is *Sister Sunday* here?" she demanded, the long shadows making the May twilight seem to stretch to impossible dimensions outside the studio's windows.

"I did not." But Colt's gaze was on Elliot, who looked, to his mind, entirely too focused on the trays of clay she was carting around.

"It is," Katy said, and her voice was accusing. "That's what sisters *do*."

"My understanding was that most sisters try to kill each other and spend their entire lives pointing out all the ways they're so different from each other that they might as well be adopted," Colt said. "Not that I'd know. Having only brothers."

Elliot looked up at that, her violet gaze direct. But bright. "Sister Sunday is sacred."

"But I'm invited," Katy told him, seemingly unaware of any undercurrents swirling around in the small building. "To the brunch part."

"Brunch," Colt repeated. "Do people really have brunch?"

Elliot straightened as if he'd issued a challenge. "Brunch is the most important meal of the week. If only because it's the best of everything. Food in any genre you like, gathered together in one."

"What if I like my food to be food, not a genre?" Colt asked.

"Dad," Katy groaned, with the embarrassed horror only a preteen girl could muster.

"Then I will weep for you," Elliot replied, looking unbothered. "Katy and I have been discussing how every woman needs to connect to her tears."

Colt crossed his arms. "That sounds alarming."

Elliot's violet gaze found his and held. "Maybe to you. Women are taught that their emotions make them weak, when obviously that's not the case or men wouldn't be so afraid of them. Emotions are strength."

She looked at him as if she expected him to argue. He

only stared right back at her, because one thing he'd discovered after all these weeks with Elliot was that he didn't, in fact, like soft things all that much. He liked tough hands, warm hearts, and kisses so hot he was surprised every day that they didn't leave marks.

Elliot nodded as if whatever expression he wore proved her point. "Powerful, fascinating women like Katy and me know that the finest expression of our strength is meeting our emotions when they arise instead of bottling them up." She didn't look at Katy then, but Colt did, and could see his daughter nodding along like this was a sermon. "Meeting them, allowing them to take hold if that's what needs to happen, and then moving on. Connection, not repression."

"It's okay to be upset about a broken promise," Katy said quietly, and she didn't have to tell Colt that she was talking about her mother's recent spate of unreturned phone calls. He knew. "It's *good*. I don't have to live out anybody's story but mine."

That space inside him that Elliot had made her own seemed to shine a little brighter, then. And oh, how it ached.

"I'm thinking my daughter doesn't need to go to a brunch of sadness," Colt said sternly, to cover it up. And to make his daughter *implode* at the injustice.

Elliot only shook her head. Pityingly. "First of all, no brunch can ever be sad, by definition. And second, *obviously*, any brunch put on by my sisters and me is magical." She looked at him archly. "I suppose you'd better come along."

And then she ignored him until he collected Katy—still moaning about the volumes of things he could never possibly understand, all of which was *wounding*—and herded her out the door.

"Settle down," he suggested when they were in the

pickup and bumping their way back toward their house. Out of sight of the pottery studio and all things Hathaway. "Maybe try connecting to things that are actually against you. Did I say you couldn't go?"

And that won him some excited squealing for the rest of the evening.

But Katy woke up the next morning on a tear. "This is *serious*, Dad," she informed him when he found her in her bedroom with what appeared to be the entire contents of her closet strewn across her bed. "Very serious. Everyone wears dresses and is *beautiful*."

"Well, cricket, I hate to disappoint you. But I will not be wearing a dress."

"You're going to have to dress up, though," Katy told him. In a voice that brooked no argument, which gave him a strange little glimpse into the kind of formidable woman she would become one day. He both liked it and hated it at the same time. "Everything will be beautiful, so you have to be as handsome as humanly possible." She shook her head like that was a tall order. "I'll help you as much as I can."

"I appreciate that," he replied, with a dryness his daughter did not seem to register.

And that was how Colt West found himself arriving to a sacred Hathaway Sister Sunday brunch, hat literally in hand, to find that it was basically like stepping into fairyland.

CHAPTER SEVEN

THERE WAS ACTUALLY a bit of a crowd for Sunday brunch, the way there was more and more these days. Georgie's manservant, Con, was hovering about, insisting on helping her, which Elliot thought was the best thing that could ever happen to her prickly sister. She hated it that much. Teddy, as ever, had invited Grandpa Jack—with or without his shotgun—and it looked like he'd deigned to appear for once, scowling down the length of the banquet table they'd created outside.

He wouldn't go *inside*, of course.

But Elliot and her sisters felt sure that he would. In time.

When Colt and Katy appeared, everyone fell silent, just long enough to make Colt look...resigned.

Elliot beamed.

"Welcome," she said, gliding over to the pair of them. For this Sunday's theme—fairy princesses, naturally—she had chosen to wear a flowing sort of one-piece thing. Probably it was called a jumpsuit, but she hated that word. She felt it fell far short of elegance, and a woman should always feel elegant in sparkly things that flowed and cried out for tiaras. "I'm so glad you came."

"This is the most beautiful place I've ever seen," Katy whispered, her eyes wide as she looked around the outdoor space they had transformed into a retreat worthy of a collection of fairy princesses. And their manservants.

Everything sparkled. And what didn't sparkle directly, gleamed.

Colt had his hands on the back of his daughter's neck, and she watched as he squeezed once, then let go. His dark gaze found Elliot. "You didn't tell us it was a party. A very pink party."

"This week's theme is fairy princesses," Elliot said. Solemnly. She held out her hands, each one glittering thanks to the tiaras she held. "I expect you to blend."

"Old Jack isn't wearing a tiara," Colt pointed out.

"Old Jack owns the land you're standing on, son," the old man retorted. "I can have you all rounded up and hauled away with a single phone call."

"Grandpa's tiara is on the inside," Teddy said.

"All that glitters," Georgie muttered, but caught the glares coming at her from all sides. "Is...extra gold within."

"Better put on that crown, boy," Grandpa Jack said to Colt, looking more pleased than Elliot had seen him in ages. It figured.

But she didn't have time to marvel over that, because Colt was taking the silly, sparkly plastic tiara out of her hand. He swept off his Stetson with great ceremony. Then he stuck the tiara on his head.

"Oh my God." Katy laughed. *"Dad."*

"We played dress-up for years, cricket," Colt rumbled at her, though his dark eyes were all for Elliot. "I taught you how to wear a tiara."

Then he reached out and adjusted Katy's, with an ease and familiarity that only underscored what he'd said.

And Elliot understood, at last, what was happening to her.

What had been happening from the start.

It wasn't uncertainty. She didn't do uncertainty.

She had always known her own mind.

The thing about Colt was that it wasn't her mind that was involved—or not only her mind, she amended.

It was her heart.

It was *her*—head to toe, mind and body, forever.

A cataclysm of pure joy.

It was everything she was and everything she would ever be, and it was as certain as the seasons. Spring might come early or late. There might be a deeper snowfall one year, a drier summer the next.

But every season would come as it should, the same each year and yet wholly original all the same.

That was how she loved this man.

That was how she would always love this man, who settled himself at the hyper-feminine fairy princess table with a sparkly tiara on his head and somehow looked as comfortable in himself as he did pounding fences or making love to her.

He caught her eye over Georgie's glorious cake display and smiled.

And it was like a sunrise inside her.

She loved him.

She *loved* him.

And when the long, silly brunch was done, Joey took Katy out in the doohickey. Everyone else left Elliot and Colt to the sparkle and the shine, the sweet May afternoon light pouring over them.

Like the sun knew, too.

"I love you," Elliot said.

Because she couldn't keep it inside her a single moment longer.

And for moment their eyes seemed fused together. For

moment, it was like the whole wide world held its breath. Birds hushed. The wind froze.

One single moment.

And then Colt shut down.

She watched him do it. She watched the heat and light in his gaze disappear.

Elliot could've taken the words back. She could've claimed it was the sugar talking, the piles of French toast, the princess cakes Georgie had made with all that life-altering marzipan.

She could have saved the moment, but she didn't. Because she'd spent all these weeks telling a twelve-year-old girl how to own what she felt. And an entire previous life fully embodying whatever choice she'd made. It was who she was.

Elliot felt a stab of something like shame that even the tiniest part of her wanted to pretend otherwise.

But she fought all of that back. She tried to arrange her face into something serene. And she waited.

Colt did not look remotely serene. He looked *volcanic*. He stared at her for a long time. Then he swallowed, almost convulsively, and she found herself watching that strong column of his tanned throat with something like despair, because all she wanted was to press her face against him, let her lips rest on his pulse, and take it back if that would make things okay again.

Even though she didn't want to take it back. She wanted to shout it to the sky.

Colt reached up and removed the tiara, setting it down on the long table with a kind of finality that made something inside her shudder.

"I told you I don't do this."

And she'd never heard that tone of voice from him before. Seething, maybe. Ripe with too many dark things, none of which she had any desire to name.

"You told me you don't date," she replied. "But then, you know, you did anyway."

"I didn't." She could've sworn the look she saw in those impossibly dark eyes of his was betrayal, but that didn't make any kind of sense. "I wouldn't call keeping secrets and sneaking around *dating*. Would you?"

"I don't sneak, Colt. Or keep secrets." She considered him. "I'm guessing you do."

He pushed back from the table and stood up. And all of his beautiful, brooding masculinity suddenly seemed to clash with the fanciful decorations. He raked a hand through his hair, and she hated that every single thing he did felt like another form of goodbye.

"We had a mutually beneficial arrangement," he told her. Gruffly. "That's it."

Elliot got to her feet because there was too much *stuff* inside of her, all of it pulling tighter and tighter and making it impossible to sit still. "Remind me, which service are you paying for in that green jar by my door?"

Colt muttered a curse beneath his breath. And he didn't spare her another glance as he wheeled around and stalked away.

Elliot trailed after him when she'd never *trailed* along behind someone in her life. But it felt like gravity. That was the force that made her follow him as he stormed out to the front of the house and then stood there, his hands on his narrow hips, practically broadcasting his fury to the fields all around. She had no doubt that if Katy had been anywhere nearby he would have scooped her up, possibly even tossed her in the back of the pickup for expediency's sake, and driven the hell away from here.

But the doohickey was nowhere in sight. That meant Colt was trapped.

And Elliot allowed herself the unworthy notion that she was *glad* he couldn't disappear the way he so clearly wanted to do.

"Is that what you think love is?" he asked, not turning around to look at her. Which meant, she supposed, he was as aware of her she was of him and had known exactly where she was as she'd followed him here. Somehow, that didn't make her feel any better. "What kind of damaged love is that? Accusing me of paying for it?"

"You're the one who left that money, Colt. I just asked you to clarify it. I already know what I feel. I've known it from the moment I marched over to that fence and got a good look at you. You turned around, our eyes met, and that was it."

"No." He shook his head emphatically. "You're a free spirit. You would do the same with anyone."

"I can't control what you think or feel, Colt," she said, fighting hard to keep her voice cool. And not to shout at him that she certainly would not *do the same with anyone*. She might like new experiences, but only Colt had ever inspired her to *get cozy*—but she refused to tell him that while he was mad at her *and* rejecting her love. "I can only tell you that I'm madly, wildly in love with you. And it doesn't really matter how little you want to hear that. It's still true."

She was vaguely aware of Georgie and Teddy coming out from inside the house to stand on the slanted porch, backing her up if she needed it but keeping their distance, too.

"Well," Colt said, his drawl washing over her almost painfully. "That's an end to it, then."

And everything inside Elliot wanted to litigate the finality she could hear in that sentence. She wanted to argue her case. She wanted to produce evidence, maybe even kiss him, since he seemed to have forgotten the magic in it.

Instead, she forced herself to stop. To breathe. To let her hands curl if they had to curl, but not to start swinging them the way she wanted to. And badly.

Because she'd spent her whole life watching her mother fight. For independence. For this job or that job. For the business connection she wanted, the relationship she didn't, and everything in between. It was an all-out war, always.

Deep inside, Elliot had always believed that love, true love, was supposed to feel the way it had when she'd met her sisters.

Like fate.

That easy, fateful, *oh here you are at last* sense of home.

She couldn't make Colt feel that way about her. But she certainly wouldn't tarnish the things she felt by getting scrappy about it.

"Just tell me one thing," she said, proud of herself for sounding so calm. "Why would loving you be so terrible?"

He turned on her then. And he clearly had no quarrel with a fight, because that's all she saw on that beautifully hard face of his. His eyes blazed with fury, his mouth was flat, and for a dizzy moment, she was tempted to confuse what she saw with the way he looked in the height of passion—

"For a thousand reasons, Elliot," he bit out. "But let's focus on one. You're not going to stay here. You've never stayed anywhere—you told me that yourself. You flit around from place to place, going wherever the mood takes you. On some level, I envy you that. Because it's not my life. It will never be my life. I don't just work on my family's ranch, I'll be the one running it one day. I will never, ever leave Jasper Creek." He blinked as if saying that out loud hurt him, but he didn't stop. "Soon enough, you'll feel the call to adventure again and you'll follow it. Because you can. You should. And I am not going to be the thing that keeps you tethered here when what you want is to be gone."

Elliot tried to take that on board. "Are you really trying to sell this as you being *noble*, Colt? Because that's not the word I'd use."

"My life is fine the way it is," Colt told her flatly. "I've got my kid. The ranch. My family. I liked our arrangement, I won't lie, but I'm sorry if you thought I was promising you more than that. I wasn't."

Elliot could hear the doohickey approaching, but she couldn't shift her gaze from Colt.

"Oh, okay then," she heard herself say. "As long as you're sorry."

Katy jumped out of the doohickey, then streaked toward them with her dress flowing behind her as she ran, bubbling over with all the things she'd seen.

And then stopped dead, standing like a triangle point between her father and Elliot.

"What's going on?" she demanded. Then she turned to scowl at her father. "What did you do?"

Elliot found she couldn't bear to be a wedge between this girl she loved a little too much and this man she loved completely. Even now. She forced herself to smile as she moved toward Katy, slipping an arm around her shoulders.

"He didn't do anything," she said. "We've talked about this. People don't have to share our feelings. It doesn't make them any less valid. Strong women aren't ever ashamed to share what they feel. Strong men like your father aren't either. That doesn't make anybody the bad guy if those feelings don't match up."

And yet, she wanted there to be a bad guy. She glanced

over at Colt to see an arrested expression on his face, and wondered why it was she hadn't cracked wide open. Why she hadn't fallen apart into a thousand pieces. She wondered how she would ever survive this. This extraordinary sacrifice. Pretending to feel the maturity she'd always felt before, in every possible scenario, and yet now thought was a terrible copout.

Because how could it possibly be mature to pretend she wasn't wracked with grief?

Still, what she did was straighten, nod at Katy, and then step back.

Out of both of their lives.

"Come on, cricket," Colt said darkly. "It's time to go."

And Elliot stayed still, like she was carved from marble, as Colt loaded his fairy princess into the pickup, stalked around the front, then slammed his way inside.

She didn't move a muscle as he backed the truck out, executed the turn so he could drive straight out, and then took off.

Leaving nothing behind but dust. And that grief she thought might take her to her knees.

"He's a bastard," Teddy, of all people, said fiercely.

"A rat bastard," Georgie agreed.

"He's a dick," Joey said flatly. "And he doesn't deserve you."

"Thank you," Elliot said quietly. "I'm in love with him. I don't want to tear him down. I want him to love me back, and he doesn't."

She didn't wait for her sisters to respond to that. She started walking, not really understanding what she was doing at first. Then, as she moved, she realized that she was going to do what she always did.

Of course.

Because there were things that words could never express—or not her words, anyway.

She flexed her fingers as she moved and, on some level, she took a great comfort in the fact that her sisters came after her, a violet-eyed parade.

"This is a great idea," Teddy said supportively. "Art always makes you feel better."

Elliot tossed open the door to her studio and marched inside, going straight through the room with her pottery wheels, and that couch where she'd spent entirely too much time over the past month and a half, and straight out back to the building across her makeshift breezeway that housed her kiln.

She only looked over her shoulder when she heard the indrawn breath from her sisters. But they weren't looking at her, they were looking past her to the shelves in the far wall.

Elliot followed her gaze. "That's right. I've been making cowboy trolls. A lot of them."

"Why are they cute?" Georgie asked.

"Trolls aren't supposed to be cute," Joey agreed.

"Because I was blinded by love," Elliot said, before Teddy could weigh in on the cuteness factor of her creations.

And then she tipped her head back and let out a sound. Raw and unfiltered. Ripe with grief and loss.

She kept going until there were tears pouring down her cheeks.

And then, one by one, she began to smash each and every one of the cowboy trolls she'd made in celebration of Colt West.

Right there against the floor, in the studio where she'd dared to dream that love might win, after all.

CHAPTER EIGHT

"I DON'T UNDERSTAND," Katy said, not for the first time.

"There's nothing to understand," Colt replied, trying to sound calm. Certain. *Parental.* When with every mile he put between him and Elliot, what he wanted to do was something out of character and crazy. Like turn the truck around. Or get out and howl at the moon—when it was still the middle of the day and there was no moon visible. He set his jaw. "We're not on the same page, that's all."

Katy was uncharacteristically quiet. Colt slid a look her way as he followed the dirt road out and around, driving far more miles to skirt Hathaway land to get back to the West ranch than it was to simply drive straight.

That felt like a metaphor. And he was a goddamned simple man. He didn't need metaphors chasing him down country roads.

Next to him, Katy was looking disconcertingly too old and too young at once. She was dressed like a fairy princess, her tiara askew on her head, as if she was still the fiercely determined toddler he remembered far too well. But the look on her face was far beyond her years.

"I already know that you and Elliot are together," she said, in a voice that was *so careful* that Colt realized in the next beat that she was…*handling* him. But he didn't have time to take that on board, because she was still talking.

"Why do you think I've been staying over at Grandma and Grandpa's so much?"

"Because you love them. And you're twelve going on twenty and want to feel independent."

"Yeah, okay, Dad. You're the one who always says that we're a team."

Colt actually slowed the truck then, out there surrounded by pine-covered hills in the distance, rolling fields, and the weight of his own regret.

Katy crossed her arms over her princess dress. "You spend so much time trying to make me feel okay about my mom. I get to try to make you feel better about stuff too. And it's stupid you think you have to be lonely. You don't."

"Where are you getting this?" He dragged his hand through his hair and realized he'd left his Stetson behind in fairyland. "You've never said anything like this before. And that's a good thing, cricket, because you don't need to worry about my social life."

"I'm not worried about your social life, Dad. *God*," said his twelve-year-old, with an aggrieved eye roll. "First I thought you were hung up on Mom. You're not, are you?" Katy shook her head when he started to respond to that the way he always did. "Don't lie to me, Dad. I'm almost thirteen."

"No," he said, matter-of-factly. "It was never like that between me and your mom."

Katy nodded. Then she held his gaze steadily. Solemnly. "How am I supposed to be happy, the way you always tell me that I should be, if you're unhappy and it's my fault?"

Colt felt his heart kick at him like it was no longer located in his chest.

"Katy. It's not your fault. And I'm not unhappy." This was the hardest part of being a father, he'd found. Not loving her. That part came as easy as breathing, and sometimes overpowered him. But Katy wasn't taciturn like her dad. She was a talker and she needed him to find words, even when he had none. So he tried. "Look, I know you love Elliot. I don't blame you. But there are...complications."

He could have sworn that his daughter's eyes got sad. For him. "You like each other," she said. "See? Easy."

"Sometimes things feel easy for a while," Colt said, as gingerly as he could. "But that's because they're not realistic. And when reality gets involved, the way it always does, it turns out it's not easy at all."

Katy sat back in her seat, her princess gown floating around her, as if to emphasize how little she thought about what he'd said. "The easier something looks, the harder it is to do well," she told him. Her dark gaze seemed to pin him to his seat. "Maybe it only seems complicated because you're bad at it."

Ouch.

Colt reminded himself that he was not having a heart-to-heart with a contemporary. The almost-woman who'd just eviscerated him with one offhanded comment was his child, and he didn't need to give her a detailed explanation about an affair that was now over.

"There's one thing I'm real good at," he pointed out as he put the truck back into gear. "It comes with a huge list of chores for you to do. And since I'm so bad at things, maybe you could do more of them."

"Whatever," his daughter muttered. "Drop me at Grandma and Grandpa's."

But even after he did that and drove back toward his own house, telling himself that he would spend the whole of his evening reminding himself who he was, he found himself sitting out there in the fields once again.

He could take the fork toward his house. Or he could head back toward Elliot.

And it turned out Colt could tell himself all kinds of things. And he could take any hit, the way he'd taken all the hits in his life so far. All of which, as he liked to tell anyone who would listen—especially his little brothers, who really didn't want to listen—he had turned into gifts.

Like Katy. His little girl.

None of this was penance. He wasn't *punishing* himself.

But what he couldn't take was that little girl calling him a coward. If not in so many words.

I love you, Elliot had said.

Big and open and entirely her, as if she expected him to cheer.

Some part of him nearly had, and that had shaken him more than anything else.

And all of his objections still stood. He might as well be the hard earth beneath his wheels. She was too many stars in the sky to count. It was who they were and always would be.

But when had he gotten the idea that it was better to cut something off before it happened, for fear of what he *might* feel down the road, than it was to actually feel it? When he had Katy as living, breathing proof that it wasn't possible to regret the things he jumped into headfirst, and to hell with consequences.

Did he really think that it was only possible to do that once?

Was that what he was teaching his daughter?

Was that what he was telling himself?

He'd spent so long congratulating himself on his duty. His ironclad sense of responsibility. He would have sworn he could never be tempted from the path he'd been on for as long as he could remember.

But maybe all that was another way to say he'd been hiding.

Punishing himself with a little penance, even.

Especially compared to Elliot, who completed him without even trying. Who was like fire and sunshine in his hands and in his heart. Who gave all of herself and made him imagine that he could do the same, but only tucked up in that pottery studio, where it didn't have to count.

Where he could pretend it was something else.

Katy might not have used the word *coward* to describe him, but Colt knew that it was the only word that fit.

He stared out at the usual glorious Oregon view. Green hills. Land rolling out golden beneath the coming evening.

The land that had made him. The land that lived inside him.

The land he tended and babied like his cattle and his horses. The land that asked everything of him, took it, and gave him so much in return.

And he got it then.

It was all love.

And once he understood that, he couldn't drive fast enough.

Colt headed across the fields this time, taking the dirt road he knew better than his own hands. And when he got to that stretch of fence that blocked him from Hathaway land, he made a split-second decision and then drove right through it.

Because it was past time he built that gate.

He pulled the pickup to a stop out in front of the pottery studio, taking in the hostile gauntlet of Hathaway sisters who stood there. They were all looking at him as if they were each imagining specific and detailed ways to cause him bodily harm.

"I come in peace," he said as he swung out of his truck.

"It's a little late for peace," said Georgie, glowering at him.

"You can go in there and see exactly how late it is," Joey said darkly. "If you dare."

There was music blaring from within, an operatic-sounding female voice above dramatic orchestration. That boded well.

"I would advise you to think very carefully about what, exactly, you think you're going to say to her," Teddy said, with a ferocity he would not have said the gentlest of the Hathaway sisters possessed. Especially since she stood there before him, clutching a chicken. "If you hurt her again, she might burn down the studio. But you'll need to worry a whole lot more about what we'll do to you."

"Happily," Georgie agreed. "Repeatedly."

"I work with a lot of machinery," Joey chimed in. Darkly.

"You're good sisters," Colt told them. He meant it.

"This is Sister Sunday," Teddy told him with a frown. "And you ruined it."

"Don't worry." He tried to sound reassuring, but didn't think he hit that mark. "I fully intend to pay all necessary fines."

"You say that now." Joey was still looking at him in that dark way that made him wonder what machinery she'd been referring to. "But I'm betting you'll sing a different tune when asked to draw down the moon tonight."

Colt took that as his cue to walk inside, pausing on the doorstep as he took in the destruction within.

The music was still going. A gray cat was sitting on the

back of the couch, cleaning its paws as if totally unaware
that it was in the middle of the storm.

There was another smashing sound from the back, so
Colt walked through the shards of broken pottery until he
found Elliot.

She was magnificent. Her cheeks were wet, her hair was
wild, and looking at her was like throwing himself face-
first into an explosion.

And loving it.

Because he could see that she felt every single thing
that he did, and the difference was, she wasn't afraid of
showing it.

She was clutching an object to her chest and it seemed
to take her eyes a long time to focus on him. Then she
scowled. And she said something, but he pointed at his
ears and shook his head.

Then watched, not sure whether to smile or not, as Elliot speared him with a look that could easily have come
from Katy. Then she stalked over to turn down the volume
button on her speakers.

The music went down to manageable decibels.

"What is that?" Colt nodded toward the thing she was
holding her chest.

Elliot clutched the object tighter. "It is the very last cowboy troll I made. I smashed all the others."

Cowboy trolls, he thought. Why not? "Why did you do
that?"

"Because they're inspired by you," she said, in her usual
direct way. "And I would very much like to smash your
face, but that route was not available to me."

And Colt laughed.

He didn't care if that was the right move or not, he just
let it out. And he watched the beautiful, magical woman

before him scowl again, even deeper. Her hand tightened around the *cowboy troll* she held as if she was considering hurling it straight at his head.

"Elliot," he said, before she tried to brain him. "Baby. I'm an idiot. I love you."

And he watched as the storm seemed to leak right out of her, deflating her where she stood.

"Damn you, Colt," she complained. "That's not fair. I'm having a *tantrum*."

"Only a man crazy in love would walk away now because he thought it might save him heartache down the road," he said. "But it's too late. I love you. As long as you're here, I intend to keep on loving you."

"You really are an idiot," she said.

That was not how he thought she'd react. "I can't say I saw that coming."

She surged toward him, then thumped him in the chest with the thing in her hand. He relieved her of it, and looked down, startled to find that what he was holding was very clearly a caricature...

Of him.

As a troll.

With a cowboy hat on.

Colt was absurdly touched.

But Elliot still looked mad.

"I spent my entire life flitting around from place to place," she told him. "That's how my mother raised me. And yes, after college, I was convinced that I wanted to live the same way—so I did. And don't get me wrong, Colt. I enjoyed myself out there. I don't see the point of living otherwise." She blew out a breath. "But I've been waiting my entire life for a place to feel like home. And nothing ever has, because I've known since I was all of thirteen that the sisters I'd always wanted were my *real* home. And that nothing would ever feel that way unless we were together."

"Elliot—" he began.

"Jasper Creek is where we belong," she told him, fiercely. "We didn't come here to play games, we came here to put down roots. *Our roots*, Colt. You don't know how lucky you are that you've never had to go looking for yours."

"Don't you see?" He slid a hand around to the nape of her neck and tugged her to him. "If you grow up with roots, you long for the sky. And I can't go out there and search for it, Elliot. I needed you to come here. I needed you to bring me the stars. That's what you did. And between the two of us, it seems to me we have everything."

And once again, the world seemed to stop.

Her gaze searched his, and he welcomed the scrutiny. He hoped she could see every last part of him. All the ways he loved her that words could never make real.

And he thought maybe she saw. That maybe she knew.

Because Elliot Hathaway melted against him at last, her violet eyes shining.

Just for him, he thought. Always for him.

"You should know this now, Colt," she said, her chin tilting up. "I don't do anything by half. If you want to come sweeping in here talking about stars and roots and *us*, I hate to break it to you, but I expect that to last forever."

And she sounded the way she always did, certain and forthright, but he could feel the tension in her body. The question there.

He aimed to make sure she never questioned him again.

"Good." He held her in his arms and he knew it would always feel just like this. Just like home. Stars above and earth below, and all the ways they loved each other in between. "Forever sounds like a pretty good start."

Then he swept her into a showy dip and he kissed her, big and wild and deep, because it was fairy princess day, after all.

And everybody who knew a fairy princess knew that the best happy-ever-afters started just like this.

Colt intended to make sure theirs was the best yet.

EPILOGUE

OLD JACK HATHAWAY waited outside the old house a year later, as close to dressed up as he got. He wasn't one for finery. If asked, he would have said he didn't have any to speak of. But even he had managed to spiff himself up for the occasion.

Because it wasn't every day that a man got to walk his four granddaughters down the same aisle.

Jack intended to do it right.

It wasn't just any old wedding aisle, of course. Not out here on Four Sisters Farm. The girls had taken their usual Sunday nonsense and turned it into a great big show of what they did best. They'd expanded. And even though he would have said it couldn't be done, they'd made something enchanted out of the yard he'd last had a fondness for when his Mary was still alive. There were chairs set up for the guests, more flower petals than Jack had personally seen outside of a storm with high winds, and Elliot had produced a friend of hers with a violin who was making the June afternoon seem to ache with hope and happiness.

Two things Jack preferred to avoid. Or pretended he preferred to avoid, these days, with this collection of determined, relentlessly cheerful descendants of his who viewed his every crusty utterance as *cute*. And fed him. And loved on him.

And made it impossible to get his hermit on as intended.

They'd brought this place alive. And maybe helped him along too, though he didn't like to admit that. He cast an eye over the old place, proud to see plants and flowers blooming everywhere, like they were auditioning for the role of prettiest. It almost seemed like the farm was the kind of fairy garden he would like to say he couldn't imagine. But he could.

Because his girls had made sure he knew. He'd attended more fairy garden teas than a grown man ought to admit.

He could see Joey's doohickey all done up in garlands of white flowers, almost making the thing look smart. He'd seen the tables laid out in Elliot's deliberately mismatched plates. He knew the party favors were little pots of Teddy's honey, sourced from her own hives right here on Hathaway land. And he could see, from his place by the front door of the old house, all the baking that Georgie had done for this day, so that not a single guest here today could possibly go without a little sweet and a lot of butter for more than a few moments.

Jack could admit he hadn't exactly been supportive of the idea. About all those cowboys hanging around, for starters.

His son Mickey had been a disappointment. Jack couldn't lie about that, much as he'd like to. Sometimes he thought it was a blessing that his beloved Mary had passed on before she saw just how big a mistake their son had made—a mistake that grew by the year, to his mind. There was a twinge in his heart as he thought that, the way there always was. Because something about these girls made him wish his boy had been better. Made him wonder what he might've done to create a man so unworthy of the title.

But today wasn't for dark clouds, or the son he'd told in no uncertain terms to stay away today. Just in case Mickey got one of his bright ideas and figured today would be a good day to show his face.

There was pain in that, but Jack was an old man. He knew by now that any life worth living came with more pain than anyone should have to bear—but if they were lucky, more than enough joy, too. He'd thought he'd lost his when he'd lost Mary. He'd been wrong.

Joy had come back for him, after all.

Times four.

He reminded himself of that when the girls' mothers took their places near him, all of them smiling politely enough in his direction. He did the same in return. Joy and pain were how it worked, like it or not. The best a man could hope was to come out of it without too much blame, and weighted toward the joy side of things.

Truth was, Jack hadn't been much for hope. Not in a long time. But this past year had changed all kinds of things on the farm, him included. He'd tried to keep a lid on things, but the girls had banded together and started falling alarmingly in love left and right.

Hell, left to their own devices, they probably all would have run off with their cowboys last summer.

Jack had felt honored to fake a little heart trouble resurgence. Well, maybe it hadn't been all that fake, but it also hadn't been medical. It had given him the opportunity to ask if they might wait until summer came around again?

And they'd agreed, because he was their rickety old grandfather, and they loved him.

He wasn't sure they'd thank him for it, but he felt better about the whole thing with a little more time under everyone's belts. More to the point, they'd given *him* the time he needed to fully take the measure of the men who thought they were good enough for his granddaughters.

He'd liked Beau Riley well enough before he started sniffing around Teddy, but his good opinion had been restored as the months passed. Because Beau was solid, and that was what his Teddy needed. He'd found Hollis Logan decent enough, until he'd taken up with Joey. But his Joey needed a man who looked like a project, like one of her machines, but could make her sweet. Hollis had done that in spades. Jack had always been a fan of Con Stone, and years ago, he'd thought he'd seen a little spark between his Georgie and her older brother's friend. He had to say, watching that spark bloom into a proper fire had been entertaining. And he'd been sharing a border with the West family for as long as anyone could remember. He had to say, it did his heart good to see his Elliot teach gloomy Colt to laugh again. Not to mention, giving him his first great-grandchild—or soon to be step-great-grandchild, anyway—in little Katy.

All told, Mary, he said, inside, where only the love of his life could hear him, *we did good.*

The door to the old house opened and Katy walked out in a shimmering gown, holding a chicken under one arm and a cat under the other.

"It's a wedding," Jack huffed at her. "Not a zoo."

The teenage girl only rolled her eyes, well-used to him by now.

"It's a sister wedding," she said, as if that explained everything. She looked down at the cat, wearing a collar today with a cushion on the top. "Jasper Junie is the ring bearer." She lifted up the baleful looking chicken, wreathed in flowers. "And Cluck Norris is the flower girl. Obviously."

"I stand corrected," Jack said, doing his best to keep his lips from twitching.

Because he couldn't think of anything sillier than a cat and a chicken marching down the aisle—with or without

Katy's help. But he knew, without a shadow of a doubt, that it was the kind of silly his girls loved most.

The kind of silly they made look sweet.

When the door opened next, the mothers sighed and Jack found himself beaming. Because they all filed out then, one after the next. Teddy holding a bouquet of violets. Joey clutching sprigs of bluebonnets. Behind them came Georgie with glorious wild roses, and Elliot with daffodils. All grown here on the farm in Joey's greenhouse, specifically for the occasion. The chairs along the aisle were marked off with bouquets mixing all four together, sister-style.

The way these girls did everything.

The flowers were beautiful, but they didn't hold a candle to his granddaughters. They all wore their own version of a wedding dress. White and off-white, cream, and what Elliot had informed him was *old ivory*. And each one of them was a sight. *Look, Mary*, he urged her inside. *Look at how beautiful they all are.*

And all of them with those violet eyes that came as a gift straight from Mary herself.

Despite himself, Jack, who had informed them all that he would feel no emotion whatsoever at this circus of a wedding, found himself getting…a little gruff.

"That looks suspiciously like a tear, Grandpa," said Teddy.

"Impossible," he barked back.

"Oh, it's a tear all right," Georgie said, moving closer, as if she was inspecting his face.

"Tears are beautiful," Elliot declared. "We should all embrace more of them."

"I'm sure Grandpa just has some dust in his eye." Joey grinned at him. "Don't you, Grandpa?"

Jack harrumphed, because he was an old man and he

could make the noises he liked. He could hear the violin playing, and could hear the guests laughing—meaning Katy had already set off, cat and chicken at the ready. His grand-daughters' mothers were close by, clearly ready to do their duty.

But first, there was what he had to do.

He opened up his arms and beckoned his girls close. They all stared at him a moment, clearly surprised at the un-characteristic gesture, but they rallied. One thing he knew about his girls was that they always rallied—whether a man claimed he wanted to be left alone or not. And when he had them all in his arms, his beautiful brides, he cleared his throat.

"I wish your grandmother was here to see this," he said, though he knew she was. He knew that there wasn't a breath he took that she wasn't a part of. She was everywhere he was, always. "She would know what to say. She always did. But you're stuck with me."

"Only place to be," Teddy said, and the other three made noises of agreement.

"I love you," Jack managed to say, though words like that had never come easily for him. He sometimes wondered if that was why…but this wasn't about Mickey. This was about the best part of his son—what he'd made, not what he'd done. "I love you all and I'm proud of you. And I'm proud of the fine men you've chosen to make a part of this family. I'm grateful that you all decided to make this your home. More grateful than you'll know." He had to clear his throat again, a time or two. While four pairs of violet eyes watched him steadily. "I want to thank you, my beautiful granddaughters, for bringing some life back to the place."

And to him, too. Jack had thought his heart attack was the end of him last year—and he'd been of the mind that getting along to see Mary sounded good to him, thank you, but his granddaughters were having none of it. They'd come here and swept him up in their parties and their Sundays, like it or not.

Oh, just admit you like it, came Mary's voice from deep inside him. *You're not fooling anyone.*

Still, he had a reputation to uphold. A man was only an old coot once—he intended to make the most of it.

"And now there's a farm store," Georgie said happily. "With streams of customers all over your land."

"I'm branching out," Elliot said, nodding. "We can't keep the cowboy trolls in stock. I might have to make other trolls too."

"I think we've planted half the valley this year," Joey agreed. "Everyone wants our starts."

"And I've been meaning to talk to you about the alpacas," Teddy said. Ominously.

"I'm talking about you," Jack said, getting back to the subject at hand. He looked at each one of them. So different, yet so fiercely linked. Even today. "I love you. That's the end of it."

Though the truth was, it was just the beginning.

Even an old man closer to an ending knew that.

And his hands were occupied, so he couldn't wipe away the moisture on his face that he was certain was from the wind. Even though, as far as he could tell, on a June day as pretty as this one, there wasn't a lick of breeze.

"Let's get you married," he said gruffly.

He let them go, grumbling as each one of them kissed him on the cheek. Then each one of his brides found her own mother, and held on. Then Jack took the front of their little procession, and, with far more dignity than the chicken and cat combination that had preceded him, he marched his granddaughters down the aisle.

Where, at the head, four strong cowboys stood waiting—each and every one of them grinning wide at the sight.

Ready for the grand and glorious future that started *right now*.

And would last forever, if old Jack Hathaway had anything to say about it.

Which he usually did.

* * * * *

Get 4 FREE REWARDS!

We'll send you 2 FREE Books plus 2 FREE Mystery Gifts.

FREE Value Over **$20**

Both the **Romance** and **Suspense** collections feature compelling novels written by many of today's bestselling authors.

YES! Please send me 2 FREE novels from the Essential Romance or Essential Suspense Collection and my 2 FREE gifts (gifts are worth about $10 retail). After receiving them, if I don't wish to receive any more books, I can return the shipping statement marked "cancel." If I don't cancel, I will receive 4 brand-new novels every month and be billed just $7.24 each in the U.S. or $7.49 each in Canada. That's a savings of up to 28% off the cover price. It's quite a bargain! Shipping and handling is just 50¢ per book in the U.S. and $1.25 per book in Canada.* I understand that accepting the 2 free books and gifts places me under no obligation to buy anything. I can always return a shipment and cancel at any time. The free books and gifts are mine to keep no matter what I decide.

Choose one: ☐ **Essential Romance**
(194/394 MDN GQ6M)

☐ **Essential Suspense**
(191/391 MDN GQ6M)

Name (please print)

Address   Apt. #

City   State/Province   Zip/Postal Code

Email: Please check this box ☐ if you would like to receive newsletters and promotional emails from Harlequin Enterprises ULC and its affiliates. You can unsubscribe anytime.

Mail to the Harlequin Reader Service:
IN U.S.A.: P.O. Box 1341, Buffalo, NY 14240-8531
IN CANADA: P.O. Box 603, Fort Erie, Ontario L2A 5X3

Want to try 2 free books from another series? Call 1-800-873-8635 or visit www.ReaderService.com.

---

*Terms and prices subject to change without notice. Prices do not include sales taxes, which will be charged (if applicable) based on your state or country of residence. Canadian residents will be charged applicable taxes. Offer not valid in Quebec. This offer is limited to one order per household. Books received may not be as shown. Not valid for current subscribers to the Essential Romance or Essential Suspense Collection. All orders subject to approval. Credit or debit balances in a customer's account(s) may be offset by any other outstanding balance owed by or to the customer. Please allow 4 to 6 weeks for delivery. Offer available while quantities last.

Your Privacy—Your information is being collected by Harlequin Enterprises ULC, operating as Harlequin Reader Service. For a complete summary of the information we collect, how we use this information and to whom it is disclosed, please visit our privacy notice located at corporate.harlequin.com/privacy-notice. From time to time we may also exchange your personal information with reputable third parties. If you wish to opt out of this sharing of your personal information, please visit readerservice.com/consumerschoice or call 1-800-873-8635. **Notice to California Residents**—Under California law, you have specific rights to control and access your data. For more information on these rights and how to exercise them, visit corporate.harlequin.com/california-privacy.

STRSMAX22